THE QUEST OF JULIAN DAY

With both of us clutching the pistol we swung in a swift half-circle. As I regained my balance I jerked up my right foot and let him have it in the groin. He gave an agonised squeal as my foot caught him but the effort caused me to stumble and I fell, dragging him down on top of me.

I had the advantage of youth, but he was tall, sinewy and incredibly strong for his years. Both of us were still clinging to the pistol as we struggled there in a heap. In twisting my head from under his I caught a glimpse of Zakri Bey. He had turned towards the street and was shouting for his men.

'Mustapha! Hassan! *Taala! Igri! igri!*' he cried. At that moment O'Kieff's teeth bit deep into my wrist.

I gasped with the pain and let go my hold on the gun. He brought it up and next second I saw his arm raised against the starry sky as he made to club me with it, but I jerked aside my head and, giving a terrific heave, flung him from me.

We rolled a yard apart and both came to rest sprawling in the filthy dust. I was on my knees a fraction before he was and, lashing out with all my strength, I caught him a smashing blow full in the face.

Dennis Wheatley

THE QUEST OF
JULIAN DAY

ARROW BOOKS

Arrow Books Limited

An imprint of Random House

20 Vauxhall Bridge Road, London SW1V 2SA

First published by Hutchinson 1939
Arrow edition 1962
Reprinted 1962, 1965, 1968, 1972 and 1980
© Brooke-Richleau Ltd 1939

Printed and bound in Great Britain by
Mackays of Chatham PLC, Chatham, Kent

ISBN 0 75 299977 X

Contents

For His Excellency

Russell Pacha

In friendship, admiration, and gratitude for the central theme of this story which he gave me by telling me about the lost legions of Cambyses one night in Cairo

1

The Birth of a Vendetta

I entered the Diplomatic Service at the age of twenty-three but was forced to resign before I was twenty-five. In view of the appalling scandal in which I was involved that was inevitable and my foolish conceit, in thinking that I could take on a far older and more experienced man like O'Kieff, undoubtedly led to Carruthers' suicide.

That was all eighteen months ago and I am now in Egypt. Recent events have caused me to feel that the time has come to jot down these notes whenever I have an hour to spare; but whether I shall live to complete them it is impossible to say. Either that devil O'Kieff or Zakri Bey may kill me before I can kill them—as I mean to do if I get half a chance—yet, even if they get me first, this record may, perhaps, help someone else to settle their account. But I had better start from the beginning.

I was christened Hugo Julian Du Crow Fernhurst, but for the last eighteen months I have been passing under the name of Julian Day; and my home is, or rather was, in Gloucestershire; a lovely old place called Queen's Acres where my uncle, an honest but unimaginative man who figures in the Army List as a Major General (retired) brought me up.

I first met O'Kieff during my last year at Oxford. He came up for a long week-end as the guest of Warburton of Merton. Warburton was not a close friend of mine although I respected his brain, and, as our sets impinged on each other's, could not avoid running into him a certain amount; but he was the fat and flabby type of intellectual and I never liked what I heard of his habits.

Sean O'Kieff is, of course, well known as an occultist; and during his visit Warburton gave a couple of shows in his rooms to which, as I was rather interested in such things, I went with a few men who knew him better than I did. The first was just a social party but the second was a midnight affair for the purpose of performing certain ritual connected with the Pan cult. into which perhaps it is inadvisable to enter here. Such matters have their unpleasant side and, I am now convinced, are decidedly dangerous, but I was young and curious at the time.

Nothing much really happened, although towards the end of the sitting there was a quite unmistakable smell of goat. It was said that Warburton's room stank of it for days afterwards and as there was no natural explanation whatever of it, this unseen manifestation of the Dark God was quite sufficient to scare most of us.

O'Kieff made himself very pleasant to me on both occasions. In the light of later events it is probable that he knew I was trying for the Diplomatic. All my friends at Oxford were aware of that and everybody prophesied that I would come through my exams with flying colours, as in fact proved to be the case, and he thought, perhaps, that I might be useful to him later on.

However, that is by the way. It was something O'Kieff said to young Bela Lazadok, just as we were restoring ourselves with drinks after that rather shattering sitting, which put me on to the fact that he was dabbling in other things besides the occult. They were speaking in Hungarian and naturally they were not to know that I understood what they were saying. It happens that I have an unusual flair for languages which is doubtless due to my rather mixed ancestry.

I am definitely British as far as nationality and feeling go. but my mother was an Austrian and I owe a great deal to my Austrian grandfather, with whom I have spent all my longer holidays ever since I was old enough to walk. He lost practically everything after the war but they couldn't take his brain or charm or culture from him, or that wonderful something which comes from having inherited the outlook of an Austrian noble in a family that goes back into the mists of time. It was to please him that I really began to read after my father died and the craving for knowledge very soon got hold of me. He was desperately keen, too, that I should acquire as many languages as possible, and those jolly holidays spent in the homes of my foreign relatives were an enormous help. In consequence. I speak French and German as fluently as I do English, and can

carry on a conversation in three or four other languages—
Hungarian among them.

'Did you manage to pick up anything worth while about
the new machine yesterday?' O'Kieff asked Lazadok.

Now I chanced to know that the Hungarian had been out
to the Morris factory the day before and that he was said to
show great promise as an engineer; also that the Morris people
were experimenting with a new type of tank engine. The question might quite well not have referred to the tanks at all and,
unfortunately, I failed to catch Lazadok's reply, but, for what
it was worth, I tipped off a friend of mine in Whitehall.

Apparently it was a lucky shot on my part. Lazadok ter-
minated his studies at Oxford somewhat hurriedly a few weeks
later and, when I next saw my official friend, I gathered that
the Government had intimated that we could no longer extend
the hospitality of Britain to the clever young Hungarian.
Against O'Kieff no sort of evidence had been forthcoming and
as he was a British subject they couldn't very well clear him
out. But it was this little passage of arms in my salad days that
put me wise to the fact that he was mixed up, to some extent at
all events, in the spy business.

That was why, when I met him again nearly two years later
in Brussels, which was my first post, I deliberately welcomed
his attempts to reopen our acquaintance. I know quite well
that it is against the rules for any member of our Diplomatic
Service to dabble in counter-espionage but I felt certain that
O'Kieff was up to no good, and I was vain enough to think that
I could outwit him; so I allowed myself to be dazzled by the
prospect of landing a fish that our Secret Service people had so
far failed to catch.

It is unnecessary to give particulars of the way in which I
thought I was leading him on while all the time he had my
measure and was only using me as a pawn. He is a strange
creature, not particularly attractive to look at; tall, thin, with
wavy, grey-white hair that looks rather like a wig; small, quick
eyes that flash behind pince-nez, a lean chin and a hard rat-trap
of a mouth. But he is immensely erudite and one of the most
fascinating people to talk to that I have ever met. When I was
away from him I disliked him intensely, but each time I met
him again for one of the many evenings we spent together, I

immediately fell under the spell of his intellect.

As with many clever people vanity was his weak spot and evidently he was so contemptuous of my power to do him any serious harm that he allowed himself the luxury of impressing me with the secret power he wielded by boastful hints thrown out from time to time. Bit by bit I learnt that he was a very big fish indeed in the muddy waters of international intrigue and one of the seven men who controlled a vast organisation which had ramifications in every corner of the globe. How, exactly, it operated he would never actually specify, but from one thing and another I gathered that they had a hand in practically every rotten game; espionage, I.D.B., organised blackmail, dope-running and even white-slave trafficking.

It may sound as if he were crazy to talk of such things to any presumably decent person; but he appeared to regard me as a disciple and when he got worked up he was really capable of making one forget the dirt that lay underneath it all. He always spoke of the intense excitement of the game in a way that distorted true perspective, and of the immense kick to be derived from pulling off a big *coup* as a result of pitting one's wits against the whole force of the Law.

Piling up profits did not seem to interest him; probably because he had everything money could buy already. His house in Brussels was beautifully equipped, and staffed with the sort of servant whom one hardly notices because he is so efficient; yet that was only one of many properties I had reason to believe he owned, although he was careful never to give me the actual addresses of the others.

This cat-and-mouse game went on for about three months and then O'Kieff told me one night that the rest of the Big Seven were due to arrive the following week for their annual conference, which was to be held that year in Brussels. I thought the time had come to get in someone more experienced than myself and confided in our First Secretary, Tom Carruthers.

Carruthers cursed me up hill and down dale for meddling in a matter that was completely outside the sphere of a promising young diplomat, but all the same he could not help showing that he was impressed by the magnitude of the thing. More, he thought that I was too deeply involved for the Secret

Service people, whose real job it was, to take over from me. Like the conceited young fool I was, I imagined that I had bluffed O'Kieff and, obviously, if we were to attempt to net the Big Seven, the time before their meeting was much too short for anyone to take my place and win their confidence.

It was, I am sure, far more with a view to keeping a fatherly eye upon me than for any other reason that Carruthers eventually consented to allow me to introduce him to O'Kieff, when I pleaded with him to allow me to do so in order that he could size up the situation for himself. Later I was to realise with bitterness and grief that by drawing Carruthers into it I had done the very thing that O'Kieff was playing for; he wasn't interested in small fry like myself.

There is no point in going into details about what followed. It was the talk of every Chancellery in Europe for months afterwards and everyone in my world has heard some garbled version of it, causing them to regard me as a figure of ridicule or a dirty little crook who had sold his country's secrets.

We met the Big Seven; Zakri, Lord Gavin, the Jap and the rest of that unholy crew. Every one of them had a name to conjure with and was far above the strata in which the police ordinarily look for criminals. They were the real Lords of the Underworld, living in affluence and power, all unsuspected by the intellectual cream of European Society into which they had been accepted on account of their wealth and dominating personalities.

On the night that O'Kieff sprung his trap I very nearly lost my life. My function as an admiring audience was ended and the fact that he had disclosed the names of the Big Seven to me was more than enough to decide him that the time had come to put me out of the way. It was only by pure chance that I did not swallow all the dope he gave me and, as it was, the doctor had to fight for my life for days.

What they did to Carruthers no one will ever know, but the Portuguese or O'Kieff hypnotised him, I think. That is the only possible explanation. He actually took several of them back to the Embassy with him on the Sunday night that he and I dined with them alone, and opened up the safe so that they could inspect all the documents that were in it.

Sir George Hogan, the Ambassador, was away for the week-end and as there were certain very important negotiations pending, the latest instructions from the F.O. were lying in the safe awaiting his return. As one of the senior members of the staff, Carruthers was always aware of the combination which unlocked the safe and, apparently, he gave them free access to it.

The nightwatchman, noticing a light in the Chancellery at such an unusual hour, went in to investigate but seeing the First Secretary with, presumably, a group of friends whom he had taken to his room half and hour before, assumed they were engaged on urgent business and walked out again.

Nothing was stolen, so they could not be charged with theft afterwards but, of course, they were able to learn a number of the most jealously guarded Diplomatic secrets regarding Great Britain's latest policy and intentions.

Everything was put back in the safe in apple-pie order and apart from my being picked up half-dead by the Belgian police in a disreputable quarter of the city next morning, which at first did not seem to have any bearing on the affair, the whole episode might have passed off without investigation if it hadn't happened that Lady Hogan was an interfering old busybody who let a ready ear to ever sort of tittle-tattle. The night-porter's wife remarked to Lady Hogan's maid that Mr. Carruthers had been sitting up till all hours with a queer lot of people in the Chancellery the night before; the maid passed it on to her gossip-loving mistress, and Lady Hogan duly asked Sir George who the queer friends were that Carruthers had been entertaining over the week-end. When Carruthers was questioned he remembered absolutely nothing about it. The night-porter was called in and described the men he had seen sitting with Carruthers round the open safe; upon which the poor fellow quietly walked upstairs and shot himself.

The scene between myself and my Chief which ensued when I had recovered and was called on to render certain explanations, can well be imagined. For all our good intentions neither Carruthers nor I had succeeded in finding out one single fact which could be used against O'Kieff, and obviously no case could be brought against him. If the First Secretary of the Embassy cared to bring a number of strangers into the Chancellery in the middle of the night and disclose our secrets to them, the case was against him, not them, and by that time. he, poor fellow, was dead and buried.

I was packed off on the next boat to England, and visited the Foreign Office for, I suppose, the last time in my life.

After questioning me at considerable length about the details of the affair, Sir Roger Thistlethwaite said in that quiet, rather over-cultured voice of his:

'I am prepared to accept your statement that you acted in perfectly good faith, but you'll appreciate that there is no course open to us than to dismiss you from the Service. It's a sad pity, you know—a sad pity. Quite a number of us here had looked on you as having— er—almost brilliant prospects.

'Quite, sir,' I replied, although I thought it a little unneces sary for him to rub it in. With my Double-First and my flair for languages, together with the facts that I am a presentable looking person, the heir to a baronetcy, the best man with an épée in my year at Oxford and quite a useful shot, all sorts of fine things had been prophesied for me. It was a foregone con clusion that I would get good posts and I myself had even begun to dream of one day averting another world war as Britain's youngest yet most brilliant Ambassador.

'What do you intend to do?' Sir Roger asked after a moment. 'I hardly know what to do, sir,' I replied.

'I fear all Government posts will be closed to you after this,' he said, 'and you'll need all your courage to live this scandal down; but you must try not to let your broken career embitter you. You're still very young, and if you take my advice, you'll fling yourself heart and soul into something else at once. Your uncle's getting on in life and you're the heir to that place of his in Gloucestershire. How about settling down there and taking the running of it off his hands?'

'I'm not particularly interested in estate management and. knowing Uncle Herbert, I rather doubt if he'll ever have me in the house again when he hears about this.'

'He can't cut you off, can he?'

'No, fortunately the place is entailed, so he can't stop its coming to me on his death; and as I inherited my father's money when I was twenty-one I'm all right for cash.'

'How about going into commerce?' he suggested. 'Lots of people do these days and you've got plenty of brains.'

15

'D'you think any decent firm would take me? Once this business gets out my name's going to stink like mud.'

Sir Roger tapped his desk thoughtfully with an ivory paper-knife. 'No, that's just the rub. We have given a new orientation to our policy, of course; always have an alternative ready for just such an emergency, and we've been working like stevedores to repair, as far as possible, the damage that has been done. But that meant communicating with every Embassy and Legation on the list and we couldn't conceal the reason for such an upheaval from the senior members of the Service. Such matters are highly confidential, but even so, there's bound to be a certain amount of talk, and it is inevitable that your name will be linked with Carruthers' suicide.'

'Naturally,' I agreed glumly. 'They'll all assume that Carruthers and I sold these secrets to foreign agents between us and that he did the decent thing by committing suicide whereas I hadn't the guts. I've got to face it, sir. My name is going to stink in the Service for generations and as the story gradually becomes common property everyone outside the Service is going to regard me as a leper too.'

'If settling down at Queen's Acres is impracticable, perhaps it would be wisest for you to travel for a bit.'

'That's what I had in mind.'

Sir Roger hesitated for a moment and then went on softly, 'Have you thought at all what line you mean to take if you run up against O'Kieff or any of his friends again?'

'I've hardly had time to consider that yet, sir.'

'You may, you know, if you propose to travel. In fact as you have money and—er almost unlimited time at your disposal, you certainly could, if you felt so inclined.'

'Are you suggesting that I should endeavour to do so?' I asked.

He stared at his blotting pad. 'I suggest nothing. It only occurred to me that you might quite reasonably feel a certain animus against these people for wrecking your career. God knows, you've plenty of cause; and I think the Government would owe a considerable debt of gratitude to anyone who succeeded in breaking up their organisation.'

'Are you inferring, sir, that if I could do so, the Government would reinstate me in the Service?'

He shook his head. 'Hardly that, I'm afraid; but it is not altogether outside the bounds of possibility that they might consider conferring a decoration on you for services rendered; which, in itself, would be quite sufficient to wipe out the stigma that is bound to attach to you as the result of this affair.'

'With help from the Secret Service it might be done,' I said impulsively.

He dropped his eyes for a moment. 'It distresses me very much to have to say so but while I, personally, believe in your integrity, others may not be quite so willing to do so; therefore any such tie-up is out of the question. You would have to act on your own.'

'In that case I doubt if I should stand much chance of securing evidence against them.'

'If you could secure evidence, well and good; but that is not essential. From our point of view it would, perhaps, be even better if they—er ceased to exist.'

'You mean . . .' I hesitated.

'I am not given to looseness of speech, young man, and I mean exactly what I said.' He seemed quite annoyed that I should question his words, yet it made me positively gasp to believe that this quiet, grey-haired English gentleman was actually suggesting that I should go out and commit murder.

I stared at him almost doubting that I had heard aright, but his mild blue eyes were now quite unwavering and he went on smoothly, 'You would have to be careful, of course, to avoid being caught; since, if you were, we could not give you any official protection.'

'I see,' I said slowly.

Sir Roger stood up. 'I need hardly stress the fact that I should, if necessary, categorically deny any suggestion that this conversation had ever taken place. But, as you know, I am one of those whose duty it is to guard the interests of the Empire, and these people are a menace not only to Britain but to law and order throughout the world. Sometimes, when such people are too clever for us to catch in the ordinary way, we have to take certain steps which we all deplore; but there it is. I don't want you to say yes or no. Just think it over, my boy. and good luck to you, whatever you decide.'

I did think it over, but it seemed a hopeless task to pit my

wits against such a vast organisation as O'Kieff's, and although
I might have succeeded in tracking down and killing one or
more of the Big Seven I had no desire to be hanged for murder.
There had not been sufficient time for bitterness really to eat
into my soul. That only came later. My brain was numbed by
the catastrophe which had shattered every interest I had in
life, and my one craving was to get away from everyone to
some solitude where I could not be reminded of the past and
could endeavour to blot the whole horrible business from my
memory.

To have gone to stay with any of my foreign relatives might
have lent colour to the rumours I dreaded, so, having resigned
from my clubs and had an unholy row with Uncle Herbert. I
spent the summer months among the lonely forests and lakes
of Finland, licking my wounds. By autumn I was drifting down
the Baltic ports, then I settled for a few weeks in Warsaw, but
winter was approaching. I hate the cold and I was beginning to
get thoroughly fed up with my own company, so I decided to
spend the winter in Egypt. The remains of the ancient Egyptian civilisation interested me enormously, but I had to avoid
numerous people whom I knew and that brought home to me
with appalling keenness the fact that I should never again be
able to mix freely with the sort of people I had known before
the crash. Each time I thought of the life I should have been
leading and everything of which O'Kieff had robbed me, my
smouldering anger against him grew. In the spring I moved to
the Balkans, working my way gradually up towards the Dal-
matian Coast, but my loneliness was becoming more than I
could bear. I began to crave desperately for some definite em-
ployment and, vaguely at first, thoughts of Sir Roger's suggestion crept back into my mind. I felt that another year of drifting would bring me to the brink of suicide, and by this time I
had realised that my own life was quite worthless; useless to my
fellow-men and a burden to myself.

It was November when I returned to London—still with no
settled plans—and only then on account of financial affairs
which I had to attend to personally. Having attended to these
I walked unenthusiastically into Cook's one morning with the
thought of planning another journey further East, and the first
person I saw leaning up against the counter was Sean O'Kieff.

2

The Quest Begins

O'Kieff did not recognise me but for that there was a very good reason. It may be that I was over-sensitive about my invidious position; many of my old friends would have stood by me, I am sure, but after receiving one or two grim disillusionments in Egypt the previous winter I had decided to spare all my old acquaintances and myself further cause for embarrassment by growing a beard. After eleven months I possessed a fine, curly, dark-brown beaver—an inconvenient appendage, I admit—but one which enabled me to walk down Bond Street without the slightest chance of recognition.

I took a place next to O'Kieff at the counter and overheard him making arrangements to sail in the S.S. 'Hampshire' from Marseilles to Egypt. My thoughts were chaotic. Killing him was one thing and, at that time, I was still not quite prepared to risk my own neck by such a desperate measure, but it did seem that this was a heaven-sent chance to keep him under observation for a spell without arousing his supicions and, perhaps, to find out enough about his activities to get him a long term of imprisonment. It did not matter in the least to me if I went to Egypt or Peru, and before he had finished fixing up his cabin I too had decided to book a passage in the S.S. 'Hampshire'.

Directly he had gone I made inquiries and learnt that the ship was sailing from Liverpool two days later. I am a good sailor and like the sea, even in rough weather, so I thought it would be a good idea to sail in her from England. I should then be well dug-in on board before O'Kieff joined her seven days later at Marseilles. The cabins on either side of his were already booked but I managed to get one two doors aft of his, on the promenade deck. Next night I was on the train to Liverpool feeling a changed man already now that after all

19

those dreary months I had once again some sort of motive for existing.

There was a blanket of mist when we nosed our way out of the Mersey the following afternoon and nearly everybody went straight down to their cabins after dinner that first night out. But the following day clear, winter sunshine and only a moderate sea brought the passengers out on deck with their rugs for the run down the Irish Channel.

Those passengers were few enough, as people returning East from leave, who form the bulk of the travellers on such liners, naturally prefer to pay the extra cost of the overland journey to Marseilles in order to get the few extra days in England. It is easy enough to lose oneself in a crowd but the very fact of our small numbers made it difficult for me to avoid the others and, as it happened, my deck-chair was put next to that of an, elderly, grey-bearded man who soon displayed a lively interest in the book I was reading.

He shuffled for a little with a couple of weighty tomes that were lying in his own lap and then leant over. 'Excuse me, but isn't that "The Thousand and One Nights"?' he asked.

'Yes,' I replied. 'I find the original version most entertaining.'

'Of course,' he chuckled. 'It's a grand book. But I commented on it because I see you're reading it in Arabic—rather an unusual accomplishment for a young man. Perhaps you're in one of the Services?'

'No. I was in Egypt for some months last winter and amused myself part of the time by learning Arabic; as I'm on my way back there now I thought a little amusing reading was the pleasantest way to polish it up again.'

'Were you engaged at one of the "digs", by any chance?'

'No. I'm afraid I'm an idle dog,' I confessed. 'I don't do any job at all.'

'I see,' he said with a rather disapproving look. 'Well, let me introduce myself. My name is Walter Shane. If you're interested in ancient civilisations you may perhaps have heard of me.'

'Of course.' I looked up with quick interest. 'Who hasn't heard of Sir Walter Shane, the famous Egyptologist? It's a great pleasure to meet you, sir.'

'That's nice of you,' he smiled benignly at me over his thick spectacles. 'And what may your name be?'

'Julian Day,' I told him; and, incidentally, the one concession the Foreign Office had made on my leaving the Service was to grant me a passport in the pseudonym I had taken, to save me unnecessary complications on my travels.

We talked till lunch-time, and a most interesting old gentleman Sir Walter proved to be; to me, at least, as I have always been fascinated by the history of ancient civilisations. He told me a lot about the various 'digs' he had superintended during his many winters in Egypt and the only thing which struck me as a little strange about him was his unnatural reticence in speaking of his plans for the coming winter.

For some years past, apparently, his daughter had been very closely associated with him in his work, and for a reason which he did not specify she had elected to remain in Egypt all through the summer. He was meeting her there and they would proceed to Luxor. But after that his plans, for a professional archæologist, were curiously vague.

At first I thought he was travelling on his own, but at lunch I saw him sitting with a youngish couple and afterwards, when he came on deck again, he introduced them to me as Mr. and Mrs. Belville. They were a delightful pair and very soon, in that astonishingly quick way in which shipboard acquaintances develop, I was on most friendly terms with them.

Their association with Sir Walter rather puzzled me at first, as although Harry Belville was a charming fellow—kind, generous to a fault and possessing a most attractive ingenuousness —it was quite clear that he hadn't got a brain in his head. He hardly knew Gothic architecture from Greek, let alone which mattered among the thirty-three dynasties of the Pharaohs who ruled Egypt for some five thousand years, and his wife, Clarissa, was little better informed on such subjects.

Her mind was much the quicker of the two but it revolved mainly round having a good time, clothes, cocktails and the sort of amusing nonsense that one reads in magazines like 'The New Yorker'. It was she who had the money. Her father had been something to do with manufacturing hats at Luton and had left her with quite a useful fortune; so that Harry, who, I learnt later, had barely enough to keep himself in cigarettes, did not have to work. Part of their charm was the obvious way they adored each other and their almost comical uneasiness if they were separated for upwards of an hour; although they had been married for the best part of five years.

He was not much to look at—a medium-sized, rather fat chap with thinning, fairish hair—whereas she was definitely attractive. Her immense vitality, piquant little face and crop of flaming red curls would have gained her plenty of admirers anywhere. I think his attraction for her lay in his unfailing good-temper and something rather stolid but extremely sound about him; because, although Harry's education had stopped short at the level of the Upper Fourth in his public school, he had an extremely good fund of hard common-sense.

By the time we rounded Gib. I had solved the mystery of what the Belvilles were doing in the company of such an erudite old man as Sir Walter. For some time past the Egyptian Government has exercised absolute control over all 'digs'. No one is allowed to excavate without a permit any more. The Government supply a portion of the funds and the labour, while making use of the European experts who come out; but any antiquities discovered in these 'digs' remain the sole property of the Government.

Sir Walter had tumbled on a new site the previous winter that he wished to investigate without the Government's knowledge or assistance. But like so many men who devote their lives to science, he had very little money of his own and, somehow or other, he had had to raise private funds for the necessary labour. He had been about the matter cautiously during the past summer in England and had apparently been unsuccessful until he had thought of approaching his daughter's old school-friend Clarissa. After consulting her beloved Harry she had agreed to put up the necessary cash and as they had never been to Egypt they decided to accompany Sir Walter on the trip.

This I gathered from half-confidences and hints, mainly dropped by Harry after we had had a few drinks together on numerous occasions in the bar. Although the business seemed a very harmless type of illegality, they would have got into considerable trouble of the Egyptian Government had found out their intentions, hence their secrecy, and I was still completely ignorant of the details of their plans when we reached Marseilles.

22

I spent the afternoon in my cabin while the swarm of passengers came on board, but O'Kieff duly joined the ship there and I saw him that night at dinner. He had not changed much in the last eighteen months except that he was a trifle greyer and his sharp features looked more than ever as if they had been chiselled out of granite.

Owing to the influx of new passengers, Sir Walter had very kindly asked me to join his table, as otherwise I should have had a lot of strangers put at the one where I had previously been sitting; and the new arrangement quite naturally resulted in my becoming more intimate than ever with him and the Belvilles.

O'Kieff was travelling alone, except for his valet, but he soon gathered a little crowd of acquaintances about him; which was hardly to be wondered at owing to his wealth and the brilliance of his conversation. I kept out of his way as far as possible and, although we passed quite close to each other on several occasions, he never showed the least sign of recognition.

I realised, though, that by sitting still I should never be able to find out what nefarious business was taking him to Egypt, so on the second night out from Marseilles I waited until he was safely ensconced in the bar, after dinner, with his new acquaintances, and then proceeded to pay a clandestine visit to his cabin

Altogether I was there for about half an hour and managed to run through most of his baggage, I did not find anything of the least importance. The reason for that was a simple one. Under his bed he had a flat, leather-covered, steel despatch box; it was obvious that he kept all his private papers in that and, of course, I had no means of opening it.

On the following night Sir Walter began to sound me about my plans in Egypt. Apparently his principal male assistant had had the misfortune to meet with an accident about ten days before the 'Hampshire' had sailed and, although his daughter Sylvia could give him all the help he required on the technical side, Harry could not speak a word of Arabic so the old man was badly in need of someone capable of helping him to deal with his Arab labour.

The Belvilles, who were present, gave it away that the three of them had been discussing the matter for some days and felt that I was just the man for the job. Sir Walter was, in fact, so keen that I should take it on, once the cat was out of the bag, that, rather ingenuously I thought, he produced a photograph of his daughter. He said it had occurred to him that I might like to see the only other member of his party, but obviously it was really shown me because he was extremely proud of her good looks and felt certain they would act as bait to any presumably unattached young man. The fair-haired, oval head which looked up at me from the photograph showed beyond question that Sylvia Shane was a remarkably beautiful girl.

'Her hair is ash-blonde, her eyes are blue and she's about eighteen months younger than I am,' said Clarissa with a mischievous little smile; and if I had needed any inducement to join their party, the company of Sylvia Shane certainly provided it.

Had the offer come a few weeks earlier I should positively have jumped at it, but my decision to try to find out what O'Kieff was up to complicated matters considerably; so for the moment I hedged:

'It's very flattering of you to want me, and in the ordinary way nothing would please me better than to join you. But I've got some business to transact in Egypt before I am really my own master.'

'Our preparations in Cairo and Luxor will take at least a fortnight,' Sir Walter said quickly.

'In that case, may I leave it open?' I asked; knowing that the probabilities were that in a fortnight I should either have got something on O'Kieff or else lost track of him.

'Certainly,' Sir Walter agreed. 'But before asking you to make any definite decision it is only fair to let you know what we propose to do.'

'There's no hurry about that as things stand,' I said.

He shook his head. 'I think I'd better tell you now because I'm quite sure I can rely on you not to let it go any further then; if you decide that you would rather not participate in this affair which is, to a very mild extent, illegal, you would feel quite free to make other plans for your winter in Egypt.'

'Just as you like, sir,' I agreed, settling back in my chair.

'You've read Herodotus, of course.'

'Yes; not recently though.'

'In any case you know enough about it to realise that whereas half a century ago Herodotus was regarded as a romancer and the prize liar among ancient historians, modern investigations have proved that he was nothing of the kind. His records of his travels sound fantastic on the face of them, particularly as many of his stories are completely unsupported by any other ancient writings. But during this century we've succeeded in digging up and translating innumerable records on stone or pottery which prove conclusively that nine-tenths of the particulars which he set down in his essays on the ancient civilisations were genuine facts. I wonder if by chance you remember the passage in which he refers to the Persian conquest of Egypt? It is in the early part of Book III.'

'No,' I confessed. 'I don't.'

'Well, briefly it was this. During some five thousand years, or perhaps even longer, Egypt, protected by her natural barriers of desert from barbarian hordes, had developed probably the most remarkable and wealthy civilisation the world has ever known. Her two greatest cities, Memphis and Thebes, each had over five million inhabitants, which makes them greater than any city with the one exception of London, in Europe at the present day. In Thebes particularly, the accumulated wealth in gold and jewels in the temples passes imagination, because it was the Sacred City of the great XVIIIth, XIXth and XXth Dynasties which conquered the whole of Palestine right down to Mesopotamia and added the wealth of many other long-civilised peoples to their own.

'Long before 525 B.C. the tide of conquest had turned and, in that year, came the Persian invasion, Cambyses descended on Egypt with his hordes of horsemen, destroyed her armies and sacked her mighty cities. Having deposed the reigning Pharaoh, Psammetichos III, Cambyses settled down to rest his legions as the new monarch in Thebes. Yet he was not content with having taken the London of the ancient world and, like Alexander who came after him, he sighed for fresh worlds to conquer.

'To the west of the Nile Valley lies the Libyan desert. It stretches for a thousand miles from north to south and is over nine hundred miles in width. That portion of the Sahara is almost waterless. Arabs cut corners off it with their caravans

25

but no human being ever succeeded in actually crossing that desert until this was accomplished in the nineteen-twenties by aeroplane.

'Cambyses learned that to the north-west of the desert there lay another mighty city inhabited by a wealthy people. Their descendants are the Senussi Arabs who inhabit the Oasis of Siwa, a great tract of fertile territory which is known in ancient times as the Oasis of Jupiter-Ammon. Greedy for further spoil, Cambyses determined to march his armies against the Senussi, but he was faced with the almost insoluble problem of crossing those three hundred miles of waterless desert.'

Sir Walter paused and, immensely interested in what he had been telling me, I asked quickly, 'Did he succeed in finding a way?'

'The victories of the Persians were largely due to the admirable staff-work they put in before initiating any fresh campaign, and campaigns were leisurely things in those days,' he answered slowly. 'Time was no object, and while he lorded it in Thebes, Cambyses prepared for his march by making good the lack of wells in a very ingenious manner.

'He collected thirty thousand wine-jars, filled them with water and despatched them with a huge caravan one day's march into the desert. There they were buried in the sand so that the water should not evaporate. The caravan then returned and picked up another thirty thousand jars which they took two days' march into the desert and buried. And so on and so on until, after many months' labour, he had established a complete chain of halting-places for his army, at each of which they would have an ample supply of water, along a five hundred mile route direct to the Oasis of Jupiter-Ammon.

'When the time came for Cambyses to march he was a sick man. He retained sufficient men with him to keep Egypt in subjection but sent fifty thousand of his finest troops off into the desert, meaning to follow them afterwards. As he considered Thebes as no more than a temporary resting-place in his great march to conquer the known world, he naturally sent with the Army the bulk of the immense spoils which he had taken from the Egyptian temples. There can be no doubt about that; otherwise we should have found them by now either in

Egypt itself or during our excavations in the Persian capital had he sent them back there.

'Cambyses' legions set out on their march but when they were two-thirds of their way across the desert their Senussi guides deliberately misled them, preferring death for themselves to opening the way to the conquest of their people. The story of their marches and counter-marches lost in the burning sand; of their last, desperate endeavour to stagger back across the endless miles to the Nile and safety is one no man will ever know. All history tells us is that not a single Persian arrived at the Oasis of Jupiter-Ammon, and that no survivor ever returned to tell Cambyses the fate of his legions. That great army, carrying with it the accumulated treasures of five thousand years of civilisation, vanished utterly, the 50,000 men in it perishing of sunstroke and thirst, lying down to die where the last stages of exhaustion overcame them; and no trace of the place where they foundered, out there in the limitless desert, has ever yet been discovered.'

'What an amazing story!' I exclaimed.

Sir Walter smiled. 'It *is* amazing, but none the less true. If you re-read your Herodotus, you'll find that he gives quite a lengthy account of this appalling calamity. But the point is that I am in a position to confirm it owing to a discovery I made during my last season's work in Egypt.'

'How in the world did you manage that?'

'I was excavating in the Oasis of Dakhla, some 250 miles west of Luxor, which was the jumping-off place used by Cambyses' army. I dug up a small steel, or memorial tablet, there. It was broken into two pieces and I had no opportunity to translate it until late in the spring when our diggings had been closed down for the year.

'The tablet had been erected by one Heru-tem, Captain of a thousand, and he recorded on it that he was a survivor of Cambyses' lost army. After many terrible days in the desert he had managed to get back to the Oasis, but he knew that the Great King would certainly kill him in his anger if he reported the appalling fate which had overtaken all his finest regiments. Very wisely, Heru-tem never returned to Thebes but settled under another name as a date-farmer in the Oasis and there lived out the rest of his life.'

'Did he give any indication as to where the army actually foundered?' I asked.

'Yes,' replied Sir Walter. 'He recorded the position of certain stars at that season, based of course, not on Greenwich because Greenwich did not exist then, but on the Great Pyramid of Gizeh, which was the Egyptian astronomical zero.'

The deck was quiet. I tried to make my voice sound natural as I said, 'That's a very valuable secret to possess.'

'It is indeed, since the greatest treasure in gold and jewels the world has ever known must still lie abandoned there. Even Harry and Clarissa don't know the actual site as yet because I only took the top half of the tablet to England in order to secure financial backing for my expedition. Sylvia has the other half in Cairo. That's why she remained there all through this summer; and without both portions nobody could learn where this enormous treasure lies.'

'I'd give my eyes to join you on this trip,' I said, 'so you can rely on me to do my utmost to get my business through in time.'

'I thought you would,' he smiled, 'and we shall be delighted to have you. Harry and Clarissa have seen the top half of the tablet already, of course, but it would probably interest you to have a look at it. As it's packed up in linen and sacking it will take a little time to unwrap, but if you care to come down to my cabin in about ten minutes I'll show it to you, and give you a translation of the hieroglyphics on it.'

'That's awfully kind of you, sir,' I said as he stood up, and, saying good night to the Belvilles, I walked as far as the companion-way with him.

I left him there and went into the lavatory. Ten minutes later I knocked on the door of his stateroom. There was no reply so I pushed it open and stepped in. I could see no tablet nor any package which might have contained it; and although Sir Walter was there he could not speak to me.

He lay dead, sprawled face-downwards on the floor, and a dark patch of blood oozed up through his dinner-jacket, round the knife that was buried up to the hilt in his back.

3

Death in the 'Hampshire'

My eyes were riveted on the hilt of the big knife that stuck out between Sir Walter Shane's shoulder-blades and the pool of blood welling up all round it. I had no impulse to turn him over and see if he were really dead. Although I could not see his face, which was twisted away from me, I knew instinctively that he was beyond all human help.

In all my twenty-seven years I had only once before seen a dead man. That was at the age of eleven, when Uncle Herbert had taken me up for a last glimpse of my father. His kind, familiar face had been no more frightening in death than in life; but this was different. I felt a little sick and swallowed hard.

I was still standing in the open doorway of Sir Walter's stateroom and stepped back on to the deck meaning to shout, but checked myself in time. The Captain would not thank me for bringing a crowd of curious passengers on the scene. Entering the cabin again, I closed the door and rang for the steward.

While I waited there I tried to collect my thoughts. It was obvious that Sir Walter had been murdered, and the reason was not far to seek. Someone had killed him to gain possession of the portion of the tablet which gave the position in the Libyan Desert where Cambyses' army had foundered; the key to the vast treasure that he had been going out to Egypt with the Belvilles to seek.

I looked swiftly round for some package which might contain the ancient slab of stone. It would be, I felt sure, a pretty bulky object, two of three feet square at least and probably several inches thick. I peered under the bed and took a quick look in the private bathroom next door, but I could see nothing which might be the memorial stone he had guarded so carefully, and it was hardly likely that he would have kept such an unwieldy thing in one of his trunks.

When the door swung open it took me by surprise and I probably had a guilty look.

'Gawd!' exclaimed the fat-faced steward, his eyes popping as he took in the situation. 'Who done it? You?'

His startled exclamation and accusing eyes brought home to me for the first time my own unenviable position in the affair. Presumably I had been the last person to see the famous Egyptologist alive, when he had left me ten minutes before at the foot of the companion-way, and certainly I was the first person to find him dead.

'No,' I muttered, pulling out my handkerchief and mopping my face. 'No. Of course not. I found him like this a couple of minutes ago. Don't stand there goggling man. Get one of the officers, or better still the Captain, and keep your mouth shut.'

'Very good, sir—very good. No offence, but it comes as a bit of a shock to see the old gent struck all of an 'eap like that.'

As the steward hurried off along the deck and I stood waiting once more, my eye fell on the photograph of Sir Walter's daughter that he had shown me earlier that evening. The turmoil of my mind was stayed for a moment as I studied Sylvia Shane's lovely features again and speculated about her. From numerous remarks the old man had let drop on the voyage out I gathered that she was devoted to him. It would be a ghastly shock when she learnt that her father had been murdered. What a grim ending to her long and dreary wait for him, through the hot and dusty summer months in Cairo, while she guarded the other portion of the tablet until he could return with funds for their expedition.

The Chief Purser arrived at that moment. He went a shade paler about the gills as he said, 'This is a terrible business, Mr. Day. How did you come to be down here in his cabin?'

I was just about to reply when the Captain and the Ship's Doctor joined us. After the doctor had made a brief examination, Captain Bingham grunted at the Purser, 'You'd best lock up here, Mr. Irons, and all of you come to my cabin.'

The next four hours were, at first, extremely trying and, as the night wore on, incredibly dreary. Harry and Clarissa Belville were sent for in due course; and the Captain, a very angry and disgruntled man at having his ship's record besmirched by such a tragedy, questioned us all in turn.

Clarissa and Harry both protested from the very start their conviction that I had had no hand in the murder. Their evidence proved that although I had not started from Liverpool in their party, and although previous to joining the ship I had been quite unknown to them, our acquaintance had ripened to a strong friendship during the voyage and Sir Walter had actually invited me to join them on their winter's digging in Egypt. They stated, too, that they were both present when Sir Walter had asked me down to his cabin a quarter of an hour before his death to see an Egyptian antique he had dug up during the previous season.

'What sort of an antique?' inquired Captain Bingham with a sharp glance in my direction.

'The half of a memorial tablet,' I replied.

'Had it any particular value?'

'The inscription . . .' I began, but Clarissa cut in quickly:

'None of us knew what the inscription was about; but the stone was an unusual one and Sir Walter prized it very highly.'

The Captain turned to me. 'Was it there when you found him?'

'No, I've never seen it.'

The Purser was sent down to search the cabin and returned to report that the tablet was not among Sir Walter's belongings; upon which the Captain pressed us for further information about it.

I soon saw that Clarissa and her husband did not wish to let out anything about their projected expedition and, as I did not see myself that the story of the lost army of Cambyses could have any bearing on the murder, I followed their lead. It was quite sufficient for the authorities to know that the motive for the crime was to gain possession of the tablet, without our divulging the secret contained in its hieroglyphics.

Captain Bingham was not a particularly intelligent man, but he went over every point again, and again and again; and showed a dogged persistence in digging up every possible fact he could about the Belvilles and myself. As they had nothing to hide, his questions did not embarrass them in the least; but my own case was very different. I was travelling on the passport of Julian Day, issued to me as a generous gesture after my ignominious dismissal from the Diplomatic Service eighteen months before. From that point I could give a straightforward account of my journeyings in Finland, Egypt and the Balkans until my return to England that autumn; but when it came to giving information about myself previous to my change of name it was by no means easy. I could only say that I had inherited a certain sum of money when I was twenty-one and, on coming down from Oxford two years later, had decided to travel.

At four o'clock in the morning Captain Bingham reluctantly brought his abortive inquiry to a close. He warned us that when we reached Alexandria the following day we must all receive permission from the police, to whom he would there hand the matter over, before we were free to go ashore; and at last allowed us to retire, weary and oppressed, to our cabins.

I had a badly needed brandy with Harry and Clarissa in their stateroom before turning in. We were all badly shaken by the night's events, and it was lucky for me they had some brandy there, as I never drink whisky. I don't like it and I don't like beer; probably because I have an exceptionally sweet palate. My drinks are cider and every kind of wine and liqueur. I am particularly fond of rich hocks and Chateau bottled Sauternes of the Yquem type and I eat a great many sweets. It is quite wrong to imagine that sugar is necessarily fattening; that is only so if one's glands are not functioning properly or one is mentally lazy. Sugar is the finest brain fuel in the world and providing one does not gorge oneself on quantities of meat one can absorb a great deal of sugar without putting on a surplus ounce of fat.

I saw with pleasure that the Belvilles' friendship for me appeared not to have weakened in the least, and their main preoccupation now seemed to be the horrible business of breaking the news to Sylvia Shane in Cairo, together with the question of Sir Walter's burial.

Owing to the climate in Egypt Sir Walter would have to be buried immediately the police had viewed his body, which seemed a good thing as it would save Sylvia the ordeal of the funeral, and Harry undertook to make the necessary arrangements. Neither of the Belvilles had the least reason to suspect any particular person of the crime and, up till that evening.

had believed Sir Walter and themselves to be the only people on board who even knew of the existence of the tablet. Very gloomily we parted for what was left of the night.

Before going to my own cabin I remained for a bit leaning over the ship's rail. It was the first chance I had had of being alone to try to think things out. All of us had been chain-smoking too, owing to our frayed nerves, and the fresh salt breeze was just the thing to clear my head before I got between the sheets.

The night was fine, the ship ploughing along at a steady eighteen knots, her bow cutting the dark sea with a soothing hiss as the great combs of phosphorescent, foam-flecked water curved up and slid along her sides to form the long track of silvery white in her wake. The sky was almost cloudless and the stars glinted brightly in the purple-dark vault overhead. The decks were deserted and, free from the bustle of the day-time, showed long, empty vistas of spotless planking fading into mysterious gloom where their ends merged into the dark-ness fore and aft.

In reply to a question from Captain Bingham, the Chief Purser had stated that there were no known crooks on board; but I knew definitely that there was at least one; that is, if such a Prince of Evil as O'Kieff could be labelled by so ordinary a word as 'crook'. What he was doing on his way to Egypt I had failed entirely to discover; but it did seem to me that, although he was certainly not the man to commit a murder with his own hand for any ordinary haul of jewels, however large, he might well be concerned in the present business.

I went over again in my mind the extraordinary story Sir Walter had told me less than an hour before his death and, fan-tastic as it sounded, I was forced to admit that it had the ring of truth about it. His word could certainly be taken that his-tory would confirm the fact that Cambyses' army having set out to make new conquests and lost its way in the vast, sandy wastes of the Libyan Desert, never to be heard of again. If Sir Walter were right about the memorial tablet he had found giving the site where those 50,000 men had perished of thirst under the merciless sun, it really did mean that one of the biggest fortunes in the world was involved.

Even the bones of the Persians would probably have disintegrated in the shifting sand and wind by now, but their spears, helmets, armour and the immense loot in gold and jewels they had taken out of Egypt would be lying in the sand where they discarded them, as they dropped to die, two thousand four hundred years ago. A million pounds would be a modest estimate for the value of that treasure; it might even run to five million, ten million, or more. O'Kieff's organisation for espionage, dope-trafficking and white-slaving, immense as it was, could not bring him such a huge fortune even in a lifetime. Knowing O'Kieff to be utterly unscrupulous, the more I thought of it the more plausible it seemed to me to suspect that he was either Sir Walter's murderer or responsible for his death.

My sole reason for sailing in the 'Hampshire' was that O'Kieff had booked a passage in her; and during those long, lonely months since he had wrecked my career the desire to get even with him had gradually crystallised into a fanatical determination to do so even at the risk of my own life. No one on board, apparently, had the least suspicion that he might be involved in Sir Walter's murder, and that suited my book. If my blind guess were correct here was a heaven-sent opportunity to secure my vengeance by bringing the crime home to him.

One fact stood out a mile; whoever now had the tablet had been concerned in the murder. Captain Bingham had naturally realised that and would take all possible steps to find it; but it could not be got out of the ship until we reached Alexandria so, to avoid upsetting his passengers, it was a fairly safe bet that he would postpone any organised search for it until then. If I could locate it before that, and I was right about O'Kieff, I might have the inestimable pleasure of personally handing him over to justice.

O'Kieff had his valet, a big, bull-necked, shaven-headed Esthonian named Grünther, travelling with him, and I thought it very likely that he also had other accomplices on board. Probably one of them had committed the murder and had already secreted the tablet in some carefully selected hiding-place until such time as it could be safely smuggled ashore.

On the other hand, O'Kieff would certainly not wish anything so valuable to be out of his possession for longer than he could help and, again, if he had done the job himself he might not yet have had an opportunity to pass it on to a confederate. In consequence, there was just a chance that he was keeping it for the time being in his own cabin. After all, there was nothing whatever to connect him with the crime in the minds of the Captain or the Belvilles; and he had no reason to suppose that anyone on board knew of his previous criminal activities.

The result of my deliberations was that instead of leaving a message that I was not to be called, as I should normally have done after such a gruelling night, I turned in to get a few hours sleep with every intention of becoming exceedingly active first thing the following morning.

It seemed that I had hardly closed my eyes when the steward roused me with my morning tea and I saw daylight flood in through the square deck window of my stateroom. I would have given a lot to turn over and go to sleep again, but I roused myself with an effort as my plan, made a few hours before, came back to me. Having drunk the tea I dragged myself out of bed to bath and dress, after which I felt considerably better. I then went out on deck and sauntered idly past O'Kieff's stateroom, which was only two doors from my own.

Having kept him under observation for a good portion of the time since he had come on board at Marseilles, I knew his habits. He was called at 8.30, the same time as myself, by his man Grünther who got his bath ready, put out his clothes and left him again about nine; O'Kieff went down to breakfast about half-past, while Grünther did not usually appear on deck again until he came up to put out his master's clothes for dinner.

I had hardly passed the cabin when Grünther came out, drawing the cabin door to after him. Taking up a position by the ship's rail I awaited events. In due course I heard O'Kieff emerge behind me but I did not turn round until he was some way along the deck.

The second he had disappeared down the companion-way I glanced swiftly to left and right. A few people were already settling themselves for the morning in some steamer-chairs further aft and one couple had commenced their 'daily dozen'. I waited until they had passed me and rounded the corner under the bridge, then I dived straight into O'Kieff's cabin.

I knew that if I were caught there rummaging through his things I should be taken for a thief, and a most unpleasant scene might follow, but I had to risk that and, with O'Kieff and Grünther both out of the way, I did not think there was much likelihood of my being disturbed. The only snag was that O'Kieff breakfasted off coffee and a roll, which occupied him less than ten minutes, so I had no time to lose.

Harry had described the tablet to the Captain the night before as a slab of granite, packed in sacking, measuring thirty-one by twenty inches, so it was much too large to be easily concealed. A quick glance round failed to show me any likely package but naturally O'Kieff would not have been such a fool as to leave it lying about where the steward would comment on it, if only as a strange addition to his luggage made since the previous night.

I picked up a large suitcase from the corner, but its lightness told me at once that the tablet was not in it. His wardrobe-trunk was locked; such trunks have drawers down one side and hanging-room the other so it might have been in the space beneath his coats. Grabbing it by the top I shook it violently, but there was no loud bump such as one would have expected if the weighty stone had been loose in its bottom.

A square leather hat-box and the flat, steel-lined despatch-case were both too small to contain it. The only other place to look was in the cabin-trunk under the bed.

I pulled it out and lifting one end found that it weighed much too heavily to contain only clothes. It was locked, but I had come prepared to force locks if necessary, and took out my jack-knife. Inserting the blade under one of the catches I gave a quick wrench. Something snapped and it sprang open the other offered equally little resistance.

It was at that second I heard the thumping of a broom against the partition of the cabin and realised with quick dismay that I had completely forgotten all about the steward. While the passengers were breakfasting he would naturally be tidying up. He had done my cabin after I had left it and I knew that the occupant of the one next door had gone down to breakfast a few minutes before O'Kieff, so the steward might come in to do his, and catch me, at any moment.

In feverish haste I lifted the lid of the trunk and peered inside. The tray contained O'Kieff's dress-shirts. Pulling it up with one hand I thrust in my other, which came in contact with a litter of dirty washing. For a moment I fumbled wildly then, right at the bottom of the trunk, my fingers touched some sacking stretched taut over a flat, heavy object. My heart fairly leapt with exultation. It was the tablet, I felt sure, and if I could only verify the fact, I had as good as got O'Kieff for murder.

I had only one hand to work with as with the other I was holding up the tray and lid of the trunk, and the tangle of underclothes prevented my actually seeing the package although I could feel the stout cord that bound it. I was just thrusting aside the dirty linen with my one free hand when I heard the slam of the door and a heavy footfall on the deck outside. The steward had done his job in the adjoining cabin. It was too late for me to get out and next moment he would catch me red-handed in the act of rifling O'Kieff's baggage.

4

Illicit Entry into Egypt

There was only one thing for it. I let the tray fall back, slammed down the lid of the trunk, thrust it under the bed and dived into the bathroom. I was not a second too soon. As I swung-to the door behind me, gripping its handle firmly so that it should not slam, I saw the curtain of the cabin entrace twitch.

Very gently I released the knob of the door and slid home the bolt, while I stood there striving to control my rapid breathing. I was safe for the moment. Even if the steward decided to do the bathroom first and found it locked he would assume that O'Kieff was still in there and clear off again to give him a chance to finish dressing. But in the meantime I was trapped. The steward would almost certainly wait about outside for O'Kieff to emerge; and when he appeared unexpectedly along the deck from the companion-way, they would both immediately investigate the question of the locked bathroom.

For what seemed an age I stood there, holding my breath as I waited for the steward to rattle on the bathroom door; but to my immense relief he set about tidying the cabin first. That left me one chance of getting out before O'Kieff made his appearance.

The bathroom window was oblong and as large as any of the others which lined the inner side of the promenade deck, but was of frosted, instead of plain glass. With quick fingers I twiddled its wheel until it slid down a little and I could cautiously peer out. The two promenaders were just passing again and another couple were lounging in deck-chairs about twenty feet further aft.

I waited for a moment until the backs of all four were turned, and got the window open to its fullest extent, slid back the bolt of the door and jumped up on to the bath. It was a tricky business wriggling out of that window feet first, but by clinging to a girder inside the bathroom, I managed it. Fortunately, I am fairly tall, five feet eleven and a half, so I was able to get my feet on the deck outside without dropping far and making a heavy thump. A girl in one of the deck-chairs turned her head to look at me but I had righted myself by that time and, although she may have wondered where I had appeared from so suddenly, she took no further notice. I breathed again.

Getting my own chair I planted it in its usual spot, outside my cabin, where I could keep observation on the entrance to O'Kieff's. My heart was still hammering as I congratulated myself on having got out of such an awkward scrape and on my luck, as I believed, in having located the tablet. Yet I could not swear that the package I had felt was actually it, and my elation was a little damped as I thought what a fool I should look if I went to the Captain with my story and charged O'Kieff with being concerned in the murder, if the thing in his trunk turned out not to be the tablet at all.

The situation was a decidedly tricky one. I had to keep on reminding myself that poor Sir Walter's death was really a side-issue as far as I was concerned. My objective was to get O'Kieff either gaoled or put out of the way altogether. Nothing could have suited my purpose better than proving him guilty of murder, but if he were innocent precipitate action might ruin my whole campaign. At the moment I had the inestimable advantage of his not having recognised me, but once I allowed myself to be drawn into personal contact with him, which would be inevitable if I charged him with the crime, it was almost certain that he would do so; and that would mean good-bye to any hope of catching him out in one of his nefarious operations during the coming weeks in Egypt. In consequence I decided that I dared not risk carrying my suspicions to the Captain.

I would have cheerfully given a year of my life for another five minutes alone in O'Kieff's cabin but, unfortunately, people were now starting to make themselves comfortable on the deck in considerable numbers, and there was little chance of its being deserted again before we reached Alexandria, where we were due that afternoon.

O'Kieff came on deck, fetched a book from his cabin and sat down to read. His lean, clever face with that unscrupulous. rat-trap mouth made an interesting study, but I knew it well enough already and had little chance to examine it further. even had I wished, as I was kept busy for the next hour or more on the unpleasant job of fobbing off all sort of curious people who wanted particulars about the murder.

I don't doubt the Captain had done his best to keep the matter dark, but it is impossible to conceal such things in the close intimacy of life on board ship, and it had leaked out together with the fact that I was concerned in it. The whole ship was agog with excited speculation and every sort of tittle-tattle.

To my great relief Harry and Clarissa put in an appearance a little after eleven. Her red curls startled the eye with more than usual violence in the brightness of the morning sunshine but her piquant features showed no trace of the trying night she had been through, except in unusual gravity. On the other hand, Harry's good-natured, rather stolid countenance gave ample indication of worry and curtailed sleep. Their arrival gave me a chance to break away from the morbid seekers after gory details, and the three of us moved to the ship's side, where we could talk without being overheard.

'Anything fresh?' Harry asked. 'We tried to sleep late, but the row out on the deck got us up much as usual.'

'Nothing official as far as I know,' I said. 'But I believe I'm on to the murderer.'

'Good God! Not really?' His blue eyes popped, while Clarissa gave a little squeal of excitement.

'Yes. It was pure chance but I happened to know that there's a crook on board. I came up against him once before, although how doesn't matter for the moment and I don't want you to give it away to anyone that I even know him. While he was at breakfast I had a look round his cabin and there's a package there which may, or may not, be the tablet. That's the trouble. I was disturbed and had to make a bolt for it before I could find out for certain.'

'We must tell the Captain, at once,' said Harry quickly.

Without disclosing anything of my own past I told them the bare facts about my vendetta against O'Kieff and my reasons for preferring not to broadcast my suspicions at the moment.

Clarissa nodded. 'All right, we'll say nothing to the Captain for the time being, since you wish it. But surely he must know that the key to the riddle lies in the tablet; I wonder he hasn't ordered a general search already.'

'That's because he doesn't want to upset his passengers. Directly he hands over to the authorities in Alex. you may bet they'll ransack everything.'

'Then if the man you suspect *has* got it, the police or customs are certain to find it in his baggage when we dock this afternoon.'

'I doubt that. He hasn't the least reason to suppose anyone on board suspects him but, all the same, he's bound to guess they'll go through everybody's stuff before we land, and he's much too clever to risk getting caught that way.'

'What will he do, then?'

'Pass it on to a confederate,' I replied. 'Probably one of the crew who could conceal it safely until the search is over and smuggle it ashore later, or lower it over the side into a boat at night. That's what we've got to prevent and where I want your help. It's much to big for him to bring out of his cabin without our spotting it. We must take turns in watching, and if he does bring it out, mark down the man to whom he hands it.'

'Of course we'll help,' Harry agreed eagerly. 'I'm jolly grateful to you, Julian, for what you've done already, and for keeping mum last night when the Captain questioned you about our expedition.'

'You're going on with it then, in spite of Sir Walter's death?'

'You bet we are. Naturally we're terribly cut up. It's simply horrible to think of the poor old chap being struck down like that; but we *must* carry on if we possibly can.'

'Why *must*?' I asked.

'Oh, for a number of reasons. For one, I'm sure he'd wish it. For another, Clarissa's got a whole packet sunk in this show. The devil of it is, though, we're scuppered before we start unless we can get that tablet back.'

'But surely you've got a translation of it?'

'No. The old man was so frightened of the secret getting out that he wouldn't have one done. It was for that reason, too, that he took only the top half of it with him to England and left the bottom half with Sylvia in Cairo.'

I nodded. 'Then we've darned well got to get it back somehow. If I'm right about it being the thing I felt in O'Kieff's trunk we will, too, providing we keep a careful watch on him.'

'Which is his cabin?' Harry inquired.

'No. 14. Just behind you to the left there. But for goodness sake don't look now.'

'Then he's the old boy with the wavy white hair like a wig?' Clarissa whispered.

'That's him; and, believe me, he's no small-time crook. He's so big that the police have never been able to get anything on him yet.'

Clarissa's blue eyes widened. 'This really is rather thrilling, isn't it?'

'I'll get a thrill all right if only I can land that devil for murder,' I muttered. 'But in the meantime I've had no breakfast except some Harrogate toffee and a few chocolates. Will you hold the fort while I find myself some soup and biscuits to fortify the inner man? I think I'll pack too, while I'm about it, so as to leave you quite free after lunch.'

As soon as I had done my packing, I rejoined them and we spent the half-hour before lunch together. They went down directly the gong sounded and came up again as quickly as they could to let me slip away. Directly I'd fed they went off to do their packing and by three o'clock, when they joined me again, Alexandria was in sight.

For the next hour we watched the city as it rose out of the flat horizon with steadily-increasing clearness. It was far larger than the Belvilles had imagined and, stretching as it does for thirteen miles in a series of bays right along the coast, it certainly is an impressive sight; but, as I explained to them, the whole city consists almost entirely of this maginficent long front. There is hardly any depth to the place at all; it tails off into masses of squalid hutments and ragged streets, in most places not more than a quarter of a mile inland.

Alexandria is not, and never has been, a really Egyptian city; it was founded by Alexander the Great after his conquest of Egypt. When the Macedonian Empire disintegrated at his death, one of his great captains, Ptolemy, took Egypt as his portion, and he and his successors ruled it from Alexandria for three hundred years. As the Ptolemys were Greeks, their capital became to Greece what New York has to the Anglo-Saxons in modern times; but long after the glory had departed from Greece herself, Alexandria radiated the light of Greek culture over all the ancient world. Romans, Arabs, Turks, French and English conquered it in turn through the centuries, so that to-day it is one of the most cosmopolitan cities in the world, but its polyglot population still contains a large Greek element and has little in common with that of the rest of Egypt.

The seven bays which make up its waterfront are not easy to identify from the sea, but I was able to point out to the Bel-villes the peninsular upon which had stood the original city where Ptolemys had reigned in such splendour, as the last independent dynasty of Egyptian Kings, until their line ended with the beautiful Cleopatra.

At the extremity of the mole jutting out from its north-eastern end we could see the ruined Arab fort of Kait Bey which marks the site where the mighty Pharos, the great light-house counted as one of the Seven Wonders of the World, once towerd to the skies; and as we drew nearer I could distinguish, among the big blocks that overlook the promenade running right round the sweep of the wide East bay, the Hotel Cecil, where we had all arranged to stay the night before going on to Cairo.

The Belvilles would have been more interested in their first glimpse of Egypt and I in telling them what I knew of Alex., if we hadn't all been so anxious that O'Kieff or Grünther, both of whom had been in the cabin behind us for the last half-hour, should not pop out of it with the tablet unnoticed by us.

The 'Hampshire' hung about outside the harbour for some time but O'Kieff and his valet both remained secluded in the cabin. All three of us felt a growing sense of excitement as the ship at last drew in towards the dock. It seemed that O'Kieff must make some move soon unless he meant to try and run the tablet through himself, but in any case the dénouement of our day-long vigil could not bow be long delayed. We were prepared to swear that nothing the size of the tablet had been brought out of the cabin since I had left it, and we intended to stick to O'Kieff like leeches once the move ashore began. I could hardly supress my impatience as I thought of the kick I'd get in watching the customs people undo that sacking-covered package in his trunk.

When one goes south to the sunshine, but does not actually cross the equator, one is apt to forget that everywhere in the northern hemisphere sundown comes early in the winter months although, of course, the sun does not set quite as early in the Mediterranean as in England. It was barely six o'clock when the ship was made fast against the wharf, but all the same I wondered vaguely if the ship's time and land time differed, as I noticed that dusk was already falling, and falling much faster than it does at home.

There was a rush of passengers with their hand-luggage to the gangway immediately it was thrust aboard, although they might have known that there would be the usual tiresome delays, quite apart from the matter of the murder, and that even normally it would be the best part of an hour before they would be allowed off.

Numerous officials came on board and, among them, a number of Egyptian police, varying in colour from light brown to coal-black negroes, with the exception of their Chief Officer who was a tall, thin, beaky-nosed Englishman, looking very smart and businesslike in his well-cut uniform and red tarboosh. Evidently the Captain had wirelessed for them to meet the ship as we saw the Chief Purser lead them straight from the gangway to his cabin.

A glorious, salmon-coloured sunset now suggested a huge bonfire somewhere behind the town, throwing the long façades of big buildings into sharp relief, while out to sea visibility was fading rapidly. While we stood there, for about a quarter of an hour perhaps, daylight disappeared and the lights about the harbour began to prick the growing gloom here and there, turning Alexandria into a fairy city.

We were watching the metamorphosis when the Chief Purser suddenly appeared with the request that Harry and Clarissa would join the Captain in his cabin.

Harry shot me a dubious glance.

'Go ahead,' I nodded, and added significantly, 'I'll keep an eye on *your* luggage.'

'Thanks, Mr. Day,' the Purser said as he turned away. 'I'd be glad if you'd remain here, as we shall be wanting you in a few minutes.'

Evidently the Captain had reported all he knew of the murder to the police and they meant to check up on our stories separately. But O'Kieff was still inside and once he emerged I did not intend to let him out of my sight whatever happened.

The Belvilles had hardly left me when the Second Purser and two stewards came up to O'Kieff's lair. I was not near enough to hear what passed between them and him but he stepped outside followed by Grünther, who was carrying his despatch case and wraps, and a moment later the stewards began to pass out his baggage while the Purser led him aft along the deck.

I waited for the stewards, my eyes glued to the precious cabin trunk as it seemed to me this was just the point at which it was likely to be spirited away to some carefully selected hiding-place below decks. Rather to my surprise, they humped it off with the other luggage; so I followed wondering anxiously what this special attention to O'Kieff portended. The little party thrust their way through the crush of passengers near the gangway and crossed to the far side of the ship which was facing away from the wharf.

The deck there was considerable less crowded, but a number of the less impatient passengers lined the rail, looking out over the harbour dotted with its innumerable small craft or haggling with the Arabs below who, packed in their flimsy boats, were endeavouring to sell them fly-whisks, fruit and a variety of junk. O'Kieff and his baggage were escorted along the deck behind the row of passengers until they came to a halt where there was a break in the rail and a shipside ladder had been lowered. With a swift glance over, I saw that a large motor-launch was waiting alongside its lowest step.

Up to that moment everything had seemed so simple. All I had to do was to keep fairly near O'Kieff when his baggage was inspected, so that if the customs people looked like letting him through without examining that package there would still be time for me to tip them off, and then, if it was the tablet he would be promptly arrested.

Now, apparently, all my calculations were to be upset. O'Kieff had no accomplice on board among the crew neither did he intend to smuggle his loot through the customs like a common little crook. As usual, he was doing things on the grand scale and had managed, somehow, to wangle special permission to leave the ship without having his luggage searched. If he really had the tablet, once he got it ashore all chance of tracing it would be gone, and, after that, all possibility of getting him for murder. In an agony of frustration I saw that he would get clean away with it unless I risked everything by intervening. But that meant facing him at once and exposing myself to recognition, which was the very last thing I wanted to do.

Just as I was striving to reach a decision it looked as if the luck had taken a sudden turn in my favour. A police sergeant came hurrying up.

'No one is to leave the ship,' he barked at the Purser.

'Good gracious, man, why?' inquired O'Kieff with bland surprise.

'It is an order,' said the sergeant.

I was just chuckling to myself at his having been caught out when he leant over the rail and spoke to someone in the launch below. Next moment a short, stout figure wearing a red tarboosh came swiftly up the ladder and stepped on to the deck. In the glow of the electric light I recognised him instantly as Ismail Zakri Bey and my heart sank like a stone.

Zakri was the Egyptian among the Big Seven whom I had met in Brussels and I saw their whole plan in a flash. Before O'Kieff left Marseilles he had arranged that Zakri Bey, who could give him diplomatic immunity from all landing formalities in Egypt, should come off to meet the ship and take him ashore. I was near enough to hear the two of them greet each other, while the police sergeant drew himself up and saluted smartly.

'Sorry to have to bring you up on deck, Bey,' O'Kieff was murmuring, 'but there seems to be an order that no passenger should leave the ship as yet.'

'That does not apply to this gentleman,' Zakri Bey said quickly to the sergeant. 'He is a friend of mine.'

'Pardon, Excellency,' replied the man, 'but it is an order of the *Miralai* that all baggage must be searched before any passenger leaves the ship.'

O'Kieff laughed, and I gave him full marks for his magnificent self-assurance, as he said, 'Well, you can search mine if you like. I haven't the least objection.'

'No, no.' Zakri shook his head. 'We have no time.'

He turned to the sergeant again. 'Mr. O'Kieff is my personal guest and I take full responsibility. Tell your officer that we had to go ashore at once to keep an important engagement. Come now,' he added to the stewards, 'put all these things in the boat.'

The sergeant did not dare to protest further, but saluted again and, to show his efficiency before such an important personage, began to shout curses at the Arab riff-raff below for the noise they were making as they endeavoured to coax piastres out of the watching passengers.

Zakri Bey's arrival on the scene caused me finally to abandon any thought of trying to prevent O'Kieff from leaving the ship. Zakri was a power in the land and he obviously did not intend to allow that cabin trunk to be opened whatever happened. If I attempted to force an issue he would simply overrule everybody, have the trunk thrown into the boat and make his peace with the authorities afterwards. Besides, if one of them failed to recognise me under the thin disguise of my brown beard it was quite certain that the other would. I could only stand there half-choking with fury at the way O'Kieff had slipped through my fingers, as he followed Zakri down the ladder.

The sergeant had passed along the deck, still shouting at the Arabs, while I leant over the rail gloomily watching the luggage being loaded into the launch. It was just pushing off when I heard a voice call up to me from the semi-darkness below, a little further aft.

'Mr. Day, sir! *Saida,* Julian *effendi*! Please to regard me! What pleasure to welcome you to Egypt again!'

I turned, and there, standing up in a small motor-boat ten yards away, was a tall figure in a long, wide-sleeved silk jibba and tarboosh, with a crooked stick hanging over one arm and two rows of enormous gleaming white teeth shining up at me out of a dark, smiling face. It was Amin Khattab, the admirable Arab who had been my dragoman during my three months' stay in Egypt the previous winter.

'Welcome, Mr. Day, sir! Welcome!' he was crying cheerfully. 'I come by train to-day from Cairo to be here to meet you.'

How he could possibly have known that I was on my way out to Egypt again passes my comprehension. I have often heard stories of Indian bearers turning up in the same way to meet ships in which their old masters were returning but such a thing had never previously happened to myself. It is just one of the mysteries of the East that native servants do often travel many miles to be on the dock for the purpose of securing their old jobs; although how they receive the news that their former employer is on a particular ship is a thing that no European has ever fathomed.

The second I saw Amin I realised that there was still a chance for me to keep in touch with O'Kieff. I had no doubt at all now that he had the tablet. Zakri Bey having come off to meet him and ensure his baggage immunity from inspection proved that, at all events to my satisfaction. Once he had the tablet ashore he could easily fake up some story to show that it had come into his possession after he had landed, So there was little hope of pinning the murder on him through it; but the tablet itself was of immense importance. The Belvilles would certainly have gone to the Captain that morning and insisted on O'Kieff's cabin being searched if I hadn't persuaded them not to. They would be as sick as mud when they learned that I had allowed him to get away with it. I knew that I stood no chance at all of getting it back forcibly from Zakri and his crew but now fate had given me an opportunity to follow them and see where they took it, that seemed the very least I could do.

The Second Purser was still standing at the gap in the ship's rail so I tapped him on the shoulder and said quickly: 'That's my old dragoman in the boat below there. I shan't be a moment, but I want to fix things up with him.'

Without waiting for his reply I pushed past him and, waving a greeting to Amin, ran down the ladder. As Amin's boat came alongside I lowered my voice and muttered to him in Arabic, 'You saw that launch go off just now? There may be trouble, as I am not supposed to leave the ship yet, but I want to follow it. Are you game to take me?'

He glanced up at the Purser and nodded. 'I am a Cairo guide, so the ship people do not know me. It shall be as you wish, my lord. Step in the boat, please.'

Without further ado I jumped down beside him. He gave an order to his boatman and the motor purred.

'Hi! Come back, there!' shouted the Purser. But I took no notice.

'Hi!' he called again. 'Come back at once! You're not allowed to land without a permit! Come back there, or you'll be in trouble with the police!'

I turned and then cupping my hands, yelled back: 'Don't worry! I'll attend to any formalities later. Ask Mr. Belville to see my baggage through the customs.'

By that time we were fifty yards from the black bulk of the 'Hampshire'. The Purser's reply was drowned among the excited murmur of the passengers near him and the shrill cries of the Arab hawkers in the crowd of boats alongside.

Zakri Bey's launch had a good quarter of a mile's start of us and was heading for the harbour mouth, but we could see his lights quite clearly and, as our boat was a good one, I felt we had a decent prospect of keeping him in sight.

'How the deuce did you know that I was on my way back to Egypt?' I asked Amin, as we settled down to the chase.

He grinned at me in the darkness and shrugged his powerful shoulders. 'It was told to me that you were on this ship by old Mahmoud who reads the sands, and old Mahmoud never lies.'

Knowing that every Arab is an inveterate believer in fortune-telling and has the sands read for him at least once a week, I did not press the question further.

We turned south-west outside the mole and ran along the curve of the coal wharf, following Zakri Bey's launch until it turned in towards the shore again. We lost it then for a bit, and had some difficulty in picking it up among the Armada of small craft that lay at anchor off a straggling line of short jetties. But Amin spotted it nosing its way along to a rickety landing-stage beyond which there were some dark sheds and a rabbit-warren of dilapidated hutments.

We followed, shutting off our engine when we got to within thirty yards of the jetty. Peering forward I saw that O'Kieff, Zakri and Grünther had already landed and were just disappearing into the dark shadows cast by the wooden buildings, while Zakri's men were still busy unloading the baggage. Pulling Amin down beside me, we crouched in the stern of the boat until the men with the baggage had followed the others up the jetty. Next moment we were alongside. 'Wait here for ten minutes and if I don't return, meet me at Hotel Cecil,' I said to Amin, and I climbed out on to the pier.

As I padded softly up the wooden causeway I was praying that if there was a car waiting in the street beyond the hutments for O'Kieff and Zakri, I should have the good luck to pick up a taxi in which to follow them and learn where they took the all-important trunk.

The jetty and its immediate neighbourhood were utterly deserted. The clanging of tram bells and the hoot of motor-horns came faintly from the street a few hundred yards away, but there was not a moving thing in sight as I entered a narrow passage at the top of the causeway where a mass of spars, anchors and other waterfront débris were littered about between two sheds.

Without a hint of warning a tall figure suddenly stepped out from the shadows and a sharp voice said, 'What the hell are you up to—following us?'

It was O'Kieff, and he was holding an automatic which pointed at my middle.

5

Hell on the Waterfront

Instead of having passed through the huddle of shacks to the street, as I had supposed, O'Kieff must have waited there at the top of the causeway to see the porters bring up his precious luggage and spotted me following them; all unsuspectingly I had walked right into his arms.

'What the hell d'you mean by poking your nose into my affairs?' he snapped, and his eyes glinted angrily behind his pince-nez.

'Your affairs?' I echoed in a tone that I hoped conveyed complete surprise. 'I wasn't following you. I don't even know who you are.'

'That's a lie! You've just come off the "Hampshire". I saw your boat leave the ship a couple of minutes after ours.'

'Well, what about it?' I bluffed. 'Why should you consider yourself the only person who has a reason for wanting to get ashore at once?'

'Who is he?' came a falsetto voice, and Zakri Bey emerged from the shadows. Evidently he had sent Grünther on with the baggage and returned to join O'Kieff.

'I don't know,' O'Kieff grunted, and signalling me with a jerk of his automatic to step out into the open space where the lights from the vessels in the basin would enable him to see me better, he added, 'Come on, let's have a look at you.'

I had no alternative but to obey and, as I did so, I wondered with acute anxiety what would happen when they recognised me. There was not a soul about except the boatmen, who were now hidden from us by the angle of the sheds; the street was several hundred yards away and a feeling of absolute panic welled up in me as I saw that O'Kieff had a silencer on the end of his gun. The 'plop' of the silenced automatic would not be heard in the street or even down at the bottom of the jetty.

When I failed to reappear Amin would not come up to investigate because I'd told him that if I did not return in ten minutes he was to meet me at the Hotel Cecil. Besides, they could easily drag my body into one of the tumble-down shacks and cover it with abandoned gear so that it might not be discovered for days and, even when it was, Zakri Bey had quite enough power with the Egyptian authorities to stymie any investigations which might lead towards O'Kieff or himself.

The night was warm but I felt myself breaking out into a cold sweat as I stood there while they peered at me in the uncertain light. It was the brief notoriety which I had gained on board in connection with Sir Walter's death that temporarily saved me.

O'Kieff stared for a moment at my bearded features and exclaimed, 'By Jove, you're the young fellow who discovered Sir Walter Shane's body after the murder.'

'That's right,' I agreed.

'You were in his party, weren't you? And your name's Julian Day. By Jove, I've got it.' He suddenly thrust his free hand into his trouser pocket and pulled out a jack-knife which he held out for my inspection.

It was my own and had the initials 'J.D.' engraved on its side. Until that moment I hadn't even missed it, but in my dash to escape being caught by the steward in his cabin that morning I must have left it on the floor.

'Your cabin was only one away from mine,' he went on grimly. 'It must have been you who broke open my trunk while I was at breakfast.'

'Honestly, you're mistaken,' I lied. 'That's my knife, but I lent it to the steward and he must have left it in your room.'

'A likely yarn! God knows what, but something's given you the idea that I had a hand in Sir Walter's death, so you decided to do a little amateur detecting. That's the only possible explanation of the knife episode and your following me ashore like this.'

'Nonsense,' I protested. 'I've got urgent business in Alex. A friend I must see before he sails on another boat to-night. If I'd remained on board I might have been held up for a couple of hours and missed him. That's all there is to it.'

'You're going to miss him anyway,' said O'Kieff ominously.

'Why?' I asked with all the truculence I could muster.

'Because I don't intend to give you the chance to interfere any further in my affairs.'

The sinister ring in O'Kieff's voice would have been quite enough to scare anyone who did not know him, but knowing him as I did, his words conveyed to me quite clearly that he meant to do me in. Next moment my fears were confirmed by his saying rapidly to Zakri in Arabic:

'I can't think what he's found out—but he knows something; and even if the young fool isn't really dangerous it's better not to take any chances. We'll settle this business with a bullet and pitch his body into one of these sheds.'

The casual way in which he spoke of killing me was utterly horrifying yet it was entirely in keeping with his character. The sweat was streaming down my face and I only just succeeded in checking an impulse to yell for Amin. Just in time I realised that I was not supposed to know what an unscrupulous man I was up against nor to understand Arabic. My only chance lay in keeping up my pretence that I was quite innocent of having followed him ashore deliberately. To shout for help would have been of little use, in any case, as his gun was still pointed at me and never wavered.

'Look here,' I said, 'I haven't the faintest idea what you're talking about and I don't know the first thing about your affairs —or want to. I got special permission to come ashore because my business was urgent and it just happens that our boatman landed us at the same jetty. I can't imagine what you're making such a fuss about.'

Zakri Bey spoke then, also using Arabic: 'I wouldn't shoot him here. One of the watchmen might find the body and his boatman knows that he landed immediately after us. There'd be nothing to connect us with his killing but the enquiry might focus attention on us and we don't want that.'

My reprieve was dictated by expediency, not mercy, yet I blessed Zakri for it and fortunately, owing to the dim light, he could not see by the relief in my face that I had understood him.

'What do you suggest, then?' O'Kieff asked.

'That we hand him over to the police.'

'But that would give him a chance to tell them anything he knows.'

'He can't *know* anything. Otherwise he would have told it to the Captain and tried to prevent your leaving the ship. At the worst he only has suspicions and with those he cannot harm you now we have the tablet safely on shore.'

'He'll talk, all the same. And, whatever charge you trump up against him, they'll let him out in a few days. If he is on to something he'll follow us half round Egypt. I'd sooner kill him now than give him a chance to spy on us further.'

'He will not talk.' Zakri gave a falsetto chuckle. 'We will take him to the Immigration Depot and have him confined there for the night with orders that he is not to be allowed to speak to anyone. To-morrow I will arrange that his landing permit is cancelled. It is quite simple for me to see that he is refused permission to make a stay in Egypt. He will be put on the next boat returning to England and that will be the end of the matter.'

Perhaps my escape from an untimely death was too recent for me to appreciate it fully, since my heart sank like lead on hearing Zakri's ingenious plan for dealing with me. I had no doubt at all that he had sufficient influence to carry it out and that no appeal I might make to the British Consul would ever be allowed to reach its destination.

'That's a very sound idea.' O'Kieff nodded and barked at me: 'Come on you! Right-about turn!'

'What's the idea?' I asked innocently, but as I spoke a little pulse was hammering furiously in my forehead and a sudden surge of anger nearly choked me. Here, face to face with me, was the man who had ruined my career, caused poor Carruthers' suicide and, I was certain now, had knifed old Sir Walter too. This was my second bout with him and it was apparently destined to end as ignominiously for me as the first had done. I was to be shipped out of the country as an undesirable alien before I'd even had a chance to get going. I had virtually had the game in my own hands that morning. If I'd gone to the Captain then, we'd have caught O'Kieff with the goods on him. but I'd bungled the whole job and the thought stung me to a frenzy.

'The idea is to give you a free ride to the police station,' said O'Kieff quietly.

He was standing within a couple of feet of me and moved his gun a fraction as he signed to me to walk on ahead of him. It was an insane risk to take, but the thought of being bested by him a second time without even a struggle made me see red.

I think he must have sensed something of my feelings, for his whole body stiffened as I leapt. But I had sprung sideways before his silenced automatic coughed and I grabbed its barrel in my right hand before he could fire again.

With both of us clutching the pistol we swung in a swift half-circle. As I regained my balance I jerked up my right foot and let him have it in the groin. He gave an agonised squeal as my foot caught him but the effort caused me to stumble and I fell, dragging him down on top of me.

I had the advantage of youth, but he was tall, sinewy and incredibly strong for his years. Both of us were still clinging to the pistol as we struggled there in a heap. In twisting my head from under his I caught a glimpse of Zakri Bey. He had turned towards the street and was shouting for his men.

'Mustapha! Hassan! *Taala! Igri! igri*,' he cried. At that moment O'Kieff's teeth bit deep into my wrist.

I gasped with the pain and let go my hold on the gun. He brought it up and next second I saw his arm raised against the starry sky as he made to club me with it, but I jerked aside my head and, giving a terrific heave, flung him from me.

We rolled a yard apart and both came to rest sprawling in the filthy dust. I was on my knees a fraction before he was and, lashing out with all my strength, I caught him a smashing blow full in the face.

He went down flat under it and the shock must have caused his finger to contract spasmodically on the trigger of the automatic. It coughed again a second before he dropped it, but the bullet thudded harmlessly into the boarding of one of the sheds.

As I scrambled up from my knees I saw Zakri coming for me; at the same moment, I caught the sound of running feet. But Zakri was a plump, effeminate man, little used to exercise of any kind and hopeless in a scrap. I side-stepped and tripped him just as his two big Arabs came pelting round the corner.

I freely confess to enjoying a scrap once I am in it but I never believe in fighting for fighting's sake, and either of those two great natives would have been more than a match for me. Almost before Zakri had measured his length in the dirt I turned and bolted for the jetty.

With blood-curdling yells the Arabs came pounding after me. As I heard the thud of their flying feet I realised that they would reach the boat right on my heels, before we had a chance to get her off. Then, in a flash, I remembered that, except for the fellows who haunt the waterfronts and make a precarious living diving for coins, few Arabs can swim at all. Shouting to Amin to untie the boat, when I was still thirty yards from it, I took a header over the side into the water.

God, how it stank! Every sort of beastliness must have collected there since Cleopatra passed that way with her lovers in her gilded barge. It was more like oil than water, and four feet down I hit the mud, which churned up in great, slimy patches all around me. But as I struck out away from the jetty, I knew my plan had succeeded.

Zakri's two men were standing there goggling at me, as helpless as two newborn babes, just on the spot from which I had dived, and the chugging of the motor-boat engine told me that Amin was coming round to pick me up.

I soon found I was counting my chickens before they were hatched. O'Kieff and Zakri came running down the causeway, and O'Kieff had grabbed up his gun. The oily water suddenly flicked up within a foot of my head as he fired his first shot at me, and I was compelled to dive into that stagnant sewer-wash again.

For as long as I could I swam under water. My lungs were almost bursting when I came up. Another couple of bullets spat at me but they were further off this time and about ten yards ahead a small sailing boat lay at anchor. I ducked again and a few strokes enabled me to get round to her far side so that she lay between me and the jetty. Two minutes later Amin came alongside and hauled me out.

His friendly, if anxious face, was a considerable comfort as I sat in the stern, trying to wring as much as I could of that stinking water out of my sodden clothes, while we chugged out towards the mouth of the basin. My own cigarettes were ruined, but he gave me one of his fragrant Egyptians and supplied me with a light. After the first few puffs I felt a little better and began to get my bearings.

To Amin's credit it should be said that with the innate good breeding of his kind—and by that I mean the very best type of Arab—he never asked a single question about these strange proceedings, of the latter portion of which he had been an eye-witness; contenting himself with the remark that there were many 'bad mens' on the Alexandria waterfront, and quite obviously he did not mean to imply that I was amongst them.

Directly I had had a chance to consider the situation I saw that I was now faced with two alternatives. I must either return to the ship or go ashore and try to pick up O'Kieff's trail. If I went back to the ship it was certain that there would be a fine rumpus about my having left her without permission. I was, after all, the principal witness in the matter of murder and the police would naturally be furious at my having gone off before they had a chance to question me. I had intended in all good faith to report myself immediately I had traced O'Kieff to his lair, and to lay before them information which, I had hoped, would enable them to raid the place and arrest O'Kieff while he still had the tablet with him; but the recent fracas on the water-front had killed that idea stone dead. Now O'Kieff knew he was suspected he would realise that the tablet was as dangerous to him as a nest of vipers and get rid of it without a moment's delay and, apart from the tablet, there was not a single scrap of evidence I could bring against him.

I knew quite well that I ought to report to the police at once but I had already made a most exhaustive statement to the Captain of the 'Hampshire' which would be passed on to them, so I did not see that I should be interfering with the course of justice by refraining for an hour or two from giving my evidence all over again.

Another thought caused me much more serious perturbation. Neither O'Kieff nor Zakri was the type of man to remain inactive. Having failed to get me they would be sure to take every possible step they could to discredit me with the police in case I aired my suspicions and reported our scrap. If I mentioned the tablet my unsupported story would then be taken as pure malice; and Zakri would ask the police to hold me until he could get an order for my deportation. If I returned to the ship, therefore, it now looked highly probable that I should not be allowed to land again at all. My vendetta would be brought to an abrupt and inglorious termination, and that was the one thing I was now determined should not happen.

I might get caught or find it expedient to try to make my peace with the police later but for the time being, while the scent of the trail was still hot, I meant to carry on.

Having reached that decision the first job was to get ashore and secure some dry clothes. I hoped that Harry would have seen my baggage through the Customs and taken it to the Cecil with his own; but I dared not go there as the hotel was the one place where the police would be certain to be waiting for me. In consequence, it seemed that the only thing to do was to confide in Amin.

He accepted my story with Oriental calm and a really touching belief in my good faith. I told him frankly that he might get into trouble through helping me, but owing to my peculiar position I had shunned all European society when I had been in Egypt during the previous winter and having spent the best part of three months with him as my sole companion up and down the Valley of the Nile we had developed a real friendship; to my delight I now found that my eight months' absence had left our friendship quite unimpaired.

He said at once that it would not be wise for him to take me to his own lodging because many guides stayed there. They were in constant touch with the European community, would have heard of Sir Walter's murder by now and would be certain to talk; but that if I would forgive the poor accommodation he would take me to his uncle, who was a tarboosh-maker and had a small house in the native quarter where he would be able to supply me with a change of clothes.

'I should be more than grateful,' I told him, upon which the boat was turned inshore and landed us at some steps further east along the waterfront, near the Arsenal Basin and adjacent to Alexandria's bazaar.

It was getting on for eight o'clock but the bazaar was still a hive of activity; noisy, smelly and vaguely mysterious, but wholly fascinating as such swarming native quarters must always be to the visiting European. The shops we passed were little more than cupboards let into the wall, each piled high with the particular merchandise of its owner so that he barely had room to sit inside it on a low stool; cobblers, carpenters, metalworkers and bakers were all working away in the open at their trades, clad in voluminous, dirty white *galabiehs* and ragged turbans, while here and there a tarbooshed merchant in European clothes stood beside his bales of brightly-coloured cottons, piles of pots or pseudo-antiques. Woolly-headed children, naked but for a single garment which looked as though it had been cut from the broad, striped stuff used for the cheaper kind of pyjamas, gambolled in the gutters. Hugely fat women swathed in masses of black material right up to the eyes, above which a wood-and-brass affair was perched uncomfortably on their noses to keep their veils on place, haggled and chattered. Sturdy negroes from the south, yellow-faced, pock-marked slum-dwellers, straight-haired oriental Jews, and scores of cripples whining for alms jostled together as they moved leisurely about their business.

The ways were so narrow that there was barely room for the donkey-carts laden with melons, tomatoes and bananas to pass; while above, the upper storeys of the houses overhung the streets so that they almost touched. Occasionally the tinny music of a cheap wireless set impinged upon the ear and a fair proportion of the trashy goods displayed would, I knew, on closer inspection prove to have come from European factories; but, ostensibly, so little has Western influence permeated this outpost of the East, the scene would still have made a perfect setting for a chapter out of The Arabian Nights.

After twisting and turning through this swarming human rabbit-warren for some ten minutes we reached a cupboard-like shop in which an old man was sitting beside a heap of large, brass cylinders that looked rather like inverted pails. It is on these moulds that the heated red felt is stretched to form a tarboosh according to the requirements of the customer in size and height.

Amin introduced the old man to me as his uncle, Abu Khattab, and said in Arabic that he had urgent business we wished to discuss, upon which the old fez-maker promptly closed his shop by shutting the two doors which flanked its sides, and led us through a narrow passage upstairs to the living-room.

It was stuffy there and had that strange Eastern smell, half sour, half-spicy, which defies analysis; but while we stood in the doorway the old man lit the lamp and threw a pinch of some powder on it which gave off an aromatic smoke that sweetened the heavy atmosphere.

Although I was no longer actually dripping, my clothes were still sopping wet, so Amin checked his uncle's desire to offer ritual hospitality until I had stripped off my things and been wrapped in a clean, white robe. Old Abu then padded away in his soft slippers to another room and, after a few moments, returned with coffee and a plate of little sweet cakes.

I sat on the divan and the other two squatted on mats on the floor. When we had partaken of the refeshments Amin proceeded to tell his uncle that for my own purposes I must be concealed or disguised until my further pleasure.

'*Fadl, effendi, fadl.*' The old fellow waved his hand with a courteous gesture placing his house at my disposal; but I did not think it fair to take advantage of his offer beyond this brief visit, so I said that as I had certain business that would necessitate my going about the city I would prefer it if they would provide me with some sort of disguise.

'Such a matter should make no difficulty,' said Amin. 'Providing, sir, that you are willing for us to cut up your most becoming beard.'

I had positively loathed that beard of mine to begin with but once I'd got used to it I had grown quite fond of it, as not only was it a most personable affair, but it had also provided me with adequate protection in numerous cases when I'd run into people who would have recognised me without it; so I was loath to sacrifice it now. But his suggestion was so sensible that I agreed at once.

'I could provide you with Arab dress,' he said. 'I have only to fetch them from a small hotel where I lodge. Also I will procure stuff for staining your face and hands quite dark. Then if you wear a tarboosh you will be taken for an Egyptian.'

'That would be fine, and the sooner the better,' I replied.

Amin hurried off and I was left in the company of the old man. Our conversation had been in Arabic and I was delighted to find that I had no difficulty at all in taking part in it. Consequently, for the next twenty minutes I continued to practise on Uncle Abu while he brought me scissors and shaving things with which I first trimmed and then shaved my beard.

When Amin got back they stained my face and hands a pleasant nut-brown; after which they arrayed me in Arab undergarments and a rich-looking, striped silk *jibba*. Amin, as I knew from the previous winter, was a vain fellow; he had a whole collection of these and never seemed to appear in the same one twice. He was bigger than myself but that was no disadvantage since the long garment slipped over the silken undervest and other clothes without the necessity of fitting anywhere. When I was fully clad, old Abu showed his broken teeth in a grin and clapped his hands as delighted as a child at the result, while Amin nodded his approval.

'No one,' he declared, 'would ever take you for a European. And now, sir, what is it that next we do?'

'My friend, Mr. Harry Belville, is staying at the Hotel Cecil,' I said. 'It's important that I should see him. But I don't think you had better bring him down here, in case he's followed. It would be best if I go and sit at one of the cafés on the waterfront and you send him along to meet me. It won't look quite so suspicious if he's seen talking to an Egyptian at a café as if he comes down to a house in the native quarter within an hour of arriving in Alex. The other thing that I wanted you to do for me is to find out Zakri Bey's address in Alexandria.'

'It shall be done, sir, just as you are pleased to direct. We will go now, if you please, to a quiet café most suitable for this.'

I thanked Uncle Abu and, not liking to offer him money, I said that I should like to send tarbooshes to a number of my friends in England and would arrange the matter with Amin: upon which we each bowed our gratitude and he saw us out into the street.

The café to which Amin took me was certainly most suitable. It was small and unpretentious but clean, and well outside the native quarter. Alexandria's population has always consisted largely of Greeks, Italians and Jews, numbers of whom have intermarried with the native Egyptians through the centuries and produced a race which varies in every shade of skin from coal-black to lily-white, so although most of the patrons in the place were polyglots, no one would have thought it at all strange to see a pure European, like Harry, sitting there.

When Amin had left me I employed myself for the first few minutes in making a list of a dozen people or so for Abu to send tarbooshes to in England; and I chuckled a bit when I thought of their surprise at receiving such a gift from a complete stranger, as I naturally did not wish to arouse old memories by sending them in my proper name.

As soon as I had done this my thoughts reverted to O'Kieff and his associates. I wondered how many of the others, besides Zakri Bey, were concerned in this attempt to locate Cambyses' treasure, and went over the unholy crew once more in my mind.

In addition to the two beauties with whom I had had a scrap that night there was the Polish Jew, Azrael Mozinsky—a huge fleshly lump of a man with the cruellest eyes I have ever seen. His only redeeming quality was his passion for music and it was said that many a poor but talented artist owed his rise to fame to Azrael's patronage and the support afforded by a small fractions of his ill-gotten millions. Baron Feldmar von Hentzen, the German, was a very different type—a great powerful brute with the typical shaven head of the Prussian bully. He hadn't the imagination of the Jew but as an organiser he was unrivalled and he possessed all the ruthless qualities necessary for carrying through a deal whatever the cost. Inosuke Hayashi, the Japanese who, it was said, controlled the Eastern drug market, was an enigma to me. Behind his thick-lensed spectacles he looked a quite harmless little man but it was utterly impossible even to guess at the thoughts which were passing behind the mask of his puckered, yellow, poker face.

Another of them was that strange little figure Lord Gavin Fortescue. He was not exactly a dwarf but his body was frail and childlike, while his fine massive head with it shock of silver hair gave him the saintly look of an archbishop. It was said that his physical abnormality, together with the fact that he was born the younger twin of an English Duke and so failed to inherit the dukedom, had embittered him to such an extent that it had turned his brain; but somehow he did not scare me quite as much as Count Emilo Mondragora, the Portuguese, who was tall and stooping with a thin hatchet face and eyes that bored through one like gimlets. It was he, I think, who must have hypnotised poor Carruthers, although perhaps O'Kieff might have been a better hand at that.

If they were all concerned in this thing the odds were hopelessly against me. But their organisation was such a vast one that I had good reason to hope the other five were scattered up and down the world occupied with their own nefarious business, and that in the present issue I was only pitted against paunchy, feline, effeminate Zakri Bey and O'Kieff himself.

These two, in all conscience, were quite enough to take on unaided as Zakri Bey had practically a free hand to do what he liked in Egypt now the British had cleared out, and O'Kieff was the master of them all when it came to brains and ruthlessness. I was still smiling a little at the thought of that fine punch I had landed full in his ugly face when I saw Amin and Harry approaching. Harry's plump face expressed such surprise and dismay when he first saw me that I had to laugh.

'Good God! You do look a guy!' he exclaimed as he sat down at my table.

Amin was standing beside us and he bent down to whisper. 'While I was waiting for the gentleman I made inquiries of a fellow-guide who lives in Alexandria and knows it well. Zakri Bey has no house here and he is not at any of the big hotels.'

'Are you sure?' I asked.

'Most sure. He is a big man, very important. If he were, my friend would be certain to have such information. But he stays, perhaps, in a friends's house. I go now, my lord, to make further inquiry.'

As he turned away I smiled at Harry. 'It must be a bit of a shock for you seeing me rigged up like this.'

'It is,' he said. 'I certainly wouldn't have known you if I'd had to pick you out from this crowd myself. You're really a jolly good-looking fellow, too, without that silly beard. But I say, old chap, you've got yourself in the hell of a mess.'

'I suppose I have rather,' I admitted. 'I imagine the police are looking for me everywhere to question me about Sir Walter's death.'

Harry's blue eyes switched anxiously from side to side, and he leaned across the table. 'It's a darned sight worse than that. Since you bolted from the ship they're quite convinced you did it. They've got a warrant out and they're after you for murder.'

6

Wanted for Murder

'After me for murder!' I exclaimed. 'You can't mean that?'

Harry's fresh-complexioned face was unusually grave. 'My dear fellow, what could you expect? You were the last person to see the old chap alive, the first to find him dead, and then without a word of explanation you skedaddle from the ship. Naturally the police think you did it.'

The last three hours had been so packed with excitements that I'd had little chance to do anything except tackle each fresh situation as it arose and none at all to speculate on what other people might be thinking of my activities. Now, I saw in a flash the fine muddle in which I had landed myself. In my anxiety to follow O'Kieff I had simply ignored the grave view the authorities might take of my unauthorised departure from the ship, but obviously it gave them grounds for jumping to the conclusion that I knew more about the murder than I had said, or even that I was the actual murderer and had lost my nerve at the thought of facing a police enquiry.

'Why *did* you clear out like that?' Harry asked quietly.

I told him about O'Kieff and Zakri Bey, upon which he said: 'Clarissa and I guessed as much when we found O'Kieff had been exempted from passing through the Customs with the rest of us. Did you have any luck in tracing him?'

'No,' I replied, and gave a brief account of my adventures since I had left the 'Hampshire'.

'It looks as if the game's up, old son,' Harry said when I had finished. 'It was a stout effort on your part, but as you lost them the longer you endeavour to evade the police the more trouble you'll have with them when they get you. I think the best plan is for you to go along with me to the police right away. After all, you *didn't* do it. so you've got nothing to be afraid of; and you can count on Clarissa and me to stand by you.'

'That's nice of you, but it's no longer as simple as all that. I'm afraid. Zakri will have been on to the authorities by this time, spun some yarn about my being an undesirable and reported how they attempted to secure me. They'll hear then that I left the ship without permission and, in consequence, am now regarded as the murderer. It's a sure bet they'll play that for all their worth because it's such a heaven-sent opportunity to divert suspicion from themselves.'

'You've got a perfectly logical explanation for all you've done.'

'Yes, Harry. But not an atom of proof with which to back up my story. The police would never believe me. It's utterly sickening to think how I've played into O'Kieff's hands, but there it is. They'll use me as a red herring, have me detained for weeks until the police have to chuck the case through lack of further evidence, and then deported.'

'The devil they will!' Harry exclaimed unhappily. 'How damnable. This business hits us pretty hard, too, because the loss of the tablet puts our expedition right out of the question.'

'I'm afraid it does, and you were frightfully keen about it, weren't you?'

'Yes. You see, it wasn't only that we were looking forward to the fun of the thing. Like most of these scientific johnnies who're always thinking in Sanskrit or some nonsense, instead of £.s.d., old Sir Walter hadn't a bob to bless himself with. Even if we didn't find any jewels he was hoping to pick up enough ancient armour and other junk to provide for his old age and Sylvia. Now the expedition's off the poor girl's left high and dry without a cent—besides which, Clarissa will be set back the best part of six thousand quid.'

'Six thousand!' I echoed. 'That seems an awful lot.'

'It wasn't all needed for the actual expedition. A couple of thousand ought to cover that after we've resold the cars and lorries we're taking; but Sir Walter had to pay up three thousand to square young Lemming, who was with him when he found the tablet.'

'But I thought Lemming met with an accident a few days before the "Hampshire" sailed?'

Harry shook his head. 'I'm afraid we rather led you up the garden there. The fact is, that though he wasn't putting up a bean, directly he heard we were going to finance the expedition the greedy devil proceeded to blackmail Sir Walter with the threat that if he wasn't given a full half-share of the profits, he would form his own expedition and go out to get the whole lot for himself. We didn't want a rival show and Sir Walter was so confident we'd get our money back out of the Persian pots and pans that we agreed to buy Lemming off for three thousand down.'

'Did he know the translation of the tablet,' I asked.

'No, but it would have been easy for him to come to Egypt and sit on our tail until we reached the place where Cambyses' army foundered. As he pointed out, there would be no witnesses to tell what happened in the middle of the desert.'

'Good God! D'you mean ...'

'I mean that he as good as threatened to collect a gang of toughs, track us to the treasure and then hold us up.'

'That explains a lot of things,' I said quickly. 'Evidently Mr. Lemming is a first-class rogue; and birds of a feather flock together. I'd bet a hundred pounds to an old top-hat that having taken your cash to keep out of the game, he double-crossed you afterwards by telling the whole story to one of O'Kieff's bunch.'

'D'you really think so?'

'I do. O'Kieff then thought out a better plan than Lemming's. He decided to travel to Egypt in the same ship as your party, murder Sir Walter and steal the tablet; which he reckoned would put paid to your expedition and enable him to go after the treasure himself without any fear of molestation.'

'By Jove, I believe you're right! And it makes me absolutely livid to think he's going to get away with it.'

'But surely you don't mean to let him, do you?'

Harry looked at me dubiously. 'I don't see that Clarissa and I can do much to stop him on our own. If we had your help that'd be different because you know these thugs, and the country and the language; but the devil of it is you're as good as ruled out of the game already!'

'Oh no, I'm not.' I said. 'I'd give my right hand to get even with O'Kieff, so if you've a mind to go after him you can count me in with you to the limit.'

'Nothing would suit my book better than a chance to get after the skunk and wring his blasted neck,' Harry asserted with a vehemence which was surprising in one normally so placid and good-natured, 'but it seems such a hopeless proposition, Julian, if you're going to be deported.'

'I don't mean to be if I can damn' well help it. That's why I've decided, now, that warrant or no warrant, I won't give myself up to the police. Once they get me I'll be slung out of Egypt, but every hour I can retain my freedom here there's still a hope of my being able to get my claws into O'Kieff.'

'D'you really think you'll be able to keep clear of the police for any length of time?'

'No, I'm afraid not. But with you and Clarissa and Amin to help me I may be able to elude them for a day or two. Fortunately none of them knows me by sight and they'll be looking for a European, anyhow, to start with. They're bound to catch me in the long run but this get-up gives me the initial advantage.'

'Well, what's the first move?'

'To find O'Kieff. As I didn't know what the regulations were in Egypt and wanted to avoid any fuss about bringing a gun through the Customs in my luggage I had mine on me when I left the ship; so I'm quite prepared to try a hold-up or any sort of burglary if we can discover where they've gone to earth.'

'You think there's still a chance of getting the tablet back, then?'

'I don't know. He's probably unloaded it temporarily just in case I tell my story to the police and they think there is enough in it to pay him an unexpected visit. But one thing's certain; he'll be in touch with whoever's got the tablet because he can't have had time to decipher the hieroglyphics on it yet. If we could trace it through him and get it back before he's able to do that it would leave him in the air. We'd get a translation done in Cairo and you could slip off into the desert without his having idea where you're heading for.'

'Yes,' Harry agreed. 'Sylvia could translate it for us. But the trouble is I don't see how we're going to set about tracing O'Kieff. Alexandria's a large city and we've only got to-night to work in. By this time to-morrow he'll be in Cairo.'

'That's just the snag,' I admitted. 'He's almost certain to be staying with Zakri Bey, and I was counting on Zakri's having a house here, but according to Amin he hasn't.'

Harry considered for a moment, then he stubbed out his cigar. 'I gather that this chap Zakri Bey is a real big noise in these parts?'

'You've said it,' I nodded. 'Like all the Big Seven he's immensely rich and right up in the stratosphere of crime where the police don't ordinarily go looking for criminals at all.'

'Is he the sort of bloke who would be accepted in the European society here?'

'Certainly. He's an Egyptian aristocrat. As a member of one of their oldest families he is *persona grata* with most of the members of the Government and many European officials.'

'In that case I think I know one line we might try. Did you ever hear of a chap named McPherson when you were here before?'

'D'you mean the cotton magnate who's said to be the richest man in Alexandria?'

'That's right. Extraordinary career he's had. When luck first came his way he was living in a flat in one of the big blocks here. He wanted more spacious accommodation and the story goes that he believed his luck was tied up in some way with his old flat, so he wouldn't leave it, but took the flat next door and knocked the wall through. After that he took the flat opposite, and another, and another, until he had the whole floor. Then he took the floor above and the floor below, and so on, until he eventually owned the whole six-storey block. Later he went to Venice, bought an old *palaccio* that was being pulled down and shipped its huge, square, marble staircase here, gutted his block of flats and re-erected the staircase in its centre; so that to-day the place is a veritable palace; huge ballroom, library, roof-gardens and all complete. They say there's not a single room remaining as it was originally except his simple bedroom on the third floor.'

'What an amazing story!'

'It is, isn't it? Anyhow, McPherson and his wife are one of the most generous couples in the world and they entertain with absolutely regal lavishness. He's an old friend of mine, and it happens that he came down to meet some people on the "Hampshire" this evening, so we ran into each other on the dock. Apparently he's got a big party on to-night—fancy dress show—and he pressed Clarissa and me to come along. Ordinarily it's the sort of invitation we would have jumped at, but in view of poor old Sir Walter's death last night it hardly seemed decent to go, so we refused. Still, I've only to ring him up and say we've changed our minds and I'm sure he would be delighted for us to bring you too.'

'It sounds grand,' I murmured, 'but I don't quite see how going to a party will get us anywhere.'

'Don't you?' he smiled. 'That's because you don't know McPherson's parties. He does things on the grand scale and every soul who matters in Alexandria will be there. If we keep our eyes and ears open we ought to be able to find out where Zakri Bey is staying. In fact, if he's such a big bug as you say, I should think he's almost certain to be there himself.'

'It's too risky. If I ran into one of those other friends of McPerson's from the "Hampshire" they'd know me again, even without my beard. Still, there's no reason why you and Clarissa shouldn't go.'

'That wouldn't be much good because neither of us knows even what Zakri Bey looks like; and nobody would ever recognise you if you came rigged out just as you are now.'

'What, like this?' I expostulated. 'But you couldn't possibly take an Arab dragoman to that sort of show.'

'Nonsense,' Harry laughed. 'Alexandria's one of the most cosmopolitan cities in the world. There'll be Greeks and Italians and French and Gyppies there every colour of the rainbow; as it's a fancy-dress dance there'll probably be at least a score of other chaps dressed as Arabs.'

'In that case, I'm all for it. What time does the party start?'

'Half-past ten; and if I know the McPhersons they'll keep it up till dawn. It's past nine now, so I'll get back to the hotel, see if they can fix up Clarissa and me with some sort of costume, 'phone the McPhersons and have a spot of food. Say we pick you up here in a car at eleven?'

'That'll do splendidly,' I agreed. 'But don't get out of the car. Stop it about fifty yards down the road, by that lamp-post there, and I'll be on the look-out for you. Now I'm on the run we must avoid being seen about together in the streets as much as possible; the police may start having you shadowed in the hope that I'll try to contact you and they'll be able to pick me up that way.'

When Harry had gone I sat on at the café until Amin reappeared. He had had no luck with his enquiries. Zakri Bey was not staying at the Royal Palace, and by personal visits Amin had confirmed the fact that he had not taken rooms at any of the big hotels. It seemed as though he and O'Kieff had disappeared into the blue and I began to fear that they had decided on a night run through to Cairo by car. It is only 13 miles and by taking the new by-pass road which runs through the desert, avoiding all the villages of the Delta, they could reach Cairo by eleven o'clock if they had left Alex. immediately after their fracas with me.

Amin took me to a small restaurant where I insisted on his sitting down to feed with me; it would never have done for him to have left me in solitary state and to have had his own food outside, as is the usual custom of guides when they are with Europeans.

He was a little bashful about it but superlatively well-mannered and I took the opportunity to watch his idiosyncrasies as he fed, and copy them, in order to fill the rôle that I was playing as fittingly as possible. I cautioned him, too, that he must not say a single word to me in English and I got in some useful practice of my Arabic during the meal.

After we had fed I thanked him again for all his help and said that if he wished to assist me further he was to report the fol-myself without my risking being seen in their company. He would then be able to carry messages between the Belvilles and myself without my risking being seen in their company. He agreed at once and, having parted from him outside the restaurant, I returned to the café on the waterfront.

One would imagine that Egypt is a place where one could count on excellent coffee but, in spite of the vast quantities of it which are consumed there, the contrary is the fact. Whether you have Turkish or French it is nearly always inferior muck and barely drinkable even in the best hotels. But I had forgotten that until the waiter in the café placed a horrid, dark and muddy brew before me. I was about to thrust it impatiently aside and order a cognac when I remembered, just in time, my rôle of Arab; and that if I wished to keep my liberty a few hours longer I must not only look but act like one, so I supped the stuff noisily with apparent enjoyment.

Fortunately I had not long to wait and with commendable punctuality Harry and Clarissa pulled up in a car near the lamp-post down the street. The driver gave me a queer look as I climbed in; but immediately I started to talk in English he realised that I was just another lunatic tricked out for the fancy-dress dance to which the Belvilles were going. Harry had managed to secure the costumes of a clown and with his round face smothered in white and red paint was quite unrecognisable. Clarissa looked charming in the short skirts and décolleté of Columbine. She was wearing a mask but her red curls would have given her away instantly to anyone who knew her. However, it was hardly likely that O'Kieff would be present at the party and as Zakri Bey had never seen her there was no chance of his associating her with me if he happened to be there.

Ten minutes in the car brought us to the McPherson palace; and palace is the only word which adequately describes that great block of flats which had undergone such a strange metamorphosis. The central staircase of shining marble soared in stage after stage right to the top storey a hundred feet above the wide hall, and as we pushed our way through the swarm of gaily-costumed guests I saw that the splendid suite of reception-rooms on the upper floors held many fine pictures and a magnificent collection of art treasures.

It was, I think, one of the most colourful gatherings I have ever seen because, in addition to the fancy-dresses, the mixed nationalities of the Alexandrians added immensely to the fascination of the scene and Alexandria too, owing once again to the mixed blood of its people, is famous for its beautiful women. The great majority of the McPhersons' six hundred guests were Europeans and there were many lovely blondes among them who, by contrast with the copper-skinned beauties brought by the Egyptian officials, appeared even more attractive; while the raven-haired Egyptian noblewomen, their great eyes shadowed with kohl, looked, as in fact they were, the prize exhibits taken straight out of wealthy pashas' harems. None of them wore veils and I noticed that nearly all of them danced appallingly badly; but the languorous way in which they smoked their cigarettes and their whole poise, when they were standing talking to their partners after a dance, made one think of scented divans and walled gardens in the soft Egyptian night.

One of these beauties arrested my attention quite early in the proceedings. She was on the small side, only about five feet two in height, but she had a lovely little figure and one of the strangest faces I have ever seen. She was dressed as Cleopatra and wore a delicate gold fillet with the royal serpent and vulture rising above her low brow. The diadem brought out the lustre of her dark hair which was curled up from the nape of her neck behind. Her skin was a golden-bronze, and she had a large, mobile mouth; but it was her eyes which were so extraordinary. They were blue and set very far apart; so that it gave one a queer sensation to look at her and one could not be quite sure if she were focusing them on one or not. In some way that I could not analyse there seemed to be something Chinese about her. Perhaps it was the great breadth of her face, which rather suggested a flatness, although she had a small, straight nose, well-pointed chin and rather high cheek bones. Very occasionally one sees the same type of face in a girl who is born of a white father and Chinese mother.

She was evidently somebody of note as several of the Egyptians—big, heavy-jowled, elderly men—whom one could spot as important officials in spite of their fancy-dress, were always hovering about her, and her jewellery was superb.

Harry danced with Clarissa while I made a tour of the rooms, then I danced with her while he knocked back a good ration of the excellent Pol Roger which was on tap in the splendid library running the whole length of the block on the sixth floor. After that all three of us went round together looking for McPherson with the idea of getting him to introduce Harry to some of the Egyptians; but when we found him none of them happened to be about and he was very much occupied in looking after some newly-arrived guests, so we had to content ourselves with his promise that he would do so later and, as it was half-past one, we went in to supper.

Luck really did serve us then. We had hardly started when

Zakri Bey came in with the girl who had those extraordinary, wide-spaced eyes, and they sat down at the table next to us with their backs to myself and Clarissa.

She was chatting away with her usual vivacity and I think a couple of hours in this gay assembly had put Sir Walter's murder, and the reason for our being here, right out of her pretty head. I tipped her off not to talk so much, so that I could listen to the people just behind us, and kicked Harry under the table so that he should get what was on and recognise Zakri Bey when he saw him again.

Zakri was talking to 'Cleopatra' in Arabic and from such scraps of their conversation as I could catch they were only exchanging the usual pleasantries.

By turning my head a little I could see them in profile in a mirror on the opposite wall, and without openly staring at it I kept watch on their reflections as constantly as I could. The mirror was a good twenty feet away and I found it a queer sensation to see them talking at that distance and at the same time to hear their voices within a foot of the back of my neck.

I strained my ears to bursting point for the best part of fifteen minutes and I was just beginning to fear that there was no hope of my overhearing anything of value when Zakri suddenly put his brown hand on 'Cleopatra's' arm and nodded towards the door.

'That's the fellow,' he said. 'The tall young man dressed as a Red Indian. He is an expert in such things and will be able to decipher it for us.'

I positively itched to turn my head and have a look at the young man in Red Indian dress; but I managed to check the impulse and my eye fell upon Harry's face opposite. It was comical enough, under the heavy grease-paint make-up and shiny pink skullcap topped by the absurd tufts of false hair that go with the costume of a clown, but his mouth was now hanging open in a positively ludicrous fashion. As he caught my glance he shut it and, bending across the table, whispered:

'Can you beat it? Lemming's here. He's just come in. Look! Behind you, there, with a little Dutch girl. He's tricked out as an Indian Chief, but I'd swear it's him.'

Naturally Harry had not understood Zakri's remark of a moment earlier because the Egyptian was speaking in Arabic.

But those two pieces of information coming right on top of each other made me fairly jump for joy. The whole thing was as plain as a pikestaff, now. Lemming had not only taken Harry's three thousand and passed the story about Cambyses' lost army on to O'Kieff, but he was also actively co-operating with the enemy. The odds were that he had either come out to Alex. on an earlier ship, or by air, so as to meet O'Kieff in Egypt and act as technical adviser to his expedition. Now that O'Kieff had secured the tablet it was to be handed over to Lemming for deciphering.

I made an angry face at Harry to stop his talking further and stole another glance in the mirror. Lemming was just sitting down at a table with the girl in Dutch costume, on our side of the room but at the far end and near the door. He was a tall young man of about thirty; a little thin, but his beaky nose, lean jaw and dark eyes suited his Red Indian get-up to perfection.

Zakri and 'Cleopatra' were now talking about some mutual friends in Paris so I listened with only half an ear, while doing my best to cover the fact that I was listening at all by carrying on a jerky conversation with Clarissa. As she was quite capable of talking enough for two at any time that part of my job was fairly easy. We had eaten all we wanted of the good things provided by the McPhersons but I meant to outsit Zakri and the girl, just in case they let fall something else, and a few minutes later my luck proved to be in again.

A huge fellow arrayed in the gorgeous costume of the Mamelukes came up to their table, smiling all over his face, and said to her:

'I see you've finished supper, and this is my dance, Princess, I think.'

She smiled back at him and stood up at once but Zakri detained her for a moment to ask:

'What time do you think you'll leave here?'

She shrugged, glanced at a wrist-watch encrusted with diamonds, and said, 'It's a quarter-past two. I think by four I shall have had enough of it.'

'If you're quite sure about that I'll tell him to call at your house for it at four-thirty, on his way back to his hotel.'

'Yes,' she nodded. 'Tell him four-thirty, and I will be there.'

Although I was positively seething with excitement I managed to contain myself until Zakri had spoken to Lemming and had followed the other two out of the supper-room. Then I told Harry and Clarissa what was on foot.

'A darned good thing I'm painted up like this,' Harry remarked, 'otherwise Lemming would have been certain to know me again and would probably have tumbled to it that we've been keeping an eye on Zakri.'

'It's lucky I've got my back towards him, too,' added Clarissa. Then she glanced at me. 'Well, Bright-Eyes, what sort of plot is the big brain hatching now?'

'The plot's already made without any hatching,' I grinned. 'All we have to do for the moment is to find out who the Cleopatra woman is and where she lives.'

'My hat!' murmured Harry admiringly. 'You do think fast!' while Clarissa gave me one of her naughty looks, which I knew quite well meant precisely nothing at all, as she purred:

'All this he man stuff is just *too* exciting, Julian. In a moment I shall be begging you to run away with me.'

'Let's dance again, then, and talk it over,' I said with a smile. 'In the meantime your nice, complacent husband can go and dig out our kind host and find out all he can about the "lady in the case".'

I knew there was no risk of Lemming's clearing off for another hour at least and Harry agreed to meet us at the buffet up in the library when he had seen McPherson, while Clarissa and I went off to dance.

Half an hour later Harry rejoined us with the information that 'Miss Cleopatra' was the Princess Oonas Shahamalek and that she lived in one of the big houses at the east end of the Rue Sultan Hussein, which is the Park Lane of Alexandria. She had been a widow for two years although only twenty-one and was said to be fabulously wealthy. Her mother had been a Persian which, perhaps, accounted for the vague suggestion of the Chinese I had noticed in her face. The Persians have traded with the Far East for many centuries by caravan, so it was quite a possibility that some distant strain of Mongol blood had come out in her.

In my excitement in getting on to Zakri Bey again I quite

forgot, for the time being, that I was a hunted man, wanted for murder by the police, and the three of us cheerfully knocked back the best part of a bottle of McPherson's admirable Pol Roger to a continuation of our luck. I had forgotten, too, that I had never had any sort of training for the desperate type of game I proposed to play and it dawned on me only when I decided it was time for us to go in search of Lemming that, although the plan I had evolved seemed fine in theory, it was going to be quite another matter to put into practice.

It was a fairly safe bet that the Egyptologist-turned-crook would leave the party unaccompanied, as he had this business call to make before returning to his hotel, and I had visualised myself holding him up before he made that call, as the first step in my new campaign. It occurred to me now that half the cars in Alexandria were parked down in the street below and that at least a dozen policemen would be keeping watch on them; added to which, from four o'clock on, any number of guests would be leaving the party. I could hardly stand outside waiting for Lemming with a gun in my hand, or slog him on the head when he appeared and carry him away over my shoulder, with such a crowd of people about. Some more subtle means of securing his person had to be thought out.

As he was a visitor in Alexandria the odds were all against his having his own car and I felt that I could reasonably gamble on his leaving in a taxi; so, having asked the Belvilles to rout round for him and keep him under observation until I returned, I went downstairs and out into the street. Just as I had feared, there were scores of cars about and practically every taxi in Alexandria was lined up in one huge rank. Walking along the line I picked out two decent-looking fellows, both of whom had good cars, and beckoned them over to me. Then I produced my wallet and put up a little proposition to them.

At first they were a bit dubious; but money talks in Egypt and they both entered into the spirit of the thing when I explained that the whole affair was only a practical joke against a man who had pinched a young woman off me for the supper-dance.

Returning to the *Palaccio* I located Harry and Clarissa sitting out on a couple of chairs on the top landing. They told me they had run Lemming to earth up on the roof-garden where he was engaged in a petting-party with the blonde in the Dutch peasant dress.

'He was re-braiding one of her plaits when we spotted them,' giggled Clarissa. 'The bow must have come off its end in the scramble and he's taking his time to tie it on again.'

I lit a cigarette and we waited patiently for them to appear. Our position was a good one strategically since, in addition to the marble staircase, McPherson had installed a lift in his converted block of flats by which they might easily have slipped down to the hall had we not kept an eye on its sixth-floor gate as well as on the stairs.

At last they came down from the roof-garden. Lemming looked pretty hot, but they may have been due to his feathered head-dress; and the Dutch maiden's make-up was distinctly out of gear, disclosing the fact that she was by no means as young as one might have thought at the first sight of her two long golden pigtails.

She retired to put her face to rights and Lemming hung about until she reappeared, upon which we followed them down to the ballroom, where they danced again, but at a quarter-past four he evidently made up his mind to tear himself away from this blonde siren as we saw him with her in the doorway scribbling a note of her address, or a date, in a little book.

Leaving the Belvilles to keep an eye on him as he was making his good-byes I promptly shot down in the lift, hurried out into the street, signalled up my two chariots from the rank and halted them just outside the front door. Three minutes later I was back in the palace waiting for friend Lemming to come downstairs. The hall was full of people and directly he reached it I went straight up to him, bowed, first touching my forehead then my chest, and smiled the ingratiating smile of the average Arab servant.

'Forgive me please, sir,' I said with a lisp, 'but you are Mr. Lemming, yes?'

'Yes. Lemming's my name.' He stared at me in mild surprise.

'The Princess Oonas has sent a car for you, sir. If you please, I lead you to it.'

'That's very nice of her. I won't be a moment,' he replied turning away.

Harry and Clarissa had followed him down to the hall. I had told them nothing of my scheme so far as I did not wish to involve them in it until I was reasonably certain that it was going to work. As Lemming left me to get his coat from the cloakroom I stepped up to Harry and whispered, 'There are two cars outside. If I can get him into the first without any fuss take the second one and follow us.'

There were twenty or thirty people in the hall, guests and servants, and in my dragoman's get-up it was quite impossible for anyone who had not actually noticed me dancing upstairs to tell if I were with either one or the other. When Lemming reappeared with a light fawn coat over his Red Indian costume I bowed to him again and, without showing the least suspicion, he allowed me to lead him out to the first of the waiting cars.

I had carefully chosen the best-looking vehicle I could find among the strange assortment on the rank. Nearly all of them had once been private cars and this was a quite presentable-looking Renault. If Lemming remarked on the taximeter that had been affixed to it I meant to tell him that the Princess' own car had gone back to the garage before I was sent to fetch him; but, if he did notice the meter, he refrained from commenting on it.

In a fever of impatience to get away I held the door for him while, out of the corner of my eye, I saw Harry and Clarissa getting into the car behind. Next moment I had clambered into the seat beside the driver and we were off.

All went well for the first ten minutes, after which friend Lemming began to get uneasy. Leaning out of the window he craned his head forward and shouted in my ear.

'Hi! Where are you taking me?'

'To the Princess Oonas's house, *effendi*,' I shouted back, although we had already left it half-a-mile behind, somewhere on our left, and were now speeding at a fine pace down the Route D'Aboukir.'

Temporarily, he seemed reassured; but a few minutes later he tumbled to it that something was really up and began to shout again. By that time we were running out through Ramleh with its many fine villas where the English colony in Alex.

mainly reside. At that early morning hour not a soul was about so I simply ignored his yelling and banging on the windows; very soon we had left the last, isolated houses behind us and were right out in the country.

When we reached a good open stretch of road, where it was unlikely that we should be surprised by natives suddenly emerging from a group of palms or hutments, I told my driver to take a side-track which ran between some fields of cotton and, after we had bumped along it for a couple of miles, I pulled him up.

The second car came to a halt just behind us. I had hardly glimpsed it before the door of the one in which I myself had travelled was thrown violently open and Lemming sprang down in the dust.

'What the hell's the meaning of this?' he roared. 'If you think you've brought me out here to rob me, you're mistaken!'

'On the contrary,' I said politely, as I stepped down from the box. 'But it's not your money I'm after—only your clothes. Look lively and get 'em off.'

7

The Egyptian Princess

'My—clothes?' he gasped glancing down self-consciously at his Indian rig.

'That's it,' I said. 'You can keep your undies and the light coat. It's those pretty feathers of yours I'm after.'

The second car had pulled up ten yards behind us and Harry and Clarissa were now watching the little scene with amused smiles. I was quite confident that I could tackle Lemming without assistance as, although I did not wish to use it, I had my gun on me; but there was just a chance that the taxi-driver might have turned nasty and I could hardly hold them both up on my own while I changed clothes with Lemming. The affair was much too important to chance slipping up, so I had thought it best to bring Harry along just in case I needed a hand at a critical moment.

'What's the idea?' Lemming snapped. 'Is this some sort of joke?'

'You can take it that way if you like,' I told him.

'I *don't* like!' he roared. 'There's more in this than meets the eye. You got me into that car on the pretence it was going to take me to the Princess Oonas.'

'True, but I've no time to argue about that now. I'm in a hurry.'

'Look here,' he parried. 'What's the game? Who the hell are you, anyway?'

'I'm the man who's going to debag you in half a minute unless you get in the cab and take off your Indian finery yourself.'

He cast a startled glance in Clarissa's direction and she tittered.

'Come on,' I said, 'unless you want to provide one of the less usual sights of Alex.'

Suddenly he swung a fist at me but I ducked and slammed in a heavy one right over his heart. He gave a grunt and crashed back into the car, collapsing on its step.

'You're a nasty piece of work,' I told him, 'and I'd like to give you a good beating-up but I haven't the time just now. Maybe I'll have the opportunity later. Are you going to get into that cab and pull your clothes off or do I push your face in?'

Panting a little he turned about quite meekly and crawled into the car. I stood by the open door so that he should not attempt to slip out the other side, and watched him while he stripped himself on his feathers and soft leather Redskin garments.

'Leave them there on the seat,' I said, when he had done; and he emerged with the light fawn coat over his underthings. It was quite a short coat, and the spectacle of his rather skinny legs protruding from beneath it gave rise to fresh titters from Clarissa. I made him remove his shoes as well, knowing that without them the stony surface of the track would delay his getting back to the main road when we had gone. Telling Harry to keep an eye on him while I changed, I got into the car and discarded Amin's long silk *jibba* and tarboosh for the Indian garments and great hood of multi-coloured feathers; after which I beckoned over Clarissa and asked her to do my face.

Fortunately the make-up I had on already was not very different in shade from Lemming's, and although mine was a little less red I hoped that the difference in tone would not be noticed if we could fake up a fair imitation of his war-paint. We had nothing which would serve as yellow ochre, but Clarissa's lip-stick was of that repulsive shade of orange which women sometimes use and she transferred some of the great blobs of white grease-paint, with which Harry had bedaubed his countenance, to my own. When she had done drawing stripes and circles on my face I looked quite a formidable Indian Brave.

I should have liked to have tied Lemming up somewhere but I feared that if I did the two taxi-drivers might begin to regard the affair as something more than a joke. We were well off the main highway so there was little chance of his being picked up and, as I knew that without his shoes it would take him the best part of an hour to walk to the nearest garage or telephone.

I felt we should have all the start we needed. Paying off the second driver, with a liberal tip, I sent him back to Alex.. Clarissa, Harry and I then piled into the other car and followed, leaving Lemming there cursing in the middle of the track.

It was nearly five by the time we reached Princess Oonas' house; which proved to be an imposing-looking mansion standing in its own grounds but facing on to the street with a broad flight of marble steps leading down from a double-doorway to the pavement.

Leaving Harry and Clarissa in the car I marched up the steps and rang the bell. In spite of the lateness of the hour the door was opened for me immediately by a smart young coloured boy in an elaborate livery on the lines of the traditional Turkish dress. He ushered me into a wide, lofty hall lit only by one hanging lantern of Moorish design which left the further confines of the place in darkness. With almost startling suddenness a hugely fat man appeared out of the shadows; approaching noiselessly in felt-soled slippers he asked my business.

'My name is Lemming,' I said. 'The Princess is expecting me.'

The fat man bowed. 'This way, *effendi*. Her Highness is above,' and wobbling like a huge, top-heavy blancmange he led the way, puffing slightly, up a broad flight of stairs.

We passed through two large reception-rooms which were positively hideous. They were packed with garish Tottenham Court Road furniture and expensive but gaudy ornaments—mostly statuettes made up from bits of ivory, brass, bronze, enamel and silver fitted together—which conflicted horribly with the soft colours of the fine Persian rugs and beautiful old Turkish hangings. Beyond the second room, however, lay what appeared to be the Princess' private sanctum, and the moment I was shown in I saw that here was displayed a very different taste.

It was not marred by a single piece of costly European junk and had an entirely Eastern atmosphere. There were lacquer cabinets on which stood numerous fine pieces of carved crystal, soap-stone, malachite and jade. One wall, rather surprisingly for a woman's room, was covered with a fine collection of arms, mainly ancient pieces of Moorish pattern inlaid with gold and ivory. A perfume-burner on a tripod sent up a little wisp of aromatic smoke, scenting the room heavily with amber. There were no chairs at all; only divans and large, low, cushioned stools.

The Princess was lying on a divan in the centre of the room. She had discarded all her jewels and changed her Cleopatra costume for a little, red, sleeveless Turkish jacket, embroidered with gold, and voluminous trousers of some white filmy material which were drawn in tightly round her ankles but cut with such exaggerated width that until she moved it looked as though she were wearing a skirt. The bright red of the jacket set off her dark beauty to perfection and lying there in the soft glow of the shaded lamps she had all the exotic allure of an houri straight out of the Arabian Nights.

The fat man closed the double-doors of the room behind me and I was alone with Oonas. It was the critical moment. Lemming had been pointed out to her only a few hours before by Zakri Bey. Had she registered his features sufficiently well under their war-paint to know that it was not he who stood before her? He and I were much of a height and I blessed the subdued light in which it was hardly likely that she would notice the slightly different colouring of our make-up. Moreover, very large eyes are nearly always somewhat short-sighted, and I was gambling on the fact that she had not seen Lemming from nearer than about twenty feet.

For a moment she stared at me haughtily, but my anxiety was relieved when she exclaimed with abrupt displeasure:

'You are late.'

She had spoken in French so I replied in the same language, 'I fear I am, a little, but I got involved in an argument and couldn't get away quite at the time arranged.'

'I am not used to being kept waiting,' she said sharply.

'I am sorry to have kept you up,' I apologised. 'But if you will give me the thing I called for I won't detain you longer. As a matter of fact, I should be pretty glad to get to bed myself.'

'I am not used to rudeness, either.'

'Really?' I smiled. 'I had no intention of being rude.'

'Some of you Europeans have the strangest manners. In this country it is considered to be in the worst possible taste for a man to declare himself anxious to get out of a person's presence the moment he is shown into it.'

She was, I suppose, so used to adulation that my abruptness had seemed quite extraordinary to her. It suddenly occurred to me that, if I had not been so anxious to secure the tablet, the last thing I should have done would have been to treat her in such a manner. We were alone there together in the middle of the night, or rather in the small hours of the morning, and any normal young man who had no special reason for wanting to get away as quickly as he could would most certainly have jumped at the chance of improving his acquaintance with the beautiful Oonas.

It flashed into my mind that perhaps that was just what she had expected me to do; possibly she had liked what she had seen of Lemming's tall figure and been pleasurably anticipating a little mild amorous dalliance with a new admirer before she turned in for the night. Yet there was no hint of invitation in her glance. Those two large, abnormally widely-spaced blue eyes stared up at me unblinkingly; and, whether she knew it or not, I felt quite certain that they possessed hypnotic power.

Anxious as I was to get through with the business I suddenly realised that I had been very near missing a marvellous opportunity to further my own plans. As she believed me to be Lemming there was a fine possibility of my learning quite a lot about O'Kieff and Zakri Bey if only I could get her to talk. Although she had not asked me to sit down I promptly parked myself on one of the low stools near her divan.

'Princess,' I said, 'I'm afraid you've entirely misunderstood me. Far from wanting to leave your presence I should count it a great favour if I might be allowed to smoke a cigarette with you before returning to my hotel. I only feared that you would be tired after the dance and anxious to be rid of me as soon as possible.'

She stretched her arms lazily above her head and gave me the suggestion of a smile. 'That's better; quite a pretty speech for an Englishman. Smoke by all means. There are cigarettes in the box beside you on the little table there.'

I took one and reaching out a plump little brown hand she struck a match, sat upright and held it for me. As I lit the cigarette her face and those extraordinary eyes were very near my own. I got a whiff of her perfume and it was some subtle stuff that I could not analyse; like and yet unlike the amber which scented the whole room.

'I consider myself a very lucky fellow,' I went on, 'in having to collect this thing from you personally. Everyone was saying how lovely you looked in your costume as Cleopatra tonight, but I am more favoured than the rest now that I have been privileged to see you in the perfect setting of your own home.'

'You like me in these simple clothes, then?'

'You look a dream—an Eastern dream such as one reads of in the old literature of your country.'

She raised an eyebrow. 'A dream induced by hashish, perhaps?'

'That I can't say as I have never tried it.'

'Really! Are you afraid to do so?'

'Oh no,' I smiled. 'Like Jurgen, I'll try any drink once.'

'Who is this Jurgen you talk of?'

'One who was a great seeker after things in general and in particular for a certain lost Wednesday of his youth.'

'You speak in riddles,' she frowned.

'Forgive me. It is the witching hour, the silence of this room and your presence, all of which have gone to my head a little. What are the effects of hashish like?'

Oonas settled herself more comfortably on her divan and half-closed her heavily-lidded eyes as she replied slowly:

'At first, perhaps, you might not like it. There is a feeling that the walls of the room are closing in until one is imprisoned by them as in a tiny cell. Then they expand again until the room seems large enough to hold the whole universe and one is only a tiny pin-point at its centre. But later there comes the sensation of limitless power and the fulfilment of one's dearest desires. For a woman, strong-limbed tireless lovers; more handsome than she could ever find in real life. And for men, women more beautiful and more expertly amorous than any they have ever possessed in the flesh.'

'One can hardly wonder then that the addicts of the drug go to such lengths to obtain supplies of it.'

She shook her head. 'Considerable quantities must be taken to ensure these dreams and frequent indulgence to such a degree plays havoc with one's mental abilities; only the weak allow it to dominate them to that extent. An occasional hashish dream does little harm; but more usually it is taken in much smaller doses which are just sufficient to stimulate normal sexual desire. Few women of my acquaintance would regard with any favour a lover who did not pay them the compliment of taking a little hashish before a meeting. But perhaps you are one of these cold, unresponsive Englishmen who has no interest in such matters, Mr. Lemming?'

'On the contrary, Princess,' I hastened to assure her, amazed but intrigued by the strangely unconventional turn the conversation had taken.

'You are fond of beautiful women?' she asked softly.

'Certainly. What normal, healthy man is not?'

'As you are a friend of Mr. O'Kieff, then, I must arrange for you to visit our House of the Angels sometime; there you will find many.'

For a moment I feared that I might offend her by even admitting the possibility that I could be attracted by anyone other than herself, particularly the girls in what I assumed to be a white-slaving joint, but on second thoughts I considered it wiser to appear to accept the invitation in the detached spirit in which it was offered.

'That is most kind,' I said, and added, with a view to getting all the information I could, 'Where is it? Here or in Cairo?'

'Neither. It is in Ismailia; down on the Suez Canal. We use it as a clearing-house for the new beauties who are being sent from the West to our depots in the East, and for the Eastern girls who are being imported from Asia into Egypt and for the cities on the Mediterranean. Practically all of them are young novices with little experience and some are quite remarkable for their loveliness. That is why we call it the House of the Angels.'

'It sounds like Allah's Paradise on Earth.'

'It is,' she nodded. 'Beauties of every nationality are gathered there for a few days only before they are sent on to begin their careers elsewhere. But, naturally, they are all at the disposal of our friends during the short time they are in Ismailia.'

'What a marvellous invitation,' I smiled, and as she now seemed to have settled down to enjoy this strange talk I thought the time had come to strike a personal note; so I went on quietly: 'But not one of them could be as lovely as yourself.

Your costume tonight as Cleopatra was sheer inspiration. Never in my life have I seen anyone who fulfilled so perfectly what my idea of the real Cleopatra has always been.'

'Cleopatra was a bad woman,' she announced, giving me a queer, not unfriendly glance.

'Are you?' I asked, looking her straight in the eyes.

'Sometimes, if I can be persuaded that it will amuse me to be so.'

'And is that very difficult?'

'Very. Plenty of people try but few succeed, Mr. Lemming.'

'You are harder-hearted than Cleopatra, then, Princess.'

'Perhaps, but I lack her opportunities. One does not meet men like Antony and Julius Caesar in these days. I would like to have had Caesar for my lover.'

'If history is to be relied upon she had many others; lesser men as far as power was concerned, perhaps, but probably much more handsome and amusing.'

She smiled again. 'You, I think, could be amusing, Mr. Lemming. There is that something in your nice, dark eyes; but you would not call yourself handsome, would you? No.'

'On the contrary,' I smiled back. 'If by handsome you mean those regular, rather girlish features which some women admire, perhaps I'm not; but I've always been told that I am decidely good-looking, so I make no bones about saying so and I'm rather proud of the fact.'

She studied me closely for a moment. 'There is certainly an attraction in the strength of your face. I like your mouth and your good chin. But I can hardly judge you to the best advantage now with all that mess of paint you have on.'

'May I come and see you again tomorrow when I'm all cleaned up?' I asked.

'Tomorrow?' she echoed. 'But you'll be in Cairo then. The train leaves as 3 o'clock and I never receive till late in the afternoon.'

Her words recalled me with a little shock. So powerful was the fascination exerted by those blue eyes of hers, set in the broad, beautiful, golden face, that for some time past I had completely forgotten the real reason for my presence there. Time was slipping by and the Belvilles would be getting anxious about me.

'Of course,' I said. 'I forgot; but you've probably been told a thousand times before that a man might even forget his own name when he's sitting looking at you.'

She laughed—a deep, musical chuckle. 'I hope that you have not forgotten yours.'

I shook my head. 'It's not quite as bad as that; and I'm here to collect a parcel from you. I do hope, though, that you'll let me see you again, maybe in Cairo.'

'There or elsewhere,' she said lazily. 'If so, perhaps I will allow you to try your persuasive powers on me—handsome Mr. Lemming. I warn you that it is unlikely they will prove adequate but, all the same, I think you're rather nice.'

She moved to stand up and I was not altogether sorry to see that the interview was ended. Attractive as she was, it would have been madness on my part to get myself mixed up with this seductive houri who resided in the enemy's camp, particularly with the police after me for murder. Yet, on an impulse as she moved away, I caught her hand and kissed it.

The moment she had left the room my glance switched to a dwarf desk-table which stood in the bay of a tall window masked by heavy curtains. I had noticed it immediately I came in and that numerous papers were scattered on it. If she came back and caught me prying into them her suspicions would certainly be aroused and she might call up her servants to detain me until Zakri Bey could be fetched. My masquerade as Lemming would then go up in smoke and my life be not worth a moment's purchase. I could only attempt to fight my way out before he arrived and that might prove far from easy.

Yet the temptation to steal a glance at some of those papers was irresistible. From the way Oonas had spoken of hashish and the House of the Angels it was quite clear that she was up to the neck in O'Kieff's organisation, and that correspondence, left lying so casually there, might easily contain valuable data to assist me in my vendetta against him.

I knew that I was taking an absurd risk as I tiptoed softly across the heavy carpet, but I banked on such a valuable thing as the tablet being locked up somewhere so that Oonas would be away a good couple of minutes getting it.

I did not dare to pick up any of the papers, so that at least she would not catch me red-handed, but I ran my eye as quickly as possible over the stuff spread out on the little table. There were five small piles of letters and, without touching them, I could only read the top sheet on each. Three were in French and two in Arabic and, to my disappointment, they were all of a social nature, but from under one pile there protruded the top half of a foolscap sheet. It was headed 'Nights of Collection from Gamal', and consisted of a long typed list of names with a date against each. The dates started from mid-November and continued at intervals of only two or three days. It was now the early morning of December the 10th and as I ran my eye swiftly down the column I noticed that against the date December 11th stood the name Yusef Fakri.

There was no indication whatever as to where 'Gamal' lived. what sort of goods the people listed were collecting or where they were to deliver them when collected, but I memorised that date and the name Yusef Fakri as it seemed reasonable to suppose that the list had some bearing on O'Kieff's nefarious activities. Another glance at the five piles of letters assured me that nothing else there would prove of assistance and I stepped back quickly, anticipating that Oonas might reappear at any moment.

Actually it was a good ten minutes before she rejoined me and when she did I was sitting, smoking quietly, on the low stool near her divan. She was carrying a large, flat package measuring about two feet by two-and-a-half. It was done up in sacking with thick cord, just as I remembered having touched it in the bottom of O'Kieff's cabin trunk, and as I took it from her I felt a glow of satisfaction at the thought that I had pulled off my impersonation of Lemming with such excellent results.

'You know where to deliver it?' she asked.

'Deliver it?' I repeated. 'But my job is to decipher the hiero glyphics on it.'

'No, no!' she shook her head impatiently. 'You are to make the translation from the photographs we had done of it as soon as it was brought in. They will be delivered at your hotel first thing in the morning. The stone itself is to be handed over to Zakri's agent directly you reach Cairo.'

My spirits sank a little. As they had already photographed the tablet it would now be impossible to prevent their learning its secret, but it was some consolation to know that having

THE QUEST OF JULIAN DAY

got it back would enable us to learn its secret too.

'I'm sorry,' I said, 'but I'm afraid Zakri Bey left me rather in the dark. I only thought that I was to take it to Cairo. What's the idea of passing it on to his agent?'

'Because he in turn will take it to Fergani the Seer, whom, it is hoped, may be able to tell us more about it after he has held it to him and gone into a trance.'

This rather unusual idea did not surprise me in view of the tremendous faith Egyptians place in the powers of their mystics and I did not like to display too much ignorance of their plans by questioning her further, but she added without prompting:

'Zakri would take it himself if he were going to Cairo and Mr. O'Kieff thinks it better not to have it with him when he leaves Alex. tomorrow; just in case the police become inquisitive seeing that his was the only baggage which was not searched before it left the ship. That is the reason they are using you for this purpose.'

'Of course,' I said at once. 'Probably Zakri Bey meant to give me instructions tomorrow morning about handing it over, but I have to be up early so perhaps you would prefer to do it now.'

'By all means. You know the Sharia Kasr el Nil, in Cairo?'

'Yes.'

'Then you will take it straight to the Banque de la Mediterranée Orientale which is at the top end, going towards the Bridge, on the left. The offices will be closed when you get there, but ring the night-bell and ask for Monsieur Carnot. Hand it over to him and he will give you a receipt for it.'

'It shall be done just as you say,' I agreed, and added on a sudden inspiration. 'Bye the bye, I'd certainly like to try a hashish dream sometime. Can you tell me whereabouts in Cairo I could do so?'

She smiled. 'As you're one of us there's no reason why you shouldn't spend an evening at Gamal's.'

At the mention of the name my heart leapt as it confirmed what I had already half-suspected. Gamal's name headed the list on her desk and so the dates of collection from him referred to consignments of hashish.

'It's on the left-hand side about half-way up the second turning on the right out of Mohammed Ali Street going from the Opera Square. The ground floor is quite a well-known carpet-shop to which anyone will direct you. Zakri will give you a card to Gamal if you ask him.'

'Thank you ever so much,' I said. 'I shall look forward to that. But I shall look forward infinitely more to seeing *you* again.'

'Good-bye, Mr. Lemming.' She looked so ravishing that I felt a sudden temptation to kiss her, but she seemed to sense it and, with an imperious gesture, extended her hand palm downwards. Submissively I kissed that instead of attempting to reach her soft, half-parted lips and, with a last smile from those strange blue eyes, I left her; congratulating myself on having got away with both the tablet and Gamal's address; but I was soon to find my self-congratulation was a little premature.

It had been very still in that dimly-lit room of hers and no sooner was I outside the door than I caught the faint sounds of distant shouting. As I crossed the first of the two long, garish *salons* I thought it was some drunken quarrel out in the street, but it grew perceptibly louder and, by the time I was striding across the parquet of the second, I realised it was coming from somewhere within the house.

Opening the far door I stepped out on to the landing and a grand hullabaloo instantly struck my ears. One glance over the balustrade was enough to show me what was happening. Half the front door stood open and wedged in it two figures were struggling fiercely—Harry in his clown's get-up, and Lemming, naked now except for his underclothes and one arm of his light overcoat. A part of the garment hung from it and it was evident that Harry had torn the rest of it from off his back. The elephantine major-domo and two other Gyppy servants were standing there near them in the hall gaping, apparently not knowing which side to take.

'Let me in! Let me in!' Lemming was yelling. 'Help me, you fools! I've got to see the Princess!'

'Stop him! Stop him!' Harry was shouting in reply. 'Can't you see he's got no clothes on? He's mad! Help me to throw him out!'

As I ran to the stairhead Lemming flung Harry from him and dashed inside. The second he saw me he began to shout again.

'That's the man! That's not Lemming! I'm Lemming! Don't let him get out! Don't let him get out!'

I had been much longer with the beautiful Oonas than I had intended when I entered the house and, including my long wait while she fetched the package, I must have been there close on three-quarters of an hour. The second I saw Lemming I guessed that he must have hobbled as far as the main road and had had phenomenal luck in getting a lift immediately on a passing car back into Alex. I saw that my delay was near proving my undoing.

For a second Lemming stood there in the middle of the hall clad only in his socks, vest and pants, pointing at me in wild accusation; but he presented such a comic spectacle that, to my immense relief, the two native boys suddenly began to laugh.

Harry, Clarissa, our taxi-driver and several other people, doubtless those who had given Lemming a lift, were now crowding into the doorway; but with my pistol and Harry's help it did not look as if I should have much difficulty in dominating the situation and securing a passage to the open street. I began to run down the stairs and was just slipping my hand under the Red Indian tunic to draw my gun when a quiet voice said behind me:

'What is the meaning of all this?' and switching round I saw Oonas standing there, gripping a large automatic in a small but very steady hand.

8

The Tomb of the Bulls

The last thing I wanted was a bullet in the back and Oonas was holding the gun as though she were no stranger to it. From my very short acquaintance with her I had already decided that she was an extremely dangerous young woman and, knowing of her association with Zakri and O'Kieff, I had not the least doubt that she would shoot me if I attempted to draw my own weapon.

She was standing on the landing at the top of the stairs; too far above me for there to be any chance of my making a spring and grabbing her pistol. On the other hand, I felt that if I could only get down among the little crowd in the hall she would hesitate to fire there, unless she were a remarkably good shot, for fear of hitting one of her servants.

'What is happening here?' she asked sharply, raising her voice to a higher pitch.

Clarissa leapt into the breach most nobly. From the open doorway she pointed at Lemming:

'This poor fellow has had too much to drink at the McPhersons' party. We were taking him home, but he insisted on stopping here for a moment because he says he's in love with you. The next thing we knew was that he'd pulled off half his clothes and was trying to batter in your door.'

'That's right,' Harry supported her. 'We tried to stop him but he'd rung the bell before we had a chance to get up the steps. We're frightfully sorry you've been troubled.'

Lemming swung round on him indignantly. 'You liar! It was your friend who lured me into that blasted car and . . .'

He got no further. I had been keeping a watchful eye on Oonas and she had turned her glance away from me to the others who were shouting at her from the hall. As Lemming swung round on Harry, I dived right on to him from the fifth stair.

We went down with an appalling bump but he broke my fall and I managed to retain my hold on the precious package.

Once again Clarissa acted with really splendid speed and decision. I had hardly launched myself on Lemming before she had spun on her heel and was pushing the little mob of curious onlookers clear of the door. Harry remained standing inside it just long enough to see me scramble to my feet, then he rushed to her assistance. One of the Gyppy boys flung himself in my path but I had my head well down, for fears Oonas should still take a flying shot at me, and it caught him in the ribs sending him spinning backwards.

The balloon-like major-domo was standing there with his little-pudgy hands raised to his shoulders, squealing in excited Arabic; but I gave him one shove with my free hand and dashed out on to the steps.

I must say that our driver proved a game fellow. He seemed to be thoroughly enjoying the night's work and the moment the fracas started he had legged it for his car to get the engine started. It was already roaring and Harry was hurriedly pushing Clarissa back into the cab as I came charging out of the house. The onlookers made an ineffectual attempt to stop me but I flung myself after my friends, tripped on the step, and landed up with my head buried in Clarissa's frilly Columbine skirts.

The people on the pavement were yelling 'Thieves! Murder! Help!' in a variety of languages and down the road I could hear a police whistle shrilling wildly; next second we were off.

By the time I had disengaged my head from between Clarissa's shapely legs, contacting, I fear, more of her delightful person than was strictly according to propriety, we were racing down the road and the shouting was dying away in the distance.

'Phew!' Harry pulled up his bald clown's pate of pink buckram and commenced to mop his painted brow. 'That was a near thing. We heard the car drive up but I never spotted Lemming until he was half-way up those steps.'

'Anyhow, you've got the tablet back,' I panted, patting the package cheerfully. 'But that young woman's a handful. I think she regards herself as Cleopatra brought up-to-date. I've never run across such a perfect example of the vamp, and she darned near hypnotised me into forgetting what I'd come for. That's why I was such a long time.'

'Really, Julian,' Clarissa said with mock severity, 'I'm surprised at you—and with a coloured girl, too!'

'Nonsense! She's not as coloured as all that. I've seen Spanish women who were a lot darker.'

'What!' she exclaimed. 'Then you did go off the deep end with her!'

'Of course not,' I protested. 'Is it likely?'

'I don't know so much. You're too good-looking to be trusted, and you had ample time.'

'You don't know me,' I smiled. 'I pride myself on being a bit of an artist where that sort of thing is concerned, and I don't believe in rushing my fences.'

She shook her head. 'Tell that to the Marines, my dear. That girl's a bad hat if ever there was one; and you're as dark a horse as one would meet in a day's march, yourself. I wouldn't trust the two of you together for five minutes, let alone for three-quarters of an hour in the middle of the night.'

'But, darling, he's never met her until an hour ago,' Harry argued solemnly in my defence; upon which both Clarissa and I went off into roars of laughter.

We were still laughing when the cab pulled up which, perhaps, was a good thing as it may have helped to reassure our driver that we really were only practical-jokers out on the spree after the McPhersons' dance.

'Where to now, boss?' he asked, and that brought us up with a jerk. A pink flush in the sky to eastward already heralded the dawn and I had to find somewhere to snatch a few hours' sleep. It was impossible for me to go to the Cecil with Harry and Clarissa or to any of the other hotels, as my description was certain to have been circulated by the police and, even in my Red Indian disguise, I should arouse suspicion if I tried to get a room without so much as a toothbrush by way of luggage.

After a moment I had an inspiration and told the man to drive us down to the Arab cemetery. I knew from my previous visit to Alex. that the place I wanted was somewhere thereabouts and in any case I did not want him to drop me actually at it. Immediately we set off again I said to the others:

'Look, here, I've found out from Cleopatra that Zakri is staying in Alex. for the time being, but that O'Kieff is going to Cairo on the three o'clock express tomorrow. He doesn't want to take the tablet along with him in his baggage. The scheme was for Lemming, who is travelling on the same train but separately, to take it. Unfortunately, though, they've already photographed the stone so we've failed in our attempt to prevent them learning its secret.'

'In that case, we've had all this excitement for nothing,' interrupted Clarissa.

'Hardly,' I protested. 'Having got the tablet back we can get a translation done of it ourselves and now that we're in touch with O'Kieff's gang we may be able to land something on him. To be honest, although I'm game to do everything I can to help you in your treasure-hunt, my main objective is to get O'Kieff ten years without the option, if not something worse.'

'What do you suggest doing now, then?' Harry asked.

'Apparently they've got some tame occultist in Cairo named Fergani, and the idea is that Lemming should hand the tablet over to him so that he can try his psychic powers on it, presumably without knowing what it is. I suppose they hope that if he does his stuff properly they may get a check-up from a completely different angle as to the whereabouts of the treasure.'

'What childish nonsense!' exclaimed Clarissa. 'Fancy grown men believing in such stupid things. O'Kieff and Co. go down with a wallop as high-power crooks in my estimation after that.'

'Not at all.' I disagreed. 'There's much more in this occult business than most people realise, and as every Egyptian believes in it, for them it's the sensible thing to do. Still, that's beside the point. We know O'Kieff's leaving for Cairo on the three o'clock train tomorrow so, providing I'm not caught by the police in the meantime, I shall go on the same train and follow him up when he gets there.'

'That's all right,' Harry agreed. 'But what d'you mean to do for the next nine hours?'

'Get some sleep in a place many people might not care about; but fortunately my nerves are pretty good.'

'And where's that?'

'The Serapeum, where they used to bury the Sacred Bulls. As there's nothing in it that anybody can steal there won't be any guardians of the place about until it's opened to the public. It means sleeping hard but that can't be helped. Directly you've dropped me, you two had better return to the Cecil and get some sleep yourselves. Amin is going to call on you for orders, as though he were a dragoman engaged by you, at nine o'clock.'

'Gawd!' murmured Harry miserably. 'That only leaves us about two hours' sleep. It's well after six o'clock now.'

'Sorry,' I said. 'But that's about all I'll get myself.'

He nodded. 'Anyway, the police told me before we left the Cecil to pick you up that Sir Walter's funeral would be round about eleven and I'll have to be on hand for that.'

'When Amin turns up,' I went on, 'tell him to buy me another set of clothes. European this time, but shabby, poor quality, second-hand stuff like you see the Greek workmen wearing here. Immediately he's done that, he's to bring the outfit along to me at the Serapeum, with some sort of snack for breakfast and something with which I can get this dark colour off my hands and face. You've already got your reservations on the three o'clock train for Cairo. I have, too, but I shan't be able to use mine as I shall be travelling second-class. Where are you putting up when you get there?'

'The Semiramis,' replied Clarissa. 'Sir Walter said it was the most comfortable.'

'And he was right,' I agreed, 'for anyone who doesn't mind paying the price. It's far and away the best hotel in Egypt. You'll be splendidly looked after there and I'll communicate with you through Amin as soon as I get a chance.'

A couple of minutes later we pulled up at the Arab cemetery, upon which I paid the driver lavishly and told him to take them to the Cecil. They wished me luck and I watched the taxi rattle away down the empty street.

As it had dropped me at the north end of the cemetery I had the whole length of the Rue de la Colonne Pompée to walk in order to reach the big piece of waste ground which lies to the south of the cemetery. In its centre there is a great, raised mound of rubble, overgrown with grass, at the summit of which rises a single tall column known as Pompey's Pillar, although actually it is believed to be the last standing relic of a temple erected by the Emperor Diocletian.

The whole site has been enclosed in comparatively recent times by the Department which deals with the preservation of Ancient Monuments as there have been discovered under the mound some large, man-made caves in which the Sacred Bulls of Serapis were buried; and during the daytime batches of tourists are now taken round the enclosure at so much a head.

The native population of the locality was already stirring but there was little traffic about yet and, after a glance up and down the street, I managed to scramble over the high fence without being spotted. Nearly a year had elapsed since I had visited the place so I was a little uncertain of my direction as I pressed forward through the knee-high undergrowth. But the dawn was now breaking and as soon as I had scrambled up on to the high ground where the tall pillar stood I was able to get my bearings.

Another couple of hundred yards down the far side of the slope brought me to the edge of a railed pit about twenty yards square and fifteen feet deep; a rickety wooden stairway led down to its bottom, where the entrance of one of the great caves showed as a dim archway in the still uncertain light.

There was nothing gruesome about the place; no heaps of mouldering bones, human skulls or pieces of rotting mummy-cloth such as I should have encountered in the catacombs which lie a little further to the south. It was just a large, dry, empty cave hewn out of sandstone, and the ghosts of the long-dead bulls, if they lingered there, had no terrors for me. Striking a match now and again I penetrated the cave for about a hundred yards and, scooping myself a hollow for my hip in the loose sand of the floor, I lay down and fell instantly asleep.

Having only had about three hours' sleep the night before and none at all for the last twenty-four hours, I should normally have slept on until any time. But there is a sort of sixth sense which warns the hunted when they are in a precarious situation, and it must have been this, I think, which caused me to wake before the first batch of tourists were brought in to see the tombs. Lighting a match I saw by my wrist-watch that it was a quarter-past nine. I had no idea what time the place was opened to the public but assumed that it would be fairly soon. I could hardly hope that Amin would arrive before ten-thirty, at the earliest, as he would have quite a lot of shopping to do after having received his instructions from Harry. But, fortunately for me, the antiquities of Alexandria are counted small game compared with the magnificent remains in the Nile Valley, so comparatively few tourists ever bother to visit them, and I hoped to be able to avoid any that might put in an appearance.

My three hours' sleep had only taken the edge off my fatigue. I had a beastly taste in my mouth and the usual mouldy feeling which follows having been up all night and then slept hard. The thought that the police were after me, too, was anything but cheering, and I was in a far from happy state as I made my way out of the cave and climbed the rickety stairs to the edge of the pit.

No one was about and I was on the side of the enclosure which overlooks the cemetery and, further off, the flimsy, stucco buildings of the modern town. Selecting a spot some distance from the pit where I could keep watch on its entrance without much likelihood of being seen, I sat down between two huge broken blocks of stone half-overgrown with nettles. One of the guardians of the place arrived with four sightseers shortly afterwards, but I was well outside their line of vision and they came and went without a glance in my direction. From that time on other couples or groups were taken down to see the Tombs of the Bulls at intervals that averaged about twenty minutes. It was not until nearly half-past eleven that Amin's tall figure approached the pit.

Being a guide himself he had free access to all such places and none of the regular guardians of a Tomb accompanies an official guide unless asked to do so. In consequence, he was alone. I watched him descend into the pit and stole a cautious glance round. There being nobody else in sight, I slipped across the broken ground and followed him down into it.

I had noted with dismay that he was not carrying any bag or parcel but as soon as he saw me coming down the wooden stairs he gave me a cheerful greeting and proceeded to produce various parcels from under his long silk *jibba*.

He had carried out Harry's instructions to the letter, thank

99

goodness, and brought me everything I needed including a couple of large ham rolls and some bananas for my breakfast. Fortunately, too, he had had the forethought to bring a candle, so, relieving him of his burdens, I disappeared into the cave while he remained to keep watch outside.

The clothes were just what I wanted; a cheap, white cotton shirt open at the neck, a pair of light, striped trousers, a shiny gaberdine coat and a straw hat which had seen better days. I was soon transformed from a Red Indian Brave into a poorer-class Greek workman, with the exception of my skin which was too dark and my face which still bore traces of war-paint. Cleaning up the mess was easy but I soon found that toning down my skin to near-white again was a much more difficult business and gathering up my abandoned garments I rejoined Amin outside the cave. We secreted ourselves in a lonely part of the large, desolate plot where he assisted me in getting the dark stain off my face and hands.

We had only just done when the musical cry of '*Haya alla 'Salat! Haya alla falah!* which is the Moslem call to prayer, came faintly to us from the minaret of a neighbouring mosque. It was midday already and I told Amin that we were to take the three o'clock train for Cairo. To avoid showing myself at the railway-station booking-office I gave him some money to get second-class tickets for us both, with instructions to meet me again when he had done so at a cheap restaurant near the station which he had suggested as being the sort of place where I would not be conspicuous in my new disguise.

Now it was broad daylight I could hardly climb over the fence again and I was a little uneasy that the men on the gate, having seen Amin come in alone, might wonder where I had suddenly sprung from if I went out with him; but Arab *boabs* are a lazy lot and we reached the street without being questioned. While I was waiting for Amin at the little restaurant my feeling of gloom was by no means lightened on seeing that my disappearance provided the chief topic of news in the morning's paper. Fortunately they had no photograph of me available which they could publish, but the paper gave a full description of my appearance and urged its readers to report me to the police at once should they happen to see me.

There was a photograph of Sir Walter and a rather stilted

account of his murder, but the paper devoted four whole columns to his career, and I saw that he was an even bigger personality in the archæological world than I had imagined.

My flight from the ship seemed to have convinced whoever was responsible for reporting the case that I was the murderer, although the statements about that were in the usual guarded language. After I had read them through I was so depressed that I had half a mind to chuck my hand in and walk round to the police-station; but now that we had recaptured the tablet and knew that O'Kieff was leaving for Cairo on the three o'clock train a certain pigheadedness made me reason, without the least justification, that if I could only sit on his tail for a few hours longer I should be able to get something definite against him.

Amin's arrival with the tickets cheered me somewhat, and worries, thank goodness, have never interfered with my appetite, so we ate a simple but hearty lunch and walked over to the station. We were there by half-past two as I was anxious to make quite certain that O'Kieff did travel by the three o'clock express and mark down his carriage so that I should have no difficulty in following him when he left the train at Cairo.

I had not shaved since the night before so with the slight stubble on my chin and my shoddy, second-hand clothes I presented a very down-and-out appearance. There were several policemen on the station but it heartened me a lot to see that none of them even bothered to throw a glance in my direction.

The Belvilles turned up soon after we arrived. I, of course, ignored them, and I don't think they recognised me as Clarissa was looking in the other direction and Harry's face remained quite blank when they passed within a few feet of Amin and myself. There were numerous other passengers from the 'Hampshire' travelling on the same train, but I was careful not to meet the eye of any of those I knew and most of them were busily occupied in saying goodbye to friends or seeing to their luggage. O'Kieff duly appeared and was installed in a first-class carriage by his valet; after which Amin and I took our seats and some ten minutes later the train steamed out.

Although I had made the journey before I found abundant interest in the passing scene. One is apt to think of Egypt as a land of sand but the Delta is the exact opposite of a desert. Its rich, black soil, brought down by the five branches of the Nile at each inundation, supports three crops a year and every inch of it is cultivated. In some ways the landscape is not unlike that of Holland; flat, green fields stretch away as far as the eye can reach to misty horizons and occasionally the prospect is broken by the great white or red sail of a boat which is mysteriously gliding through the fields on some unseen canal.

In detail, though, the two countries are entirely different. The triangular sail of an Egyptian *felucca* has little resemblance to that of the Dutch barge; the distant spires one sees in Holland are minarets or the white domes of small mosques set among groups of palms in Egypt; and the gay bungalows with their neat gardens of the Dutch hamlets are replaced by Arab villages of incredible squalor.

Provincial towns and villages alike in Egypt all have a strangely unfinished appearance owing to the flat roofs both of houses and hovels upon which huge mounds of long reeds are left to dry; skinny chickens peck about in the rubbish and ragged garments from the family wash are hung out on lines. On the ground floor whole families herd together with their live-stock in indescribable filth and confusion. Yet outside the villages one often sees a charming vignette of peasant life; a line of supple, straight-backed women in dark robes walking in single file with pitchers or great bundles balanced on their heads; a small, naked child leading a hump-necked bullock, or a woman perched on the hindquarters of a donkey with a child in her arms just like a picture of the Virgin Mary, during the flight into Egypt.

It was dark before we got to Cairo and the myriad lights of the Egyptian capital twinkled in the crisp air on either side as we steamed in. Amin and I were out of our carriage almost before the train had stopped. Passing the barrier at once I sent him to secure a car while I waited within a few feet of the ticket-collector for O'Kieff and Grünther to come through.

Uniformed *kavasses* from all the big hotels were on the platform but that gave me no guide as O'Kieff waved them all aside and was escorted by a private dragoman to a handsome Rolls. Running round to the place where Amin was waiting I jumped into the car he had engaged and told the driver to follow O'Kieff.

As soon as we were clear of the station yard the Rolls turned right instead of towards central Cairo. After a few minutes we passed the Museum and crossed the Nile by the famous Kasr el Nil bridge. On reaching the west bank we turned left and were soon out on the fine open road to Gizeh.

In the old days Cairo's European quarter was concentrated on the island of Gezira which lies in the middle of the Nile, and the race-course, golf-course and polo-grounds of the Gezira Club, which is the centre of British social activities, still occupies many acres of it much to the chagrin of the Egyptians. But numbers of the more wealthy European residents have now built houses in fine gardens out along the Gizeh road and I imagined that it was for one of these that O'Kieff was making. However, we could see his car ahead of us on the long straight road and it showed no signs of slowing down.

We followed him for mile after mile until Cairo's suburbs had been left far behind and I knew there was only one place for which he could be heading—the Mena House Hotel which nestles at the foot of the Great Pyramid. Sure enough his car turned in to the semicircular drive before the wide verandah. I pulled our man up before we reached the gates and Amin and I got out.

Telling our fellow to wait, we walked on as far as the hotel drive and I was just about to turn up it when I remembered that, in my poverty-stricken get-up as a Greek workman, I was in no fit state to enter a *de luxe* hotel where crowds of visitors were sipping their before-dinner cocktails after a welcome bath and a long day's sightseeing. I would have given anything for a bath and a drink myself, but I knew that I must do without either. Amin, too, was barred from entering the hotel by the regulation current throughout Egypt by which all dragomen report to the hall-porter when they wish to see their employers and await their pleasure on the steps of the terrace.

However, Amin was well-known among the other guides and the house-boys of all the principal hotels in Egypt. So I said to him: 'Look here, I want you to have a chat with one of the porters and find out the number of the room that O'Kieff's been given. Also where abouts it is, if possible. D'you think you can do that?'

'Why yes, sir.' he replied at once. 'I will speak with my friend

Hussein, the boss boy of the terrace waiters. He will be able to tell me what you wish to know.'

I waited outside the gate for the best part of a quarter of an hour before Amin rejoined me.

'The gentleman had reserved a suite,' he said. 'It is on the first floor at the back. Come with me, sir, and I will show you.'

We turned into the fine gardens on the right-hand side of the hotel and walked down an avenue of palm trees.

'There, that is it.' Amin suddenly stopped and pointed. 'All five windows where the lights are, on the first floor. Four windows from the corner of the building. The gentlemens is up there now, I expect.'

'Good,' I said. 'That's all I want to know. The next thing is for you to drive back in the car to Cairo, go to the Semiramis and ask for Mr. Belville. Tell him we've traced O'Kieff out to Mena House and that I am remaining here for the moment; but that I hope to see him some time before he goes to bed tonight. They would never let me into the Semiramis dressed like this but he is taking care of my luggage for me so I want you to ask him to put one of my lounge-suits with a shirt and collar into a small suitcase and bring it back with you. I could easily change behind the bushes. You'll find me waiting for you either where the car is now or somewhere about here in the garden.'

When Amin had gone I sat down on a bench to keep observation on O'Kieff's lighted windows. As usual, he was doing himself well. Those first-floor rooms overlooking the tennis-courts and garden were about the best that were to be had in the hotel. The other side faces a sandy slope which is hardly compensated for by the fact that some of the windows give an uphill view of the Pyramids.

Occasionally I could see shadows moving behind the blind and I guessed that Grünther was unpacking for his master. O'Kieff was doubtless enjoying a bath and he seemed to be taking his time about it. I waited patiently, knowing that sooner or later they would both go down to feed, but I could not altogether suppress a rising sense of excitement at the contemplation of the scheme I had in mind.

The previous night I had obtained a package under false pretences; now I intended to add burglary to my crimes. It would be quite an easy climb up to one of those first-floor windows and once O'Kieff's suite had been vacated I meant to pay a clandestine visit to it. I had seen from his luggage on the station that he still had the flat, steel-lined despatch case with him, and it was that which I was after. If I could only secure it and break it open we might find enough incriminating documents inside to hang a regiment.

The night was warm, the air soft, the atmosphere fragrant from the perfume of the night-flowering shrubs in the carefully-tended garden. Most of the hotel guests were occupied over dinner. The dragomen and outdoor servants were all on the far side of the building, and during my time of waiting only two couples passed me, in both cases much more interested in each other than myself.

I must have sat there for well over an hour when the lights in O'Kieff's suite were switched out one after another. I gave its occupants five minutes to get downstairs and then crossed the gravel path. Entering the shrubs in the bed beneath the windows I clutched a convenient drain-pipe and hauled myself up by it until I could get my hand on the window-ledge of what I believed to be the sitting-room. My movements were screened by the avenue of palm trees which ran parallel to the side of the hotel and in spite of my light-coloured suit no one could have seen me unless they had been walking along the path immediately below.

With my knees still clutching the drain-pipe and clinging to the window-ledge with one hand I was able to use the other to ease up the catch of the already open window and pull it out as far as it would go. I wriggled a little further up the pipe, hung out sideways from it; then, thrusting myself off, I sprang for the sill, landing with my chest against it and my head inside the window.

For a moment I hung there kicking, but with another violent heave, I jerked myself up until I was half in and half out of the room.

It must have been the slight noise I made myself and the efforts of the last few moments which prevented me from hearing the approach of footsteps; but I was still kicking wildly in my endeavour to wriggle over the sill when a voice exclaimed:

'Here he is! Here he is! Quick, Mustapha, grab hold of his ankles while I get the police!'

9

Shock Tactics

I made one last violent effort to wriggle through the window even as my mind registered the fact that the voice which had spoken was a woman's. Her words suggested that she had been definitely looking for me, but I had no time to wonder who she was or how she could have got mixed up in the police hunt as, at that second, her companion sprang.

I felt his large, muscular hands close firmly about my ankles and a violent jerk as his whole weight suddenly straightened my legs and wrenched me clean out of the window. I came sailing backwards in a flying curve and landed with a sickening thud in the flower-border. The shock drove all the breath from my lungs and I lay there gasping like a landed fish while the native who had pulled me from my precarious hold, but had fallen with me, released his grip on my ankles, twisted like a snake and flung himself on my prostrate body.

'Well done, Mustapha! Well done!' came the woman's excited voice. 'Can you hang on to him while I get help? If the police haven't arrived yet I'll get some of the hotel porters.'

'Yes, *sitt*, yes,' panted the brawny Arab who was now straddling my chest, 'but I would rather that they find him dead when they arrive. It might easily happen in a fight and he deserves death, this murderer of my master.'

'Hi! Wait a minute,' I managed to gasp with swift apprehension.

'No, Mustapha, no,' the woman said at the same moment. 'I know how you feel, but I forbid you to harm him. The law will deal with him as he deserves.'

As she turned swiftly to go for help I caught a glimpse of her over the Arab's shoulder. She was a tall, slim, long-limbed girl with ash-blonde hair, and I recognised her instantly from

the photograph Sir Walter had shown me on the 'Hampshire' as
his daughter Sylvia.

'Miss Shane!' I called. 'For God's sake wait a minute. This
is all a horrible mistake.'

She halted abruptly and turned to look down into my face,
asking with quick curiosity, 'How did you know my name?'

'I'll tell you that and plenty of other things that'll interest
you—if only you'll order your man to get off my chest.'

'Is it likely, now I've had the luck to catch you? Anything
you want to say you can say to the police.'

I saw that she was about to turn away again and in a last,
frantic effort to stop her, I called, 'if you hand me over to the
police bang goes your last chance of catching your father's
murderer.'

'You murdered him yourself!' she cried harshly. 'You brute!
I—I could . . .' Suddenly she burst into a torrent of tears.

'Please,' I begged. 'For goodness sake! I didn't kill your
father. I swear I didn't— but I'm doing my damnedest to get the
devil who did.'

For a moment her shoulders shook as the sobs racked her;
but with surprising will-power she checked the outburst which
ceased as suddenly as it had begun. She rubbed the back of one
hand across her eyes and asked in a voice which showed that
her resolution had weakened a trifle:

'Who did kill him, then?'

'If only you'll let me get up, I'll tell you everything,' I said.

'All right,' she agreed grudgingly, 'but you, Mustapha, hold
him tightly in case he tries to escape.'

The Arab got off my chest and allowed me to stand, but he
took up a position behind me with a firm grip on my coat
collar.

I must have looked a pretty unpleasant sight, facing her like
that; unshaven, dishevelled, and with mud from the flower-bed
plastered all over my tawdry clothes. It was an ignominious
position, too, being held out for her inspection by the brawny
Mustapha like something the cat had dragged from the dust-
bin. As a matter of fact I could have taught *him* something, had
I wished. His firm clutch held nothing but the collar of my coat
so by slipping my arms out of it I could have left it in his grip
and made a dash for liberty. I didn't care to chance that, as

they would certainly have shouted for help and brought half the hotel staff out in a hue and cry after me, but the knowledge that I could make a bolt for it, if I wished, gave me back my confidence and, realising that to employ shock tactics was the only line which might save me from immediate arrest, I promptly reversed our rôles in the conversation.

'Now,' I said with some sharpness, 'you'll first tell me how it is you came to be looking for me here.'

'You *are* Julian Day, aren't you?' she asked quite mildly.

'Yes,' I agreed. 'I'm Julian Day and I was a friend of your father's. I'm also a friend of the Belvilles. *They* know I had no hand in the murder. I spent all last night with them.'

'Oh,' she exclaimed, rather weakly. 'I haven't seen them yet.'

'So I imagined. But they came in on the evening train and the sooner you do see them, the better. Now, how did you know that I had arrived in Cairo, and how is it you were able to recognise me by the seat of my pants when I was hanging out of that window?'

'It was Mustapha here, my dragoman. He's a bosom friend of your man Amin and he knew Amin was going down to meet a Mr. Julian Day at Alex. on the "Hampshire" yesterday. Your name was front-page news in every paper this morning. Directly we saw you were wanted for the murder we thought Amin might be able to give us some information about you. So we met the train from Alex. this afternoon and, although your disguise seems a pretty good one, we felt certain that the man with Amin must be you.'

'Good work. I congratulate you. What did you do then?'

'We followed your car. But we were unlucky and had a tyre burst, just by the Zoological gardens, and we feared we had lost you. On the off chance that you'd come out to Mena we came on here and questioned the porters. Amin had gone back to Cairo, they said, but we described the man who was with him and one of the loungers by the gates said he thought that he'd seen you stroll into the garden about an hour ago.'

'You've missed your vocation,' I grinned, my admiration tempered with just a touch of sarcasm. 'Then you came along to hunt me out, I suppose?'

'Yes, having 'phoned the Cairo police, I was too impatient to wait for them. We feared you might . . .'

'Good God! You 'phoned the police? They're on their way here, then?'

'Yes. Of course.'

'Then for goodness sake let's get out of this while there's still a chance. If you let the police arrest me, you won't stand an earthly chance of getting the man who really did the murder.'

'But how do I know . . .' she began uncertainly.

'Come on,' I said impatiently. 'You've *got* to trust me.'

'I don't see how . . .' she began again, and Mustapha cut in quickly, 'No, *sitt*, no! He is an evil mans. You must *not* trust him.'

'You keep out of this,' I snapped, jerking my head round. 'You're going to do exactly what I tell you. Miss Shane and I are going up towards the pyramids where no one is likely to look for us, so that we can have a little talk. Meanwhile you're to stay here until Amin comes back. You'll keep out of the way of the police and directly he arrives you'll bring him along to us. We shall be by the IVth Dynasty tombs on the far side of the Sphinx.'

Before he had time to express surprise or dissent, Sylvia gasped indignantly, 'Is it likely that I'd leave him behind and go off into the blue with you alone? You must be mad, I think, even to suggest it.'

'All the same, that's what you're going to do,' I told her; and with one swift jerk I had my automatic out of my pocket.

'Don't be frightened,' I said as her eyes opened wide in sudden consternation, and reversing the gun so that I held it by the barrel I extended it towards her as I asked, 'Have you ever handled one of these before?'

'Yes,' she said. 'I always carry one if I'm motoring alone outside Cairo.'

'Right,' I smiled. 'Then you'll know how to shoot me with it if I start any funny business when we're up by the pyramids?'

'I've told you that I wouldn't dream of going up there alone with you. It's too great a risk.'

'Nonsense!' I said angrily. 'Can't you see that my handing over my pistol to you is a perfect guarantee of my good faith? Is it likely I'd do that if I were really responsible for your father's death? Of course not! I could have shot Mustapha with it a couple of minutes ago and you as well—immediately you told me that you'd already summoned the police.'

'That's true, I suppose,' she admitted.

'It is: and when you hear what I've got to tell you I'm certain you'll realise how wise you were to trust me.'

'All right, then. I'll chance it. Let him go, Mustapha.'

'You understand what you're to do?' I said swiftly to the Arab as he released me. 'Wait here for Amin, who's bringing me out a change of clothes. The two of you are to join us as quickly as you can outside the tombs of the IVth Dynasty Kings. Come on,' I added to her, 'you had better follow me, then you can keep me covered with that gun, if you want to. But for mercy's sake leave the safety-catch down or you may let it off by mistake.'

Next minute I was trotting round the back of the hotel with her after me. We reached a steep bank on its far side beyond the kitchens and made our way up on to the flattish plateau of hard sandstone beyond. Fortunately there was no moon but the stars gave quite sufficient light to see by as we stumbled over the uneven ground parallel with the road which curves up towards the Great Pyramid of Kheops and the slightly smaller one of Khephren which actually looks larger from that angle because it stands on somewhat higher ground.

She continued to keep behind me so I knew that her suspicions were by no means fully allayed, but I felt I could congratulate myself on having wriggled out of an appalling mess, at least for the moment.

Keeping well away from the road I hurried on, glancing behind now and then to assure myself that I was not making the pace too hot for her; but she showed no sign of fatigue and with her long legs it looked as though, for a mile or two, she was capable of covering the ground as quickly as I could.

Within ten minutes we had reached the base of the Great Pyramid. It was silhouetted against the night sky and, not having seen it for the best part of a year, I could not help being impressed again by its magnificence in spite of my anxious state of mind. They say that it covers fourteen acres of land, and is close on five hundred feet in height, which is well over four times the height of Grosvenor House, Park Lane. But it does not look that height, which is probably on account of its shape. It is said that it took a hundred thousand men thirty years to build, but the idea that it was erected by slave labour is a misconception. They only worked on it for about six weeks each year after the principal harvest was over. Apparently the peasants used to come in from all parts of the country for a sort of annual *fiesta* and the people of the different townships used to have competitions as to which contingent should drag the huge blocks of stone up the ramps into position quickest. The work was done with songs and laughter as a willing tribute to a great ruler who fed the people from his abundance and entertained them with every sort of merry-making after their labours each night.

When it was completed, with its smooth, white, marble surface shining in the sun, it must have been a really lovely thing. But a few hundred years ago the Arabs tore off the polished facing, to use the marble in building the Sultan Hassan Mosque, leaving its sides all jagged with the four-foot-deep blocks of sandstone exposed like giant sets of steps.

The most impressive thing about it is its solidity and strength. When the Arabs removed the casing they only destroyed a tiny fraction of it and I doubt if there is enough gun-cotton in the world to blow it up even if some vandal wished to do so. Even an earthquake could do no more than crack it and one has the feeling that when London is again a brickless, water-logged marsh and New York once more a barren island, the Great Pyramid will still be standing. It saw the dawn of civilisation on this earth and it will look upon the last sunset of the world.

In front of it there is a small police post and I wondered why Sylvia had not got men from there rather than wait until police could be sent out from Cairo. But perhaps it was not occupied at night, or she thought it better to communicate at once with headquarters. To avoid passing near the police post I kept to the right of the Great Pyramid and went right round it, sticking close to its huge base. Our way was made harder by heaps of shaly rubble and deep ditches from past excavations but, finding there was not a soul about, when we got round the far side of the Pyramid I ventured on the track which winds down towards the rear of the Sphinx. From Mena House the Sphinx is about half an hour's walk in the day-time and considering our detour we did well to reach it in forty-five minutes. Turning left behind the great, squatting beast I strode swiftly down the rock ramp which runs along the far side of it until I reached the shadows thrown by the great stone gate leading in to the IVth Dynasty tombs. The Antiquities people have put up an iron-barred gateway and this was locked, but I had no wish to go any further so I halted and turned to face my captor.

The light was better here than it had been among the shadows of the garden at Mena House and on our way I had had little chance to study her at all closely. Portraits can be deceptive, particularly where young women are concerned, but the one I had seen of her on the ship did her no more than justice. She really was a damnably attractive-looking girl. I remembered Clarissa saying that her eyes were blue, but they looked dark at the moment, and with the upturned bow of her eyebrows, aided no doubt by make-up pencil, they contrasted strikingly with her very fair hair which was ruffled slightly from her exertions. She was standing a good couple of yards away, still covering me with the gun.

'Cigarette?' I asked, fishing out my case and offering it to her.

She hesitated a moment and I grinned. 'Afraid I might rush you and snatch the pistol if you get too close?'

She shrugged, and coming a step nearer, extended her hand. 'I've taken such absurdly big chances already to-night, it doesn't seem as if one more will make much difference.'

'Fine. I'm glad about that. Because, you see, that pistol isn't loaded, so I could quite easily have taken it from you any time I wished.'

'What?' she exclaimed.

'Yes. I was afraid you might spot that owing to its lightness; but evidently you're not quite so used to handling weapons as you would have me think.'

She laughed then, a soft, low gurgle that was good to hear. 'You must think me an idiot for having let you fool me like this.'

'Far from it. I give you full marks for brains and for pluck. Running me to earth at Mena when the whole Egyptian police-force had failed to track me down was a first-class piece of work.'

'Oh, that was Mustapha mostly, and a little luck. For that matter, it's you who really come off with flying colours. You're still a free man and could do what you liked with me out here without anyone hearing my shrieks.'

'Really?' I said. 'I'm very easily tempted.'

'How dare you?' she said. 'I didn't mean that.'

'Of course you didn't; forgive my nonsense. But what I'd like to be certain of is whether you still think it possible that I murdered your father?'

'No,' she said decisively. 'I am quite convinced now that it wasn't you.'

'Why?' I asked. 'You were quite convinced I *had* done it half an hour ago, and you've had nothing but my bare word to cause you to alter your opinion since.'

'I don't know. Call it "feminine intuition" if you like. But from the way you speak and act, I have a feeling that you're quite incapable of committing such a horrible crime.'

'That's good. Let's sit down, shall we?' I motioned her towards a near-by slab of stone and as we sat I casually relieved her of the automatic. Pressing the button on the upper part of the butt, I removed the clip of bullets from it and quietly held them up for her to inspect.

'Oh, dear!' she groaned in mock distress. 'So it *was* loaded after all.'

'Yes,' I said. 'Sorry I had to lie to you about it, but I can't afford to take chances.'

'That's another lie. You knew quite well I wouldn't have tried to shoot you unless you'd turned really nasty. You pulled that bluff merely to impress me.'

'Quite right,' I laughed. 'But don't you consider that a compliment? Unless you're a liar too, you'll confess that you were impressed.'

'Of course I was,' she agreed quite frankly. 'And if you want the truth, you've done little else but impress me ever since we ... er ... met.'

' "Met's" the word,' I agreed cheerfully. 'But it's you who are to blame because you're so remarkably well worth impressing.'

'Hadn't we better talk about Father?' she said stubbing out her cigarette. 'You know, that's what we came out here for.'

113

'True. Although with the pyramids and stars and all, on a night like this, I could wish that it was something else.'

'You've conveyed that quite sufficiently already, Mr. Day. But I'm not in the mood for that sort of thing, or in the habit of entering into flirtations with complete strangers. If you don't mind, until Mustapha and Amin turn up, we will confine our conversation to facts.'

'I do mind. But on the other hand I can see that your suggestion is quite reasonable. I'll tell you now, as briefly and clearly as I can, how I got drawn into this.'

For the next ten minutes I gave her a pretty thorough outline of everything I knew about the business from the moment of my meeting her father in the 'Hampshire' up to the point of her discovering my trying to get into O'Kieff's window at Mena House that night.

She did not ask me a single question and sat silent for a moment or two afterwards. Then she said:

'Am I to understand that the Belvilles will vouch for all this?'

'Yes. As soon as I get a change of clothes which will make me a little more presentable, we'll do our best to evade the police, who must be hunting for me all round Mena House by this time, and return to Cairo, where Harry and Clarissa themselves can tell you exactly the part I've played.'

'Why did you set out for Egypt in the first place?'

'Because I knew this man O'Kieff was sailing in the "Hampshire" and I want to get even with him over a past affair.'

'What sort of affair?'

'That, my dear, is nothing to do with you.'

'Tell me something about yourself. Who are you? What's your background? What d'you do?'

'Sorry. None of that enters into this affair, so I don't propose to tell you.'

I felt her stiffen slightly, and her voice hardened a trifle as she said, 'You realise, I suppose, that your reticence is highly suspicious? No normal person has any objection to talking about themselves.'

'True,' I agreed. 'But I am a wolf in sheep's clothing. I have a huge, horrible, gory skeleton in my cupboard, which eyes such as yours are far too beautiful to look upon.'

'You can cut out the "beautiful eyes" part,' she said coldly.

'In the first place they are not particularly big and you haven't even seen them properly yet. But unless you've really got something to hide I don't see why you should be anxious to conceal your past.'

Although I had tried to skate over the matter by treating it lightly, the skeleton was a grim and sordid fact, and she was quite justified in wanting to know something about me. I relaised that by digging my toes in I was only converting her good impression of me to a bad one. But I had no alternative; so I stuck to my line of semi-comic nonsense.

'If I were to tell you who I am and what I've done you would shrink from me as though I were a leper. People who snatch the coppers from a blind man are simply nothing compared with me, and I live by preference on the immoral earnings of women. I'm a dope-runner and a blackmailer and, up to date, I have bigamously married seventeen old women to get hold of their savings. Now, are you satisfied?'

'No,' she said firmly. 'I'm not. You haven't done one of these things. You're not that type of man at all; but you're hiding something. And it might have a bearing on Father's death. That's why I have a right to know what it is.'

'That's where we differ. I'm sorry to disappoint you, but I maintain that *no one* has a right to dig in to another person's affairs.'

'All right,' she shrugged. 'We'll leave it like that for the moment.'

We fell silent after that and whereas a quarter of an hour before it had seemed that a spontaneous mutual attraction bid fair to smooth away the strangeness of our situation, there had now developed a definite tension between us. I was quite glad when, across the angle of the great pit which had been dug all round the Spinx, so that its lower limbs may now be seen, I caught a movement in the shadows which I felt fairly confident was caused by Amin and Mustapha.

As there was always the odd chance that it might be a couple of police scouting for me even as far away from Mena House as this, I wasn't taking any risks. I grabbed Sylvia by the arm and made her crouch down with me behind some big rocks. But Amin and Mustapha it proved to be and we came out again to meet them.

Amin had seen Harry and had duly returned with a blue lounge suit of mine, shirt, collar and tie; also a pair of my own shoes. I changed into these at once behind the rocks and reappeared feeling a little more like my old self, except for the fact that I still had twenty-four hours' growth of stubble on my chin.

Mustapha reported that two trolley-loads of police had come dashing up within five minutes of my leaving Mena House with Sylvia. They had surrounded the whole hotel and garden and instituted a thorough search but, of course, failed to find us.

Amin had arrived back while they were busy drawing the grounds and questioning the hotel servants. Mustapha had been extremely anxious for his mistress's safety but it seemed that a few moment's conversation with his old friend, Amin, had set his fears at rest. They had decided between themselves that Mustapha should tell the officer in charge that Sylvia had made a mistake about the Greek workman whom she had thought was me, and had gone back to Cairo leaving him to apologise to the police for having brought them out there on a wild-goose chase. The officer had cursed Mustapha roundly for not having Sylvia's message earlier, but the dragoman had excused himself by saying that he had been in the kitchen quarters having some supper when the police had turned up and that he had only just learned of their arrival. The police had then piled into their trolleys again and returned to Cairo.

This was the best piece of news I had had that evening, as I had been badgering my wits in vain to find some means of securing either Sylvia's car or my own from outside Mena House with the police swarming all round it. For a moment I even considered making a second attempt to get into O'Kieff's room, but dismissed that as much too risky. He would certainly have finished his dinner by this time and might already be back in his suite or go up to it at any moment. Moreover, in spite of my change of clothes there was a chance now that some of the hotel porters might recognise me as the man for whom the police had been looking.

There still remained the possibility that somebody had spotted Sylvia's car and, in consequence, the police officer had not accepted Mustapha's story entirely but had left a couple of men to keep a watch on it, so on second thoughts it seemed wiser that neither of us should return to Mena House if it could be avoided.

'Are you game for half an hour's walk?' I asked Sylvia.

'Why?' she enquired.

'Because I think it would be best if we sent Amin and Mustapha back to collect the cars and were to meet them ourselves a mile or so away from Mena on the Cairo road.'

'D'you know your way across this bit of country in the dark?' she asked a little dubiously.

'With the lights of the main road stretching for miles right in front of us it's impossible to miss it.'

'All right,' she shrugged, and having given careful instructions to the two dragomen, we set off.

If Sylvia had realised what she was letting herself in for I doubt if she would have agreed to accompany me, seeing that our relations were by no means of the best at that moment; but when we started neither of us was aware what a difficult piece of ground we had to traverse. There was never any question of our losing our direction as we could see the lights on the road the whole time, but getting there was the very devil.

A little way in front of the Sphinx we came to the *gebel*, as they call the natural embankment which forms the confines of the Nile valley and runs, several miles inland, more or less parallel with the actual banks of the river. The ground shelved away sharply beneath us forming almost a cliff-face where it marked the division between the flat lands below, which are flooded by the Nile during the inundation period, and the arid desert on the edge of which we were standing.

The drop was about forty feet, but we had to get down it somehow and, I must say, Sylvia was game enough not to complain when I led the way down the shaly sandstone slope. We slipped and slithered, clutching at projections of crumbling rock here and there, but managed to reach the bottom in safety. The next five minutes proved easier going but after that we came upon fields of lucerne and cotton where the soggy soil hampered our progress badly and at times we were bogged in it almost up to the ankles. Dykes, small and large, seemed to bar our path in all directions. Some we were able to cross by plunging down their slimy banks and wading through the few inches of water in their muddy bottoms; others were so wide and deep that we were forced to make tedious detours to find bridges over them. It was a hellish business but at last we reached an Arab village on the banks of the big dyke that runs alongside the main road.

What I had estimated at half an hour's easy walk proved an hour's exhausting travail and although Sylvia did not complain her temper was by no means improved by the time we had crossed the last bridge and reached the cars which the two Arabs had brought to meet us.

My bright idea had ruined a pair of shoes for Sylvia, and both her stockings and her dress were in a shocking mess, so I felt very small indeed as I tumbled into her car, leaving the two guides to follow in Amin's taxi. She still said nothing but I could tell by the reckless way she drove me back to Cairo that she was livid with rage and that our hour of floundering round in the mud had cost me the last remnant of any prestige I had managed to earn for myself during the early part of our talk together.

It was half-past ten before we reached the Nile bridge. At the city end I pulled Sylvia up and waited for the other car to halt behind us. The great block of the Semiramis, with its fine outlook over the river, was only just on the other side of the road, but I felt that we could not possibly present ourselves there in our present condition; so I suggested to Sylvia that she had better go straight to her hotel and change before seeing the Belvilles, while I cleaned myself up as well as I could and joined them later.

Leaving her there I drove off with Amin to another part of the city where an acquaintance of his duly shaved me, cleaned up my suit and got some of the mud off my shoes. Meanwhile Amin secured a room for me in a small *pension* near by and, having told him to report to Harry at nine-thirty the following morning, I took another taxi back to the Semiramis.

I was by no means happy at the idea of entering Cairo's great luxury hotel, and felt I should have been wiser if I had got the Belvilles to come out and meet me somewhere, but none of the people in the 'Hampshire' had seen me without a beard, and the police had no full description of me as I was at the moment.

118

Fortunately Harry had had the sense to go straight up to his room after dinner and there was no question of my having to wait in the lounge as he had left instructions that a visitor he was expecting was to be shown up straight away. I found that Sylvia had arrived before me and that the Belvilles had already given her their version of her father's death and my activities; while she had given them particulars of how I had spent the few hours since my arrival in Cairo. So we were all up to date about the situation.

Harry poured me out a welcome glass of champagne and kind Clarissa had had the forethought to order a large supply of sandwiches to be sent up. Neither Sylvia nor I had had any dinner and when I was shown in she was tucking into them as though she had not fed for weeks.

I had hardly had time to sit down before she asked acidly: 'And what, exactly, does our clever Mr. Day intend to do now?'

'Since your intervention prevented my getting away with O'Kieff's despatch-box tonight I've hardly had time to think,' I replied with equal lack of cordiality. 'Unfortunately, too, by butting in the way you did you've made it next to impossible for me to show my face out at Mena any more. However, there is still Gamal's, the dope-distributing depot, the address of which Princess Oonas gave away to me when she thought I was Lemming. We might get a lead to something there. Anyhow I mean to pay Mr. Gamal a visit tomorrow night.'

'She said you'd have to get a card from Zakri Bey,' Harry objected.

'True, and that's impossible. Still, I'll probably be able to wangle my way in somehow.'

'But Julian, dear, if they find out who you really are they might kill you,' Clarissa protested hastily. 'We can't let you deliberately walk into a place like that.'

'Why not, since there's a chance of my finding out something? I shall be carrying a gun remember.'

'I don't like it,' declared Sylvia, who had curled up with her long legs under her on Clarissa's bed.

'It's nice of you to be concerned for my safety,' I said. 'But I'm pretty capable of taking care of myself.'

'I'm not the least concerned for your safety,' she replied. coldly. 'I mean I don't like the whole business. You appear to think this man O'Kieff was the murderer and you must have been mixed up with him before because you know quite a lot about him. Yet you flatly refuse to tell us anything about yourself. For all we know you may be another crook who's quarrelled with him.'

'Oh come, darling,' Clarissa exclaimed in a shocked voice. Sylvia shrugged. 'I'm sorry if I put it rather bluntly. Mr. Day seems to have made good use of the fortnight on board to exercise his fascination on you and Harry, but it's had no time to work with me yet, and I'm simply going on the facts. None of us knows a single thing about him.'

'Well, if you don't like *my* way of handling this,' I said, 'what would you suggest yourself?'

Her beautifully-chiselled Anglo-Saxon features were set and her eyes hard as she stared at me. 'You are wanted by the police in connection with my father's murder. If you *are* an honest man and completely innocent you will give yourself up at once.'

I shrugged. 'If I do, bang goes any chance of my getting anything on O'Kieff. After the dance I've led the police they're certain to detain me for some days until they've definitely satisfied themselves that I didn't do it and then Zakri will have me deported.'

'I honestly can't see that you're likely to get much by going to this dope-den tomorrow night,' Harry said thoughtfully.

'Can't you? We know Gamal is mixed up with Oonas and Zakri, therefore also with O'Kieff. I want to meet a few more members of the gang if possible, so that we may be able to identify them if we come up against them later. That's why I am determined to visit Gamal's place.'

'That's all very well,' said Sylvia. 'But there's one thing you seem to have forgotten. Let's accept your word for the moment that you had nothing whatever to do with Father's death. The fact remains that owing to your having left the ship without permission the police naturally believe you are the murderer and they're wasting all their energies trying to find *you* when they should be concentrating on somebody else. It isn't fair to them to go on giving them a lot of bother for nothing like this. Besides, since you got the upper half of the tablet back from this Egyptian Princess, somebody obviously brought it ashore last night. As everybody else's baggage was searched that certainly points to O'Kieff, but the police know nothing whatever about that yet. They're much more likely to be able to pin the murder on him—if he did it—than you are. That's why I insist on your giving yourself up to the police and telling them everything you know.'

'I see your point, but giving myself up virtually means giving up my chance of getting even with O'Kieff; so I'm afraid I can't oblige you.'

'To hell with that! I'm not the least interested in your private quarrels, Mr. Day; but I *am* concerned in bringing my father's murderer to justice. If you won't do the decent thing I'm going to have you arrested.'

'That's easier said than done.' I sneered, angry, in my tired state, at the lack of sympathy she seemed to be showing.

'All right,' she said, sliding off the bed. 'But you won't be able to keep on the run without assistance very long. Harry and Clarissa won't help you against my wish, I know, and Amin will be useless to you once the police are told he's been supplying you with changes of clothes.'

'No,' I agreed slowly. 'I doubt if I could keep my freedom for twenty-four hours entirely on my own.'

She nodded her ash-blonde head. 'I'm glad you appreciate that because it's all I'm going to give you. Since you're so keen on it you shall have your chance to visit Gamal's tomorrow night if you're prepared to give me your word that you'll surrender yourself to the police immediately afterwards; if not, I'm going off here and now to tell them all I've learnt about you.'

I knew that I was up against it. Since I was unable to tell her the truth about my wretched past it had risen up to shackle me. Unless I should have phenomenal luck on the following evening O'Kieff would have won his second round against me without lifting a finger.

10

Dope

'It's nice to know that you attach some value to my word.' I said acidly.

'I'll take it for what it may be worth,' she replied.

'I shrugged. 'You have it then. I'm so dog-tired I simply couldn't stand up to a police enquiry tonight and twenty-four hours is better than nothing.'

Harry, looking like a P. G. Wodehouse character, stood there fingering his little wisp of flaxen moustache and goggling at us with his round, blue eyes. By way of showing his sympathy he poured me another glass of champagne and, tired as I was, as I took it from him my weary brain began to turn over this new situation.

I attributed the fact that I had so far managed to evade the police to no particular cleverness on my own but entirely to the frequent changes in my appearance. Having landed the previous evening at Alex. as a well-dressed, bearded Briton, I had become within an hour a clean-shaven Arab dragoman; by half-past four in the morning I was a Red Indian Brave and by half-past eleven a poor Greek workman; nine hours later, out by the Pyramids, I had changed yet again, but my last metamorphosis had brought me much nearer to the original than I cared about.

It is true that I still sported the sallow skin of the Greek and that the loss of my beard would prevent any casual shipboard acquaintance knowing me again at first sight; but in all other respects I was once again my normal self and even the better-class Levantines living in Cairo do not usually wear Saville Row clothes.

'Harry,' I said, 'will you do me a favour?'

'Of course, old man.'

'My own suit fits me much too well. D'you mind lending me

one of yours so that I can go about without being quite such an easy mark for the police tomorrow?'

'By all means,' he agreed. 'Take your choice out of the little lot in the wardrobe.'

Harry was a few inches shorter than myself and a good deal fatter; he also had a passion for large checks which I rarely wear, so I selected a pair of grey flannel trousers, a white-and-green check jacket and a Fair Isle pullover.

As I packed the things into my small suitcase I said to Sylvia, 'You've had a long and trying day, Miss Shane, so perhaps you'd like me to see you back to your hotel.'

'Thank you,' she said without enthusiasm. 'I'm staying at the Continental, but I don't want to take you out of your way.'

'That's no distance,' I replied. 'And this time I really can promise not to lead you into a swamp.'

Clarissa showed by the lack of warmth in her goodnight to Sylvia that she was quite definitely on my side and she made her feeling patent by exclaiming:

'Julian, dear, I simply must give you something to take with you for luck. What shall it be?—I know!'

Running to her jewel-box she came back with a golden sovereign which she pressed into my hand. 'The image of St. George and the dragon. You'll be St. George, you see, and O'Kieff the dragon. If you carry that tomorrow night it will remind you that both Harry's thoughts and mine are with you.'

'A St. George who has no history,' Sylvia remarked with a cynical little laugh.

I ignored the gibe and thanked Clarissa for her sweet thought just as nicely as I knew how; after which Harry insisted on seeing Sylvia and myself downstairs.

We went out by the side-entrance opposite the Kasr el Nil, by which I had come in, and were fortunate in not having to pass anyone except a solitary native servant. There were no taxis outside so we started to walk along until we could pick one up.

It was late now and the broad street was empty except for a few passing vehicles, pedestrians hurrying homeward and the ragged beggars who infested Cairo by night as well as by day. The growing good will that had marked the first part of my talk with Sylvia out by the IVth Dynasty tombs had completely evaporated. My inability to speak about my past and the dance I had led her through the cotton-fields seemed entirely to have destroyed her earlier impulse to regard me as a friend and we walked along side by side in uneasy silence.

Just as we were passing a side-turning a whimpering cry caused us to pull up and stare down at it. A few feet away a hefty Arab was belabouring a small boy with a heavy stick.

'Excuse me a minute,' I said, and stepping forward I caught the Arab's wrist. With one swift wrench I forced him to drop his stick, at the same time giving him my left, hard, in the pit of the stomach. With a choking gasp he collapsed into the gutter while the small boy ran off into the darkness. Next moment I had rejoined Sylvia and we were walking on.

'More heroics for my benefit, Mr. Day?' she inquired sarcastically.

'Certainly not,' I replied with some heat. 'It's only that I don't like to see small children hurt; but I suppose, to you, that sounds only an extremely pompous statement.'

'No,' she said slowly, 'and I take back what I said. It was mean of me and quite unjustified. I can't make you out at all, though.'

'Why? I'm a perfectly normal person.'

'Is it normal for a man who is being hunted by the police to risk attracting their attention to himself by entering into a street brawl?'

'I'm afraid I hadn't thought of that,' I confessed. 'Perhaps it was silly of me but I acted on the impulse of the moment. I'm not used to thinking of myself as a criminal.'

'So it seems. Yet you're certainly hiding something. That's what puzzles me so.'

An empty taxi cruised past us but it hardly seemed worth while to take it now as we were more than half-way to the Continental.

'I'm hiding nothing,' I assured her, 'which could have the least bearing on your father's death.'

We covered another hundred yards in silence then she said suddenly, 'I'm afraid you think I'm being very hard on you, Mr. Day.'

'No,' I replied. 'It's just that my objective is a more sweeping one than yours, that's all. You're out to get your father's

murderer, whoever he may be, and you'll be satisfied with that.
To the best of me belief, I'm after the same person for the same
thing and for many other crimes as well. But I'm using larger
maps than you because I know him to be one of the heads of a
great organisation for evil and I want to do my best to cripple,
that, if not break it up, in the process of getting even with him.'

'If you discovered that the murderer was not O'Kieff but one
of his people you'd let him go rather than spoil your chance
of pinning something on O'Kieff himself later, wouldn't you?'

'Yes, I would. Unfortunately this dragon is the sort of beast
that can grow fresh talons by the dozen overnight and I want
to strike off its head, not one of its claws.'

'I suppose you're right about that and perhaps I'm taking a
narrow view,' she said more gently. 'You see, I only learnt
about Daddy's death this morning and I was most terribly fond
of him. I've got enough of the primitive in me to want to get
the actual brute who struck him down and I feel the police
stand a far better chance of doing that than an amateur like
yourself.'

'I quite understand,' I assured her, 'and, tired as I am, I'd
go to them myself this minute if it didn't mean me being thrown
out of Egypt. It's bad enough having to cash in my checks
tomorrow night.'

We had reached the steps of the Continental. The broad
terrace overlooking Ezbekiyeh Gardens and the Opera Square
was in semi-darkness but the bright light from the doorway of
the hotel fell on her lovely face as she turned and held out her
hand:

'I'm afraid I *am* being hard, but I just can't help it. Please
don't think too badly of me.'

'I don't,' I smiled.

'All right, then. When you've got Harry's clothes on and
have collected a tarboosh nobody's likely to pay much attention to you. Just to show there's no ill-feeling, come and have
a cocktail with me here to-morrow evening at six. I'd like
to see you again before you risk yourself in that place of
Gamal's.'

'Does that mean you've abandoned your theory that I'm
probably a crook?'

'Not necessarily. There are nasty crooks and nice ones and

I don't mind entertaining the more pleasant variety providing they don't actually try to do me down.' With the suggestion of a smile she left me and disappeared into the hotel.

From the rank in the square I took one of the ancient open carriages, called *arabiehs,* that ply for hire in Cairo at all hours. It was not far to the cheap *pension* where Amin had taken a room for me but on the way the gentle clopping of the old horse's hoofs nearly sent me to sleep and by the time I had climbed to a third-storey room my legs were almost giving under me.

It was over sixty hours since I had woken in my cabin on the morning of the day that Sir Walter was murdered. That night I had only four hours' sleep and nearly twenty-four hours later I had managed to snatch another three hours in the Tomb of the Bulls. For the last thirty hours I had been a hunted man and continual excitement had sustained me, but now I was all in; pulling off my clothes I flopped into bed, sinking at once into a deep and dreamless sleep.

It was after midday when I woke; the streets of Cairo were dangerous for me and, since there was nothing I could do until the evening, I just turned over and dozed for the best part of the afternoon.

The bathing accommodation at the *pension* was far from being all that I could have wished, but I made do with it and, much refreshed by my long sleep, I dressed myself in Harry's clothes and went out to make a few purchases.

I got a bright-blue, soft-collared shirt, a tarboosh, a green tie with white camels printed on it and a ghastly pair of lemon-yellow leather shoes with long, pointed toes. I then drove to Groppi's, the famous *patisserie* in the Sharia Kasr el Nil, where I purchased two boxes of their huge chocolates for Sylvia and Clarissa and let myself go on a fine selection of sweets for myself. My eyes have always been bigger than my tummy when let loose in a good sweet-shop and, although I knew quite well that I should never be able to eat them all, I could not resist buying my favourite fondants, caramel moue, almond brittle, nougat, fruit jellies and violet chocolate creams, and I had positively to drag myself away or else I should have left with another half-dozen boxes.

Returning to the *pension* I put on my new items of attire

and, regarding myself in the spotted mirror over the old-fashioned, marble-topped washstand, congratulated myself upon my appearance. Harry's clothes were not too conspicuously full round the waist but both the sleeves of the coat and the bottoms of the trousers were a good couple of inches too short for me which made them look like ready-mades. With my yellowish complexion and flashy haberdashery I now looked a typical middle-class Egyptian and no one, I think, would have suspected that I was an ex-member of His Britannic Majesty's Diplomatic Service or a product of Eton and Oxford.

The only thing that bothered me was a slight cold. Like a fool I had not troubled to dry my feet properly after getting them soaked when wading through the cotton-fields with Sylvia the previous evening and it looked as if I was going to pay the penalty of my carelessness.

When I arrived at the Continental the terrace was crowded with a hundred or more people sitting over their evening drinks and watching the multi-coloured life of Cairo pass in the street below. Clarissa and Harry were at a table with Sylvia. Harry recognised his own coat as I came towards them but the two girls looked quite startled for a moment until they realised the identity of the flashy young stranger who bowed before them.

My green tie with the camels on it caused quite a lot of laughter, but I was not too conspicuous as at least half the men on the terrace were Egyptians wearing tarbooshes with European clothes and I might quite well have been a minor official or a merchant who had been asked along to discuss some deal in the jewels or antiquities which make up so much of Cairo's trade with wealthy European visitors. The chocolates were accepted with cries of glee by Clarissa and more appreciation than I had expected by Sylvia, although, I learnt later, she rarely ate sweets.

She was looking pale and tired; quite evidently feeling the reaction from the day before and beginning to realise fully the fact that she had really lost her father. To distract her from her grief as much as possible during the day I learnt that the Belvilles had made her show them some of the sights.

Harry found Cairo disappointing; a shoddy, second-rate capital, he called it; and it is quite true that although it has many fine modern buildings these are much too dispersed to be effective. Even in the main streets they are so often separated by blocks of tawdry shops, and the hundreds of fine old mosques, in which lie the city's true glory, are invariably surrounded by the tumble-down structures of the poorer inhabitants.

Clarissa, however, was thoroughly enjoying herself. She had bought every sort of useless nonsense in the Mouski that morning. The narrow alleyways and long, dark shops of the Bazaar had intrigued her so much that neither Sylvia nor Harry had been able to persuade her that she could buy the same sort of junk cheaper in Birmingham or Hamburg.

In the afternoon they had visited old Cairo where the three religions have been practised side by side in amity for centuries. At the Jewish synagogue they had seen the oldest copy of the Torah in the world, said to have been penned direct from that which was kept in the Temple of David at Jerusalem. In the Coptic Christian church they had visited the tiny crypt believed to have been the place where the Virgin sheltered with the Holy Child during her flight into Egypt. But the Mosque of Amr seemed to have intrigued Clarissa even more particularly the story that one of its three hundred and sixty-six columns had travelled all the way through the air from Mecca upon being struck by Mohammed with a whip and that the Faithful believe the whole mosque will fly back there one last Friday in the month of Ramadan. Although normally deserted, its great courtyard is packed to suffocation with thousands upon thousands of believers on each of these holy anniversaries.

'Just think of it!' she said. 'The whole thing rising up into the air like some huge magic carpet and whisking away across the desert down the Red Sea.'

'And wouldn't the people in it have a fit if it did!' Harry grinned. 'Now darling, you've talked quite enough nonsense. Let's hear what Julian intends to do if he's still set on making this mad expedition tonight.'

'There's nothing much to tell you,' I said, 'because my plans are quite nebulous. All I know is that Gamal's place is part of the dope-distributing organisation and I'm going to pass the evening there on the off-chance that I can find out a little more about it.'

'What time do you expect to get away?' Sylvia asked.

'Goodness knows. I may not even get in, but If I do I shall stay as long as possible.'

'Well, we're dining at Jimmy's,' she announced. 'So if you do get slung out or get away by a reasonable hour, perhaps you'd like to come on there.'

'I envy you,' I said. 'His curried prawns are the best food in Egypt, but I doubt if I'll be through before midnight. If I find out anything that's worth while I'll telephone you whatever hour it is and we'll arrange a meeting. If not, we'd better meet here at, say, ten-thirty tomorrow morning.'

'What d'you want us to do if you fail to turn up?' Harry asked anxiously.

'If that happens I don't suppose I shall be terribly interested but as you're to see the police in any case, they'll doubtless do their best to find my mangled corpse.'

'Don't, Julian!' exclaimed Clarissa.

'Sorry,' I laughed. 'I was only joking. It's a thousand-to-one against my running into anyone at Gamal's who would know me and I promise you I'm the very last person to get myself into trouble for the mere fun of the thing.'

Harry ordered another round of champagne cocktails but our conversation had become disjointed and uneasy. All three of them made half-hearted attempts to persaude me to change my mind about going to Gamal's but I was pig-headed and, since my project looked like spoiling their evening, I decided that the best thing to do was to drink up and leave them. Harry made me promise that I would ring up whatever hour I got back and they all wished me luck.

I was by no means so certain as I had made out that I would not run into bad trouble and while I was dining alone at a small restaurant I had a distinct attack of cold feet. But I knew this was my last chance of striking at O'Kieff so like it or not, I had simply got to take it.

I gave myself till half-past eight, then I made my way along Mohammed Ali Street and entered the second turning on the right. The district was by no means a pleasant one and it was thereabouts that numerous British officers had been assassinated during the troublesome times when the Egyptian National-ists were adopting Terrorists tactics in order to secure Home Rule for their country.

E 129

I found the carpet shop without difficulty. The door was shut but I could see a light gleaming through its lattice, so I banged upon it loudly and after a moment an Arab in a white *galabieh* opened it, standing there quite silently while he waited for me to state my business.

'Is Gamal *Effendi* in?' I asked, and he nodded.

'Who wishes to see him, master?'

'He would not know my name,' I said. 'But tell him, please, that I come from Yusuf Fakri.'

'*Ayoua,*' he bowed. 'Please to step in and wait here.'

He shut the door behind me, slid-to the bolt and left me standing in the dimly-lit shop. A number of rugs were hanging on the walls and at the back of the place there were several of the looms at which one sees small boys busily hand-weaving in the day-time. In the centre of the floor there were two great stacks of carpets nearly three feet in height and I formed the impression at once that the place was not merely a blind but that a genuine carpet business was conducted there.

After a couple of minutes the servant returned and led me upstairs to his master; while we went through the usual Arab greetings I took quick stock of the dope-trafficker.

Gamal was a fat, heavy man of fifty-odd with grizzled hair showing at the sides of his head where it was not covered by the tarboosh. His skin was dark and slightly pitted, doubtless from smallpox in infancy. There was nothing particularly villainous-looking about him but I noted that his eyes were very quick and lively. The room in which he received me was obviously his office and that in itself seemed rather a give-away; it was much too well-equipped with every sort of Western business gadget to belong to the owner of the musty, old-fashioned carpet shop downstairs.

'You come from Fakri?' Gamal said, pushing a box of cigarettes across his desk towards me.

'Yes,' I replied. 'My name is Daoud el Azziz, and I am Yusuf's cousin. He has the fever tonight and has sent me in his place.'

I knew from the list I had seen on Oonas' desk that a man called Yusuf Fakri was due to collect a packet of dope from Gamal that night and I was taking a big risk in passing myself off as Yusuf's cousin; but it was the only means I had been able

to think of which would get me into the place without a card.
If Yusuf had collected the stuff earlier in the evening I should
find myself in the soup within a couple of minutes but I counted it almost a certainty that they would do their work late at
night and by making my call at 8.30 I was hoping that I had
forestalled him. It was an anxious moment as I watched Gamal
covertly to see his reaction to my story.

He frowned but to my relief said, after a moment, 'So the
young fool's taken a spot too much again, eh?'

'No, no, Mr. Gamal!' I hastened to protest. 'Believe me,
poor Yusuf is really ill. He ate bad fish, I think; anyhow it is
some sort of poisoning. He was sick and weak as a dog when
he sent for me this evening and begged me to report to you and
offer my services in place of his own for a job that he had to
do.'

'What sort of a job?' Gamal enquired.

I shrugged and spread out my hands in a truly Oriental
gesture. 'Mr. Gamal, he told me nothing; only that you relied
on him and that if you were willing to let me take his place I
could earn some good money.'

'I bet you've got a pretty shrewd idea what Yusuf does, or he
wouldn't have sent you,' said Gamal quickly.

'Well, Mr. Gamal,' I fluttered my eyelashes coyly and smiled
at my feet. 'Yusuf knows I'm to be trusted. And although he's
never let on to me, I've got my own ideas how he earns his
cash.'

'You've guessed anyhow that for a few hours every couple
of weeks he risks seeing the inside of a prison?'

'Nobody ever gets paid good money for doing nothing,' I
said sententiously. 'We've all got to live, haven't we?'

'That's true enough,' Gamal nodded. 'And you're the sort of
boy who's prepared to risk a spell on those lines yourself, eh?'

'Yusuf didn't say so but I'm sure that's why he picked me.
I'm game to do anything you wish, Mr. Gamal—if the pay's
right.'

He stared at me very hard for a moment with his little,
black, beady eyes, evidently wondering whether he could trust
me, but my story was plausible enough and, in view of Oonas'
carefully-arranged roster of collectors, he probably had no one
else to hand that he could send in Yusuf's place. Without say-

ing anything further he stood up and went out of the room.

I was beginning to get a little anxious as it suddenly occurred to me that he might be telephoning somewhere to check up my story and if he did I should be sunk. I slipped my hand behind my hip and loosened my gun so that it would draw easily, knowing that if Gamal *was* checking up my only hope of getting out of the place alive would be by acting before he could.

The moment the door opened my fears were set at rest; he had only gone to get the dope and he threw a large brown-paper packet, which evidently contained it, on to the desk.

'There's the stuff,' he said sitting down again. 'You'll be paid tomorrow. Where d'you want the money sent?'

'Send it to Fakri, Mr. Gamal. He told me he was putting me on to a good thing and naturally he wants his split. All I'd like to know is the total you're paying for the evening's work.'

'Two hundred piastres. Split it how you like. Now about delivery. You're to take the stuff to the City of the Dead. Do you know the building they call the House of El Said?'

I shook my head.

'Well, you know the police-post. That's more or less in the centre of the city.'

'Yes,' I said, and he leaned forward to draw a little diagram on a sheet of paper.

'Here's the police-post. You don't have to walk right into it as it's the only place in the whole area where there will be any lights. Directly you've located it, take the main road back to modern Cairo and go down the sixth turning on your right coming from the police-post. Two hundred yards down it you turn right again; there are roofless buildings on both corners. Next to the one on the left is the burial house of El Said. The family keep it in some sort of repair and the shutters are painted green; you can't possibly miss it because it's the only house thereabouts that has any shutters to its windows at all. Just beyond it you'll find what used to be the side entrance, which is recessed into the wall. Sit down in there and nobody'll see you even if they pass within a foot of you. Your opposite number will come straight up to you and say, "I'm a stranger from Assiut and I've lost my way. Can you direct me back to the city?" upon which you will reply, "I'm a stranger too, but I come from Suez." By which each will know that the other is all right. You then hand him the package and make your way home. Is that clear?'

'Perfectly,' I nodded. 'He says he's from Assiut and I say I'm from Suez. What time am I to be there?'

Gamal glanced at his watch. 'It's barely nine yet and you're not due at your post till twelve-fifteen. Why the devil did you come so early?'

'Yusuf said it would be best for me to do so in case you didn't care to take me on, as then you would have plenty of time to find somebody else.'

'I see. That's all right, then. What are you going to do in the meantime?'

'Oh, hang around. Have coffee somewhere.'

'Oh no, you're not,' he said promptly. 'Not with that packet of stuff in your possession. It might be pinched off you or you might get mixed up in some shindy. You had best stay here. I can't have you in this office but you can sit downstairs in the shop and if you leave at half-past eleven that will be quite time enough.'

'Just as you say, Mr. Gamal,' I agreed submissively.

'Another thing, young man,' he went on. 'Once you've done your job, forget it. If one of my people drops out I might be able to use you and you can make some easy cash on trips like this. But you're not to come near this place again unless you're sent for. You're not to speak to your opposite number, either, except just the words I've told you; and I wouldn't advise you to have any bright ideas about following him through innocent curiosity when he goes off because if you do you'll get a knife in your back.'

'You don't have to worry, Mr. Gamal. I'm grateful for the job and want to work for you again, so I won't do anything but just what you've told me.'

'That's the way,' he nodded. 'Now you'd best go downstairs. Turn to the left at the bottom.'

As he opened th office door for me Gamal shouted to his servant and told the man to provide me with a paper to read while I was waiting. I thanked him and, descending, settled myself on a pile of carpets in the musty shop, soon after which I was given a copy of *El Mokattam*, the leading Cairo paper.

The light was dim and the print bad but I made a pretence of studying it while I thought matters over. Although I had failed to think up a way of penetrating to the inner portion of the dope-den where the hashish-addicts congregated I felt I had done far better. Having made Gamal's acquaintance I should know him again anywhere and as he had swallowed my story I was temporarily, at least a member of his organisation entrusted with a consignment of the drug. That would enable me to contact my opposite number and, I hoped, trace him, when I had handed it over, to some other depot in the chain. Moreover, although I had not been given the run of the place, quite fortuitously I had actually been ordered to remain within sight of its door for two and a half hours and so would have the opportunity of observing everybody who came in and out of it without arousing the least suspicion.

However, there was one most unpleasant snag. Yusuf's illness was pure invention in my part and it was a hundred-to-one that he would turn up in the normal course of his duties to collect the packet of dope that I was holding. Immediately he appeared the cat would be out of the bag and I would find myself up to my neck in trouble. For a moment I was tempted to try to make my get-away as soon as I could but I saw that if I did that Gamal would be certain to suspect me and, having ample time in hand, send some of his people to beat me up when I appeared at the rendezvous in the City of the Dead at twelve-fifteen. Obviously I had to hang on where I was as long as I could do so with reasonable safety. As Yusuf did the job regularly it would be bad luck if he put in an appearance before eleven at the earliest, so I determined to stick it out till then.

It soon became obvious to me that the carpet shop was used only as a business entrance to the premises and that there must be some other, probably through a court at the rear of the buildings, to which the hashish-addicts came to indulge in their dope-dreams.

The results of my vigil were most disappointing. Only two people knocked on the street-door and were admitted by the Arab servant. One was a short, thick-set, bespectacled Jew, evidently a regular visitor as he nodded to the Arab and hurried upstairs in a most business-like manner without even asking if Gamal could see him. The other was a heavily-painted woman of about thirty who had the appearance of a French prostitute. She too hurried up to Gamal's office as though she had urgent business to transact and both left again within a few minutes of their arrival.

It occurred to me that the place probably consisted of two houses backing on to each other and connected only by a secret entrance through the partition wall; so that if one of the patrons gave the place away to the police and it was raided Gamal would remain quite unmolested in his room above the carpet-shop, which was the real nerve centre of the business. Actually I should have learnt little if I had been in the addicts' side of the house and I congratulated myself on having got into this quieter but infinitely more important section of it.

It was a weary business sitting there pretending to read the Arabic newspaper, but my boredom never lasted for more than a few moments as it was constantly punctuated by the thought that Yusuf might arrive on the scene or, having arrived by some other entrance, be actually closeted with Gamal plotting my destruction.

At last I saw by my wrist-watch that it was eleven o'clock. As far as I knew Gamal had not given any instructions to his man to prevent my leaving before half-past so I stood up and walking to the door began to unbolt it.

At that moment there was a loud knock and I opened the door to find a young man standing on its step. He was about my own age and I almost laughed as I noticed the striking resemblance of his clothes to those I was wearing. They were, of course, of much more shoddy material than Harry's but he also had on a check jacket, grey flannel trousers and a pullover with a flamboyant tie. I was just patting myself on the back for the excellent choice of garments I had made for the part I was playing when the Arab servant came up behind me and said to the young man:

'Good evening, Mr. Fakri.'

Either the servant was extraordinarily slow-witted or, more probably, Gamal had not told him that I was supposed to be taking Fakri's place; otherwise that fat would have been in the fire there and then. As it was I saw that Yusuf, after one glance at the parcel I was carrying, had begun to eye me curiously. It was obviously no time to linger. I smiled broadly at Yusuf.

thrust my way past him with a cordial 'good evening' and nodding good night to the servant, stepped out into the street.

I did not dare to look back but I had the impression that they were staring after me and talking together excitedly on the doorstep. The moment I had turned the corner into Mohammed Ali Street I took to my heels and ran.

It was an unpleasantly close shave but there were still plenty of people about so I had no difficulty in losing myself and a few minutes later I was back in the Opera Square considering what my next move should be.

Undoubtedly by now Gamal and Yusuf would be entering into angry explanations and aware of the trick that had been played on them. What would they do? Most probably they would believe me to be either a dope-thief or a police spy. I was carrying a package which, judging by its weight, probably contained £500 worth of hashish—a fine haul for any thief—and I knew that there were a number of these operating in the drug market, their line being to sell the precious dope back to the organisation by devious channels.

If Gamal and Co. put me down as a thief they would be sick as mud but there was nothing very much they could do about it. On the other hand they might believe me to be a police spy, in which case they would be burning papers as hard as they could go in anticipation of a raid; but they would also know that the police have a habit of following up any information they are lucky enough to get hold of and would naturally endeavour to rope in the man who was due to collect the dope in the City of the Dead that night. If it was too late to warn him, Gamal might try heading him off in which case there was a chance of my coming into collision with his people at the rendezvous; but I decided that I must risk that. If luck was with me they would be too scared to do anything and I should have a clear field to meet and follow my opposite number.

I put in half an hour over a couple of drinks at a small café; then I took an *arabieh* to the mosque of el Hakim which lies on the north-western outskirts of the present Cairo.

The Egyptian capital has been shifted several times since its foundation. The original town, now called Old Cairo, that Clarissa had visited that afternoon, lies to the south-west on the Nile bank near the Island of Rodah and was founded by

General Amr, the commander of the Caliph Omar, about the middle of the seventh century; but the old city was later abandoned for new and more beautiful suburbs to the east which rose on the slope of the Mokattam Hills where the magnificent Citadel now stands. Later again the fashionable quarter moved north; but at one period in the Middle Ages a terrible plague afflicted Cairo so that its inhabitants died by the thousand, and as the corpses were too numerous to be carted to the cemeteries, people were buried where they died in their own houses. The ravages of the plague were so severe in this northern city that it was entirely deserted by the living and henceforth became known as the City of the Dead. Afterwards a new city rose between the Citadel on the east and the Nile where it flows past the Island of Gezira on the west; and this now is the heart of modern Cairo.

After the plague had passed, the richest citizens who had survived found that they had two houses, one in the new city and one in the City of the Dead; so the practice arose of using the City of the Dead as a cemetery. Further bodies were buried beside the victims of the plague in the old family mansions there until the custom became such a well-established one that the Government decreed that every Mohammedan family in Cairo must own a burial house in that quarter.

This has led to the strange phenomenon of the dead city now having suburbs, which stretch away into the desert and towards Abbassia in the extreme north. They are the queerest suburbs imaginable since so many of the original houses have fallen in that the Government does not insist on proper houses being built; the present-day purchaser of a site need do no more than lay the foundations of a house and build an outer wall about three feet high. The result is acres and acres of land covered by long, straight streets intersecting each other every few hundred yards and composed of thousands of partially-built houses differing only in their state of completeness and design.

The City of the Dead is a most grim and desolate place even by day as no one ever goes there except funeral processions and an occasional sight-seer. By night it is the haunt of thieves and vagabonds and no place for any honest man to enter, unless he wants his throat cut; apart from one night in the year when the surviving members of each family occupy their house and spend their night in prayer for the departed.

Unlike its new suburbs, the streets of the original city are narrow and twisting. Its buildings are sinister beyond description; gaunt, roofless and falling into ruin so that through the gaps in the fallen walls and the squares that once held windows can be seen innumerable Arab tombs crowded together on the floor of each empty room.

I had never visited it by night and, frankly, I dreaded the ordeal, knowing that its police patrols could do no more than keep a watch on its main thoroughfares. It would take a full brigade of troops to police that network of lanes and alleys which spreads over so many acres.

It was five minutes before midnight as I paid off the driver of my ramshackle carriage near the mosque of el Hakim; a quiet neighbourhood where few people were moving at this hour.

I lit a cigarette and stood puffing at it until the *arabieh* had driven off, then I turned north-east and walked a few hundred yards between two rows of dilapidated houses, inhabited by poor Arabs, until they gave way to mounds of rubble and blank, crumbling walls which cut the skyline in a jagged silhouette. The road sloped upwards and it was here that the city of the living gave place to the City of the Dead.

Behind me I left occasional street-lamps and the faint rays of friendly light coming from partially-curtained windows. As I mounted the hill and looked back I could see over the rooftops. The individual lights in the nearer houses had become pin-pricks and now blended with a hundred thousand others making a reddish glow above the whole broad expanse of modern Cairo. But up the hill in front lay impenetrable darkness unlit by a solitary gleam in any direction; except if one looked upwards over the line of crumbling walls to the stars which twinkled in the darkened sky. Behind me I could hear the subdued roar of the city's night life; in front it was as silent as the grave, and when I say grave I speak literally, for upon either hand graves lay in every room of every house by hundreds upon hundreds throughout the length and breadth of that desolate, eerie city.

I advanced with extreme caution, listening with all my ears for the faintest sound which might disturb the stillness. I had no desire to run into a police patrol as they would be certain to question, and might arrest me, since they would regard anyone found there at such an hour as being up to no good. Yet I was even more afraid of being surprised and fallen on by one of the gangs of toughs which were said to lurk in the ruins. Preferring the lesser evil of being challenged by the police I kept well to the centre of the road. The shadows at its sides which would have concealed me were fraught with too many unknown dangers.

When I reached the top of the hill I turned left into a long straight thoroughfare and, hand on gun, heart in throat, walked down it for half a mile until I saw a faint glow ahead of me. I went even more cautiously then, knowing it could only be the bivouac fires of the police-post. A few minutes later I came to the end of the street and, carefully ensconcing myself in a heavy band of shadow, I peered round the corner into the old square which used to be the centre of the city. In it there were now a wooden shed, two army tents and about half a dozen of Essex Pasha's famous white racing dromedaries tethered near by. A bivouac fire was burning in the centre of the encampment and a dozen Egyptian police were squatting round it.

Silently I turned away and retraced my steps, counting the turnings between the ruined houses as I went. All the time I kept to the centre of the road and my hand on my gun as, although I had not seen a single sign of life except at the police-post, that was no evidence that I had not already been spotted by cut-throats who were stalking me and liable to leap out of the shadows at any moment.

At the sixth turning on the right I turned downhill again and took the first turn to the right as I had been instructed. The road was of a fair width but only by comparison with some of the noisome alleys I had passed on my way up from the modern city. I found the house of El Said without difficulty, since it was easily identifiable by the shutters. I found, too, the niche by the old side-door where I had been told to wait but I did not pause there; instead I took up my position about twenty yards further on in a patch of darkness which gave me ample cover. Then I waited with beating heart and the best patience I could muster.

My watch showed me that it was just on the time appointed

but the minutes dragged by with leaden feet and not a sound broke the stillness. I was just beginning to think that Gamal had managed to warn my opposite number in time, and that he would not turn up, when the clicking of a loose stone caught my ear. It was followed by a stealthy tread.

At first I could see nothing but after a moment I discerned a movement in the shadows near the entrance of the turning which led to the main street; but it seemed to me that it was too diffused to be one person and, staring into the darkness, I suddenly became aware that four figures were approaching.

The thought, 'why four instead of one?' flashed through my racing brain and then that these men were nothing to do with Gamal but one of the gangs which I feared so much. They reached the nook where I was supposed to be and entered it which told me definitely that there were Gamal's people. Next moment they broke out into excited chatter; yet their voices were semi-hushed and I sensed that the grim spell of the place was on them even as it was on myself.

Evidently they were surprised and annoyed to find the place empty. Abandoning their former caution they stepped back into the road where, by the faint starlight, I could see them for the first time with some clearness. The silhouette of one of them struck me as vaguely familiar; then I identified it as that of Yusuf. I guessed at once that on learning he had been fooled Gamal had sent Yusuf and several of his people to stop my opposite number keeping the tryst and, on the assumption that I might be a police spy, ordered them to find out if I had kept it with the idea of assassinating me. Even as the thought came to me it was confirmed by my catching the flash of starlight on steel and I saw that one of the stalkers was carrying a drawn knife in his hand.

I thanked my gods that I had had the sense to conceal myself at some little distance from the rendezvous but I was none too happy at the thought that I could not retreat from where I stood without showing myself. With the idea of making myself safe from any surprise attack I had selected an angle where two high walls met; the deep shadows there concealed me perfectly but my situation would be a desperate one if it occurred to them that I might be hiding somewhere near by and they started to hunt for me. My only consolation was that there were so many equally good hiding-places within a hundred yards of where they stood they would probably consider any search quite futile.

I could hear them debating together what to do next, and even caught the words of one who declared that as I had failed to keep the appointment it was senseless to linger there and that they had best get back to make their report as quickly as possible. With a sigh of relief I saw them turn away and set off towards the entrance of the lane.

They had not gone ten yards when a frightful tickling started in my nose. The wretched cold I had caught the night before had been bothering me all the evening. I gritted my teeth, whipped out my handkerchief and buried my nose in its folds but, in spite of my superhuman effort to suppress it, a violent sneeze burst from me. Instantly Yusuf and his companions swivelled round, paused for one moment and then, drawing their knives with excited cries, came dashing towards me.

11

A Desperate Business

I was cornered; I could not retreat and there were four of them. If they used firearms it was certain that I should be massacred where I stood within the next two minutes. My one hope was that they would rely upon their knives and that I might be able to break through them if I could survive their first attack.

One of them pulled a torch out as he ran and flashed it into the dense shadow where I was crouching. The sight of me, caught in the beam, drew a cry of triumph from Yusuf. Momentarily the light of the torch blinded me and as the man who held it switched it off I could see nothing. After that one cry of triumph they fell sinisterly silent and I could only hear the soft padding of their feet as they came racing at me in the blackness.

I had drawn my gun and I fired at point blank range, dead ahead into what I believed to be the middle of them. A scream of pain told me that my bullet had found its mark and the flash of the gun showed them to me. Two negroes, an Eurasian with a hooky nose and small beard, and Yusuf—evidently the most cautious of the four as he was well behind the others. Which one I had hit I could not tell but I thought it was one of the negroes.

They fell upon me like an avalanche and I fired again at that very second but I must have fired wide as there came no answering cry to my bullet.

As they came at me I attempted to side-step but one of the negroes caught me off my balance. In my left hand I was gripping the packet of dope by its string handle and I swung it violently at his head, catching him full in the face, but his impetus was much too great for the blow to have any material effect. It saved me momentarily from his knife, which glanced over my shoulder, but the force of his attack sent me spinning sideways and I fell heavily to the ground.

The Eurasian was on me like a tiger-cat but I kneed him in the stomach and wriggling free rolled over and over down the slope still clutching my automatic. The loose dust swirled up all round me getting in my mouth, eyes and nostrils. My thigh was hurting where the Eurasian had kicked me and as I tried to get my breath the filthy dust made me choke and splutter.

The second I stopped and tried to rise they were on me again cursing and shouting; my gun exploded ineffectually and was knocked out of my hand. I caught the flash of a knife but jerked myself aside and the blade struck sparks out of the stones in the roadway. One of them clutched my throat and bore me back-wards; I could no longer see which of them was actually on top of me as we were all in one writhing bundle, kicking and slashing at each other in wild confusion. A pain like the searing of a red-hot iron ran across my forehead as a knife gashed it.

Even as I lay there wriggling beneath them, lunging out with fists and feet, grabbing handfuls of hair or turban, the beastly stench of their unwashed bodies strong in my nostrils, with half of my brain I was thinking what a lunatic I had been not to foresee that Gamal might send several of them after me. If I died there I knew that I had only myself to blame. A fist smashed into my face and I felt the hot and sticky blood from my nose run down over my mouth and chin.

The hand that gripped my throat was powerful and mus-cular; I fought with the strength of desperation but the grip tightened and I began to feel an intolerable pain in my chest while my limbs weakened. The stars above me went out. Everything was black, then red with whirling catherine wheels and streaks of fire. I squirmed and twisted but evey movement was weaker than the last and I knew that I was done.

As though from a great distance I heard the report of fire arms but it did not mean anything to me at that moment. The hand on my windpipe was suddenly withdrawn. My protruding eyeballs eased back into their sockets, the catherine-wheels gave place to a red mist and then to blackness again.

After a second I realised that the weight of my attackers had been withdrawn from my bruised and aching body. I could see the stars above and was lying there huddled in the gutter. A great commotion was going on all round me; someone trod on my chest and stumbled, pitching over my prostrate body; there were more shots, the flash of torches and an authoritative voice shouting staccato orders in Arabic. A hand grabbed me by the collar of my jacket and I was lugged roughly to my feet.

Still dazed and semi-conscious I looked about me and enough of my wits had returned by then for me to realise that I owed my life to the intervention of the police.

There were about twenty of them armed with rifles and automatics and commanded by a native officer. Yusuf, the Eurasian and one of the negroes were already being manacled. One of the police snapped a pair of handcuffs on my wrists and pushed me roughly towards them. The second negro was lying sprawled in the middle of the roadway where I had shot him; he was groaning slightly which gave me a little hope that I might escape being charged with manslaughter.

At the end of the lane a police-van had driven up; a stretcher was got out of it and the wounded negro carried to it. After a curt order from the officer the other captives and myself were hustled to the van and four policemen got into it with us. The doors were locked and it was driven off down the hill.

Some twenty minutes later we arrived at Police Headquarters. Our names were taken by a sergeant and I gave mine as Daoud el Azziz; after which the officer duly charged us with trafficking in illicit drugs. We were searched but I had no papers on me and had decided that it would be best to hold my peace for the moment. When the formalities were over we were led downstairs and I was pushed into a small cell.

The place was clean but there was no means of switching off the blue-bulbed electric light. I was only thankful that I had been given a cell to myself and not confined with the others who could certainly have beaten me up, if they had had half a chance, as being the cause of their own arrest. Yusuf had glowered daggers at me while we were standing in front of the sergeant's desk and he had good reason for his fury. Seeing that the police had found the packet of dope in the gutter it was quite certain that Yusuf and Co. were in for a good long spell of prison.

My head was aching abominably but I sat down on the narrow bed and began to consider my own position. My firing. I thought, must have brought the police on the scene and they would assume that a quarrel had broken out among the dope-traffickers, so I should be brought up with them for examination next morning. That did not worry me much since I had a perfectly good explanation as to how I had become mixed up in the affair. On the other hand, that explanation meant giving away the fact that I was the man the police were hunting for in connection with Sir Walter's murder, and it was quite certain that I should have considerable trouble with a lot of angry policemen for having led them such a wild-goose chase instead of having come forward immediately I had landed in Alexandria.

My only consolation was that in any case I had promised Sylvia that I would surrender to the police the following morning so I was only really anticipating what was in store for me by spending the present night in a cell.

To my annoyance I found I had run out of cigarettes; doubtless I could have bought a few off one of the warders if I had cared to try but I had some of Groppi's soft caramels in my pockets so I made do with those instead. They were a bit squashed through my rough-and-tumble but that had not impaired their delicious flavour and I only wished that I had come through the business with so little damage. I was bruised all over; my right leg hurt me badly where the Eurasian had kicked me and the gash on my forehead was now stiff and painful.

Having cleaned and bathed the cut by dipping my handkerchief in the pitcher of water I lay down on the hard bed, covered my eyes to shield them from the light and drifted off into an uneasy slumber.

I was awakened the next morning by the warder bringing breakfast—coffee, bread and a piece of sausage—not a very appetising meal but quite edible and sustaining. No one came to ask me any questions and I had half a mind to try to get permission to ring Harry up, as I feared that he and the girls would be worrying about me. But I felt it was certain that I should be interrogated in the course of the morning and it would be better to wait until then.

About ten o'clock a warder unlocked the door of my cell and motioned me to step outside; a couple of armed police were waiting there and they led me upstairs to an office room where a spectacled man was working. He took no notice of me for a moment or two, then got up and went into another room next door; when he came out again he was carrying a large sheaf of papers and he said to me in English:

'His Excellency will see you now. Please go inside.'

Somewhat to my surprise the two policemen saluted and retired while I walked forward unaccompanied into the further room.

It was a big apartment and there was no one in it except a solitary Englishman seated behind a desk. He was a very fine-looking man of between fifty and sixty; tall, broad-shouldered with grey hair and blue eyes. From the reference to 'His Excellency' I knew at once that this must be the famous Essex Pasha, the Commandant of the Cairo Police and the terror of all dope-traffickers.

I was rather intrigued at the thought that he should consider the previous night's affair of sufficient importance to question me about it himself but he took the wind completely out of my sails by saying amiably:

'Good morning, Mr. Day. Come and sit down.'

I stared at him a little rudely, I fear, but I did as I was bid while exclaiming, 'So you knew who I was all the time!'

'Yes,' he nodded, 'and it's just as well for you that we did. You wouldn't be alive now if my people hadn't been shadowing you last night.'

'By Jove! I had no idea that you were on to me before the scrap, sir. Then it wasn't the sound of my shots that brought the police on the scene?'

He smiled a little bleakly. 'Admission No. 1. It was you who shot the negro. We thought as much but we weren't quite certain. He died early this morning so we shall now have to add that to the other charges against you—and it's becoming quite a formidable list. Illicit entry into Egypt, failure to report to the police when advertised as wanted for questioning in connection with Sir Walter Shane's death, being concerned in the traffic in illicit drugs, giving a false name to the police when arrested and now—manslaughter. You have quite a lot to answer for, young man.'

'I know it,' I sighed. 'And I'm afraid I've given your people a great deal of trouble but I hope to be able to convince a Court that I had good reasons for acting as I did.'

'I see.' His firm mouth hardened. 'So you prefer to reserve your defence. That must be as you wish, Mr. Day; and of course I can have all these charges brought forward formally But I was hoping that you would have been prepared to talk frankly to me.'

'The situation's a bit unusual, isn't it?' I said. 'One way and another I have been led to believe that you, or the police rather, believe it was I who killed Sir Walter Shane. If that is so, oughtn't I to consult a solicitor before I answer any questions? Please don't think I've any idea that you're trying to lead me into a trap. I'm asking your advice now, sir; and I really would be grateful for it because I know that I've got myself into a shocking mess, although I assure you I had no hand in Sir Walter's death.'

'Of course you hadn't.' He sat back suddenly with a great roar of laughter. 'I know that. Your own actions since you landed are proof enough. If you were the murderer you would be in Suez or Port Said by now trying to get out of a country that's too hot to hold you—not running round Cairo getting yourself mixed up in a scrap with drug-traffickers, or sitting on the terrace at the Continental calmly having drinks with your friends. I've a very shrewd idea what you've been up to, Day, and if I'm right you can count me as your friend; but there are a lot of gaps that I've got to fill in yet and you'll lose nothing by being absolutely frank with me. I've no intention of charging you with murder and, although I make no promises at the moment, I think we might even drop the lesser charges if you are prepared to tell me exactly what part you've played in this unpleasant business.'

'If that's so, sir,' I smiled, 'you've taken ten years off my age. I only wish I'd known this yesterday. If I had, I would never have attempted to play the lone hand I did last night.'

'But it was your performance last night which really convinced me you weren't the man who did the murder; so perhaps it's just as well things have panned out as they did. Now, start from the beginning and tell me everything. Take your time and have a cigarette.'

As I helped myself from the box an overwhelming sense of

147

relief swept over me. Since Essex Pasha was already persuaded that I hadn't committed the murder, there was a real possibility that he would believe the rest of my story, strange as it might sound; and I knew without even having to think about it that here was a man I could trust absolutely.

He was not only an Englishman whose integrity was beyond question and one of the most famous police chiefs in the world, but also a high official of the Government who, while understanding the intricacies of Egyptian politics, would never allow himself to be browbeaten or side-tracked by a rotten little rat like Zakri Bey. I knew the only way I could hope to convince him that I had not dreamed the power and menace of O'Kieff's organisation was to withhold nothing of importance, so I told him my real name and the reasons which had led me to assume that of Julian Day.

He nodded slowly. 'So that's who you are. I remember hearing about that tragic business at the time and I knew poor Carruthers slightly. This is extremely interesting. Go on.'

I then gave him particulars of my trip out to Egypt on the 'Hampshire' and all that had happened since. The only thing I concealed was the reason for the Belvilles' proposed expedition and the actual matter which lay hidden in the hieroglyphics on the stolen tablet for which Sir Walter had been murdered; but Essex Pasha picked upon the point at once.

When I had done he sat back and placed his finger-tips together. 'You've told your story well and, as the Egyptian part of it checks up with certain ideas of my own, I'm quite prepared to believe the whole of it. There's one thing, though, Day —it would be best, I think, if I continued to call you by your assumed name—this tablet must have been of some very special significance for O'Kieff to murder, or instigate the murder of Sir Walter in order to get hold of it. I should like to hear a little more about that tablet.'

I smiled but shook my head. 'There I can't help you. sir. Solely because it's not my secret. The thing *has* a special value, of course. In fact, it's *so* valuable that it certainly provides a perfectly adequate motive for Sir Walter's murder, but I can honestly assure you that the knowledge of its secret would not assist you in your investigations in the least.'

'These archæologists are a queer lot.' His blue eyes twinkled.

'And they sometimes find the regulations of the Egyptian Government for the protection of its buried treasure extremely irksome. Naturally, if it came to my knowledge that Sir Walter or his friends had been contemplating any illicit digging it would be my duty to report it to the proper authority. However, it's hardly my province to go into that side of it at the moment; so I won't press you on that point.

'My business is the murder and, since most of the crime in Egypt is linked up with it, even more particularly the suppression of the Drug Traffic. I've had my eye on Gamal for some time but nothing definite that I could bring against him. The people who attacked you last night are small fry, of course; but we'll see to it that they get good long sentences. Where your efforts have proved really valuable is in drawing my attention to the Princess Oonas and Zakri Bey. She's an exotic creature but I was not aware that she had any interests outside her love-affairs, and although Zakri is an untrustworthy intriguer it's never been suggested that he was mixed up in this. Both of them have plenty of friends in high places but from now on I shall be able to keep an eye on them, if you're right, we shall doubtless get them in the long run.'

'Just how powerful is Zakri?' I asked.

'Very powerful indeed.'

'Powerful enough to get me slung out of Egypt? That was the idea, you know, and it was for that reason I went to such pains to evade the police.'

'I don't think you need worry. All sorts of people try to pull all sorts of wires in this country and very often they succeed; but I've served the Egyptian Government for so long that I think I can say they place considerable trust in me. If I vouch for you personally, very strong reasons indeed would have to be adduced against you before anyone could bring pressure to bear for the cancellation of your permit to remain here.'

'That's very good of you, sir,' I said.

'No. I naturally expect you to refrain from any rash undertakings. But, as you may know, it's been my life-work to stamp out this Drug Traffic which is the curse of Egypt, and you've succeeded in enabling me to catch Gamal and stop one more hole in the wall, so I owe you something for that.'

'It's nice of you to put it that way,' I smiled at him. 'And, of course, I'll take no further steps against O'Kieff and Co. without consulting you, Why is it, though, that the Egyptians seem to have this craving for dope more than any other race? Have they always been like that?'

'No. Dope was almost unknown in Egypt until the building of the great dam above Assuan which was completed in 1902.'

'What on earth has the dam got to do with it? I always thought that huge inland lake which is held up there by the gigantic barrage was the absolute making of Egypt.'

'So it was, commercially. In bad years it saves the country from famine and it enables the peasant to grow three crops a year instead of two. It's made vast fortunes for the cotton merchants, but it's ruined the health of Egypt's people.'

'Do. please, explain,' I said.

'It's this way. When the Nile inundated the country naturally only once a year, the ground dried up during the dry season and was baked hard by the sun which killed a certain bacillus or parasite that is in it. Now that the land can be kept irrigated through the dry season by releasing water from the great reservoir at will large areas of it never dry up at all. The crust may appear hard but the earth is not sterilised by baking to a sufficient depth; underneath it still remains moist and soggy because no proper drainage system was established, as it should have been according to the advice of the experts, when the great dam was built. In consequence the parasite that I was speaking of is not killed off every year but has increased and multiplied in the damp subsoil until the whole land is riddled with it.

'Owing to the low state in which the *fellaheen* live, it's impossible to prevent them from drinking unfiltered water and they get this bug in their tummies. The Arabs are a very strongly sexed people and, curiously enough, while the bug does not seem to have any effect on the women it saps the virility of the men and makes them virtually useless as lovers and husbands.

'Soon after this disease first started amongst them they discovered that hashish would temporarily restore their sexual vigour. Urged on by their women they began to take it regularly and within ten years of the completion of the dam the dope-taking habit had gripped two-thirds of the population. That's the whole story.

'We're getting it under but it's a hard fight; and as long as they can get it in they'll take it unless the Government can be persuaded of its folly in repudiating our engineers' original plans and institutes a proper drainage-system.'

'That's extraordinarily interesting,' I said. 'And now, since you are being so kind, would you tell me how, the police in Alex. having failed, you succeeded in getting on to me so quickly?'

He smiled again. 'The people in Alexandria didn't have much chance did they? And we had a little more time to go into the case. It was obvious that you and the Belvilles were very friendly while you were on the ship and that they didn't believe you were the murderer, so it was a fair bet that, if you were innocent, sooner or later you would get into touch with them. I had them met at the station and followed to the Semiramis. Then Sylvia Shane's telephone message came through that she had located you out at Mena. She denied that afterwards but I felt there was something fishy about it and when it was reported that she had turned up with a young man to see the Belvilles at the Semiramis later that night I felt fairly certain it was you. We could have pulled you in then, of course, but I wanted to know what you were doing in Cairo when, if you had been the murderer, you would almost certainly have been trying to get out of Egypt through one of the ports. We had you covered all the time you were asleep in your *pension*, while you were having cocktails at the Continental and later, when you went to Gamal's. When you left his place carrying a package and took to your heels in Mohammed Ali Street we had a pretty shrewd idea what you were up to and I arranged for a special force of police to be drafted out to the City of the Dead directly you entered it. I'm sorry you very nearly got knifed but we wanted to pinch the other people who contacted you there, so my men had to wait until they were quite certain that it was you the other four were after.'

'Wonderful,' I grinned ruefully, 'and to think that I flattered myself that I was fooling you all the time!'

'What d'you intend to do now?' he asked.

'With your permission, sir, I propose to resume my own

identity and move to Shepheard's. I should like to telephone the Belvilles, too, because they must be very worried about me.'

'Telephone them by all means if you wish, but I expect Sylvia Shane will already have told them where you are. I thought your friends might be anxious as to what had become of you so I rang her up first thing this morning to tell her we had you safely here.'

'You know her, then?'

'Oh yes, I've known her for years. She plays the best game of tennis of any girl in Cairo and she's a beautiful dancer.' His blue eyes twinkled again. 'Nice girl, Sylvia—isn't she?'

'Very, I should think, when one gets to know her,' I parried cautiously. 'But I've only seen her in rather trying circumstances.'

'You mustn't blame her for wanting to come to me in her trouble rather than relying on a strange young man of unknown antecedents.'

'I don't in the least, sir, and I should never have attempted to persuade her to do otherwise if I hadn't been so desperately anxious to get my own back on this devil O'Kieff.'

'Well, there's a chance that you may be able to do that yet. I'll have our records searched but I feel certain I've never come across him, under that name at all events. I can have him watched, of course, and if only I can tie him up in some way with Gamal there might be a case to bring against him. But that's unlikely as Zakri Bey is obviously the middle man between the two and it's going to be difficult enough to get anything even on him. In the meantime I can't interfere with O'Kieff at all. Have you any other line which you can follow up with a view to landing him?'

'I'm afraid I haven't,' I confessed. 'But he hasn't come to Egypt for his health and the Belvilles will be moving down to Luxor in a day or two, and I'm hoping that he'll show his hand again when we get there.'

'All right, then.' Essex Pasha stood up. 'If you find out anything of interest, let me know; and above all, remember that the law is stronger than you are. Don't go and get yourself into trouble with it, but use it to lay these rogues by the heels if you possibly can. There are a few formalities they'll want you for outside and if you'll send your passport round by hand this afternoon I'll have it visa-ed for you. Good luck.'

I thanked him whole-heartedly for his kindness, and all that he was doing for me, and when I walked out of his office a free man I felt an altogether different being. That interview had done far more than relieve me of my fear of being deported or even possibly charged with Sir Walter's murder. It was the first time since the tragic termination of my diplomatic career that I had confided my whole miserable story to anyone; and it is impossible to describe the immense feeling of buoyancy and restored self-confidence it gave me to know that Essex Pasha had believed me and shown that I might count him as a friend.

The formalities he had referred to consisted of identifying Yusuf and the other prisoners at the police court proceedings against them and giving a précis of my evidence concerning them and Gamal, which I duly signed, to the proper authority.

Afterwards I telephoned the Belvilles and Sylvia but they were all out so I left messages asking them to lunch with me at Shepheard's Grill at half-past one. I then returned to my *pension*, got the stain off my face, changed back into my own clothes and moved to Shepheard's. I was still stiff and bruised from the previous night's scrap but after the luxury of relaxing for half an hour in a fine hot bath I felt infinitely better physically as well as mentally.

My message to Harry had included a request that he would bring the rest of my baggage round with him when he arrived for lunch, but my own clothes that Amin had brought out to me at Mena served for the time being, and when I walked down to the lounge a little after one o'clock I had, for the first time after nearly three days of costume parts, assumed my normal appearance.

I took a table on the terrace and at a quarter-past one Harry and Clarissa turned up. Sylvia had told them early that morning that I was safe at Police Headquarters so they had gone sight-seeing with her and visited the Citadel from which to see the maginificent views over Cairo. When they had got back to the Semiramis they had duly received my message about lunch and had come along early as Sylvia had asked them to drop her, on their way, at the Continental so that she could tidy up.

Clarissa was most solicitous about the cut on my forehead and both of them were anxious to hear about my adventure on the previous night. When I had told them about it, and something of my interview with Essex Pasha that morning, they were overjoyed to learn that things had gone so well and that I was now a free man again, able to move about without subterfuge just as I wished.

It took the best part of half an hour to tell my story and although it was a quarter-to-two by the time I had finished, Sylvia had not turned up. After glancing at his watch Harry exclaimed:

'I wonder what can have happened to that girl. She's taking her time, isn't she?'

Clarissa laughed. 'You silly! She's beautifying herself for the conquering hero. You can't expect her to hurry over that.' And I ordered another round of drinks.

Soon afterwards a porter came up and gave me a telephone message which had just come through. Miss Shane was terribly sorry but she would be unable to lunch as she had been sent for on urgent business by the police.

We could only imagine that Essex Pasha wanted to question her in order to check up on my statement to him. It was disappointing that she was unable to join us but it could not be helped, so we went in and I was able to enjoy the first really decent meal I had had for days.

We sat on the terrace afterwards until about four o'clock. In Egypt all roads lead to Shepheard's and the coming and going of its patrons, who include members of every nation under the sun, together with the colourful street-scene below, provides a fascinating spectacle which always makes one want to linger there unless one had urgent work to to.

It was Harry who suggested that Sylvia must soon be back and that we might stroll along to the Continental so as to be there when she got in.

The two hotels are in the same street and only a few hundred yards apart so a few minutes later we had exchanged the terrace at Shepheard's for the terrace at the Continental. Sylvia had not returned and we ordered tea.

It was getting on for five o'clock, I think, when we first became vaguely anxious. Three and a half hours seemed a long time for an interview with the police and as Sylvia had intended lunching with us it was reasonable certain that she would get in touch with us as soon as she was free. It occurred to me that I might have received only a portion of her message and that something about meeting us later somewhere might not have reached me, so I went inside to the hall-porter's desk and made him repeat it to me in person.

I found that the message had been given to me just as she had given it to him and he was quite clear about what had happened. She had come in at about ten minutes past one and gone up to her room. At half-past a police officer had come in and enquired for her. She had come down in the lift a few minutes later and the two of them held a short conversation together within sight of the porter's desk; after which she had given him the message to be telephoned to me and gone off with the *bimbashi*.

There was nothing particularly queer about that. it was only the length of time she had been away which puzzled me somewhat and I decided to ring up and find out if she was still at Police Headquarters.

After a little delay I managed to get on to Essex Pasha and to my surprise he knew nothing whatever about the matter. He said that he had certainly not sent for Sylvia and he knew of no reason why anyone else should have done so; but he promised to make inquiries at once and ring me back as quickly as he could.

When he rang through again it was quite evident that he was as worried as I was.

'Nobody here knows anything about this business,' he said quickly. 'You had better hang on where you are. I'm coming round at once.'

A quarter of an hour later he was with us. Tall and distinguished-looking, he swept off his soft black hat with the flourish of an eighteenth-century courtier as I introduced him to Clarissa, but the gay twinkle in his blue eyes which had made him seem so friendly in the morning was no longer there. Quietly but with extraordinary speed and efficiency he took charge of the situation. Within two minutes of his arrival the manager had been fetched and we were upstairs in Sylvia's room.

The place was in chaos and looked as though a tornado had swept through it; cupboards and trunks had been broken open. the mattress dragged off the bed and ripped from end to end. the carpet rolled aside and half the floorboards pulled up. Her clothes and belongings were scattered in wild confusion everywhere.

I knew at once that what I had been fearing for the last twenty minutes had happened. Sylvia had been lured away in order that O'Kieff's people could ransack her room for the other half of the tablet. Probably they had hoped to secure it by some more subtle means until one of Zakri's spies—perhaps even a police official in his pay—had told them that Essex Pasha had had a long interview with me that morning and then released me. The news that they would not be able to have me deported, as they had hoped, and that I was free to continue my fight against them had doubtless forced their hands and made them decide upon immediate action.

'What were they hunting for?' Essex Pasha asked me sharply.

'The other half of that memorial tablet I told you about this morning,' I said at once.

'Well, they haven't got it,' Harry cut in. 'Sylvia told me yesterday that it's lying in the vaults of her bank.'

'How about a translation of it?' I asked. 'I suppose she made one?'

'Yes. But fortunately they haven't got that either. She gave it to me to read last night, together with a rough translation which she did of the first half of the tablet in my room at he Semiramis after dinner. I've got them both in my pocket at the moment.'

'But where have they taken her?' I exclaimed. 'That's what matters.'

Essex Pasha had already sent for the floor waiter and the chambermaid. His questions elicited the fact that two Egyptians who were not staying in the hotel had been seen coming down the corridor from Sylvia's room at about half-past two. Their description was taken. and that of the bogus policeman, from the hall-porter downstairs.

In the manager's office Essex Pasha got on the telephone. passed the description of the three men and that of Sylvia to his people and ordered a general notification to be sent out to all stations. Then he sat back and said glumly:

'I'm afraid that's all we can do for the moment. But what puzzles me is why they should have troubled to kidnap her. They could easily had kept her under observation until she was safely out of the hotel for a few hours and have ransacked her room during her absence.'

'I think I can tell you,' I said miserably. 'They must have realised it was only a fifty-fifty chance they would find the tablet here or a translation of it. They kidnapped her so that if their raid was unsuccessful they would be able to force her to sign a letter authorising them to collect the tablet from anyone to whom she had passed it for safe-keeping.'

He gave me a sharp glance of approval and looked at the manager. 'D'you know where Miss Shane banks?'

'Yes, Excellency. Miss Shane has been staying with us for many months and her cheques are always drawn on the Anglo-Egyptian Bank.'

'Get me through to the manager, will you? If he's gone home have the call made to his private address.'

For a few moments we stood about silent and anxious until the bank manager was located. Essex Pasha told him there was reason to believe that Sylvia Shane had fallen into wrong hands; crooks who might exert pressure upon her to sign certain documents; and that if anybody arrived at the bank on any sort of business in connection with her they were to be detained on some plausible excuse and Police Headquarters notified immediately.

'Well, we've blocked them there,' he said when he had finished. 'But that doesn't get us far. I'll turn every man I've got on to the job; but the devil of it is that we haven't got a single line to indicate where these thugs may have taken the poor girl.'

'I don't know,' I said, and as I spoke I was half sick with fear, 'but I may be able to tell you that too. Have you ever heard of a white-slaving joint down in Ismailia called the House of the Angels?'

12

White-slaved

'The House of the Angels,' he repeated. 'Yes, I have heard of it. There have been vague references to it from time to time in some of my people's reports, but it's evidently a pseudonym for some other place and only referred to under that name by the inner ring. Are you certain it's at Ismailia?'

'Yes,' I said.

'Tell me all you know about it.'

I related my conversation with Oonas and her offer to give me the run of the place when she believed that I was Lemming.

'Why should you imagine they would take Sylvia there?' he asked when I had finished.

'Well,' I hesitated. 'It's a beastly thought, but Sylvia's good-looking, isn't she? And the place is not an ordinary brothel but a depot through which they bring Asiatic beauties for the houses in the Mediterranean ports and ship white women to the East. It makes one sick even to think of it but, since white-slaving is part of their business, mustn't one face the facts and assume that having taken the risk of kidnapping Sylvia, directly they've bullied her into signing the letter to the bank, instead of releasing her they'll white-slave her as well?'

He nodded. 'I'm afraid that is so. I only asked you to see if you were reasoning on the same lines as myself.'

'How simply frightful!' Clarissa exclaimed. 'We must stop them! We must! We must!'

Essex Pasha took no notice of her. He was already on the telephone again asking the operator to get him on to Police Headquarters in Ismailia. As he hung up the receiver he glanced at his watch.

'It's now twenty-to-six,' he said. 'So they've had four hours' clear start. There is a direct road to Ismailia but it's a pretty poor one so it's almost certain that they'd take the first-class road down to Suez and go north along the Canal bank from there. Suez is eighty miles and roughly a three-hour run. Ismailia is another fifty but the road, being in the Canal zone and kept up by the Company, is the best in Egypt so they'd cover that stretch easily in an hour and a half. At that rate they're not due in till about seven so there's just a chance that we might catch them on the open road.'

When his call to Ismailia came through he gave quick instructions for police cars to be sent out on both the Canal road and the desert track with orders to search all cars approaching Ismailia from either direction. The Ismailia police had never heard of the House of the Angels but they promised to make every possible effort to locate it.

'Is there nothing else we can do?' I asked as he hung up the receiver.

'I'm afraid there isn't, yet awhile,' he said slowly. 'A general call will have gone out by now from Headquarters, so every policeman in Egypt will be on the look out for her; but we must wait until we get some reports in. Unless they told her some extraordinarily plausible story its hardly likely she would willingly let them drive her out of Cairo. The probability is that they ran the car into some cul-de-sac or courtyard in the city and gave her a shot of dope to keep her quiet. If they had wanted to get away quickly they would have left her lying in the back of the car as though she were asleep; in which case it's almost certain that one of the men at the police barriers will have noticed her and be able to tell us by which road the car left the city. Or, again, since they would normally have to stop somewhere for petrol, a garage-hand may be able to tell us something when the police make their inquiries.

'On the other hand, after having doped her, they may have thought it worth while to expend a little extra time in dressing her up in the black clothes of a native woman with a veil over her face and hair so as to prevent anyone recognising her. But even if they did that, we have the description of the car she left in and of the man she left with and, as there isn't a great deal of motor-traffic on the roads outside the city, there's still a good chance that the barrier police will be able to give us some information.

'I only wish there were something else we *could* do, but this is a case where we just have to leave it for the police organisation to function; and although it may seem a poor consolation to you at the moment I can tell you that when the police-net is spread nation-wide like this, the odds are all in its favour.'

'But we can't just sit here like this doing nothing!' Clarissa cried. 'At least we can go down to Ismailia.'

'We've no proof at all that they're taking her there,' I said. 'It was only my idea.'

'It's a very logical one, though,' said Harry. 'God forbid that I should add to the gloom we're all feeling, but having kidnapped her it's a hundred-to-one against these people letting her go again. If they did she would be able to describe them, and the place to which she'd been taken, to the police afterwards. They wouldn't dare risk that, so they'll try to get her out of the way somehow. This white-slaving depot offers an excellent way of disposing of her and means that they'll get a good round sum in hard cash for her as well. They'd never be such fools as to stick a knife in her with such an alternative ready to their hands.'

'I quite agree with you,' Essex Pasha nodded.

'Then I'm going to Ismailia,' declared Clarissa.

'You can't do more than the police can,' I remarked.

'No, but I can be on hand when the poor child's rescued.' replied Clarissa promptly. 'And after such a frightful experience she'll need another woman to look after her.'

'Good for you,' I admitted, and turned to Essex Pasha. 'You've no objection, sir, I suppose, to our going down to the Canal?'

'None at all. I think Mrs. Belville's idea a very sound one. You had better go *via* Suez and I'll telephone the police there that you're on your way. If you go straight to Police Headquarters they'll give you any news that may have come in while you are making the trip, and pass you on to the police in Ismailia.'

I thanked him and asked the manager if he could get me a car with a really good driver.

'Yes, Mr. Day,' he said. 'You shall have my own man who's a first-class fellow. I'll telephone for him to come round at once.'

'It would be best if you sent him to Shepheard's,' I said, 'as

I'm going there right away to collect a toothbrush. Then I'll pick up Mr. and Mrs. Belville from the Semiramis.'

The manager accompanied us out on to the terrace and I found Amin and Mustapha there. Although it was barely half-an-hour since we had discovered Sylvia's disappearance, news travels fast among the native servants and they had both arrived to offer their services. Poor Mustapha was in a frightful state. He adored his young mistress and was almost incoherent as he pleaded volubly to be allowed to get his hands on the rogues who had entrapped her. On learning that the car we were to have was a large Buick which would hold five beside the driver, we decided to let the two dragomen accompany us.

We split up then—a very gloomy and unhappy party—our only consolation being that Essex Pasha himself had the matter in hand and we knew that he would do everything that was humanly possible to trace Sylvia. He drove off back to Police Headquarters while the Belvilles took a taxi to the Semiramis and the two dragomen accompanied me to Shepheard's.

Inside ten minutes I had thrust a few things into a small suitcase and was leaving Shepheard's again. The Belvilles were already waiting for me at the Semiramis so we got off without delay and it was barely six when we passed the railway-station on our way out of Cairo.

The road to Suez runs through Heliopolis, a less fashionable suburb of Cairo than Gezira or the district along the Mena road which is on the exactly opposite side of the city. A few moments after leaving the huge block of the Heliopolis Palace Hotel on our right we pulled up at the police barrier for the number of our car to be taken, as is the custom with every vehicle proceeding into the desert. The number is then telephoned through to the police at the next town so that if the car does not arrive within a certain time it is known to have broken down and assistance can be sent out to it. Having passed the barrier we roared away along the straight flat road in to the open plain.

The country was as different from the fertile fields of the Delta as one could possibly imagine. Not a tree, not a house, not an animal nor even a blade of grass was to be seen in any direction; only the ribbon of road clearly marked on either side by large, cylindrical kerosene containers, looking rather like dust bins, which had been filled with sand and whitewashed so that by night a car's headlights could pick them up clearly and there was no danger of its running off the road.

On either side of us stretched the empty, yellow plain, broken here and there by a distant line of hills or an occasional undulation. This Eastern desert is not a waste of sand such as the uninitiated traveller expects to see, but a waste of stone varying in colour from gold to dark brown. It was at one time a sea-bed and the darker patches are caused by great quantities of loose flints scattered over the windward side of every rise while such loose sand as there is gets blown from among them to form long streaks of golden-yellow on the lee of the hills or in the shallow valleys.

It was Harry's and Clarissa's first experience of the desert and both agreed that in spite of its bareness it had a strange fascination of its own, filling one with a desire to leave the road and penetrate the waste to see what was on the far side of each low line of hills, although one knew perfectly well that the new prospect beyond them would be exactly the same and that one might continue mounting ridge after ridge for hundreds of miles without finding the slightest difference in the alternating patches of darkish flints and yellow, shaly sandstone.

We were all too anxious about Sylvia to talk very much or display interest in any other topic, and after a while the desert scene grew monotonous. The road is well kept and we made good going but even so we were all fidgety with impatience to reach our destination.

In the whole eighty miles, with the exception of police-posts, we passed only one human habitation. It was just half-way between Cairo and Suez to the left of the road and some distance from it. By that time the light was fading but out on a low range of hills we could see a great, rambling building like a fortified palace surrounded by high walls. Amin said that he thought it was an old Coptic monastery.

Soon after, the sun set behind us, casting strange shadows over the broken plain; then darkness fell and we roared on into it eating up the miles, our headlights flashing upon the whitened kerosene tins but for which we should have had to proceed at a snail's pace for fear of running off our course.

At a quarter-to-nine we pulled up at the police barrier outside Suez. A sergeant jumped on our running-board and directed our driver to the Miza Hotel where we were met by an English officer of the Egyptian police. He introduced himself to us as Major Longdon and told us that Essex Pasha had telephoned him to expect us and that he had taken rooms for us at the hotel. We asked at once for news of Sylvia but he said that he was sorry he had none to give us. All the cars that had come in to Suez from Cairo that afternoon or direct to Ismailia by a second-class desert road had now been checked up. There were, all told, only fifteen of them and the police had satisfied themselves that every one of these was owned by a reputable person and that none of them had been used to bring the kidnapped girl from Cairo.

This looked, on the face of it, as though my idea that she might have been taken to the House of Angels was entirely wrong and that we would have done better to have remained in Cairo; particularly as the Ismailia police had so far failed in their efforts to locate any house which might be the secret white-slaving depot.

Major Longdon was a tall, thin, bony, rather tired-looking man with a bronzed complexion and a network of little wrinkles round his eyes but his smile was pleasant and we very soon realised that behind his lazy manner he concealed a quick brain and an attractive sense of humour.

He led us in to the Miza, which was a very modern building, and gave us a welcome drink while our things were carried upstairs. The hotel was quite a small one and practically deserted. Longdon said, while we were quenching our thirst, that he did not think there was any point in our going on to Ismailia unless we had further news and that the accommodation at Suez was somewhat better.

I had not been in Suez before and as it is one of the half-dozen towns in Africa that even a schoolboy might be expected to name I had imagined it to be quite a big place; but its sole claim to fame lies in its connection with the Canal and it is, in fact, little more than an overgrown village.

As Longdon told us, few passengers either join or leave the ships that pass through it; ninety-eight per cent of the people who are changing ships at all do so at Port Said so even the hotel accommodation is limited and provincial. Until a few years before, the old Belle Aire Hotel on the opposite side of the street had been practically the only place for European visitors to pass a night. Longdon had fixed us up at the Miza because he thought the new beds there would be better but he proposed that we should dine with him across the way, at the Belle Aire, because it was run by a Frenchwoman whose cuisine was considered to be the best in Suez.

After our drinks we went up to wash, and, to my amazement I found that I had two double-beds and one single at my disposal. The two double-beds—and they were big ones at that —occupied a good portion of the bedroom. There was a modern, private bathroom leading out of it and then a verandah room which overlooked the street but was enclosed with wire gauze against mosquitoes and could be used as a sort of sitting-room as, besides the single bed, it contained a sofa, a couple of armchairs and a table.

When I got downstairs again I asked Longdon the reason for this munificence in the case of a single man, upon which he laughed and said:

'Lots of Egyptians come down here for their holidays and it's the custom in Egypt that if a man takes a room in a hotel he considers himself entitled to accommodate the whole of his family in it. In consequence, as the average Egyptian family numbers about eighteen, two double-beds and a single one can't really be considered any too lavish.'

The Belle Aire provided us with an excellent meal of the type one might get at an hotel in any small French provincial town; but it was a gloomy session in spite of Longdon's efforts to entertain us.

The thoughts of all of us were naturally on poor Sylvia and what she might be going through while we were sitting there. Our by no means amicable discussion after our first meeting out at Mena two nights before and an hour over cocktails the previous evening were the total extent of my acquaintance with Sylvia so I did not know her sufficiently well to count her as a friend. Yet the very idea of any decent girls being subjected to the treatment she was likely to receive in the House of the Angels was enough to make me frantic to prevent it. I had no personal interest in her whatever but I chafed horribly at being unable to raise a finger on her behalf.

Although there seemed good reason to suppose that I was wrong in my idea that she had been taken to Ismailia, somehow I still had a feeling that I was right in my surmise. O'Kieff and Co., as I had every reason to know, were very clever people and, to my mind, the fact that the police had accounted for all the cars which had come through from Cairo that afternoon did not really amount to much in this particular case. With such important personalities as Zakri Bey and the beautiful Oonas in the organisation there might well be lesser fry—well-to-do merchants and so on—whom the police regarded as quite above suspicion. The thing that worried me most was their failure to locate the House of the Angels. If Sylvia was there, immediate action was the only thing which could save her.

I didn't know very much about the white-slaving game but I did know that the first act is to break the spirit of any unwilling victim. The usual procedure is a beating of sufficient violence to make the girl incapable of any endeavour to escape through the sheer misery of her physical condition; after which she is forcibly raped by the heftiest thug in the house, which ordeal naturally has the effect of throwing her into such hopeless dejection that she no longer has the vitality even to attempt planning a get-away for many hours. The victim is then normally half-starved, beaten and raped again systematically for a number of days until her will is so broken that she consents to receive a client upon the promise that if she does so her daily beatings shall cease, her hunger be appeased and that she can count henceforth on more comfortable conditions.

I know doctors say that the rape of a fully-grown woman is next to impossible; and that most of such cases which come before the courts are due to vigorous wooing coupled with over-persuasion where the girl has suffered a revulsion of feeling afterwards, wept out the story to indiscreet friends and then been cajoled or bullied into bringing a case by her indignant parents to save the family name in the eyes of the neighbours. But Sylvia's situation was very different. She would be in a place where she could scream her head off without anyone hearing her and, even if she was still in a state to put up a feeble resistance after being beaten half-unconscious, there would be plenty of people about ready to hold her down.

In her case too there was not even the hope that she would

be kept at Ismailia for several days. They would naturally be anxious to get her out of Egypt as quickly as possible. I visualised with a horror that made my palms of my hands wet, that poor girl being subjected by the native servants of the house in the night that was now approaching, to every brutality which might rob her of the initiative to endeavour to get a message through to us. The following day, or night at latest, she would almost certainly be drugged, smuggled aboard a native craft and shipped down the Canal to a port on the east coast of the Red Sea where she would be sold by secret negotiations into the harem of some wealthy Arab sheik, and all trace of her lost for years or perhaps for ever.

It was a hideous thought and one which I strove to put from me but, try as I would, I could not evade the fact that although the smug, self-righteous ruling caste of Europe elects to ignore it, a similar fate does still overtake tens of thousands of young women annually, and that if that was the way Zakri had planned to get rid of Sylvia, she would fare no better than any of the others.

While we were trying our poor best to do justice to a créme caramel Longdon was called away to the telephone. He returned to say that he had been talking to Essex Pasha. There was no news which could definitely be associated with Sylvia; police spies of every kind were hunting feverishly for traces of her through all the black spots of Cairo, so far without result, and the police-posts on other roads out of the city had been no more successful in their search for a car that might be suspect than those on the roads running east to Suez and Ismailia; but the air port police had reported a private 'plane with two men and three women on board as having left at a quarter-past three ostensibly for Alex. The three women had been dressed in native garments and were wearing veils; one of them had been supported by the other two and the party had declared that they were taking her home after a serious operation. As the 'plane was not leaving the country there were no passport formalities so no one had questioned her or examined her closely, but it was thought, in view of the circumstances, that this might possibly have been Sylvia in a semi-conscious state after having been doped so that she should not talk or call for assistance.

This news was far from cheering as, if the woman was Sylvia, it now looked as though they might have flown her right out of country direct to one of the Red Sea ports, in which case our chance of rescuing her was almost nil and, although I did not express my opinion, I felt that the poor girl would be better dead.

Better news came through twenty minutes later, while we were still sitting over our coffee; or, if not better, at least news which gave us something to occupy our minds and take them temporarily off our more dismal speculations. The police at Ismailia telephoned to say they thought they had located the House of the Angels. The officer in charge at Ismailia said he was waiting for definite confirmation that the house was the right one before issuing orders for a raid; so we decided to leave at once in the hope that we might arrive in time for it if it was made.

I went with Longdon in his car and the others followed in the one which had brought us from Cairo. For the first few miles out of Suez the road twists through native villages, palm groves and well-cultivated fields, but soon we were on the magnificent highway running parallel with the Canal which is kept by the Company.

The distance from Suez to Ismailia is about fifty miles and after about twenty the road leaves the Canal to follow the shores, first of the Little Bitter Lake, and then the Great Bitter Lake, through both of which the Canal passes. On these long, straight stretches we went all out but it was half-past eleven before we reached Ismailia. On entering the town Longdon drove straight to the French Club where, he said, the Ismailia Chief of Police had promised to have a man with the latest news for us.

When we stepped out of the cars Longdon was greeted by the Chief of Police himself, a sandy-haired, moustached man named Major Hanbury, to whom he introduced us.

Major Hanbury said that he had suggested our coming to the French Club as it would be more comfortable for us to wait there than in his office. The house had proved to be the right one but the raid had not yet been made as time was needed for the police to take up their positions, but it was provisionally fixed for eleven-forty. He led us into the Club and offered us drinks in a big, cheery-looking bar with many little tables and gaily-painted, semi-comic maps upon its walls. There was only a sprinkling of people about and none of them took any notice of us, so directly the drinks had been ordered Major Hanbury gave us details about the result of his enquiries.

None of his men had ever heard of the House of Angels before that afternoon but once they had got on to the place it had proved to be the residence of a wealthy merchant named Suliman Taufik which stood in its own grounds on the northern outskirts of the town. Taufik was an influential and ostensibly respectable man and for that reason Hanbury had hesitated to order a raid on his house without some confirmation of the belief that it was being used for illegal purposes but, since his telephone call to Suez, he had managed to trace two of the native servants who were taking an evening off in the town. On questioning them he had elicited the information, under considerable pressure, that young women of many nationalities were brought to the place, generally at night, and remained there as guests for a day or two before being spirited away again.

Having considered that good enough to justify the issue of a search-warrant, his juniors had been busy for the last hour collecting all their available forces for the purpose of surrounding the house before the raid was made. When he had finished his drink he stood up and said that he must now be upon his way.

'If I may, I would very much like to come with you,' I said. 'If there's a scrap there can't be too many of us and in any case you'll need somebody to identify Miss Shane—if she's there.'

'I'd like to be in this thing too,' Harry added promptly.

'You can come if you like,' the Major agreed. 'But what about Mrs. Belville? I'm afraid we can't have ladies mixed up in this business.'

Clarissa sighed resignedly. 'You men have all the fun; although it can't be any joke for poor Sylvia. But never mind, I'll be all right here. Only for goodness sake take care of yourselves. Don't go getting shot or anything.'

Hanbury smiled. 'You needn't worry, Mrs. Belville. I've raided plenty of places before and we've more than sufficient men to deal with any rogues we may find in Taufik's house. It would be miserable here for you waiting on your own but I think I can solve that problem. There are some friends of mine at that table over there—Geoffrey Chatterton and his sister. If I may, I'll introduce you and they'll look after you while we're away.'

The introduction was duly effected. Chatterton, I gathered, was in the Irrigation Department—a tall, bronzed young man with a ready smile; his sister was a plain but pleasant woman of about thirty.

Hanbury just told them that we had some rather tricky business to transact which might take the best part of an hour, and asked them to entertain Clarissa in our absence, to which they readily consented. We left her with them and piled into the two cars outside, taking Amin and Mustapha with us.

Ismailia is quite a small town so the drive was a short one and we left the cars on its northern outskirts a few hundred yards from a long wall, some little distance from the roadside, which Hanbury pointed out to us as the place we were going to raid.

His junior officers reported to him that the place had been surrounded and instructions were given that, while sufficient men were to be left outside to catch anyone attempting to escape over the walls, the rest were all to come in over them on hearing one long blast from his whistle. He gave them ten minutes to get back to their posts and then, supported by a sergeant-major and six native policemen, our group walked quietly towards the main gateway.

When we were still some distance from it Hanbury detached the sergeant-major and one of the policemen, telling them to get over the wall fifty yards to the right of the gate and tackle anyone in the porter's lodge should the porter refuse us admission. As soon as they were out of sight on the far side of the wall we advanced to the main gate and hammered on it.

For a moment or two there was no response, then the covering of the grille in the great- old-fashioned structure was lifted and a pair of dark eyes peered out at us.

'What do you want?' asked a voice in Arabic.

'To see Suliman Taufik Bey,' replied Hanbury.

'He is from home,' replied the *boab*.

'When is he expected back?'

'I cannot say. He spends much of his time in Cairo and has been gone from here some days now.'

'Then I wish to see whoever is in charge in his absence.'

'Everyone is in bed at this hour,' said the man surlily.

'All the same, you'll let me in,' snapped Hanbury, and drawing his revolver he suddenly thrust it into the grille so that the barrel was within an inch of the *boab's* nose adding, 'Don't move. I'm a police officer, and you will be charged with obstructing me in the execution of my duty if you make any resistance.'

The man's eyes goggled with fright but he did not attempt to shut the covering of the grille and remained staring down the threatening barrel of the revolver.

'Hussein!' Hanbury called, raising his voice. 'Are you there?'

'*Hadra, effendi!*' came the gruff voice of the sergeant-major.

Hanbury spoke again. 'Secure this man and get the gate open.'

There was a slight scuffle as the porter was pulled away from the grille, followed by the noise of heavy wooden bolts being thrust back, and one half of the massive gate swung open.

With cautious footsteps, our pistols in our hands, we made our way up a long, straight drive bordered by palm trees to the front entrance of the house. It was quite silent but lights were burning in some of the upper windows. The building was a fairly modern one, probably erected somewhere in the eighteen-nineties. In a whisper Hanbury directed us to take up positions on either side of the front door where we should be concealed in the shadows. He then went up the two steps alone and rang the bell.

It clanged hollowly somewhere at the back of the house and we waited there holding our breath until someone should come to answer it. After what seemed an interminable time footsteps shuffled on the far side of the door. It was opened a crack and I could just see a native servant peering suspiciously round it.

There was a short, muttered conversation in Arabic and I caught the words '. . . your master . . .' and '. . . warrant to search these premises . . .'

At that the servant endeavoured to force the door to again but Hanbury had his foot in it and next second the blast of his whistle screamed loud through the still night as he flung his weight against the door.

At the sound we all leapt from our cover to his assistance. The door gave suddenly and Hanbury fell headlong inside it with Longdon and one of the policemen on top of him. Over their prostrate bodies I saw the servant grab a lever which was fixed to an iron box on the wall. As he wrenched it over an alarm-bell somewhere in the centre of the house suddenly shrilled with a frightful clamour.

Hanbury was on his feet again but the servant was racing down the passage shouting at the top of his voice and deaf to our commands to halt.

We poured into the narrow hall-way and as we did so I could hear the thudding feet of the police reinforcements who had come in over the walls and were now pelting across the garden to our aid.

Hanbury led the way after the flying servant towards the back of the house, two of his men following him. Longdon and the sergeant-major dashed into a room on the right where a dim light was burning. I headed straight for the stairs, taking them three at a time, my gun in my hand and Harry after me.

As I reached the bend I saw a group of men on the landing above who were dashing down to meet us. One of them raised his pistol and fired. The bullet whistled past my cheek and buried itself in the wall.

I fired in reply and at that moment the lights went out.

13

The House of the Angels

There followed in the next few moments the most terrifying experience that I have ever been through. On the previous night I had had not time to be really frightened; Yusuf and his fellow cut-throats had fallen on me too quickly for me to think of anything but bracing myself to meet their attack. Although they had rushed at me out of the darkness there had been no horrid interval in which I was directly menaced by an unseen enemy; as they had not used firearms I had not had to face the threat of being suddenly stricken down from a distance in the dark. Once their first rush was over, all my wits had been occupied in a purely physical endeavour to dodge their knives and force them from me, limb pressed to limb, until the moment when I practically lost consciousness.

The present encounter was utterly different. How long it was after the lights went out before the fight started again, I cannot say; probably not more than a couple of minutes at the outside, but it seemed an eternity. Downstairs it had been renewed almost immediately; shouts and the trampling of feet came from the rear portion of the premises into which the native servant had disappeared. They were followed by the crash of shots coming distant and muffled from somewhere out in the grounds. But I remained silent and motionless, crouching on the turn of the stairs. There were armed men, I knew, up there on the landing no more than ten feet away from me; I had not the least cover and they could hardly fail to hit me if they fired at the place where they had seen me standing before the lights went out. I could not retreat without making a commotion, as Harry and some of the police were blocking the staircase in my rear, and I knew that at the least sound a hail of bullets would come crashing at me from above.

The Stygian blackness into which the whole house had been plunged was not as great a handicap to the enemy as to myself, since they could retreat without giving away their position whereas I could not; yet it was probably because of it that they held their fire, waiting for me to move, in order to make quite certain on annihilating me with a fusilade before the flashes of their pistols revealed the place where they stood to the people behind me.

The palms of my hands were moist, my forehead was damp and I had an awful, tight feeling in the pit of my stomach. I knew that at any moment I might be riddled with lead and I tried frantically to think what it was best to do.

For a second I was buoyed up by the delusion that, knowing the police had broken in, the men on the landing above had taken advantage of the darkness to slip away in the hope of making their escape by some other exit; but almost as soon as the thought came to me I knew I was only fooling myself. I'd seen, by the one glimpse I'd had of them, that they numbered five or six at least so they could not possibly have beaten a retreat without my hearing them. They were up there waiting —waiting for me to move before they fired the shots which would tear my flesh and send me reeling back to die in tortured agony.

I suppose if I had been a real he-man I would have dashed up those stairs into the darkness firing right and left; but I simply could not bring myself to do it. I have always had a particular horror of being shot in the face and the mental images of my own features pulped and bleeding which my mind conjured up absolutely paralysed me.

Suddenly it came to me that to lie down was my only chance of escaping at least some of their bullets. Harry was not directly behind me, but partially covered by the turn of the stairs, so it was unlikely that the first burst of bullets intended for me would harm him. With infinite caution I stooped and extended my hands until they touched a higher stair, then I bent my knees until they touched another and, lastly, turning me head sideways, I lowered it between my shoulder blades until it was below the level of the stair on which my hands rested and my right cheek was pressed flat upon the stair-carpet.

It was, admittedly, an ostrich-like position as my shoulders were still fully exposed to any shots fired low but I make no excuse for my cowardice; I crouched there sweating with sheer blue funk while I waited for some move on either side.

It was at last, precipitated by Longdon, although that 'at last' was probably no more than a hundred seconds from the time the lights had gone out. His voice came sharply from the hall below.

'Come on, there! What are you waiting for? Up you go!'

I clenched my teeth and the nails of my left hand bit into my palm, but I did not budge. In my right I was still clutching my automatic.

There was a mutter of voices at the bottom of the stairs, then one of the police leaned past Harry and pushing an arm round the banisters sent a pot-shot flying up into the darkness above. His gun was hardly a foot behind and two above my buried head and the explosion sounded like the Crack of Doom.

'There! There!' I heard Harry cry. He had evidently seen the enemy in the flash of the policeman's pistol, but his shout was cut short by a thunder that seemed to rock the staircase. The enemy had opened fire, aiming at the flash, and it was that which doubtless saved me.

A banister-rail splintered with a tearing sound. Bullets thudded into the plaster behind me and the stench of cordite was strong in my nostrils. I knew then that I had to move; I did not even think about it, but jerking myself erect I pelted up the stairs firing as I went.

The darkness was alive with flashes. How I escaped being hit I shall never know. There was a scream from somebody in front of me as one of my bullets hit a man, and a curse from one of the people behind who had stopped one from above. Next second I was up on the landing right in the thick of it.

One of them slashed at me with a fist that held a pistol but in the darkness he could only guess at the position of my head and the blow took me on the shoulder, sending me spinning sideways. I turned and pistoled him where he stood. Someone else fired an instant afterwards and by the flash I saw the horror on my victim's face. His eyes were bulging from his dark face and his tongue was hanging out as he slipped down on to his knees.

For a moment the firing was so continuous that the flash of the guns was enough to give me some idea of the geography of the place. From the landing a passage ran the whole length of the house; fifteen feet from the head of the main stairway another staircase led up through a narrow arch to the second floor. A dozen figures were milling wildly on the landing but I caught sight of one who was firing into the mêlée from a vantage-point on the lowest of the upper stairs. I only saw his face for an instant but I knew those lean, jutting features too well to be mistaken. It was O'Kieff.

It had not even occurred to me that we might find him there and my heart positively leapt with exaltation at the thought that he, of all people, was fast in our trap.

Once in the scrimmage I had too much to think of to be frightened any longer and now all sense of personal danger left me entirely. At the sight of O'Kieff I literally flung myself into the mob and sent a great Arab hurtling backwards in my endeavour to get at the man I hated so bitterly.

The firing had lessened now and it was almost impossible to pick out friend from foe. The bodyguard on the House of the Angels had proved bigger than we had bargained for and, besides those who were putting up a fight downstairs, there must have been at least eight or ten of them on the landing when I had first charged it.

Half a dozen hand-to-hand conflicts were in progress as I barged and fought my way towards O'Kieff. Flashes still coming at fairly quick intervals showed him to me standing there—the one calm figure in this wild gun-fight—picking his human targets with quiet deliberation as each flash revealed the mêlée to him.

At last I was through the screaming, cursing mass; still miraculously unharmed, except for a slight gash in the upper arm where a bullet had seared it, and that my right ear felt the size of a cauliflower from a blow that had descended on it in the darkness. I raised my gun, aimed carefully for the place at the bottom of the upper stairs where I knew O'Kieff was standing, and waited for the next flash.

It came, and from him, giving me a perfect target. I

squeezed the trigger; in the pandemonium I did not even hear it click, but nothing happened. I squeezed again and again; then I realised that my magazine was empty.

With frantic fingers I slipped out the empty clip and rammed home a new one but, just as I raised the gun again, another flash showed me that O'Kieff was no longer there; he had abandoned the fight and fled upstairs. I flung myself forward and hurtled up them after him.

On reaching the top of the next flight I could hear his light, swift footfalls as he raced along an unseen passage. It was black as night up there but at that very moment the lights came on again; evidently Hanbury had got control of the situation on the ground floor and found the main switch. After the darkness the lights blinded me for a second, then I saw O'Kieff twenty yards away at the far end of a long, narrow corridor. I jerked up my gun and fired.

Till then I don't think he realised that anyone was after him and, for a second, I thought I had scored a bull as he halted dead in his tracks. But I was mistaken, for he instantly swung round and fired in reply. Both of us were normally good enough shots to have killed each other at fifty feet but his bullet went wide too, whipping past my ear. The light was not good as only a single small bulb lit the whole of the long corridor and, in addition, our recent exertions had left us breathless, upsetting our aim.

Before I had time to get in another shot O'Kieff dived through a nearby doorway and there was a loud metallic clang. I raced down the passage and hammered on the door but I knew then that he had escaped me. It was a steel door with a spring lock and it cut me off from him completely.

Evidently there was a second staircase somewhere behind it and I could only hope now that he would be caught by the police on the lower floor or out in the grounds. Nevertheless, I burned with such hate against him that my one thought was to get downstairs again as swiftly as I could to ensure that every possible effort should be directed towards cornering him.

I rushed back to the staircase up which I had come but, to my surprise and fury, I found that a door which I had not seen in the dark had closed at the end of the passage, cutting me off from it. This door was also made of steel and I guessed in a flash that it, and the one through which O'Kieff had disappeared, must be operated by electricity. He had obviously closed and locked them both simultaneously by pressing a controlling switch before he fled down the further stairs, making me a prisoner in the upper floor of the house.

It was barely a minute since O'Kieff had disappeared from view. As I stood there panting for breath and fuming with anger a dull explosion reverberated through the house; it sounded as if a bomb had been thrown somewhere on one of the lower floors but there was no repetition of it and the steel doors cut off any sounds of further fighting.

Along the upper passage there were five or six doors on either side and I was just wondering what next it was best to do when, one after another, four of them opened a few inches in as many seconds and were promptly shut again. At the nearest I caught a glimpse of a young negress who gave me one terrified glance before slamming her door and locking it.

The sight of her gave me just the impetus I needed for fresh action. Evidently it was up in these rooms that the 'Angels' of various nationalities were kept before being exported from East to West and West to East, and they had all been thrown into a dither by the sounds of the firing. If Sylvia were in the place at all she must be somewhere among them.

In two strides I was outside the door; lifting my right foot I brought it down crashing with all my force against the lock. The wood splintered and the door flew open; but the little negress had completely disappeared.

The room was comfortable and well-furnished; a couple of trunks stood in one corner, a dress and some undies were neatly folded on a chair and the bed-clothes had been tossed aside, suggesting that the girl had been asleep when the riot started.

At first I feared that in her terror she had thrown herself out of the window but a quick look under her bed showed me that she was crouching there.

'Don't be frightened,' I said in Arabic, thinking that the language she would be most likely to understand. 'Come out of there. I'm not going to hurt you.' But she only glared at me like a wild animal and suddenly began to whimper.

Thrusting my hand under the bed I grabbed her by the arm and began to drag her out. She fought like a tiger-cat and gave me a nasty bite on the wrist before I had managed to pull her from her hiding-place and on to her feet. Apparently she had been sleeping naked and only thrown on a wrap when she got out of bed to investigate the din below. The wrap had got badly torn in our struggle and now dangled wide open from one of her shoulders exposing her whole figure.

Negresses mature young and although she was probably not more than fifteen she was perfectly developed with the sort of lithe, rounded young body that an artist would have given anything for as a model. She was black as your hat with an almost bluish tinge on her velvet-soft, ebony-skin and evidently she had already been groomed for marketing, since she was clean as a new pin and smelt faintly of some pleasant perfume.

I did my utmost in both Arabic and French to reassure her and try to get her to talk sense, as my one anxiety was to learn from her as quickly as I could anything she could tell me about the place and which room Sylvia was in, if Sylvia was there; but my efforts were quite unavailing. She would only jibber at me in her own barbaric tongue, so after a moment I let her go and dashed out into the corridor again to try the door opposite.

It was locked so I applied the same process as before and burst in. The room was furnished like the other but sitting on the bed was a white girl, a pretty enough young thing of about twenty, but I saw at once that she lacked the perfection the negress as her ankles, which protruded from beneath her dressing-gown, were somewhat on the thick side. That was hardly surprising as young negresses are ten a penny and Zakri's crowd would only skim the cream of the slave cargoes which, in spite of the efforts of the International Police, are shipped almost nightly through Abyssinia over to Arabia.

The girl was calmly smoking a cigarette and was perfectly self-possessed. Her pretty mask of a face suddenly dissolved into a rather sickening leer as she asked in French:

'What is the excitement, *cheri*? Are they having trouble with some drunks?'

It was clear that in spite of her youth she was not a new hand at the game but naturally most of the white girls sent East are shop-soiled goods.

'I'm with the police,' I said at once. 'And this place is being raided. Can you tell me anything of a fair-haired English girl who was brought in here today?'

She let out a filthy expletive which seemed, somehow, peculiarly shocking on the lips of a young girl of carefully tended appearance and seeming innocence; then she gave a resigned shrug of her slim shoulders. Evidently she knew enough of this business to realise that the worst that could happen to her was a short spell in prison. She smiled again.

'What misfortune! I thought it was only a few foolish ones letting off their guns and that Monsieur was a customer. I am dying of *ennui* in this place and would have welcomed a little diversion; especially with *un beau garçon comme Monsieur.*'

I ignored the compliment and repeated, 'Can you tell me anything of a fair-haired English girl who was brought here today? If you can, I'll ask the police to make it easy for you.'

She shook her head. '*Mais non*. This is a very unusual establishment. We girls aren't even allowed to see each other and we're only here for a night or two before they send us on our way.'

'Thanks,' I nodded and strode out of this particular little spider's parlour. Back in the corridor I heard somebody battering on the steel door which shut me off from the staircase up which I had come. I could only hope that they would find some means of forcing it quickly and, since I could give them no assistance from my side of it, I began to shout for Sylvia as a quicker way of finding her than by breaking in the door of every room. Although I bawled her name at the top of my voice half a dozen times there was no reply, so I had to go back to my original method.

This time I went to the far end of the corridor and smashed in the lock of a door there. Its occupant was a beautiful little Chinese. She looked as fragile as Dresden china, sitting up in bed with her pretty, unpainted face and dark hair which had been carefully curled. She was calm but anxious as he betrayed by a little quiver in her voice when she spoke, with obvious hostility, in halting English.

'Go 'way! You no makee anything here. Madame say no visitors dis place. Go 'way out!'

'I'm sorry,' I smiled. 'But I'm not here for that sort of thing.

179

I'm looking for an English girl that I believe was brought here today. Can you tell me anything about her?'

The little Chinese shook her head. 'Me no see. You spik Madame. P'laps she tell.'

I wasted no further time on her but dashed from the room and attacked the door on the far side of the passage.

To my surprise it did not give at the first assault and, on examination, I found that it was of stouter wood and had two locks.

I went at it again with a running kick, planting the flat of my foot with all my weight behind it over the two keyholes. It creaked and the locks loosened in their sockets but it did not give and I had to fling my whole weight at it twice again before the wood splintered and it flew wide open.

The room was in darkness and no sound came from it, so I fished round by the doorway for a light switch. My fingers found it and pressed it down.

The light flooded an absolutely bare apartment. There was not a stick of furniture in it and only a worn carpet on the floor; at the first glance I saw that the window had heavy bars across it.

In the first glance, too, I saw Sylvia. She was lying flat on her back in one corner without a stitch of clothing on. As I think I have said before, Sylvia was a tall, long-limbed girl with a naturally graceful carriage, and in Cairo I had much admired her figure; but there was nothing beautiful about her nakedness. She lay sprawled in an ugly, unnatural attitude, one arm twisted awkwardly under her and the other dangling limply across her body hiding the curve of her breasts. Her head was propped up against the wall so that her chin rested on her chest and her silver-gold hair hung lank over her face. A great purple bruise disfigured one of her thighs and clots of dried blood encrusted her right shoulder.

My consciousness barely took in the fact that she was nude because I was half-stunned by the appalling thought that I had arrived too late and that I was staring only at her corpse which had been thrown down there; but, as I moved towards her, she moaned and turned over.

In a second I was beside her, pillowing her head against my

arm and searching with my free hand for the flask of brandy in my hip pocket.

She moaned again when I forced a little of it between her lips then, as the spirit coursed down her throat, she coughed and a little colour flooded back into her dead-white cheeks.

I gave her another sip of the brandy but she feebly raised a hand and tried to push the flask away, opening her eyes as she did so and staring at me.

I saw a flicker of recognition enter them and she smiled very faintly while I strove to comfort her with those silly, meaningless phrases which burble to one's lips when one is trying to reassure someone who has suffered an accident or is in great pain.

I don't think she realised then that she was naked as she lay quite placidly in my embrace; but *I* realised it and knew that I must do something about it as quickly as I could to save her feelings when she fully regained consciousness.

'I won't be a second,' I said, propping her up against the wall, but a sudden look of stark terror came into her blue eyes. With surprising strength she grabbed my hand and moaned:

'Don't! Don't leave me!'

Knowing what I was up to I paid no heed but shook off her grip with a reassuring smile and ran out across the passage into the Chinese girl's room. She probably had a number of garments in her wardrobe and her trunk but as nothing suitable was visible I just grabbed her bedclothes.

'Sorry to bother you,' I said with an apologetic grin. 'But I want these. You can get some of your own clothes on. The police will be up here in a moment.'

She let out a falsetto screech as I ripped the blankets off her bed and sliding out of the other side spat at me furiously, but I took no further notice of her and hurried back to Sylvia.

Evidently she had realised why I had left her by then as she was sitting up cross-legged with her head in her hands and her back turned towards me.

'Here, cover up with these,' I said, draping the bedclothes round her. 'I'll get you some proper clothes as soon as I can.'

With a little shiver she huddled into the blankets and extended a hand over her shoulder. 'Please, may I have some more brandy?'

I was perspiring from my exertions but I realised that it must have been pretty chilly up there, lying about without any clothes on. Thrusting the flask into her hand I left her again and hurried down the corridor to the French girl. She was still sitting on the edge of her bed quietly smoking.

'Well, where are the police?' she smiled. 'I believe *Monsieur* was only fooling and that they've given him the run of the place to pick whom he likes up here. But why make such a fuss about it? I'll show you a better time than any of these coloured women. Come over here and talk to me, *cheri*.'

'The police are here all right,' I assured her grimly. 'If you listen you can hear them working on that steel door at the top of the stairs. In the meantime I want the loan of some of your clothes.'

'My clothes!' she echoed. 'Why? For some special *funnibizznes?*'

'Don't be silly,' I said. 'But give me some of the things in that trunk. A suit of undies and a coat and skirt if you've got one.'

'*Monsieur* is a little mad, I think,' she sniffed.

'Thanks, I'm quite sane,' I retorted. 'But I've found the girl I was looking for and the swine who runs this place had locked her up stripped to the skin.'

Her hard little face softened immediately. '*Pauvre petite*,' she murmured, standing up. 'So she is a new girl and unwilling. Such treatment is the first step and most of us go through it. Of course I will find things for her.'

As she spoke she went to the wardrobe and fished out a pair of step-ins, a silk dress and a little coatee. 'Here, take these. I will bring stockings and other things in a moment.'

'Thank you ever so much,' I smiled as I received the garments from her. 'I'll see to it that you get an easy deal from the police for this.'

She shrugged disdainfully. 'The police! I am not afraid of them. But when one is in trouble, one is in trouble; and it is for that reason only I lend my clothes to your little friend.'

Her attitude left me awkward and abashed but I had no time to bother about that and quickly took the things along to Sylvia. Giving them to her I asked if she felt strong enough to get into them.

182

'Yes,' she said. 'Just go outside for a moment, will you?'

'Right,' I said. 'Some shoes and stockings will be along in a minute.'

As I stepped out into the corridor I noticed that the banging on the steel door had ceased and I wondered what had become of the rest of the raiding party; but when I thought of it I realised that all my smashing-in of doors and swift questions to these women had happened so quickly that it could be barely five minutes since I had chased O'Kieff upstairs. The police would have had plenty to occupy them during so short a time; the probability was that only a stray member of the party had followed me and, finding the door too much for him alone, he had now gone to get help. I was anxious to get Sylvia out of the place and into Clarissa's care as quickly as possible but it was clear that we were cooped up there with the 'Angels' until our friends could release us.

It was just then that I first noticed the smell of smoke. I was still sniffing uncertainly when the door of the room next to Sylvia's was flung open and a young Jewess came dashing out. She was shouting something in a tongue that I did not understand but a billow of smoke that followed her as she ran from the room told its own story. O'Kieff must have fired the place on his way out and we were trapped up there in the top storey.

14

Heru-Tem; the Man Who Came Back

On each of my dashes along the passage several of the doors in it had been opened a crack but on my appearance they had shut each time with the rapidity of a row of tickled oysters. There had been something vaguely reminiscent of a French farce in those kimono-clad figures peeping from their doorways, but now that the house was on fire I had an uneasy feeling that tragedy was only lurking round the corner.

The piercing shrieks of the Jewish girl brought the French trollop and the sullen little Chinese out into the passage. One by one the other doors opened and, altogether, eight girls emerged. In spite of the urgency of the situation I could not help being momentarily amused by the thought that the 'Angels' might quite well have been the elected representatives of a respectable international beauty contest; except for the fact that some of them were more scantily clothed than is permissible at a public appearance.

They were certainly a hand-picked bunch and did not look at all like *filles de joie*; that, of course, was on account of their youth. I doubt if any of them were over twenty and the three Europeans among them were probably the only ones who had had any actual experience of the business. In addition to Miss France, Miss Africa, Miss China and Miss Palestine there were a red-headed piece, a High Yaller with golden hair and two brunettes who looked as though they had a Mediterranean origin. I learnt later that the first was English, the second a half-caste German from Tanganyika and that the other two hailed from Greece and Turkey respectively.

They were all yammering at the tops of their voices in a babel of tongues as they crowded round me and I suppose many men might have found the situation a slightly—shall we say—trying one; but I'm not the least ashamed to admit that, ever since my Oxford days, I've always preferred girls to ball games and as a number of very charming damsels have devoted quite a lot of their time to improving my education, young women either singly or in bunches have no terrors for me. If I hadn't been somewhat anxious about the extent of the fire below I should have thought it rather a joke to find myself responsible for the safety of this strange collection of beauties.

With a familiarity which some say breeds contempt I thrust them hastily aside and pushed my way into the Jewish girl's room, from which the smoke was now swirling in big billows It was next to the hidden stairs down which O'Kieff had disappeared and the seat of the trouble was at the foot of the wall abutting on to the staircase. Evidently he had had a special store of incendiary material already prepared there and the explosion I had heard was the bomb with which he had ignited it, otherwise the fire could not have got a hold so quickly. Dense clouds of smoke were welling up from the crack between the floor-boards and the skirting and through them I could see the red flames flickering as they ate hungrily into the well-seasoned wood.

Snatching up a pitcher of water from the washstand I sprinkled its contents over the blankets on the bed and piled them on the place where the fire was fiercest but the heat was so intense that they only served as a temporary check. Coughing and sneezing from the smoke I made my way to the window and shut it, then staggered back out of the room pulling the door shut behind me.

'Silence!' I yelled in stentorian tones to the alarmed beauty chorus; after which I repeated in every language I could muster, 'Don't be afraid. The police are below and there are plenty of them to rescue them. Get your clothes on as quickly as you can.'

That seemed to reassure them somewhat and they ran off to their respective rooms, except Miss France, who was holding the other things she had promised to get for Sylvia.

Sylvia came out that moment and with a word of thanks relieved her of them. As the French girl hurried back to dress I caught Sylvia's eye and both of us quickly averted our glances. The form of education administered so delightfully by my fair friends in the past had not included 'correct approach to a young woman of one's acquaintance who has passed the last ten hours being initiated into the first stages of white slavery preparatory to being shipped off to Arabia, and who knows that one is aware of how she has been spending her time.' The last thing I wanted to do was to pry into the details of what she had suffered but it was evident that she could not feel natural with me until she had given some account of the events which had preceded my finding her and I was almost inclined to welcome the fire as a postponement of the first awkward exchanges concerning her abduction.

As Sylvia turned back into the room I hurried to a solitary window at the extreme end of the passage and, reaching it, thanked all my gods to find that it was not barred. Throwing it open I thrust out my head. I could see figures moving in the garden but it was clear that the fire had spread with great rapidity as flames, smoke and sparks were issuing from the window immediately below me. I hailed the people in the garden and Longdon's voice came back.

'That you, Day? We thought you had been scuppered. How many others are up there?'

'Sylvia Shane and eight of the "Angels",' I yelled back. 'We're trapped up here by a steel door at the top of the stairs. Can't you manage to force it?'

'No!' he cried. 'We've been trying to for the last ten minutes, but nothing short of dynamite will shift it. There are no ladders here so you'll have to make a rope of sheets.'

'Right ho!' I bawled and shut the window, but I was none too happy about the task before me. It would take time to do as he suggested and get all nine women safely to the ground, and a steady stream of smoke was already percolating into the corridor from under the crack of Miss Palestine's door.

Sylvia was the first out as she had already been partially dressed when the alarm of fire was given. She looked sick and ill but not frightened although she again glanced quickly away from me which, seeing the state I had found her in, made me dread more than ever hearing even a vague reference to what she had been through.

Immediately I had told her what we had to do she set to work knotting together the bedclothes I had got for her from Miss China, while I ran from room to room collecting others.

By and large, the girls behaved better than might have been expected, with the exception of Miss Palestine. She had gone off with Miss Greece to borrow some garments and, on her return, wailed throughout the whole of the proceedings. The others buckled to very gamely, once they understood what was wanted of them, and with so many willing hands we soon had a thirty-foot rope of sheets stretched out along the corridor. I tested each knot myself while they pulled a bed out of the nearest room to which I firmly secured one end of the rope.

As Miss Palestine was giving so much trouble I decided to get rid of her first, and tied the other end of the life-line twice round her body.

She was in such a state of terror that in spite of our efforts to persuade her she flatly refused to go out of the window; but the situation was becoming too serious to waste much time in arguing with her so, getting the other girls to take the strain on the rope, I picked her up bodily and pushed her out feet first.

I wanted Sylvia to go next as she was so weak from the ordeal she had been through but she wouldn't hear of it and, once again, I dared not waste time arguing. The flames were now licking under the door of the bedroom where the fire had first appeared and the whole corridor was so thick with smoke that we could no longer see the full length of it.

As Sylvia wouldn't go I sent down the little negress, since her wide staring eyes showed an abject fear although she had remained dumb the whole time like some frightened animal. After her, we lowered Miss Greece, Miss England and Miss Turkey but each operation took several minutes and I was still left with the Mesdemoiselles France, China, and Tanganyika, besides Sylvia.

By that time our eyes were smarting so badly that we could hardly see; while fifteen feet behind us we could hear the roar and crackle of the flames as they ate up the door and licked at the wall opposite. I'm not exactly a panicky person but I was getting distinctly worried at the rapid way the fire was gaining.

As Sylvia still refused to go down, I sent the High Yaller and, on turning to select the next, found that the beautiful Chinese had fainted. Gasping and stumbling we hurriedly tied the life-line round her and pushed her inanimate body out of the window.

The heat was simply appalling; sweat was running down our faces in streams and as we staggered about half-blinded I began to fear that the rest of us would never get out in time. To us, waiting there, panting for breath in the stifling atmosphere, it seemed that each time we lowered the life-line it was longer before it came up again. While I attended to the rope and took the strain when each of the girls was lowered, I made the others keep their heads thrust out of the window so that they could get as much fresh air as possible, but I was feeling near the end of my tether.

I cursed myself for not having had the foresight to tie a damp towel over my mouth and nose, but I had had no time to think of that and now I was paying the penalty. With every breath I drew the acrid smoke tore at my lungs until it seemed that my chest would burst with the frightful pain that racked it. Behind us now there was one solid sheet of flame and I knew that it would take another six minutes at least for the remaining three of us to reach safety. My movements had become slow and clumsy and although I fought with all my will it seemed as though my brain was going. I doubted if I could stave off unconsciousness even for another two minutes.

It was Sylvia who saved us. She saw how things were with me as I staggered and nearly fell in my effort to tie the life-line round Miss France. Leaning out of the window she called down that we were done unless someone could come up to help us. At that moment Miss France fainted and fell on to me but somehow or other we managed to bundle her out and keep some sort of check on the life-line as it jerked through our hands; after which I remember nothing until I came to in the garden.

It was Longdon who had swarmed up the line and got out Sylvia and myself both of whom were unconscious by the time he reached us.

We were all so done-in that it was as much as we could do to stumble into the cars and, a few minutes later, the beds that Hanbury provided for us; so it was not until the following morning that I had a chance to talk things over with any of my friends.

In the confusion resulting from the fire O'Kieff had escaped and the dozen prisoners, including the 'Madame' of the place, that Hanbury had captured were small fry, mainly consisting of Arab servants and strong-arm men. Three of their people had been killed in the scrap and five others dangerously wounded; while our party had sustained six serious casualties including two dead and Mustapha, whose right arm had been broken by a bullet. As the 'Angels' were nearly all apprentices at their trade it was hoped that they were not beyond permanent rescue and they were being sent to Cairo where arrangements would be made for their transport to the countries of their origin when relatives, who would be responsible for them, had been duly contacted.

Harry seemed to have enjoyed the scrap, in spite of the fact that he had been temporarily knocked out and had a bump on his forehead the size of a hen's egg; at all events he certainly enjoyed basking in Clarissa's obvious hero-worship when she came down to join us for lunch.

She told us that, all things considered, Sylvia seemed better than might have been expected; and when she had been asked if she would like to remain in Ismailia for a few days to recover she had declared she would much rather go back to Cairo that afternoon where she could have her own things about her.

The doctor who had been called in the night before to look after us had given her a sleeping draught, so she had slept well and her main complaint, apart from the fact that she was stiff and sore, seemed to be that she had developed a violent cold. So far she had given no account of what had happened during the time she had been a prisoner but, whatever had occurred, it was cheering to know that she hadn't broken down under it and was apparently putting a brave face on the matter.

After lunch she came downstairs in clothes that Hanbury had borrowed for her. They fitted badly and she was looking very groggy but she declared that she was ready to make her statement to the police. We suggested that we should retire but she said she had no objection to our remaining while she told her story.

Under the impression that she was being taken to Police Headquarters she had driven off with the bogus police officer and, just as Essex Pasha had postulated, the car had turned off from the main road into the courtyard of a private house where the gates were immediately closed behind it. Directly she had started to enquire the reason, several people had come out of the house and dragged her into it; holding her down they had pulled up her skirt and given her an injection in the thigh. After a few minutes she had lapsed into unconsciousness and she remembered nothing else until she found herself, dressed in native garments, lying back in the seat of an aeroplane.

Hanbury nodded at that point and remarked, 'It was the information from the Air Port Police in Cairo which enabled us to trace you. We had never heard of the House of the Angels here and were completely baffled; but the suspect 'plane with the sick woman on board had not arrived in Alexandria, which made it look pretty fishy. It occurred to me then that there's only one man here who runs a private 'plane and that's Suliman Taufik. He doesn't use the Ismailia Air Port but keeps it in a private ground near his residence. On enquiry I found that it had flown over and landed there at a little before four in the afternoon. The time of the flight tallied with the trip from Cairo and so did the description of his 'plane when I got on to the Air Port Police there. That more or less settled the matter in my mind but I checked up afterwards that Suliman's place *was* the House of the Angels by pulling in some of his servants.'

Sylvia nodded. 'Thank God you did. Anyhow, that's what happened; by the time they got me to the house the dope was beginning to wear off a bit. In a room downstairs I was confronted by a man whom I recognised at once, from Ju—Mr. Day's description, as O'Kieff.'

She shivered slightly and went on quickly, 'He's a horrid person; cold as a fish and with eyes like a snake. He threatened me with all sorts of pains and penalties unless I would sign an authority to my bank for them to hand over the lower half of the tablet—the one I've had ever since it was discovered—to his representative.

'At first I refused, of course, so they took me upstairs for a little gentle persuasion. I decided then that discretion was the better part of valour and signed the letter they wanted. Afterwards they took my clothes and locked me up so that I couldn't get away, and it was like that Mr. Day found me.'

'You've, er—got nothing else to charge them with?' Hanbury enquired a little awkwardly.

'How d'you mean?' she asked calmly.

'Well—er—so far we have abduction, illegally administering a dangerous drug with criminal intentions and enforcing the signing of a document under pressure of threats. As they beat you up I think we ought to add assault and, er . . .' he looked away in embarrassment. 'I don't want to press you now but perhaps the assault charge might need some special qualification which you would rather prefer through a Police Matron.'

'Oh no,' said Sylvia looking him straight in the eye. 'You're quite mistaken about that. Nobody even laid a hand on me.'

I saw at once the line she was taking and quickly came to her assistance.

'What's more,' I said, 'Miss Shane told me when I found her last night that the bogus police officer who took her off in the car didn't accompany them in the 'plane to Ismailia. I feel quite certain, too, that it won't be the least use your holding any identity parades of your prisoners because, owing to the state she was in, Miss Shane would not be able to recognise the women or the other two men who did accompany her in the 'plane from Cairo.'

Hanbury turned and gave me an angry look. 'Thank you, Day, but I'm not questioning you, and I should be obliged if you would keep your views to yourself.' But Sylvia smiled and remarked quietly:

'He's quite right. Actually it's a fact that the bogus policeman wasn't on the 'plane and I do feel quite convinced that I should never be able to identify any of the others.'

'Well, if that's the way you feel,' Hanbury muttered, 'we can't even charge anyone with the kidnapping or anything else for the present.'

'That's it,' I said. 'But the "Angels" will be able to give you all the evidence you want about the house being a white-slaving joint so you can jug your prisoners quite satisfactorily without bringing Miss Shane into it at all.'

He smiled then. 'Yes, I see the situation; since I can do that I won't press Miss Shane further. She's been through a ghastly time and the last thing I want to do is to embarrass her with the further ordeal of having to come forward as a police witness. I shall have to, though, if we manage to lay our hands on O'Kieff or the bogus policeman.'

The meeting broke up then and Clarissa went up to pack

her few things while Harry settled for us all with the doctor. I had already packed and Sylvia had nothing but the borrowed clothes she stood up in so, while Longdon and Hanbury were comparing notes, we wandered out into the garden.

'I've so much to thank you for I hardly know where to start,' she said as soon as we were out of earshot.

'If you feel that way,' I smiled, 'you might start by calling me Julian. You almost said it just now, you know, when you were making your statement to Major Hanbury.'

'All right—Julian, then. I naturally think of you that way because that's what Clarissa and Harry always call you. I *am* grateful, though—terribly—for everything.'

'It's Essex Pasha and his lieutenants you have to thank really. It was they who located you.'

'It was you who thought of the "House of the Angels". It was you who actually did the he-man stuff and were the first to find me in that filthy brothel. It was you who would have saved me first from the fire, if I hadn't insisted that those poor little devils should be lowered before me; and it was you who really saved me just now from the horror of having the whole story in every paper in Egypt as a result of having to give evidence against the prisoners. I'd already made up my mind that I wasn't going to admit to any assault charge but I hadn't thought about an identification parade and you tipped me off about that most skilfully.'

'I saw no reason why you should be dragged through the Courts when it wasn't necessary,' I said. 'As for the other part of it, anyone else would have done as much; it was only that I happened to be on hand. I'm glad, though, that I was, from a selfish point of view, as at least it gave me a chance to prove that I'm out against O'Kieff every bit as much as you are. May I take it that in spite of my mysterious past you will really trust me in the future?'

'Yes, of course you may. I feel rather ashamed now that I ever doubted you; but you must admit I had good reason to. Still, your past *is* entirely your own affair and I don't mind a bit now if you'd rather not talk about it. The one thing I *do* know about you is enough. You're quite the bravest man I've ever met.'

'Please!' I protested, feeling my cheeks redden 'It's nice to know you think that but horribly embarrassing to be told so to one's face.'

'Nothing like as embarrassing as being found stark naked in a brothel,' she said a little grimly.

'I hardly noticed that,' I said hurriedly.

She gave a queer little laugh. 'That's a pretty poor compliment. As a matter of fact I'm very proud of my figure. 'It's rather humiliating to learn that you didn't even notice it.'

I guessed at once that she was trying to make a joke of the thing in order to hide her embarrassment and get it off her mind so that she wouldn't feel shy about it when she was with me in the future. So I quickly took up the line she was playing.

'I'm rather a connoisseur of figures myself and from what little I did see I should think you're a prize-winner every time. But to be quite honest, I was too upset when I first found you to think of anything like that because I was afraid you were dead. And afterwards, as you may remember, I was much too occupied to take in any details. I could only thank God you were alive and hope that you hadn't suffered too much during the hours before we found you.'

'I mean to try to forget that,' she said. 'It was damned unpleasant being beaten and I was scared stiff that they'd ship me down to one of the Red Sea ports, as they threatened, before anyone could trace me. But at all events "the worst" didn't happen.'

We both burst out laughing then because 'the worst' seemed such a delightfully comic expression.

'Thank the lord for that!' I smiled. 'I've got some idea of the usual drill in such places and I was terrified they'd put you through it.'

'They meant to,' she admitted. 'And that was after they had beaten me up and I had agreed to sign the paper, but I managed to keep my head and save myself.'

'I give you full marks, then. I'm dead certain I could never have thought of a yarn that would have got me out if I'd been in your shoes.'

She lit a cigarette and puffed at it gently. 'It was rather a thin story but it served its purpose. I told them I was sick with, er—tuberculosis shall we call it—positively riddled with it—so they decided to wait for a medical examination.'

'By Jove!' I cried, swinging round and looking at her with admiration. 'That was quick thinking with a vengeance. You say I'm a brave man but anything I did was just child's play compared with the nerve required to put over a thing like that. You made a better showing in the fire than I did, too.'

She shrugged and smiled at me. 'Let's call it quits, shall we, and stop throwing bouquets at one another. I still feel horribly weak, though, so if you don't mind we'll go back now and sit down until the cars turn up.'

Ten minutes later, having said goodbye to Hanbury and the doctor who had attended us, we set off back to Suez. Sylvia travelled with the Belvilles in our hired car while I went with Longdon again in his.

On the right of the road a few miles outside Ismailia we passed the magnificent war memorial to the Forces of the Empire who served in Egypt during the Great War. It is set up on a rise with nothing but the blue sky and limitless desert behind it which makes it one of the most impressive I have ever seen; but it struck me as strange that it should have been erected in such a desolate spot where few people ever see it instead of on a well-chosen site in Cairo, and I asked Longdon the reason.

'It's because it was just at this point on the Canal that we repulsed the Turkish invasion,' he replied with a queer little smile.

'Invasion?' I echoed, puzzled. 'I had no idea that the Turks actually penetrated into Egypt during the Great War.'

'Yes,' he laughed. 'A corporal and five men in a rowing boat.'

'But how on earth did such a queer little force break through our lines?'

'There wasn't any line to break through,' he replied. 'Until Allenby took command most of the generals out here weren't very bright. The first concern of the British in Egypt was naturally to defend the Canal in order to keep it open for our shipping. As there were no Turkish troops within two hundred miles of it at the outbreak of the war we could easily have established our lines on the Turkish side of the water; but, incredible as it may sound, the idiots actually decided to defend it from the rear. They left it so that the Turks could walk right up to it without opposition and the Canal itself was in no-man's-land.

'Fortunately for us, Johnny Turk's supplies broke down so he had to fall back through lack of water and ammunition almost as soon as he got there; but if he'd had another twenty-four hours' leeway he might easily have sunk some of the ships in the Canal with his artillery. If he had, it would have taken us weeks to get it clear again and, in the meantime, all the reinforcements on their way from Australia, India and the East would have been bottled up in the Red Sea and rendered completely useless to us.'

'What a crazy show,' I murmured.

He shrugged. 'Anyhow, most of the muddlers are as dead as Queen Anne now and the staff officers picked for their brains these days. I don't think there's much likelihood of the present lot trying to defend important strategic points from behind if there does come a "next time".'

The afternoon was fine and we raced on in the sunshine through the beautifully-kept Canal Zone which is under the administration of the immensely wealthy Suez Canal Company. The dues on shipping are so high that they sound almost prohibitive but they are worked out to a scale which would make it just a trifle more expensive, whatever the tonnage of the ship, in extra fuel and wages to take her round South Africa.

There is no expense in connection with operating locks along the Canal as the engineers under de Lesseps who built it found, to their astonishment, that the ocean level is exactly the same in the Red Sea as in the Mediterranean, and this naturally adds enormously to the Company's profits; on the other hand, every time there is a severe sandstorm in the Canal Zone it costs the Company £20,000 to dredge out the sand which is blown into the Canal.

As the Canal is banked on either side its waters cannot be seen from certain portions of the road and, just as we were passing the southern end of the Little Bitter Lake, this gave rise to a most queer illusion. In front of us lay, apparently, the un-broken desert valley, yet, with smoking funnel and flags aflutter, a big liner in the distance seemed to be ploughing its way through a sea of sand.

By half-past four we were in Suez where we said goodbye to Longdon and I got into the other car. We had had to leave Mustapha in the hospital at Ismailia on account of his shattered arm and with Amin sitting next to the driver there was a seat inside for me. Sylvia was now feeling the reaction of her ordeal and looked pathetically ill and weak. She slept fitfully most of the way back to Cairo and our journey was uneventful.

The manager at the Continental had had a new room prepared for her and all her things moved into it, so Clarissa took her straight up to bed. The rest of us also were pretty done-in and after a scratch meal, for which we had very little appetite, we made an early night of it.

The following morning I had an interview with Essex Pasha and gave him a verbal account of what had happened; although, of course, he had already received official reports from Hanbury and Longdon. Sylvia was too ill to come downstairs that day so I lunched with the Belvilles, and Amin took us to see a few more of the sights of Cairo in the afternoon. On account of my adventure there two nights before Clarissa was anxious to visit the City of the Dead so we drove through its desolate, uncanny, empty streets and afterwards visited the tombs of the Mamelukes.

Until Sylvia was well again we could not do much to prepare for the expedition which the Belvilles were still set on making; and for the moment I had come to a dead-end in my vendetta against O'Kieff. Zakri and Oonas were reported by the police to be still in Alexandria. Suliman Taufik, the owner of the now defunct House of the Angels, and Gamal had both been arrested; but O'Kieff had left the Mena House and entirely disappeared. It was a considerable satisfaction to know that I had at least dealt the enemy two most effective blows, in packing up one of their dope-dens and their de luxe white-slaving depot but, for the time being, as there did not seem to be any further way of getting at them, I filled in my time by going round with Harry and Clarissa.

On the second day after our return from Suez we went to see the Tutankhamen treasures in the Egyptian museum. I had seen them before but the Belvilles were utterly amazed, like most people who see them for the first time, at their variety and magnificence. The coloured reproductions of them which have appeared on postcards and in periodicals give but a poor idea of the actual treasures, since only a score or so of the most important objects have been selected for that purpose. The whole collection numbers over 1,700 items, each of which has some special interest on account of its uniqueness or beautiful workmanship, and fills two huge galleries; but perhaps the most staggering thing about the collection, as compared with other Egyptian antiques, is its perfect preservation. The gold and gems, the wood carving, ebony, ivory and alabaster are as fresh and bright as though they had come from the craftsman's shop only yesterday.

That afternoon the Belvilles drove out with Amin to see the Pyramids, which they had not yet visited, while I put in a few hours writing up this journal; but we arranged to meet again that night to see the Continental Cabaret, which is the best show of its kind in Cairo, and when we met there Clarissa said that Sylvia's doctor had agreed that she would be well enough to get up the following day.

The next morning the four of us got down to business. Sylvia was looking a little subdued, I thought. She had lost the hardness which had seemed to me such a prominent feature of her make-up at our first hectic meeting, and I liked her better in this chastened mood. I was glad to see that she greeted Harry and myself without the least embarrassment and that she looked fairly fit again; no worse, at all events, than if she had been confined to her room for a couple of days with a severe cold.

Harry produced the notes she had loaned him and she read them through for us. They began with the translation of the front of the top half of the tablet which ran:

'I, Heru-tem, make obeisance to thee, Osiris, Lord of Abydos, King of the Gods, Ruler of Eternity, whose names are manifold, whose transformations are sublime, whose form is hidden in the temples, whose Ka is holy. Homage to thee, Hathor-Isis, Divine Mother. To thee also, Horus, Royal Hawk, Great Son, Protector of Warriors. Intercede for me, Heru-tem, when the time of my trial cometh before thy august

197

Father in the dread hall of Maāti. For behold, I am a just person. I know the names of the forty-two assessors of the dead and can justify before them without fear.

'I was full of goodness and of gentle character and a ruler who loved his town. The hungry did not exist in my time even when there were years of famine. For behold, I ploughed the fields both north and south; thus I found food for its inhabitants and I gave them whatever it produced. I did not prefer a great person to a humble man: not a daughter of a poor man did I wrong, not a widow did I oppress. There was not a pauper round me; until the coming of the Persian there was not a hungry man in my time.

'Behold, I fought gallantly; I led my men into battle.'

It was here that the stele had been broken; the translation of the lower part of its front continued:

'In my chariot I was a mighty man. My arrows sped fast. I wielded my mace tirelessly, crushing the skulls of Pharaoh's enemies.

'It was the will of the Great Ones that Pharaoh should be chastened in my day. Pharaoh submitted to the Persian and the people knew a humiliation such as had never come upon them before in the whole history of the land. The gods were mocked; their statues were thrown down; the treasure of ages was looted from the temples; the shaven priests were sacrificed as an offering to strange gods; the tears of the people were more abundant than the waters of the Nile.

'In Thebes the Persian proclaimed himself Pharaoh and Lord of the Two Lands. His flail smote the peoples of the North and the peoples of the South. He commanded thy servant, Heru-tem, to appear before him. His captains had made known to him my strength and my valour. To take service under the Persian was abhorrent to me yet, behold, I did this thing that by his favour I might protect and feed the people of my town.

'There came a time when even the wealth of Thebes was not sufficient to satiate his greed. He styled himself King of Kings and willed that no people should escape the weight of his sceptre. Travellers filled his ears with tales of rich cities

which lay beyond the desert to the West. He planned to lead
his host out of Egypt for their conquest. The riches of the
distant Oasis of Amon enticed him. For many months he
made preparations for his journey, yet when the time came the
Great Ones willed that he should not march with his army.

'The wealth of the land was collected at Thebes. The host
was sent forth and behold, I, Heru-tem, was among them,
being a captain of a thousand. The Persian lay sick and was
to follow after. We journeyed through the Oases on the west
bank of the Nile (of Kharga and Dakhla); then for many days
across the sands by the way which has been prepared for us.
Each night we halted at the cisterns (water jar dumps) which
the advance-guard had placed against our coming; without
them we should have died of thirst.'

The translation was here continued from the back of the
upper portion of the stele

'We deviated neither to right nor left but marched in a
straight line as is the manner of the Persians.

'For twenty-two days we saw no man, nor wild life, nor
vegetation. For water we relied upon that which had been
buried; our food we carried with us. Three days more and
we should have reached the great Oasis; but the false Gods
of the Persians bore them not up; their guides betrayed them.
On the twenty-third day we were diverted by a ruse from the
line we should have followed. That night we failed to come
upon a cistern. The guides fled in the night and made off
secretly to the Oasis. For two days and two nights we marched
and counter-marched, striving to find our path. The third day
we turned back upon our tracks. Men were dying of thirst
when we found again the last cistern at which we had halted.
There was a half-ration of water for the men but none for
the horses. The chariots with their loads of treasure had to
be abandoned. The soldiers mutinied; many officers were
slaughtered.

'With me was the priest-astronomer, Khnemnu. Each night
he had taken observations of the stars. These are the readings
for the place where the treasure of Egypt was lost; the place
where the army of the Persian was stricken by the Great Ones

in their wisdom; so that of itself it fell to pieces, its thousands dying in terror and confusion.'

There followed a date from the old Egyptian calendar and numerous astronomical figures which meant nothing to us; but Sylvia said that Sir Walter had worked them all out during the previous spring and, reducing them to modern tables, had satisfied himself that the catastrophe had occurred in approximately Lat. 28° 10″ N. Long. 25° 33″ E. It was here, too, that the break in the tablet occurred again so that some of the date was on the upper part and the atronomical observations on the lower. In consequence the site of the treasure could not be calculated unless one had both halves of the tablet. Sylvia went on with the translation of the back of the lower portion which read:

'By thy grace, O Lord of millions upon millions of years, I, thy servant Heru-tem, chanced upon eight large water-jars buried apart from the rest. Five others (men) were with me. We watered our horses and escaped into the night leaving the dying army. Our water lasted six days and on the seventh we found another cistern. For a time we remained there regaining strength from the surplus left by the army. We set out again but the sand betrayed us. Khnemnu had many years and was the first to die. My companions followed him to thy bosom. O Lord Osiris. Count it unto me that although I was weak I gave each a burial according to the rites with such sustance as I had. I alone reached the Oasis (of Dakhla).

'The people gave me back my strength and I remained with them. Had I returned to Thebes to make known the loss of the whole army the Persian would have killed me. The people of the Oasis honoured me for my wisdom and made me a ruler among them. They gave me groves of date palms and I prospered. Behold, I dealt fairly with them; I gave them good counsel. For a score of years I lived happily among them.

'Guide my feet in the Hall of Truth, O Ruler of Eternity. O Lady Hathor, have compassion upon a simple man who has protected the weak. O Horus, Royal Son, intercede for a soldier who has not shirked danger. Order it that when my heart is weighed in the scales against the feather of Maäti that it may not depress the balance. See to it that my entrails

200

are not cast before Am-mit, the Eater of the Dead. Grant thou that I may sail down to Tattu like a living soul and that I may live for ever among the blessed in the Fields of Sekhet-Aaru.'

As Sylvia ceased we all sat silent for a moment. Those simple sentences brought 'the man who came back' strangely near to us. Actually he had died many centuries before Christ was born; yet it seemed as though the mists of time had dissolved for a moment and that he might have returned out of the desert only yesterday, so clear and convincing was the record which had come direct from him to us moderns of the age of steel.

Sylvia then produced the lists which she had made out before our arrival of things which she considered it would be necessary for us to take on our expedition. As Harry read them through carefully I suggested a few additions and we divided amongst us the work of getting them together. The vehicles for the convoy had been shipped out on the 'Hampshire'; the tents and most of the stores had already been ordered, but if we succeeded in finding the spot where Cambyses' army had foundered we should naturally want to dig up as much of the treasure as possible before returning; and once we left the Oasis of Dakhla behind we should be entirely cut off from any source of supply.

That meant we had to budget to make ourselves self-supporting for about five weeks in the desert and must carry with us an innumerable variety of items. As I listened to the long lists I soon saw why it was that, quite apart from the three thousand pounds Lemming had blackmailed out of her, Clarissa had had to sink such a large sum in this expedition.

As Mustapha was *hors-de-combat* I had warned Amin to be on hand and suggested that, if he was willing to go on the expedition, we should send him to Luxor ahead of us to select the men to go with us. We called him into conference and after I had promised, as was only fair, that if his licence as a guide was taken from him by the authorities, should it be discovered later that he had been involved with us in illegal digging, we would pay him an adequate sum in compensation. he willingly agreed to accompany us.

Although his general occupation was to show transient tourists the antiquities of the Nile Valley, on many occasions he had taken visitors with more leisure upon camping expeditions into the desert, so he went through our lists again with us and added a few more items which his experience told him might prove useful in emergencies. Once we had told him that it was buried treasure we were after he was delighted as a child at the whole idea of the trip. I knew we couldn't have a better man to pick the personnel of our caravan and it was arranged that he should start on the following morning for Luxor, where we would join him with our vehicles and stores five days later.

When he had left us I found there was still time before lunch to walk up to Groppi's and order myself a special supply of sweets, in hermetically-sealed tins, for the expedition. Five weeks is a longish period and as I strolled up the Kasr el Nil I was happily contemplating the vast assortment that I should be justified in buying at one fell swoop; together with the various kinds and their respective quantities.

I was just outside the Anglo-Egyptian bookshop and had got as far in my mental list as *Feuilletés Pralinés,* those delicious satin cushions striped like golden wasps which have thin layers of chocolate between their sugar instead of a solid chocolate centre, when I chanced to glance at a big limousine which had pulled up at the kerb owing to a traffic block. In it, large as life and twice as beautiful, was the Princess Oonas.

She was not looking in my direction and I did not realise for the moment that she would be unlikely to recognise me even if she saw me, since her last view of me was with the paint-daubed face of a Red Indian, so I swung round and dived into the bookshop.

A smiling Arab in European dress came forward to ask in what way he could serve me but I waved him hurriedly aside and, staring at the car, wondered what I could do about it.

Here was the trail once more; if only I could follow it. Sooner or later it was certain that Oonas would contact O'Kieff or Zakri Bey and, although the expedition to try to find Cambyses' treasure had now fired my imagination. I could rarely forget for long that, as far as I was concerned, it was only a fascinating side-issue.

With my mind in a whirl I stood gaping at the car until the traffic was released and it moved on. Suddenly I saw that whatever happened I must not lose track of Oonas now I had found her again. A bicycle was leaning against the kerb outside the shop.

'Is that yours?' I asked the bookseller quickly.

'It is my son's, sir,' he replied in some astonishment.

'Right!' I cried. 'I promise I'll bring it back and pay you for the loan but I've got to borrow it.'

In one leap I was across the pavement. Seizing the handle-bars I jumped into the saddle and began to pedal for dear life after the fast-disappearing limousine.

15

The Ancient Valley

Luckily there was another traffic block further up the street
so I managed to catch up the car before the jam moved
on again, but by that time we were within a hundred yards
of the Nile bridge and evidently the car was going over it
towards Gezira. Once it had crossed the river and reached
the open road I knew I should never be able to keep up with
it. I cast frantic glances right and left in search of a taxi but,
just as it happened, there was not a single empty one in sight.
In desperation I adopted the old errand-boy's trick of grabbing the back of the car with one hand so that it would tow me
along.

A policeman shouted at me angrily but I took no notice and
at a terrifying speed for a push bike, I was carried over the
bridge. On the grid of the car there was a big pile of luggage so
I assumed that Oonas had only just arrived in Cairo and was,
perhaps, going out to Mena House, since O'Kieff had put up
there during his short visit; but at the far side of the bridge
the car turned left along the Nile bank.

Another minute and it started to slow down; coming to a
halt opposite the landing stage where the tourist companies
keep their flat-bottomed steamers which take parties of visitors
to Egypt up and down the Nile. I pedalled on for another
hundred yards and dismounting from the bike took up my
position under a tall palm tree to watch events.

Oonas got out of the car and after her another woman whom
in my excitement I had not previously noticed. She was evidently a maid, as she was carrying a rug, a beauty box, and
various other items of Oonas' equipment. They both walked
down to the wooden landing-stage and up the gangway on to
one of the steamers that were moored there; upon which the
native stewards came running off to fetch the baggage from
the car.

Leaving the bike under the palm tree I strolled over to the wooden wharf and asked the man who was superintending the loading of the baggage what time the ship was due to sail.

'In a quarter of an hour, *effendi*,' he replied. 'We leave at one o'clock.'

'Are you full up?' I enquired.

He shook his head. 'Business is not what it was, *effendi*. In the old days every cabin was booked weeks in advance and if a passenger wanted to give up his cabin he could sell it at a premium. But in these times there is not so much money in the world and only in the high season are we fortunate enough to fill all our cabins.'

'Thanks,' I said, and slipping him five piastres, I hurried on board to see the purser.

He was a swiss and proved very amiable. He agreed at once that if I wished to come on the trip he could fix me up in a cabin with a private bathroom. 'But,' he said, 'how about your baggage. You have none, apparently, and we are due to sail in ten minutes.'

I pleaded with him to delay his departure just for half an hour. At first he refused but when I pointed out that, seeing the ship was not full, my passage money meant a clear profit to his company, he consented; although he laid it down very firmly that if I was not back by half-past one they would have to sail without me.

Fortunately, knowing that I might find myself in some unusual situations in my campaign against O'Kieff, I had landed in Egypt with a large sum of ready money on me which I kept in a money belt strapped round my waist, so I promptly undid it and paid my passage as an earnest of good faith.

Once on the shore again I seized the push bike and putting every ounce into my flying feet streaked across the bridge back to the bookshop, where the owner was unfeignedly glad to see me and his son's cycle again. I offered to pay for the loan of it but he would not hear of this and seemed a most friendly fellow, so I bought half-a-dozen of the latest novels and told him to send them to Sylvia at the Continental.

Ten minutes had gone but in a further five a taxi got me back to Shepheard's where I had the hall-porter send up men for my baggage right away. Another ten minutes went in cramming my things into my trunks just anyhow and while the porters were carrying them downstairs I scribbled a note to Harry: 'Oonas on Nile boat leaving 1.30 today, didn't see its name. Am going too. Trip to Luxor takes six days. You'll be just in time to meet me there arriving same day by rail. Love to Clarissa and Sylvia. See you in Luxor. Julian.'

As I had stayed for some weeks at Shepheard's during the previous winter, the management knew me well enough to trust me for my bill and promised to send it on to the Winter Palace at Luxor. I left the note for Harry with the porter and dived back into the taxi. It was sixteen minutes past one when I left Shepheard's and twenty-seven past by the time I got back to the wharf. I was on board with two minutes to spare. It was only then I realised that I could easily have made all my arrangements at my leisure and by hiring a car for the twenty-miles' run to Sakkara have joined the ship there any time up to five o'clock that afternoon; but that's the sort of fool I make of myself when I act on quick decisions.

None of the passengers was about when I reached the ship and as the purser showed me to my cabin he told me that they had all gone in to lunch; so I left my unpacking till afterwards and went straight down to the dining-saloon on the lower deck.

It was a long, narrow room, the width of the ship and roughly a third of its length; about thirty people were feeding there but several tables were still vacant and I was given one to myself. Oonas was seated facing me on her own at a table about fifteen away.

As I sat down I looked straight across the intervening table, which was occupied by two elderly women, at Oonas and saw that she was looking at me, as indeed were most of the other people. Doubtless they had been summing up their fellow-passengers at this first meal of the voyage and, having had a quarter of an hour to study each other, it was natural that they should now concentrate their attention covertly upon the solitary late-comer.

Oonas' face showed no trace of expression as her large blue eyes swept over me and then transferred their gaze to the other side of the saloon. Knowing she was short-sighted I had not expected for one moment that she would know me at the first glance. The all-important test would come later, when I first spoke to her, as my voice was much more likely to give me away than my appearance. If she remembered it as that of the man who had impersonated Lemming my six-day trip was almost certain to be wasted, but if she did not know me again there was a reasonable chance that I might become sufficiently friendly with her to learn quite a lot of interesting things.

The other passengers looked a dull lot; there were more women than men and most of them were middle-aged or elderly, the majority, from such scraps of conversation as I could catch and their style of dressing, appeared to be Americans. There was only one really good-looking girl among them and she was deep in conversation with an equally attractive young man, which suggested that they might be honeymooners as later I found to be the case.

The ship had cast off directly I had come aboard so we were now chugging up the river and I turned my attention to the colourful spectacle outside the windows. I should explain, perhaps, that these Nile steamers have little resemblance to an ordinary ship. They are three-decker paddle-boats with flat bottoms, drawing only a few feet of water, and are almost entirely composed of superstructure, so one gets an equally good view of the passing scene from any of the three decks and it is rather as though one were being propelled along the river in a glorified house-boat. The lower deck contains the dining-saloon and engines; the main deck is mostly cabins, with a comfortable bar at the forward end, and the upper deck is divided into de luxe cabins aft with a drawing-room and a glassed-in observation-lounge forward. For anyone who is a bad sailor but finds life on shipboard attractive in other respects a Nile boat provides the perfect vehicle, since during the whole passage the river is as smooth as a mill-pond yet one gets the illusion of ocean travel from one's immediate surroundings.

The food proved better than I had expected although, owing to my own lateness, I was hurried through lunch to catch up with the others. When dessert was served a gorgeously-robed Arab appeared, took up his position at the end of the saloon and bowed theatrically to right and left of him, clapping his hands for silence. He then began in a loud voice:

'Ladies and gentlemens, I am Mahmoud, your guide for the

Nile voyage. Each night we anchor some place in the middle of the river where you sleep very comfortable away from the little biting insects. Each day we go ashore some place and I show you, please, many interesting things.'

He then proceeded to give, for the benefit of the uninitiated, an abbreviated and somewhat facetious history of Ancient Egypt.

'The Nile Valley, ladies and gentlemans, has been inhabited very long time. Desert very difficult to cross on west side and east side also make it no fun for bad mens to raid the Egyptian peoples. They develop the civilisation untroubled by invaders for many many centuries and learn to make many beautiful things.

'The history of these people is in three parts, yes. Altogether thirty-three Dynasties of Kings rule over the Egyptian peoples for four thousand years; but not all these Dynasties matter very much, oh no!

'First come the Old Kingdom. Many of you in Cairo visit the Pyramids, perhaps. The Great Pyramids you see at Mena are built in the time of the Old Kingdom by the Pharaohs of the IVth Dynasty. The Vth Dynasty Kings also very powerful. This afternoon we visit Sakkara where we see the Step Pyramid and tombs of the VIth Dynasty, also very powerful. It finishes, this wonderful Old Kingdom, about 2,600 years before Christ.

'There is then civil war. For 500 years history is black-out. We only know that at latest the Princes of Thebes, which we now call Luxor, conquer all the land and become the XIth Dynasty which found the Middle Kingdom. The XIIth Dynasty follows, also very great people. At Beni Hassan I show you some of the XIIth-Dynasty tombs but much trace of the Middle Kingdom is not left, oh no, because they build not so big as the Old Kingdom and where they make temples those who come after build on top.

'The XIVth Dynasty is what we call Shepherd Kings. They come from no one knows where, Palestine perhaps. They are not Egyptians and they conquer all. The Middle Kingdom is finish.

'Another 400 years goes away, poof! There comes another Dynasty of pure Egyptian Kings, the XVIIIth. This is the start of what we call the Empire because they rule in Egypt and conquer Sudan and Mesopotamia also. In it there reigned the great Hat-shep-sut, the Queen Elizabeth of Egypt. She, what you call, wear the trousers and put her husband and son right in the back place. Also then reigned Tothmes IIIrd, the Napoleon of the ancient world. With the XIXth Dynasty we have Seti I and Rameses II called the Great, because he put up so many statues to himself. After come the XXth Dynasty with many other Pharaohs bearing the same name, Rameses, but not so great. With them finish the XXth Dynasty and the Empire, about 1,100 B.C.

'Of the Empire we have many remains. You see, perhaps, the treasures of Tut-ankh-amen in Cairo. These are of the Empire XVIIIth Dynasty 1360 B.C. At Luxor and other place I show you many fine temples of Empire period; greatest in Egypt. Also tombs in Valley of Kings, XVIIIth, XIXth and XXth Dynasty.

'After the Empire much troubles again. Later come the Persians and the Greeks. The latest make new capital at Alexandria and found the last Dynasty of Egypt before the Roman conquest, number XXXIII. It last 300 years and end with Cleopatra; what a girl, eh! The Ptolemies build much. I show you their temples at Dendrah and Edfu; best-preserved in Egypt but very decadent. The true history of Egypt, ladies and gentlemens, lies in those Dynasties of which I tell you, the IVth, Vth and VIth of the Old Kingdom, the XIth and XIIth of the Middle Kingdom, and the XVIIIth, XIXth and XXth of the Empire.

'This afternoon at three o'clock we make excursion by car to Sakkara, visiting the two colossal statues of Rameses II, the beautiful alabaster sphinx, the Serapeum where are the tombs of the Sacred Bulls, also those of the Old Kingdom nobles Ti and Ptah-Hotep with their very nice coloured scenes depicting the life of Egypt five thousand years ago. Afterwards we return by way of the site of ancient Memphis which was the capital of old Egypt; we come on board for nice-cup-of-tea and continue our voyage. You all have your tickets for visit the ancient monuments, yes. You bring them, please. No tickets no in; no galloping donkeys. Thank you very much. Much pleasures, ladies and gentlemens.'

I knew at once that I for one was not going to enjoy Mr. Mahmoud's ministrations as guide, philosopher and friend. He was doubtless quite a good fellow in his way but any real interest in his job had probably long ago been undermined by dreary repetitions of parrot-learned lectures delivered mainly to abysmally ignorant tourists who did not know the first thing about Ancient Egypt. His ingratiating semi-comic style of address had doubtless been developed as the best method of getting good tips out his simple-minded charges, but I could see that he would be little use to any Europeans who had read, even casually, a certain amount about the Egyptian civilisation.

When we went ashore that afternoon my impression was confirmed. At each of the places we visited he reeled off his patter interspersed with jokes which were doubtless hoary with age but nevertheless raised a laugh among the tourists, many of whom had only just arrived in the country; but the thing that annoyed me most was that he didn't even know his stuff thoroughly. He was correct in the main but his knowledge of Egyptian history was extremely sketchy and when he was questioned about the lesser gods of the vast Egyptian pantheon he got hopelessly confused; while about the symbolism of the religion and its wonderful inner meaning he knew absolutely nothing. I suppose that didn't make the least difference to the majority of his audience but I found it intensely irritating and after a while I wandered off on my own.

I had visited Sakkara before and done it very thoroughly with Amin, spending several days out there the previous winter; but the paintings in the tombs showing the Egyptians hunting, fishing, counting their cattle, dancing and harvesting are so fresh, so colourful and of such infinite variety that I was only too delighted to have the chance of visiting them again. I remained there while Mahmoud took the crowd to see the Tomb of the Bulls, which is far bigger than the one in which I had taken refuge in Alexandria, but merely a series of great man-made sandstone caves without any paintings or carvings on its walls.

On our way back we passed through the acres and acres of beautiful palm groves which now cover the site where once stood the mighty city of Memphis with its five million inhabitants. Not a brick or stone remains of that once teeming city which for thousands of years thrived and flourished as the great metropolis of the Nile Valley; but the cars pulled up in the middle of it and we got out to see the two colossal statues of Rameses the Great, who flourished about 1250 B.C.

One statue is badly cracked and Mahmoud informed us that the damage had occurred during the great 'erti-quake'—that was how he pronounced it—of A.D. 27. The earthquake he referred to was an extremely serious one and damaged many of the statues and temples throughout the whole of the Nile Valley but it happened, as I knew quite well, not in A.D. but in B.C. 27 and, by this time, thoroughly irritated with the man, I said so.

He smiled deprecatingly and assured me I was wrong, upon which I promptly bet him a pound that I was right and offered to verify the fact from a guide-book when we got back to the ship; but he wouldn't take me.

It was, perhaps, a little unkind of me to have made him look a fool in front of the goggle-eyed group who were hanging on his every word and to undermine their faith in him for the rest of the voyage; but one good thing came out of this little passage of arms.

I had studiously avoided attempting to make any contact with Oonas during the excursion, but at the moment when I had contradicted Mahmoud she had been standing only a few feet away from us. As the party moved off, she left her maid who had been tagging round behind her all the afternoon, and came up beside me.

'I am so glad,' she said in halting English, 'that you tick off that stupid man. It is an insult that people of intelligence should be expected to listen to him.'

'Thanks,' I said. 'It's nice to hear you say that because I was feeling rather a cad about it. To most of these people it doesn't make the slightest difference in what year the earthquake happened and I suppose he's doing his job as well as he knows how.'

'That is no point at all,' she went on hurriedly. 'These peoples come to visit my country and learn about its great past. They should be told right even if they are stupids who have not so much knowledge of history.'

You can imagine how delighted I was that she had contacted

211

me herself and, quite obviously, regarded me as a complete stranger. Regardless of tourist etiquette, by which each person having secured a seat in a car sticks to it throughout the whole journey, I calmly got into the one in which she had been going from point to point and studiously ignored the old gentleman whose seat I had taken.

'So you're an Egyptian?' I smiled at Oonas. 'It's rather surprising to find anybody who actually lives in the country making a trip like this with a bunch of tourists.'

She laughed then. 'Is it not the same the big world over? The foreigner in London, he runs to see Westminster Abbey and the Tower but the Londoner who lives there all his life, no, he never makes the visit. I have lived most of my life in Egypt but what do I know of our great monuments? Nothing at all. A year ago I read a novel which is about Ancient Egypt. I become interest in the old time of my country and read more —big, serious books about it. I go to Luxor last winter and I become fascinate by the wonderful things there. Now I go again, but by the Nile ship, so that I can make visit the places I have not seen on the way.'

This statement showed Oonas to me in a completely different light from that of the beautiful little vamp I had met in Alex.; but, after all, because a person is mixed up in criminal activities that is no reason whatsoever why they should not have interests outside their work, like other people. Evidently Oonas had brains and a serious side to her character, and since she was going to Luxor it was quite reasonable that she should have chosen this way of making the journey.

When we got back to the ship tea was served in the observation-lounge while the steamer pushed off and began to chug its way again up the river. Quite naturally Oonas and I sat down to a table and had tea together. It was then she asked me if I spoke French and when she learned that I did it was agreed we should speak it as that made conversation so much easier for her.

The only male on board, other than myself, who might have intrigued her was the handsome young American, but he was glued to his good-looking wife so I had nothing to fear from possible rivals and I began to congratulate myself on my good fortune. Here was an exceedingly beautiful young woman who had interests in common with my own and it was my particular job to get to know her as well as possible. It seemed that business might be combined with considerable pleasure.

We parted to change for dinner but got together again immediately afterwards for coffee and liqueurs, and she said at once how stupid we had been to eat the meal at separate tables when we might quite well have shared one between us. I had thought of that already but I wanted Oonas to make the running, at all events to begin with, so that she could have no possible suspicion that I had any motives for wanting to see as much of her as possible, other than those normal to a young man on meeting an attractive girl, but it was decided then and there that for the rest of the voyage we should have our meals together.

I soon found that in addition to beauty this little Egyptian princess had a quick, lively mind and an excellent education. The fact that she was not pure white did not bother me in the least as she was an aristocrat to her finger-tips and her abnormally large blue eyes put her right outside the category of a 'coloured woman.' She was rather small, coming only up to my shoulder, but she had the right sorts of curves just where they should be and was extremely soignée. I have always been interested in women's clothes and I could see with half an eye that all her things came from the best places. The lovely flame-coloured thing she was wearing that evening positively screamed Schiaparelli.

We anchored off El Wasta that night at about eleven and most of the passengers drifted off to their cabins. Oonas and I sat on for a little while, but when she said she thought it was time for bed I did not press her to stay up longer as I knew that we had plenty of time before us.

The second day of the Nile voyage is the least interesting of the whole journey as there are no ruined temples or ancient monuments on either bank during the hundred-mile run; but I was much more interested in Oonas than in Ancient Egypt by that time and we spent a delightful day together.

Immediately after breakfast I secured a couple of armchairs right in the very front of the observation-lounge where one could get an uninterrupted view of the ever-changing scene as it unfolded on the approach of the steamer. I had a job to retain the extra chair as half-a-dozen people tried to grab it off me and showed barely-veiled resentment when I insisted that it was already taken; but I had not the least interest in any of the other passengers and stuck to it like a leech until Oonas put in an apprence and, I was pleased to see, came straight over to me.

It was one of those days all too rare in most life-times when one has nothing to do and all day in which to do it; and what could be fairer than to spend it in the immediate vicinity of an exotic beauty who is quite prepared to give one her undivided attention?

She told me a lot about herself, her travels abroad and her home-life in Alexandria; but she made no mention whatever of Zakri or anything which appeared to have the least connection with the people I was after and I was much too wily to ask her any leading questions so early in the game.

For the time being I was content to take what the kind gods had sent me and watch the broad, calmly-flowing river with its picturesque native craft. Long vistas of cultivated country stretched to the ridge of hills which marked the beginning of the desert on either side, and in the fields unhurried labourers were tending their crops with just the same primitive methods that had been used season after season for countless generations by their ancestors.

Occasionally we passed a grove of date palms near which there nestled a mud-walled village where noisy children stopped playing in the dirt to hail us from the river-bank. Every mile or so we saw a water-wheel with a game little donkey staggering round and round it; or that even more primitive method of irrigation in which half-a-dozen natives, stripped to the skin and sweating in the sunshine, levered buckets of water on long poles from stage to stage up the river-bank until it could be poured into the channels of the fields.

It is virtually slave labour, as they continue their monontonous task from dawn to dusk for about eightpence a day, but perhaps even such a dreary existence has some compensations. Storms are almost unknown in that sheltered valley, where it is always spring or summer, so a mud hut which costs nothing to build and can be erected in a couple of days is adequate shelter thus disposing of the problem of rent. The mild climate makes clothes unnecessary, except for a single cotton gown, and the fertile land with its modern irrigation system makes the more common kinds of food incredibly cheap and abun-dant. The standard of life of the peasantry is amazingly low but they are always laughing and joking together and if they lack the benefits of cinemas and night-schools at least they do not have to worry themselves about gold-standards or gas-masks; and they are not even aware of the existence of Czechoslovakia, Spain or China.

One of the most fascinating things about the Nile voyage is the splendour of the sunsets; nowhere else in the world have I ever seen such unbelievably fantastic colouring and they are no rare phenomena but, owing to the almost unchanging climate, occur regularly day after day. As the sky is nearly always cloudless the sunset lasts for the best part of half-an-hour while the scene gradually changes, the bright, hard blues and yellows of sky and sand taking on softer hues in the even-ing light until at last the outstanding objects on the west bank are silhouetted, as though cut from black cardboard, against the gold-and-orange glory of the dying sun which sinks un-seen into the desert beyond.

While Oonas and I were watching it that evening a small caravan of some twenty camels, moving in single file, passed along some high ground on the western bank towards a small palm grove which fringed a native village, and the beauty of that silent procession in the distance against the flaming sunset utterly defies description.

That night for dinner we split a bottle of champagne and afterwards decided that we would get our coats and sit out on the deck where we could talk more freely than in the crowded lounge. Since the previous afternoon we had spent some four-teen hours in each other's company and we had discussed a vast variety of subjects, from Egyptology to Paris fashions, and from Chinese ancestor-worship to, inevitably, love. So it was not unnatural that having once reached that all-important topic, whatever else we touched on while we sat there watching the rise of the Egyptian moon, we should come round again and again to the old, intriguing mystery.

When I asked Oonas if she ever thought of marriage, she told me that she had been married at the age of sixteen; had been a widow at nineteen and was now twenty-one. Having inherited a fortune which made her independent she had stoutly resisted all her family's efforts to marry her off again; not, as she said with enchanting frankness, because she had found the connubial state unattractive, but because she had definitely made up her mind that for the next ten years, at least, she was not going to tie herself to any one man. In response I made it clear that while I too was all for the bliss which some aspects of marriage implied, I certainly had no intention of tying myself up to one woman yet awhile.

Having put our cards on the table we fell a little silent, but it was a pleasant silence warmed by the fact that each of us was unquestionably attracted to the other and, knowing it, dwelt happily upon the possibilities of the situation. For my part the knowledge that Oonas was mixed up in O'Kieff's organisation, and probably in some respects an extremely unscrupulous young woman, interfered in no way with my feelings. If I could get anything out of her which would help me against O'Kieff, so much the better; if not, I meant to regard the trip as a holiday and I saw no reason in the world why I should not make the most of her obvious liking for me.

When at last we stood up to go to bed I suddenly took her in my arms, lifted her right off her feet and kissed her. For a delicious moment her soft, warm little body clung against mine as she freely gave me her mouth but, after that moment, without the slightest warning she suddenly bit me viciously in the lower lip. It was a sharp and most painful warning that she really was the little vixen I believed her to be. As I dropped her she sprang away from me, dodged behind the seat where we had been sitting and ran off to her cabin laughing hilariously.

I had half a mind to follow her and administer the spanking she undoubtedly deserved but, on second thoughts, I realised that she was a sufficiently old hand at the game to know that anticipation is half the pleasure in a love-affair. She was, I felt certain, perfectly willing to be taken but only in her own time and tonight she had let me go just as far as she meant me to.

The following morning I bagged the two best places in the observation-lounge again but there was no opportunity to use them as we had set off from Minia, where we had anchored for the night, shortly after dawn and soon after breakfast pulled

216

into the river bank at Beni Hassan, where we were to go ashore.

Oonas appeared on deck just as the little crowd of tourists, loaded down with cameras, binoculars, fly-whisks and parasols, were filing down the gangway. I saw her quickly suppress a wicked little smile as she noticed my slightly swollen lower lip when she wished me good-morning, but I made no mention of our encounter that night before and immediately dropped into my rôle of escort.

Beni Hassan is not a particularly exciting spot as there is little there to see except a long terrace high in the cliff above the village where there are about thirty or forty XIth and XIIth Dynasty rock tombs; in consequence there are no cars to be had in the place and the excursion has to be made on donkeys; which are brought in from their work in the fields by the peasants as a Nile steamer makes a call. Oonas evidently knew the drill as her lower limbs were encased this morning in a pair of workman-like jodhpores and she carried a little riding-switch.

The donkeys are, of course, hired *en masse* by the companies that run the ships but their owners seem to live from visit to visit on the anticipation of a tip and each donkey appears to have at least three owners. It was as though Babel had broken loose on the bank of the river, as dozens of Arabs urged each passenger to take *their* donkeys, and the confusion was added to by scores of others endeavouring to sell neacklaces of beads, fake antiques, hand-made rugs and all sorts of other junk.

I managed to secure two of the less flea-bitten-looking animals for Oonas and myself and without waiting for the others we set off up the track to the rock tombs which looked like so many windows in a vast façade. Conversation was almost impossible as we had six or eight Arabs of varying ages jabbering about us, urging on the donkeys when we wanted them to walk or grabbing their reins and pulling them back when we had settled into a comfortable trot; without ceasing they sang their own praises in our ears—old gentlemen that they were 'best fellow donkeyboy,' and urchins screaming for *baksheesh* or cigarettes.

This wretched pestering is one of the things which the traveller to Egypt has to set off against the glory of the sunsets and the interest of the ancient monuments. Wherever one goes one is beset by these hordes of beggars who destroy half one's pleasure in visiting the sights and, for the ordinary traveller, there is no way of getting rid of them, since a present of money only incites them to yelp for more.

It is, however, possible to silence them and drive them off if one is sufficiently acquainted with their native tongue. I was just about to launch into a stream of Arabic when I suddenly remembered that Oonas was not aware I could speak it and it occurred to me that an occasion might arise later where that might stand me in good stead if I continued to conceal my knowledge of the language from her. As it happened, my reticence that morning was to save my life only a few hours later and the beggars were dispersed without any effort on my part. Oonas, who obviously regarded them only as human cattle, began to lay about her with her riding-switch while she hissed out just what she thought of them, their fathers, mothers and remotest ancestors; not forgetting the kind of offspring they were likely to produce in time to come.

We visited only three of the tombs; they were just a series of large, square chambers hewn out of the living rock and their wall-paintings had little of the beauty of those at Sakkara which had been made many centuries earlier. In the old days Egypt was divided into thirty *nomes* or provinces and Beni Hassan was the capital of the Gazelle Nome. The best-preserved tomb there is that of one, Kheti, who lived during the Middle Kingdom, about 2100 B.C., and was the *monarch* or governor of the nome. The next most interesting is the somewhat larger one of a Prince Khnem-hotep which has among its paintings a representation of the migration of Asiatic tribes into Egypt. Mahmoud told us that it was supposed to be Joseph and his brethren, but this idea has been exploded long ago; although it is the first known painting of beared Semites being received into the Land of the Pharaohs.

We lunched on board while sailing up the river and, at three o'clock in the afternoon, halted at Tel-el-Amarna where we were to go ashore again.

Here, on the east bank, the desert runs right up to the Nile and it is that which has saved the ancient city from complete destruction. All the other cities of the old civilisation were built in fertile regions so when they fell into decay the land was ploughed over or planted with palms, wiping out all trace of them entirely; but here there was no object in ploughing up a waterless, sandy waste and so after 3,000 years the lower walls of row upon row of the brick houses which formed the streets can still be seen.

There are the ruins of the palace, too, quite near the river bank, but apart from these relics of the long-dead city there is very little of interest to the casual traveller. Tel-el-Amarna does have, however, a very special interest for anybody who has read even a little about Egyptian history.

When the New Empire was at the height of its magnificence under the mighty XVIIIth Dynasty which ruled from the Sudan right across to Mesopotamia, a nobleman called Iuaa and his wife Thuau were responsible for altering Egypt's destiny. They were not pure Egyptians but foreigners who had been ennobled and their daughter Ti became the queen of Amenophis III. When that Pharaoh died this foreign Queen and her parents brought up the new Pharaoh, her young son Amenophis IV, in strange doctrines.

She taught him that the Egyptians were wrong to worship many gods and that there was only one God who was the father not only of the Egyptians but of all peoples; and that he was represented in the solar disc which gave warmth and light to all. The young Pharaoh became a fanatical convert to his mother's belief, changed his name to Akhen-aton, meaning 'Beloved of the Sun's Disc,' ordered his people to observe the new religion and defied the mighty priesthood of the old gods in his capital of Thebes.

The history of Egypt for the next decade is the story of the so-called 'Heretic' Pharaoh's struggle against the priests of Amen. It was on finding that he could not subdue them in his capital that he decided to build a new city for himself further down the river at Tel-el-Amarna.

Akhen-aton was certainly one of the great reformers of the world and many people have compared the religion he preached with Christianity, since its main tenets were love, simplicity and naturalness; although it differed from Christianity in its intense devotion to every form of beauty in this present life. Akhen-aton's reign was not a long one but he left an indelible mark upon his country because he revolutionised art and favoured the faithful portrayal of all things in a natural manner as opposed to the conventionality and symbolism which had been enforced upon all Egyptian artists by the priesthood for centuries.

Having built his new city at Tel-el-Amarna with extraordinary speed he went there to live the life of a dreamer and philosopher; but, in the meantime, his great empire was falling into decay. He would give his generals no instructions for the defence of his cities in Palestine but talked to them only of brotherly love or kept them waiting for days in his antechambers refusing even to see them.

On his death he was succeeded by his young son, who had been brought up in his doctrine, but by that time the remnants of the Egyptian armies had been driven back into Egypt and the whole country was falling into chaos. The boy soon fell under the power of the old priesthood who took him back to Thebes and rechristened him Tut-ankh-amen; but his reign was short and while still in his teens he was buried in the now world-famous tomb. The 'heretical' doctrines had meanwhile been suppressed; an able general called Horemheb became the next Pharaoh, founded the XIXth Dynasty and drove out the Semitic invaders; but Egypt never recovered the rich cities and great territories in Asia that had been lost to her by the dreamer Akhan-aton.

Oonas and I secured a couple of strong-looking donkeys, drove off the local beggars and rode through the palms fringing the top of the river-bank to the ruins of the 'Heretic' Pharaoh's palace. From this point we could survey the whole site of the dead city, which occupies a wide, flat area broken only by rows and rows of low mounds where the buildings used to be, and is ringed in by a horse-shoe of hills the centre of which was about five miles distant.

Mahmoud was rallying his party to ride right across the plain to inspect some rock tombs in the hills, but we were sick both of his patter and the crowd so, having talked it over, we decided it would be much more fun to visit Akhen-aton's own tomb, which lies a mile or two further inland. In the light of later events I feel sure it must have been Oonas who first made this suggestion but she put it so skilfully that, at the time, I was quite under the impression it was my own idea.

As the crowd trotted off after Mahmoud accompanied by ninety-eight per cent of the male population of the village we turned aside and, producing some piastres, I asked Oonas to bribe our donkey boys to leave us to our own devices. She spoke to them in Arabic and with broad grins on their faces they took the money, pointed out the way and stood aside while we cantered off together.

The track to Akhen-aton's tomb passes through a gap in the hills, then follows a shallow *wady*. Even in the strong sunlight it was a little eerie there, as once we had left the native village behind us there was no sign whatever of the hand of man and we might have been a hundred miles from any human habitation, but the rocks on either side were full of colour while here and there were patches of tiny desert daisies and dwarf shrubs which manage to exist in some waste places entirely without water except the little they can absorb from the nightly dew.

The way was longer than I had thought and although our animals were game little beasts we had to walk them most of the way, so it must have been a good hour-and-a-quarter from the time we left the river bank before we reached our destination.

A solitary mud-walled dwelling, which had round the edge of its roof a decorative row of things like inverted water-jars which are used for nesting pigeons, stood about a hundred yards from the iron gates of the tomb. A tousled-haired girl who was making bread outside it brushed the crawling flies from her eyes and went in to get her father. He was a villainous-looking fellow and emerged carrying an ancient fowling-piece, perhaps as a symbol of his tomb-guardianship, but having begged a cigarette he accompanied us to the tomb and unlocked it. We tethered the donkeys to a rock and went inside.

The tomb was hardly worth a visit except for the fact that it once contained the remains of a man who started a new religion and still makes his personality felt through the artistic revolution which he brought about, whereas countless other monarchs who reigned centuries after him have passed into complete oblivion.

The wall-paintings were not in very good repair and they did not consist of portraits of the Pharaoh making offerings to a long line of gods and goddesses, as is usual in the tombs of the Egyptian Kings. Instead there were numerous representations of the sun's disc with rays in the form of straight lines radiating from it, each of which had a hand at its end, symbolising the light and life given by the sun to the Pharaoh, his family and all living things. When we got outside I tipped the tomb-guardian and he went off to his hovel. Then, as on looking at my watch I found that time was getting on, I said I thought we ought to start back right away.

Oonas did not share my view. She said that it was barely half-past four and that as the boat was only going up to Beni Mohammed to anchor for the night, after leaving Tel-el-Amarna, she saw no reason why we should hurry.

'It will take us an hour and a quarter to ride back,' I said, 'so we won't make it much before six. I doubt if the party will remain ashore for more than three hours so we'll only just do it by leaving now, as it is.'

'Are you afraid that the boat will sail without us?'

'Oh, no,' I smiled. 'However late we are it won't do that. They may think we've got lost and send out a search-party from the village, but it would be as much as the Purser's job is worth to leave two of his passengers marooned in a place like Tel-el-Amarna.'

'Well, then,' she pouted. 'What are you worrying about? The ride has tired me. You are unkind and have no consideration. I must rest a little before I mount that silly animal again.'

'It isn't that I want to hurry you in the least,' I assured her. 'But if the ship is due to sail at six and has to wait for us, think of the tittle-tattle it's bound to cause among the passengers.'

'If it is that you are frightened of, you'd better go back alone,' she shrugged. 'I can find my way without you.'

'As though I care what those stuffy people say about me! They are only a stupid rabble. But I waste my breath in arguing with you. It is obvious that you must be tired of my company since you are in such a hurry to get back on board.'

'Now, really!' I protested. 'That's utter nonsense and you know it.'

'Well then, forget the stupid ship and let me rest for a little while. My poor legs are absolutely giving under me. Come and sit down here.'

I will confess that I did not really need very much persuasion. She looked such a forlorn little figure standing there in the silent, deserted valley and her face was quite adorable under her dark, curling hair. What did it matter if the ship's departure were to be delayed for a little and we were to provide a crowd of people in whom we had not the least interest with matter for a mild scandal?

'As long as you're game to stay here, I am,' I smiled as she sat down in front of a big boulder. 'But I don't think your back can be very comfortable against that rock. Wouldn't it be nicer for you if you leaned against my shoulder?'

Suiting the action to the word I put my arm round her and she nestled her head down on my chest.

'No biting this time,' I said softly.

She laughed. 'You must take your chance of that.'

I took it, with results extremely satisfactory to all concerned, and we snuggled down together warmly embraced in the loose, soft sand.

How long we remained like that I don't really know; however long it was the time was all too short, because Oonas and I were no novices at the delightful game we were playing and, within limits, she let me love her to my heart's content. It is a game that cannot be played indefinitely when there is a limit, though; and it was she who broke the party up by saying:

'We've lots of time before us, darling, and I'm afraid I'm a little too sophisticated to be quite contented with a bed of sand. I think we ought to get back to the village and that wretched ship.'

We kissed again and, standing up, shook the sand out of our clothes, mounted our donkeys and rode back down the valley. The time had passed quickly as it always does on such occasions and although we hurried our donkeys as much as we could, before we got back the sun was beginning to set.

I knew that by this time the Purser must be cursing us wholeheartedly and visualised the gossip-avid passengers lining the rail as they watched for our return; but there was one thing I had not bargained for. When we reached the palm-fringed bank above the place where we had come ashore the ship was no longer there.

223

16

Old Nick's Own Daughter

I knew well enough that we were shockingly late and had no valid excuse to offer; although with Oonas' shapely arms arms round my neck I would not have been human if I had insisted on breaking up our party at the tomb earlier. But that was not the point. For all the Purser and that facetious fool Mahmoud could know we might be lost somewhere out in the desert, with night approaching. They were responsible for us and it was positively disgraceful that they should have gone off like this. I could only imagine that it was sheer slackness and that they believed we had come aboard with the other passengers. Fuming with rage I considered the position. The ship was due to anchor that evening at Beni Mohammed and although I had no map with me to check the distance I was under the impression that it was a good thirty miles upstream. How to get back on board that night presented the devil of a problem.

'We're in a proper mess!' I exclaimed as we brought our perspiring donkeys to a halt on the outskirts of the village.

To my surprise Oonas suddenly laughed.

I turned in my saddle and looked at her. 'It's all very well, but being stranded here is no joke. If this were a bigger place we could hire a motor-boat and catch them up, but you can see for yourself that there are only a couple of sailing-craft down by the river. We could get across in one of those and the railway's probably not more than two or three miles inland from the other bank; that's about our only hope.'

She shook her head. 'No good, my dear. All we could do on donkeys would be to reach some local halt and trains only stop at such places once a day, at most.'

'In that case we won't be able to get back to the ship until tomorrow at the earliest. I'm afraid your reputation will be in ribbons by that time.'

'How nice of you to be so worried for me; but you have no need to be. I do not care two hoots what those people think.'

Her indifference to possible scandal certainly made things easier for me but, all the same, I was far from being happy about the turn things had taken. I make no pretence whatever to being a saint and, seeing the way things were shaping between us, I was perfectly capable of having deliberately planned that we should miss the ship but, now that it had happened fortuitously, I had a curious feeling of responsibility for her. I think she almost read my thoughts, as she went on with a wicked little smile:

It doesn't seem to have occurred to you that most men would consider themselves extremely lucky at having to spend a night on shore alone with me. This little adventure might prove rather fun, you know.'

Not wishing to appear a prude. I hid these strange reactions, which puzzled even myself, by protesting quickly: 'My dear, it's the sort of thing I would have given my eyes for if we hadn't landed up in this miserable little dorp. I'm sure you don't like fleas and lice any more than I do. What I'm really worrying about is where we can spend the night.'

She shrugged and cast a glance at the village, which consisted of no more than a score of native hutments:

'Allah will provide.'

A crowd of men and boys were already hurrying towards us and Oonas questioned them as they came running up. The ship had waited for an hour past its proper time of departure but when we had failed to return the Purser had left a message with the local Sheik to say that if we were not back by sundown a party was to be sent out to find us. He had asked him to express his regret at having to leave us behind and say that he dared not delay the sailing of the ship any longer; otherwise she would not be able to get into her proper anchorage at Beni Mohammed before dark. That was a reason for his sailing I had not thought of and, of course, it *was* the passengers' responsibility to get back at the proper time after each excursion.

The Sheik, an old man with a friendly twinkle in his rheumy eyes, came hobbling up with the aid of a long stick, and I asked Oonas to enquire from him about the possibility of trains; but it seemed that her gloomy forebodings were justified. The nearest halt on the far side of the river was a place called Deir Mowas but trains only stopped at it three times a week. A south-bound train was due the following morning but until then we were stuck.

He had, however, one cheering piece of news for us. Oonas' maid had left the ship just before it sailed and was now in the village with her mistress' luggage. We asked the Sheik what accommodation there was to be had and the none-too-clean old man placed his house at our disposal with the lordly courtesy of one offering a palace.

Dismounting from our donkeys we followed him along the bank and through the mud-walled village, accompanied by the entire population of screaming children and ragged *fellaheen*, while black-clad, veiled women peered curiously at us from the low doorways of the houses. Oonas' maid met us in a sort of lane, which could certainly not be dignified by the name of street but seemed the only thoroughfare between two groups of hovels. She was a quiet, colourless female—probably Syrian —and, although I had seen her about, I had hardly noticed her during the time on the ship, yet she evidently had her wits about her as, in addition to bringing off Oonas' luggage, she had made my steward put a few things in a bag for me when she had learnt that the ship was sailing with out us.

The Sheik's house, when we reached it, proved to be a single-storeyed building and, as far as I could judge, it only contained two rooms. The outer one was full of women but the Shiek drove them out with kicks and curses while we sat down on the rush mats which covered the floor. The place stank abominably of goats and was littered with filth of every description. What the inner room was like I did not see but I was already convinced that to spend a night anywhere in that hovel would be absolute torture.

Coffee was served to us and while we drank it Oonas and the Sheik carried on a leisurely conversation. I did not pay much attention but presently I caught the word 'tents' and almost immediately afterwards Oonas turned to me.

'We're in luck,' she said. 'Since last winter he has been storing some tents for a party of excavators and they have not returned here yet. It was a little difficult to avoid offending the old man by saying we would rather not sleep in his house but I insisted that, rather than inconvenience him, the tents should be set up outside the village for us.'

'Thank God!' I murmured. 'What a marvellous break. My ankles are beginning to itch already where the inhabitants are biting me and I was trying to resign myself to being eaten alive here.'

'I'm afraid you'll have to put up with that for a bit,' she shrugged. 'He is having his fatted calf cooked and we shall mortally offend him if we don't remain here to eat it.'

It was abominably hot in the low, fusty room as there was a fire on the floor near the doorway and no other ventilation for the smoke, which made our eyes smart horribly. The Sheik left us to give orders about erecting the tents and for three-quarters of an hour we had to put up with the heat and stench as well as we could while the meal was being prepared.

When it arrived the 'fatted calf' turned out to be a large dish of pigeons. There were no plates, knives or forks and the big, round platter was just set down in the centre of the room, while Oonas, the Sheik, his eldest son—a wall-eyed man of about forty whom he had introduced to us—and myself squatted round it. The dish was served by the simple expedient of the Sheik's placing his hand in the centre of it and presenting us with a pigeon apiece, which we proceeded to tear limb from limb with our teeth and fingers.

I was a little leary of the flat slab of bread which was handed round for us to tear pieces off as I had so often seen similar loaves being prepared in the dirt outside native huts where they were smothered with flies and where all the filth near by got blown onto them; but I avoided eating the crust and found the inside unexpectedly good, although unleavened bread is terribly filling and, after a few mouthfuls, I had to give it up for fear I should not be able to do justice to the rest of the food provided for us. As it was, one pigeon would have been ample for my requirements but three apiece were pressed upon us and I knew enough of native customs to realise that our host would consider himself insulted if we did not gorge ourselves to the limit.

The pigeons were followed by a dish of tiny hens' eggs and

sweet corn which we sopped up with the unleavened bread, all dipping into the dish as hard as we could go; then came goat's-milk cheese and a sticky, undefinable sort of sweetmeat. More coffee was served, after which Oonas belched politely and bowing to the Sheik said, *'Mahbruk!'* meaning, 'Congratulations on the excellent meal you have provided.' As she did so she nudged me slightly so I promptly followed suit and our hosts demonstrated their satisfaction in a similar manner.

The old boy then clapped his hands loudly and that seemed to be the signal for which the entire population of the village had been waiting. In a second the room was filled by natives of all ages scrambling for the remains of the feast, with excited cries and hectic laughter, while our host led us outside.

The fresh night air was like perfumed wine after the noxious odours in the Sheik's living-room and I sucked in great, deep breaths of it as we followed the old man along the bank to a spot about forty yards above the river, where the tents had been pitched among a grove of palms.

There were two of them; an ordinary, bell-shaped, Army tent and a spacious-looking marquee. I assumed at once that the former was for me and I was immediately relieved of an uneasiness which had been growing in me for the past hour. As I was not supposed to know Arabic I had been unable to inform the Sheik that Oonas and I were not related; so I had feared that if she too had failed to inform him of that fact the sleeping arrangements made for us might prove extremely embarrassing.

In normal surroundings I would have felt that Oonas was perfectly capable of taking care of herself and therefore fair game if I could get her; but being thrown together for the night like this was quite a different matter so I had made up my mind that I ought to do the decent thing and suppress any impulse to take advantage of the situation. I'm not saying that my resolution would have held if it had been suggested that we shared a tent and she had showed no objection, but now it seemed that the cup of temptation was to be removed some thirty feet and two thicknesses of canvas from me. Of course, there was always the chance that Oonas might find it necessary to come and borrow some matches from me during the night but, even at the risk of disappointing her, I had no intention of thinking of an excuse for paying her a visit.

My reactions can be imagined, therefore, when Oonas' maid suddenly appeared in the entrance of the bell-tent and I saw that she had taken possession of it. Before I could readjust my feelings the Sheik had led Oonas and me into the marquee and, from a remark he made at that moment, it became quite clear that he believed me to be her husband.

I only just checked myself from disillusioning him in time; as to have done so would have given away the fact that I understood Arabic. Oonas, I noted with mixed feelings of elation and anxiety, ignored his reference to our married state and began rather hurriedly to praise the furnishings of the big tent. I myself was considerably surprised by their opulence because I had always believed that excavators lived hard when they were working on a 'dig'; but the marquee disabused me of such notions.

It was divided into two halves by a curtain across its centre; but this was draped back at the moment disclosing a sleeping-apartment in which Oonas' bags had been stacked and her things laid out for the night. The half in which we stood provided a pleasant anteroom containing a large table and a number of comfortable chairs. Rugs were spread on the ground in both compartments and I noted that the excavators' surplus stores had also been placed at our disposal, as a selection of civilised drinks had been set out. They even included several bottles of champagne which, I assumed, were 'overs' from a stock the archæologists kept for celebrating Christmas, birthdays, etc. Both ends of the marquee were lit by shaded oil-lamps which gave a pleasant subdued light.

There was no bed in the anteroom and I began to wonder if, as a result of my new-found scruples, I should have to pass an uneasy night in one of the chairs. The old Sheik was salaaming before us. He touched his forehead, then his heart as he murmured :

'Blessed be the name of Allah. May he bring you joy in the darkness and many beautiful children.'

We bowed in return as he backed out; then, to test the lie of the land, I said to Oonas, 'What was he muttering about?'

'Wishing me the one thing I don't want,' she shrugged. 'Lot's of babies.'

I laughed, a little unconvincingly, I fear; and we fell silent. After having thought of half-a-dozen things most suitable to the situation which I might have said, or done, in slightly different circumstances, I remarked lamely, 'Well, here we are.'

'Yes, here we are,' Oonas repeated, a hint of mockery in her lovely blue eyes. 'What about a drink?'

We had not dared to touch the water which had been offered in the Sheik's house as it would have meant certain enteric to Europeans so we had to make do with coffee and I had a first-class thirst. 'Grand,' I said, and I opened up a bottle of champagne.

Oonas was sitting down in one of the chairs by the time I had poured her a glass. Pouring myself another I sat down too. She got up at once and, coming over, perched herself on my knee.

I don't think I've ever felt so uncomfortable as I did during the next ten minutes. I've always rather prided myself on my technique but now that I did not feel justified in using it I was utterly stumped. What she thought of me, after my fervour in the afternoon, God alone knows. We kissed, but not properly. I simply dared not risk it and I could not find a word to say.

At last, in sheer desperation, I began to talk Egyptology; but she cut me short by standing up and saying with marked politeness:

'I think I shall go to bed now. I'm afraid, though, you won't be very comfortable here.'

'Oh, I shall manage,' I muttered. 'Good night; happy dreams.'

'Thank you,' she smiled, 'and—er, the same to you.' Upon which she disappeared through the curtains and drew them to behind her.

I suppressed a giant sigh and began to wonder if I was really laying up treasure in Heaven for myself or behaving like the most colossal fool. I derived not an ounce of satisfaction from my self-imposed restraint and where, I suppose, my self-esteem would have risen considerably if I had been a really 'nice' man, it had gone right down to zero.

The final indignity to my manhood came when the curtains

parted a few inches and Oonas flung out a pair of my silk pyjamas that her maid had collected for me from the ship.

Sadly and silently I undressed and put them on. With fury in my heart I drew two chairs together and thought of the wretchedly uncomfortable night I was condemned to spend on account of my own asinine scruples which, at the moment, I felt would have disgraced even the little prig who features as the hero in 'The Fifth Form at St. Jude's'.

I positively ached to abandon the crazy attitude I had taken up, dash through the curtains and babble out all sorts of apologetic nonsense as I seized Oonas in my arms. It was a deliberate insult to her beauty that I should remain where I was, acting the part of a tongue-tied fool. Yet, having taken up the line I had I simply could not bring myself to abandon it; and whether that was strength or weakness I have not the least idea.

I tuned down the lamp to a glimmer and had picked up my coat to put it on, knowing that later the night air would grow chilly, when the curtains parted again and Oonas appeared framed between them.

Her face did not give the least indication as to whether she was amused, contemptuous or angry. She just said quietly:

'You haven't done your exercises yet.'

'Aha!' I exclaimed, utterly taken aback. 'Exercises!'

'Yes. I do mine every night. Don't you?'

'Er, no. I'm afraid I don't,' I replied a little weakly.

'You should, then; they are excellent for the figure. If we had foils we could fence for a few minutes, as that is the best exercise of all, but as we haven't, running will serve instead.'

'Running!' I echoed. 'But you can't run here, in the marquee, and . . .'

'Can't I?' she cut me short. 'You just watch me. Over the chairs, under the table, round and round, bending, jumping, tumbling sideways and running on again. That's just the thing to keep you fit. Anyhow I'm going to.'

'Well,' I murmured, utterly amazed at this entirely new side of herself that Oonas was presenting to me. 'If you feel that way I wouldn't dream of stopping you.'

She moved forward, coming right up to me. She had very little on but I was hardly conscious of that as she looked me calmly in the face and said, 'I'm fitter than you are. I bet you couldn't catch me.'

'Don't you believe it,' I laughed, and I instinctively made a grab at her but she slipped away and dodged round to the other side of the table where I could not get at her.

'Come on,' she said. 'I challenge you.'

'Right!' I cried. 'I'd get you or any woman within two minutes in the confines of this tent.'

With a little laugh she leaned forward and, blowing down its chimney, put out the lamp. Next moment her voice came mocking and alluring from the far side of the tent:

'Try it! Catch me! Catch me if you can!'

In all the days of my life I have never experienced greater excitement than in that chase. Perhaps it was the primeval hunting instinct, which is still strong in the roots of every man, coming out in me; but I knew that I had to get her or for ever be dishonoured in my own estimation.

Oonas was not an athlete; physical exertion is anathema to her type, and I doubt if she had run a mile in the last five years; but she was extraordinarily quick and agile. Again and again I nearly caught her but she slipped through my outstretched hands. There were no corners to the marquee so I could not drive her into one and when she came up against the central dividing curtain she slid under it, so I had to follow her to the other side. She seemed to sense the obstacles in the dark better than I did and I was constantly barking my legs against the chair as I made wild rushes forward. For twenty seconds at a time I would lose her completely and stand trying to hush my panting as I listened for her softer breath, until her mocking voice came from just up against the wall of the tent, but she had evidently pulled off her dressing-gown as she flung it in my face and eluded me while I was struggling to free myself of its folds. A moment later I touched her back and grabbed her nightdress but the flimsy chiffon tore from top to bottom as she wrenched herself away, and I was left with a yard or so of the filmy material dangling from my hand. The whiff of her perfume I got from it nearly drove me insane and I knew that she was now standing there in the darkness only a few feet away from me without a stitch of clothing on.

Eventually I caught her, although I half-believe she allowed me to in the end, and when I did she turned suddenly, flung herself into my arms and glued her mouth to mine. I could feel her heart hammering in her chest just beneath my own and I crushed her warm, palpitating little body to me. All the scruples I had had were now cobwebs in the wind. Like Jurgen and countless others before me I did the manly thing. Picking her up in my arms I carried her to bed.

Later I knew that I ought to have suspected something from the beginning. Even if the way in which Oonas had deliberately delayed our return to the boat had not made me think, the handsomely-appointed marquee and the supply of champagne should have done so; but there is no doubt about it that she had practised a mild form of hypnosis on me. I knew quite well that I was not really in love with her, yet her beauty exercised such a fascination over me that in her presence I was capable of thinking of little else.

It was still early when we had taken possession of the marquee as the rising and setting of the sun is always the signal for waking or sleeping among the native peoples and our meal with the Sheik had been served shortly after sundown. What time I woke I have no idea but the marquee was in pitch darkness so it was evidently still the middle of the night. It must have been Oonas getting up that roused me since I knew at once that she was no longer there by my side, although she had moved so stealthily that she had not betrayed her going by a single sound. Once roused, my brain became instantly alert and, although there was no apparent cause for it, something seemed to tell me that I was in imminent danger.

I slipped out of bed at once and, striking a match, looked through the curtained division of the marquee. Oonas was not in the outer compartment so I tiptoed softly towards the entrance; just before I reached it I caught the sound of voices. Standing there in the dark, I listened with all my ears. It was Oonas speaking to her maid through the flap of the other tent and it was evident that I must have followed almost on her heels as she had only just succeeded in rousing the woman from her sleep.

As I could not hear distinctly I moved a few steps forward, but that was my undoing. I tripped over a tent-rope in the dark and fell sprawling on the ground with a terrific bump.

'Who's that?' came Oonas' voice in a quick, excited whisper.

'It's only me, darling,' I admitted lamely. 'I woke up to find you gone and wondered what had happened to you.'

'But I only left you for a moment,' she protested. 'Go back to bed, my sweet. I'm just coming.'

There was nothing for it but to beat a retreat but as I turned away I heard her say hurriedly to her maid in Arabic:

'You understand? I like this Englishman and I will not have his throat cut. I am not afraid of Zakri's anger and the arrangements for the killing are to be cancelled.'

This was a jolly thing to hear from one's paramour in the midst of a night of love. It was flattering and, in the circumstances, somewhat comforting to learn that I had made a sufficiently good impression upon Oonas for her to decide that she would not have me done to death, but my blood literally chilled and little beads of perspiration broke out on my forehead as I thought of the cold-blooded treachery she had evidently contemplated.

It was clear now that she had known who I was all the time or, at all events, tumbled to it pretty quickly. She must have planned this ruthless betrayal of me in detail during our first evening on the ship and sent instructions to Zakri Bey before we sailed the following morning.

Her calculations had evidently been based quite correctly on the assumption that two days of her company would be sufficient for her to get me in the state where I should be eager enough to sleep with her. Tel-el-Amarna, which consisted of no more than a miserable village, provided a perfect place for her to arrange matters so that we should miss the ship and have to spend the night together; and Akhen-aton's tomb was an admirable objective with which to lure me away from the rest of the party. If there had been an hotel in the place my death would have proved far more difficult to account for afterwards; but since she was much too fastidious to sleep in a native hovel she had had the marquee and its furnishings send down by rail; or, more probably, brought by somebody who had given the local Sheik his orders and instructed him in his lies about their being the property of excavators.

When I thought of the way in which she had even provided champagne with the intention of thoroughly enjoying herself for a few hours before she had me murdered, her cold-bloodedness seemed almost unbelievable, but reconsidering it I saw that the whole thing was absolutely in keeping with the 'Eastern Queen' idea, in which rôle she obviously fancied herself.

It was clear that she just didn't think on the same lines as a European girl and that her Western culture was merely a camouflage. Mentally she was in the same state as her prototype Cleopatra who, history relates, often abandoned herself to the embraces of a handsome slave but had him strangled the morning after in order that he should not become a nuisance or boast about it afterwards. Evidently I had been cast for the rôle of the handsome slave but as I had done my stuff particularly well I was to be reprieved for the moment; just as the Caliph in the Arabian Nights, who executed his Queens at the rate of one each morning, reprieved the beautiful Scheherazade because she could tell a good story.

I lit the lamp and opened another bottle of champagne while I wondered whether it would be best to tackle the beautiful little viper that had been nestling in my bosom and give her the good beating she thoroughly deserved, or to say nothing about it. Presumably the plan had been for half-a-dozen lads from the local village to break in and slaughter me, as killers can be bought for about fourpence a time in Egypt; but now that their orders had been cancelled it seemed that there was nothing to fear from that quarter. If I beat her up she might still call on these bravoes to slit my throat at the first opportunity; whereas, since she had no idea that I knew Arabic, she could not be aware that I had understood her instructions to her maid or knew anything of her original scheme for the conclusion of her night's entertainment; so, providing I didn't start anything myself, I was quite safe for the moment.

I had hardly poured myself a glass of wine before she came back into the marquee as serene and smiling as a seraph and as good to look at as the No. I Lady of the old Zeigfield Follies who used to be picked from the likely lasses of all America.

Coming straight over to me, she curled her arms round my neck and drew my head down to hers. Very soon I was wondering if I could really trust my ears or if they had deceived me. It seemed utterly impossible to believe that this starry-eyed young thing scarcely out of her teens could have plotted such a black betrayal; yet, all the time, I knew it was so.

We took the bottle into the inner sanctum and drank some more of the sparkling wine. The flawless beauty of her began to get hold of me again. My knowledge of the truth about her should, I suppose, have made her personality repellent to me but, now that she was lying there beside me displaying all her charms in the soft glow of the shaded lamp, it did not do so. In fact, she was such a delectable morsel that in spite of her treacherous little brain I could cheerfully have eaten her. During the interval that followed, upon which I will not dwell, apart from her caresses I was only conscious that the whole of my secret inner being rocked with silent, semi-insane, gargantuan laughter at the thought that I was capable of such monstrous cynicism.

The bottle and our amorous dalliance having come to an end we went to sleep again; but the night still held its unexpected excitements. I woke at the sound of angry voices coming from the entrance of the marquee. Oonas woke at the same moment. Slipping from my arms she jumped out of bed, pulled on a robe and said hurriedly:

'It must be the Sheik and the people from the village. They got drunk after we left, I expect. Leave this to me. Do not come out whatever you do, my sweet, because when these people are drunk they are sometimes difficult and they have a hate against the English.'

Believing it to be the Sheik creating a fuss because he feared to lose his blood-money now the orders for my assassination had been cancelled I let her go, assuming that she would easily be able to get rid of him by paying him off but, as a precaution, I jumped out of bed myself, lit the lamp, looked to my automatic and started to scramble into my clothes.

The curtains dividing the marquee were drawn but it was evident that our visitors had forced their way into the ante-room. I could hear Oonas quarrelling with them and suddenly, with a violent shock, I realised that their leader was not the Sheik at all. That high-pitched, feminine voice could only be Zakri Bey's.

Oonas was putting up a grand show. She was threatening

everybody with death and damnation if they did not clear out and leave her in peace, but Zakri was angry and persistent.

'I will not allow your fads and fancies to interfere with our arrangements!' he piped, as with feverish haste I now hustled on the rest of my clothes. 'This man is a danger to us and after tonight we will see to it that he is a danger no more. You can have all the men in Egypt for your lovers if you like. But Day must be eliminated. Stand aside, now! Or you'll make it necessary for me to have my people lay hands on you.'

I waited to hear no more but dived at the skirting of the marquee and, wrenching it up, wriggled underneath it.

The moon had long since set and the stars were paling but there was just enough light for me to see by and, since I could glimpse the palms ahead, it was certain that my would-be murderers would be able to spot me if any of them were looking in my direction. I prayed to all the gods that the whole party was in the marquee as I took to my heels and ran for dear life along the high bank above the river. I had hardly covered fifty yards before I heard Oonas give a frantic cry of warning.

'Julian! Julian! Save yourself or these men will kill you!'

Her shout was followed by the sound of shots. I stopped dead in my tracks; but only for a second. However unscrupulous Zakri might be he was not the sort of man to risk possible trouble for himself by shooting down a woman like Oonas without due deliberation; especially when it would be so easy for him and his men simply to thrust her out of the way. Evidently she had snatched up a small automatic, which I had noticed among her kit, and it was *she* who was firing on *them*.

A hundred yards from the tent I paused for breath and looked desperately round me for some place to hide, but the ragged line of palms gave little cover and beyond it lay the barren desert. By the faint greyness which lighted the sky in the east I knew that dawn was approaching. At most I could not cover more than a couple of miles before sun-up and wherever I might try to conceal myself among the shallow ruins of the dead city which stretched on either hand across the plain, my enemies only had to send a man up a palm tree to pick me out; after which I should be hunted till I dropped and shot down long before I could reach the hills.

For a moment I thought of doubling back, while the semi-darkness lasted, behind the marquee to seek shelter in the village; but the sound of the shots would have brought the whole place to life already. The Sheik was almost certainly in Zakri's pay and even if he had been willing to hide me nine out of ten of his people would have been ready to betray my refuge for a few piastres.

No hope lay in that direction but, as I glanced back, I noticed the dark bulk of a motor-cruiser close into the river bank where it shelved up to the marquee. It was evidently that in which Zakri and his thugs had arrived ten minutes earlier; if only I could secure it I should be able to cross the Nile and reach safety on the other side. Without a second's hesitation I plunged down the steep slope towards the river and drawing my gun raced along the sandy foreshore towards the cruiser.

When I was within twenty yards of it I saw a single man standing in its stern near the wheel; he spotted me at the same instant and let out a sharp challenge. It was his life or mine so I blazed off three rounds dead at him.

With a yelp of pain he slumped down in the boat and next moment I was scrambling over the gunwale into her. He was whimpering in her bottom but there was no sound or movement from any other part of the boat. My luck was in; he was the only man they had left on watch there.

As I jerked the poor fellow to his feet fresh shouting came from the marquee up on the bank a hundred yards away. Zakri and his people had heard my shots and were scrambling down the slope to get me.

With one terrific heave I flung the wounded man over the side into the shallow water. Grabbing the controls of the boat I pushed over her power lever and turned her nose out from the bank. A shot smacked into the woodwork of the cabin amidships; another crashed through the glass of a window and sent its splinters flying all about me. I threw myself flat on the bottom boards in the stern and let her run blind for a few moments while Zakri's gunmen peppered her. As the light was still uncertain they ceased fire before I reached mid-stream and I was safe; but only for the time being.

Standing up I headed her for the opposite shore and, when I got to within twenty feet of it, I found an axe and hacked a jagged rent in her bottom boards; then, scrambling out into the shallow water, I turned her round and pushed her off again with her engine still running. If she had not been holed by Zakri's people she certainly was now and she would sink before she ran ashore.

It gave me a vicious satisfaction to think that Zakri's evening out had cost him his fine motor-cruiser for which, I reckoned, he would not have paid much less than £1,000. But my own situation still gave me acute anxiety. We had ascertained the previous evening that the thrice-weekly train from Deir Mowas for the south left at eleven o'clock that morning. Long before that time Zakri and his party would have crossed the river in one of the native sailing-boats and so be able to catch me up at the station. Zakri was a power in the land; the station-master at this wayside halt would be only an unimportant Egyptian official. I could hope for little help from him if Zakri found me there, declared I was an escaped criminal and that it was his business to arrest me. I should be carted off into the desert and duly shot.

After a little thought I decided to take a gamble. I had no idea how far it was to the next station or halt along the line. It might be five miles, ten, or even twenty. There was no likelihood of my getting lost once I struck the railway-line; if the halt was any great distance I should miss the train and be stuck there for a couple of days but if I could get there in time I should stand a much better chance of boarding it without being caught by Zakri.

I set off inland up the track and while I was covering the first quarter of a mile I weighed up the respective merits and disadvantages of making for the halt to the north or the halt to the south of Deir Mowas.

If I turned south I should be moving in the direction in which the train was going and, therefore, gain anything from twenty to forty minutes' leeway; but, as against that, when Zakri failed to find me at Deir Mowas he would not wish to stay there. It was almost certain that he would take the train south to Assiut, as from there, even if he really wanted to go north, he would be able to get a *rapide* back to Cairo. If he and his people were on the train when I tried to board it they would certainly see me and get out; in which case I should be caught and no better off than if I tried to catch it at Deir Mowas.

On the other hand, if I made north I should be moving against the direction of the train and considerable lessen my chance of catching it; but at least I should be able to board it without being seen by my enemies.

In consequence, I turned up a track through the cotton-fields that led north-westward. By this time the sun was rising and in beauty the scene rivalled the sunsets of the previous days. The whole of the east bank of the river was bathed in gold and salmon-pink as though the desert where Oonas and I had lingered the previous afternoon were the site of some gigantic conflagration; but I had little time to give to contemplating such glories of nature and, pushing on, reached the railway-line after half-an-hour's hard going.

Once the sun was up I began to feel its heat and the next two hours' trudge was a gruelling business after the exhausting and adventurous night through which I had just passed; yet by nine o'clock I had real cause for jubilation. Across the fields I spotted the white dome of a small mosque and a cluster of buildings huddled round it near the railway-line. When I reached it I discovered that the place was called Masara, and I had achieved my objective with the best part of two hours to spare.

There was no hotel but a tiny shop supplied me with a breakfast of coffee, eggs and fruit after which I sat down patiently to await the coming of the train. When it arrived I took a ticket for Assiut, which was as far as it went, and as soon as it left the station I locked myself in the lavatory.

Being a local train it was naturally a short one and it had only two coaches devoted to first and second-class compartments. The odds were that Zakri would join it at Deir Mowas so I dared not show myself until we reached Assiut; otherwise, since there were no Europeans upon it to whom I could appeal for assistance, he would haul me off the train at the next way-side halt. Fortunately the journey is no more than fifty miles but, even so, as we stopped at each halt for the best part of ten minutes it took nearly two hours.

It was only by changing lavatories twice on the way that I managed to avoid being drummed out by the conductor or showing myself yet, when we at last pulled into Assiut, I found that the discomfort of my journey had been worth while as Zakri and his men *were* on the train. On opening the door a fraction I caught a glimpse of them and I waited patiently where I was until they had had plenty of time to pass the barrier.

There was no point now in rejoining the Nile steamer so I decided to make for Luxor at once; as the Belvilles were due there the next day but one. There remained the question of getting back my baggage but here my luck had really served me well.

I recalled the schedule of the Nile voyage. On the fourth day the steamer was due to leave Beni Mohammed in the morning and arrive at Assiut about 9 o'clock. Since Assiut is one of the principal towns in Egypt the tourists were to come ashore for a drive through the big Coptic quarter, which is a feature of the place, be taken to inspect a carpet-factory in the bazaar and then up into the hills, beyond the town, where one can get a fine view of the city and the great, white stone barrage which is the only dam between Aswan and Cairo. That meant they would be ashore for several hours and, as far as I could remember, the ship was not due to sail again until about teatime. All I had to do was to drive down to the quayside and collect my things; afterwards I should just have time to catch the one good train of the day from Cairo which left Assiut for Luxor at a little before three.

The ship's passengers were all on shore so I escaped their curious glances and any impertinent enquiries as to what had happened to Oonas and myself the night before; but I should have liked to give the Purser a good dressing-down for having left without sending Mahmoud to look for us and I had no opportunity to do so as he was also ashore, buying supplies.

Perhaps that was just as well as I soon learnt that I should only have looked a fool if I had tried. My steward gave it away that Oonas had told the Purser before she left the ship that we intended to spend the night as the guests of the local Sheik; after which we meant to rejoin the ship at Assiut. There was obviously no reply to that and it explained everything; the maid being put off with all Oonas' baggage and the reason they had not troubled to look for us. The ship had left Tel-el-

Amarna at its normal time and the message from the Purser about having to get into Beni Mohammed to anchor before dark was a pure invention with which the Sheik had been primed. I packed my bags as quickly as I could and returned to the railway-station.

Zakri was not on the train so he evidently intended to return to Cairo but, in any case, I had no fears of him now, as the express was packed with Europeans and I knew he would never have dared to start anything in their presence. We got into Luxor at 8.50 and driving straight to the Winter Palace I sat down to a belated and most welcome dinner.

The previous twenty-four hours had been, to say the least of it, strenuous, so directly after the meal I went to bed. As I tucked the mosquito-curtain in under the edges of the mattress and snuggled down between the cool sheets I wondered if I should ever be able to get O'Kieff and Zakri. I had managed to damage them quite a bit in the past ten days but that had only been retaliation. It was hopeless, I knew, to try to prove that they had attempted to murder me on the previous night; the local Sheik and his people would never dare to give evidence against them and I was a long way yet from being able to carry the war into the enemy's camp. But at least it was pleasant to feel that for the moment I was out of danger again. Within three minutes I had fallen into a heavy, dreamless sleep.

It was pitch dark when I woke and what had roused me I had no idea; but I knew with a horrid, tense certainty that there was someone in my room and that they were moving stealthily towards my bed.

17

The Midnight Visitor

For a moment I lay quite still, staring into the darkness; I could not see a thing but I knew in the very marrow of my bones that someone was standing only a few feet from me. I felt absolutely certain that if I stretched out my hand I would be able actually to touch them through the mosquito-netting. Although I could not see even the faintest outline of a form it seemed to me that I could hear the low breathing of my sinister visitor, yet I could not have sworn to that because my heart was pounding so hard that the blood was drumming in my ears.

I had felt so safe when I had gone to bed that I had not even troubled to lock my door, much less put my automatic under my pillow. In the marquee on the river-bank the night before my enemies could have done away with me almost with impunity; enquiries as to my whereabouts would not have started until three nights later when the Belvilles found that I failed to arrive on the Nile boat at Luxor. After the murder my body would have been carried to some lone spot and thrown down the bottom of a steep ravine; within a day the ghoulish attentions of vultures, kites and pariah dogs would have rendered the manner of my death unrecognisable; the following night the jackals would have completed the business. Oonas would have told some plausible story—perhaps that I had quarrelled with her—in any case, that I wandered off and failed to return. and that all search for me had proved unavailing; upon which she had assumed that for some reason of my own I had abandoned her and gone off upstream in a river boat. Days later, when a proper search was instituted, a police patrol would probably have come upon my remains and reported that I had broken my back through falling down a gully. The village people might suspect otherwise but they would be much too frightened to air their suspicions.

But here, in Luxor, in the great Winter Palace Hotel where several hundred guests were staying, it was a totally different matter. It would be as great a risk for anyone to attempt a murder as it would be to do so at the Savoy Hotel in London. I had been justfied in assuming myself perfectly safe, yet, as I lay sweating there, I felt that I was in imminent danger and any second I feared that an unseen knife would suddenly descend through the mosquito-curtains, to bury itself in me. I dared not move for fear of precipitating the blow; I could only wait, thanking God that I had awakened in time, which at least gave me the chance of flinging myself sideways as the blow fell.

I fought to control the beating of my heart so that I could hear better and the soft breathing beside me became definitely perceptible. Then I felt a gentle tugging under my left-hand side and I knew that the unseen visitor was very carefully pulling the mosquito-curtain out from where it was tucked in beneath my mattress. The assassin feared, perhaps, that the folds of the netting might entangle his weapon and so was going to lift it before striking.

It took every effort of will I possessed to lie there rigid but I managed it and stealthily drew my right arm free of the bed-clothes so that I could lash out when the time came for me to throw myself aside.

Something touched the bedclothes just above my left elbow and ran lightly up my arm; very gently a hand was laid upon my shoulder. Next instant the unseen presence had leaned forward over me and warm breath fanned my cheek. In a flash it came to me that the figure was too near to strike effectively at that moment. With a terrific heave I jerked myself up and, throwing my right arm wide, cast it out to encircle the head bent above me. In one violent movement I had grabbed the person that menaced me and pulled him down with all my force on top of myself.

There was a muffled cry as a head came sharply in contact with my shoulder, then Oonas' voice: 'Julian! Don't! It's me! you're hurting!'

With a sigh of overwhelming relief I eased my grip and

struggled up into a sitting position. For all I knew she might have been on the point of attempting to murder me when I seized her but she wasn't carrying any weapon or I should have felt it, and I was certain now that if she tried any tricks I should be quite equal to dealing with them. I stretched out my hand to switch on the bedside light but she was in the way and she pushed my hand quickly back again.

'I'm sorry I gave you a fright,' she said softly. 'It's awfully cold out here. Move over, darling, so that I can get into bed with you.'

I hardly knew if I could believe my ears in view of the manner in which we had parted early that morning; but without waiting for me to reply she pulled the bedclothes aside and, putting one arm round my neck, wriggled down beside me.

'How the devil did you get here?' was all I could think of to ask just then.

'The same way as you did, my sweet, by the train that came in from Cairo this evening. But you were in such a hurry at the station you didn't see me, and directly I got here I went straight to my room. As a matter of fact, I didn't want to see you again until we could talk things over in comfort without being disturbed.'

'But you weren't on the local train from Deir Mowas,' I objected, 'and I sank Zakri's motor-launch, so how on earth did you get to Assiut in time to catch the express?'

I felt her shrug her shoulders. 'I telegraphed up the line from Deir Mowas and made them stop the express for me. It picked me up there about half-past one.'

'By Jove, you've got a nerve!' I murmured.

'It needed none. Only a little influence. After all, this is my country and I am a princess in it, you know. But you don't seem very pleased to see me, Julian.'

'If I'd known I might expect you I would have had the champagne on the ice all ready for Your Highness,' I said sarcastically; but she did not seem to get that so I added, 'And a nice bowstring ready to strangle you with in the morning.'

'That would have been very unkind and also very stupid.'

'Unkind!' I echoed. 'And what right would you have to complain if I did decide to wring your neck? You know perfectly well that's the fate you intended for me. You got in touch with

Zakri Bey after our first night on the ship and had him rail those tents and the bubbly wine down to Tell-el-Amarna. You told the Purser that we were to be the guests of the Sheik there for the night and then deliberately led me off to Akhen-aton's tomb so that the ship should sail without us. The whole affair was a skilfully-laid plot to ensure my murder. Do you deny it?'

'No, darling, no. But I arranged it all before I really got to know you.'

'What difference does that make?' I asked angrily. 'The fact remains that you hatched a scheme to bring about a man's death and let him make love to you knowing quite well that your friends were going to kill him.'

Oonas sighed, and, pulling off her dressing-gown, snuggled herself down even more closely beside me.

'I'm a bad woman, darling,' she said in the voice of a penitent child. 'I am a very bad woman. There is no doubt about it. But I cannot help being a bad woman, can I?'

There did not seem to be much reply to that line of attack and rubbing her cheek against mine she went on softly:

'It is all true—every bit of it. I quite meant to have you murdered. You see, you have been causing a great deal of trouble to many friends of mine and so we all thought it would be much the best thing for everybody if you were put out of the way. But then, you see, I fell in love with you and I couldn't help that either, could I?'

I was at a loss for any appropriate answer to that one, also. Of course it might have been quite untrue, but few men are so armour-plated as to be entirely unwilling to believe such a statement when it is made by an exceedingly beautiful young woman; and as I was pondering the matter, she went on again.

'I know it was very wicked to think of having you killed but life is very much cheaper here than it is in England. Where I was wrong was in not realising sooner how much I loved you; but it wasn't until last night that I suddenly knew how you had stolen my whole heart out of my body, and then it was too late to alter the arrangements. When I left you to speak to my maid it was to cancel the orders and I had no idea then that Zakri would come himself to see the business settled. When he turned up I was terrified for you, my darling; but it was I who saved you. I shouted at the top of my voice. "Julian, Julian!

Save yourself! They are going to kill you!'" and I shot three of Zakri's men to give you time to get away.'

That part of her story, at least, was true enough as I well knew; although it was overhearing her remark to her maid which had warned me in the first place and enabled me to get my clothes on directly Zakri arrived with his bravoes, which was a good five minutes before she called out to me and the shooting started.

'That's all very well,' I said. 'But your having changed your mind at the last minute does not alter the fact that you originally intended to have me murdered.'

'But, Julian, that is unfair!' she protested. 'You are being most unreasonable. In Alex. you pass yourself off as one of our people and steal that tablet from me, which it had taken us so much trouble to get. You come to Cairo where you steal our dope and cause poor Gamal to be arrested so that his place is closed up and a lot of our men will be given long terms of imprisonment. You go to Ismailia where you break into the House of the Angels, wrecking the whole of our business there. Through you it is burnt down and eight young women, who cost us quite a lot of money, are taken out of our hands, and lots more of our people are imprisoned by the police. If you go about making such a nuisance of yourself—what can you expect but that people will want to murder you?'

Her attitude was a little staggering but, looking at things for a moment from her angle I quite saw her point. If I hadn't interfered with them in the first place they would not have interfered with me but, as it was, they clearly had considerable reason for wishing me out of the way.

I stretched out my arm behind Oonas' head, switched on the light and picked up a violet cream fondant. She blinked a little and turned to look at me, those heavily lidded, widely-spaced blue eyes of hers only six inches from my own.

'You aren't angry with me any more, are you?' she pleaded. and leaning forward suddenly she kissed me on the mouth.

'I don't quite know,' I confessed, drawing back my head. 'I've had no previous experience of young women who make up their minds to have me killed in cold blood one day and tell me that they're in love with me the next.'

She laughed. 'Then, my sweet, you don't know what real love

is like. All your experience must have been with those sticks of Englishwomen. I am quite different and when I feel a thing I feel it with all my being. When I counted you an enemy I would have gone to any lengths to bring about your death. But now that I love you I am yours body and soul.'

'How did you manage to find out who I was?' I asked. 'Did you recognise me right away as the man who visited you dressed up as a Red Indian in Alexandria?'

She shook her head and her dark curls danced with the movement. 'No, I didn't know you. But you are not very clever, my darling. You didn't introduce yourself to me that afternoon at Sakkara, but having met such an attractive young man I naturally enquired who he was directly I got back to the ship. They told me his name was Julian Day and as you've been the principal topic of conversation among my friends ever since you landed in Alex., that was quite enough. One look at your eyes afterwards, of course, and I knew you again for the man who had posed as Lemming.'

It was my turn to laugh. How I could ever have committed such a crass stupidity as to give my own name to the Purser on the boat, I cannot think. The whole time we had been on board I flattered myself that I had taken her in completely while actually I had as good as pinned a label to my chest which shouted to the housetops who I was.

'Well,' I said. 'What are we going to do now?'

'Unfortunately there is no champagne,' she murmured. 'But at least we could put out the light.'

'Wait a minute,' I said quickly. 'I'd like to know a little better where we stand. The fact that you're in love with me is very flattering, but how long is it going to last? From the way you talk of them it seems you still approve of all the activities of your friends, whereas, quite obviously, I don't. What guarantee have I that during the next clash you won't change sides again and administer poison to me in my morning coffee?'

She really looked genuinely shocked at the suggestion and protested hotly: 'But, Julian, how could I do such a thing now that I love you? Before it was quite different. As for the things that my friends do, what difference does that make to us? They must make their living somehow but, for myself, I am rich enough not to have to worry. I have found it amusing to be

248

mixed up in their clever plots. But now I am on your side and I will plot for you. I think I could even arrange to have Zakri murdered, if you like.'

I passed a hand over my eyes as I tried to take it in. Here was this young woman, who had been plotting my death only a few hours ago, now anxious to murder somebody else on my behalf. Could such a violent change of heart possibly be genuine? It may have been partly the extraordinary fascination which her enchanting person had over me whenever I was in her presence; but I honestly believed she meant it.

The fact was, that although to all outward seeming she appeared a sophisticated and cultured girl who would be received anywhere in the Western world, underneath she was in some respects as simple as a child, and her emotions consisted entirely of the barbaric loves and hates suited to a woman of the dark ages.

If I was right, she would prove an invaluable ally and could give me information of the first importance which really might enable me to get O'Kieff and the rest just where I wanted them. In any case it seemed that if I took her at her word she could hardly refuse me a certain amount of data upon which I could check up afterwards; so her apparent passion for me opened up a prospect of carrying on my vendetta which I would have been positively mad to have thrown away.

I took her little, heart-shaped face between my hands and looked straight into those marvellous eyes. 'Oonas,' I said, 'are you prepared to prove your loyalty to me by telling me all you know about O'Kieff's and Zakri's organisation?'

'Yes,' she said. 'Tomorrow morning I will answer truthfully any questions you like to put to me. Now, can we put out that horrid light?'

The following morning things did not pan out quite like that because, having left me when the first, faint light began to creep through the curtains, she did not emerge from her own room until lunch-time.

I had spent a lazy morning myself, getting up late and exerting myself no more than to go out and buy a few things I needed temporarily until I could retrieve the rest of my kit from Oonas, who had brought it on to Luxor with her.

Having learned of my arrival the night before Amin was

waiting patiently to see me on the steps of the hotel. To tell the truth Oonas had occupied my mind so fully that I had forgotten all about him and, having no explanation of my unexpectedly early appearance in Luxor ready to my tongue, I simply told him that I had changed my plans. As Mustapha was still detained in hospital at Ismailia by his shattered arm I assured Amin that I should not need his services for the next four days and that he had better continue with his work in preparation for the expedition; but I took him with me to assist me in my shopping.

We did not have to go far as two rows of shops flank the entrance of the great hotel and really form part of it as they are situated under the wings of its front terrace. They are mainly antique-dealers, bookshops which deal in a great variety of photographs and postcards, and travel-agencies; and except for this single terrace there is no other European shopping centre in the town. There was no sweet-shop among them and all I could procure were some bottled sweets from the English chemist. As the sight of Oonas, on her way to the Nile steamer five days before, had prevented my ordering a big supply from Groppi's, I was considerably irritated by this but if I could have seen ahead a little I would have realised that this was a trifle compared with the irritations I should have to face in the next few days.

The first hint of them came when, having just started my lunch, I saw Oonas sweep into the dining-room like the Princess she was, and the head waiter bowing deferentially before leading her to a table. She smilingly ignored his gesture towards one in the window and walked straight over to mine instead.

The fact that we had shared a table on the Nile steamer, not to mention our activities of the preceding night, perfectly justified her in doing so without any invitation, but, as I waved the waiter aside and placed a chair for her myself with a smiling greeting, a little devil somewhere at the back of my mind suggested to me that perhaps I hadn't been quite such a clever boy as I thought.

It was clear that I had definitely saddled myself with this beautiful little wanton for as long as the two of us remained in Luxor. How would the Belvilles view that when they turned up? I could hardly hope to persuade them that Oonas had be-

come a reformed character overnight and was now completely
trustworthy when, in the cold light of morning, I did not
really believe it myself. Again, it now occurred to me that,
although I might succeed in getting a certain amount out of her
about Zakri and Co., it would be only what she chose to tell me
whereas, having constituted me her cavalier, she would have
much more opportunity of finding out things about our own
activities, whether I wanted her to or not. I wondered, too,
what Sylvia would make of her and had an uncomfortable
feeling that neither of them would like each other one little
bit. Doubtless I should have thought of all this before but I fear
that Oonas' blandishments on the previous night had played a
big part in obscuring my judgment and this was my first
awakening to the very tricky situation in which I had landed
myself.

All unaware of my miserable forebodings of trouble to
come, Oonas chatted away with the utmost gaiety all through
lunch while I managed to mask my inward thoughts and play
up to her very prettily.

It soon emerged that whatever else about her might be
phony her interest in Egyptology certainly was not. She was
genuinely disappointed that our having left the ship prema-
turely had deprived us of visits to Abydos, one of the most
ancient shrines in Egypt and the centre of the Osiris cult; and
Dendra where the great temple, although dating only from the
decadent Ptolemaic period, is the best-preserved in Egypt;
and she was determined to make up for lost time now she was
in Luxor. Without consulting me in the matter she had already
ordered a car to take us out to Karnak that afternoon.

'That's grand,' I said. 'But, you know, I want to have a
serious talk to you and the earlier the better.'

'Of course, darling,' she agreed as though butter wouldn't
melt in her mouth. 'But we can talk just as well while we're
walking round the temple.' So, for the moment, I left it at that.

It is from Luxor that one views the remains of hundred-gated
Thebes which was, perhaps, the greatest city in the whole of the
ancient world. It is not as old as Memphis but first became
of importance when the Pharaohs of the Middle Kingdom
selected it as their capital about 2100 B.C. After the fall of the

XIIth Dynasty it suffered a temporary eclipse of a few hundred years, during the rule of the Shepherd Kings, but it rose again to an almost unbelievable magnificence under the New Empire when the Pharaohs of the XVIIIth Dynasty held sway there as the sovereign lords of all the lands and cities from the frontiers of Abyssinia to the Persian Gulf. Unlike Memphis, which has been entirely obliterated, Thebes still has innumerable temples standing which testify to the greatness of its builders.

On the east bank of the river, where the temples of Karnak and Luxor still stand, flourished the city of the living which was larger than the Paris, Berlin or Rome of our day; while on the west bank there was another city—that of the dead—which provides even greater interest. It is here, in this vast necropolis, many square miles in extent, that besides many other temples, there lie the famous Valley of the Tombs of the Kings, the Valley of the Queens and the Valley of the Nobles.

Karnak is about twenty minutes' drive from Luxor and it is there that the greatest temple of all times was erected to the gods. Its area is so great that St. Peter's in Rome and the whole of the Vatican could be set down inside it without anywhere touching the boundary walls. The remains consist of innumerable pillars, colossi, pylons, obelisks, courtyards and shrines, since it is not one but many temples built or reconstructed by many Pharaohs from the XIth Dynasty right up to the erá of the Ptolemies; so that building was going on there over a longer period than from the time Christ lived on earth to the present day.

The great temple which rises in its centre is that of Amen-Ra; one-hundred-and-fifty-six huge columns tower above one in its main hall like a forest of stone and on the ground occupied by the base of each twelve men could form a group without being unduly overcrowded. In the old days every inch of surface was brightly painted so that the whole place was a blaze of colour; great flags fluttered a hundred feet high above its pylons; its mighty gateways were of bronze and copper, the sacred images of solid gold encrusted with precious gems. Now all that splendour has departed but the temple still remains immensely impressive and awe-inspiring.

It takes several days to view Karnak thoroughly but both of us had been there before so after spending an hour in revisiting a few of our favourite spots we sat down to talk on a great stone scarab beside the sacred lake.

Oonas proved much more forthcoming than I had anticipated. She knew little about O'Kieff and nothing at all of his six great confederates, with the exception of Zakri. But of him she was able to tell me a great deal. She gave me chapter and verse about his dope-trafficking activities, the addresses of various depots where the stuff was stored, and the channels by which it was smuggled into Egypt from Japan, which is now the centre of its manufacture; more than enough, in fact, for me to realise with a glow of satisfaction that I as good as had him in the bag. But my self-congratulation was a little premature, as she suddenly said:

'What hard luck it is for you, darling, that you're no longer in a position to make use of all this.'

'What!' I exclaimed. 'Why on earth not?'

She stared at me in surprise. 'But, Julian, they know by now that I have thrown them over and become your mistress. If you were to pass anything that I've told you on to the police and they acted on it Zakri would guess at once that it was I who had betrayed him and they would kill me.'

This was a snag that I had not foreseen and her reasoning was certainly plausible enough.

'We could get you police protection,' I murmured after a moment.

She shrugged contemptuously. 'The only protection I should get from the police would be about ten years in jail. Surely you see that I am so deeply involved in all this that if you went to the police the first thing they would do would be to arrest me. No, Julian. You can do nothing on what I've told you unless you want to see me dead or imprisoned.'

With bitter disappointment I admitted to myself that she was right. Even by turning King's Evidence she could only hope for a mitigation of her sentence and anxious as I was to prevent her continuing her career of crime, it was unthinkable that any act of mine should place her life or freedom in jeopardy. Yet I had a worrying idea at the back of my mind that she had deliberately tricked me and would never have told me a single thing if she had not realised from the beginning that she could afterwards head me off from using any information she gave .

me. I may have been doing her an injustice but I had a shrewd suspicion that while she had developed a genuine passion for myself she still wanted to remain in with her unscrupulous friends, so she had thought up this clever little plot by which she could eat her cake and keep it too.

'What d'you suggest I should do, then?' I asked rather gloomily.

'Why, it is simple, isn't it?' she smiled. 'Since Zakri is your enemy, we must arrange to have him murdered.'

I swallowed hard and looked down at the ground. There was something really terrifying in the way in which this beautiful little creature with the smiling face under the big, floppy hat spoke so calmly of having people done to death. I knew it was illogical to jib at the proposal as I had made up my mind long ago that if any one of the Big Seven gave me an opportunity to kill him and get away with it, I would shoot him out of hand; yet that was somehow different from plotting the assassination of one of them with the assistance of a young woman barely out of her teens while we sat there smoking in the sunshine.

'I'll have to think about it,' I said, standing up rather hurriedly. 'Let's go and have a look at that little temple on the other side of the main building; the one where there's that marvellous statue of the Cat-Goddess Sekhmet.'

I thought there was just a touch of cynicism in Oonas' smile as she agreed and she made no further reference to her proposal for Zakri's murder either then or that evening when we were back at the hotel.

That night at dinner she positively surpassed herself as a delightful and entertaining companion. The fascination she exerted had certainly got me again and my worries of the afternoon receded right into the background. I do not seek to excuse my weakness where she was concerned but in some justification of my curious mental state it can at least be urged that those blue eyes of hers certainly possessed a hypnotic quality. I drank in her beauty like a drug and I simply could not keep my own eyes from her face even when she was not looking at me because, even in profile, her features and the very set of her head were utterly ravishing. Perhaps, too, a great part of her power lay in the extraordinary rare combination of qualities which she possesses; she had the subtlety, the humour and the knowledge of a woman of the world clothed in a physical body which, having only just reached maturity, had all the freshness, the satin skin and the very essence of glorious youth.

I knew Harry, Clarissa and Sylvia would be leaving Cairo that night and their arrival in Luxor would mean endless complications but I refused to think of that for the time being. I was in such a state that I hardly cared what they thought or said, and I abandoned myself without reservation to another night with Oonas which was even more hectic than the last.

It was that temporary, mad absorption in her to the exclusion of all else which made me forget that the Cairo express got into Luxor at 7 o'clock in the morning. Fond as I was of Harry and Clarissa I would not have got up to meet them at such an early hour in any case, but a little forethought might have told me that as we had all booked our rooms together the hall porter was almost certain to inform them that I had already arrived.

As the Nile boat was not due in until that evening they would naturally be most anxious to hear what fresh turn in the situation had caused me to change my plans and come hurrying on to Luxor before them.

With a casualness that was typical of her, Oonas had neglected to lock the bedroom door when she had joined me, shortly after I had turned in, and we were lying side by side in blissful early-morning drowsiness when there was a sudden, sharp knock on the door, a rattle of the handle, and it flew open. Harry stood there framed in it, his good-natured, fishlike face wreathed in smiles, as he exclaimed:

'Hullo, Julian, old boy! Fancy you getting here before us!'

Next moment he caught sight of Oonas through the mosquito-curtain and with a single ejaculation of 'Good God!' he pulled the door shut again.

'Who on earth was that?' asked Oonas quickly, sitting up.

'Harry Belville,' I said. 'I told you last night, if you remember, that my friends would be arriving in Luxor this morning.'

'Yes, of course,' she agreed. 'Do you think they'll like me?'

'I am sure they will,' I replied with a conviction I was far from feeling and I wondered miserably what wretched complications the day would bring.

18

The Green-eyed Monster

A line of Kipling's flashed into my mind: 'I've taken my fun where I found it and now I must pay for my fun.' That about summed up my own situation but before I could attempt to deal with anything else I had to cope with Oonas, so I said:

'I'm awfully sorry he barged in here like that. But it must be ever so much later than I thought. I ought to have seen to it that you got back to your room a couple of hours ago.'

She shrugged. 'It doesn't matter, darling, but it's lucky I managed to get a room in the same corridor. If you keep a look-out till the coast's clear I can easily slip along there now without any of the servants seeing me.'

As soon as she had gone I bathed and dressed, thinking matters over while I did so. On second thoughts I decided it was rather a good thing Harry had found Oonas and myself tucked up together. He was not the sort of chap to conceal anything from his wife so it was a pretty safe bet he would tell Clarissa and that would save me quite a lot of troublesome explanations. By being presented at once with the *fait accompli* they would know exactly where I stood and Clarissa was such a good sport I felt confident I could rely upon her treating the situation tactfully. I wondered if she would pass the glad tidings on to Sylvia and I rather hoped she wouldn't.

As there was nothing whatever between Sylvia and myself it was nothing to do with her whom I chose to sleep with; yet I liked her a lot so I naturally wanted her to think well of me, and I could not get away from the feeling that she would disapprove intensely. However, that just had to be faced, and having finished dressing I went downstairs to find them.

They had only had coffee and rolls on the train so they were just finishing a second breakfast in the restaurant. The greetings of them all were very friendly so I sat down to tell them of the way I had struck up an acquaintance with Oonas on the Nile boat and my subsequent adventures at Tel-el-Amarna; only suppressing the fact that I was actually in bed with her when Zakri and his bravoes arrived at the marquee to murder me. I then went on to explain that Oonas had experienced a change of heart, done her best to save me by a last-minute warning, and that I was now playing her for all I was worth to get such information as I could about the enemy.

As I told the story it sounded credible enough but I knew quite well that I was painting the picture with roseate hues and I felt distinctly guilty about it. They all listened in intent silence while I recounted the particulars of my escape and confided themselves to a few polite, non-committal remarks when I went on to speak of Oonas.

When I had finished there was a rather awkward silence until Harry said: 'Amin came to meet us on the train and he tells me the six cars we're taking on the expedition and most of our supplies have arrived from Cairo. They're in the station yard and we thought of going along to check them over. Would you care to come?'

'There's no need for us all to go,' Clarissa cut in. 'You and Sylvia can manage quite well between you. Julian can stay here and show me the famous garden we've all heard so much about.'

The front of the Winter Palace Hotel looks out over the Nile and has a magnificent view of the Libyan Hills in the distance but behind it there is one of the loveliest gardens in Egypt. It is a much-advertised feature of the place and covers many acres. The part immediately overlooked by the hotel windows consists of numerous varieties of palm and other tropical trees, grass lawns, gay flower borders and groups of flowering shrubs; while the further portion of the demesne is given over to avenues of fruit trees, mainly bearing grapefruit, oranges and tangerines which are picked as required, fresh from the trees, for the hotel dining-room. Half-a-score of native boys are employed to water it morning and evening, so it presents an ever-green and colourful oasis in the middle of the dusty little town.

As soon as the others had gone I led Clarissa out into it; upon which she took my arm and said:

'Now, Julian, what you've been telling us will do very nicely for Sylvia but I want to hear the *real* story.'

'There isn't very much else to tell, except what you can guess for yourself,' I parried.

'You've fallen for the beautiful Oonas, haven't you?'

'Well . . .' I hesitated. 'I suppose I have. It's rather difficult to explain. There's no question of my marrying her. If there were, I'd set out on an expedition to the North Pole rather than go through with it, because, as sure as God made little apples, our attraction for each other can't possibly last; but at times I find her absolutely irresistible.'

'I can quite understand that,' Clarissa conceded handsomely. 'I thought her one of the loveliest little things I've ever set eyes on when I saw her at that fancy-dress dance in Alex. But do you really believe in this "change of heart" business? It doesn't sound quite in keeping with her character.'

'I honestly don't know,' I confessed. 'At times I believe she loves me so much she'd let me jump on her with hob-nailed boots if I wanted to; and at other times I'm quite convinced she means to double-cross me at the first opportunity.'

'I should think you're probably right about both things,' Clarissa said wisely. 'Any woman can see with half an eye that your little friend is sex incarnate. When she's all het up about a man she would probably risk prison or stick a knife into any one for him; but once she's cooled off, her brain gets control again and we've pretty good reason to know that all her real interests lie in the enemy's camp.'

'You've hit it. "The leopard cannot change his spots" or Oonas her criminal mentality. As a matter of fact, owing to her temporary aberration about me, she actually offered to get Zakri murdered for us yesterday.'

'Did you accept?'

'No. I'd have liked to, but I hadn't got the guts. I'm afraid the truth is that I am an awful weakling in lots of ways when it comes down to brass tacks.'

'Not weak, Julian dear, just very human,' Clarissa murmured kindly, giving my arm a friendly squeeze. 'Have you succeeded in getting anything out of her yet?'

'Nothing I can use without bringing her into danger.'

'I thought as much. She's clever, Julian, so watch your step. You've caught a bad go of the old measles and you won't be better till you get it out of your system. Have as much fun with her as you like but for God's sake don't trust her.'

'What a grand person you are, Clarissa,' I smiled. 'You've clarified all my vague ideas and put the whole issue in a nutshell. You couldn't have been sweeter about it, either. But tell me, now, what's the most tactful line to take? In the ordinary course of events I should join up with you now that you've arrived, but at the moment I'm sharing a table with Oonas. Are you game to meet her or would it be best if we kept the two parties entirely separate?'

'Of course I'll meet her and I shall be charming to her; but I think it would be best if you kept to your own table and don't bother about us too much for the next few days. She's certain to be jealous and possessive so that'll leave you quite free to amuse her and, at the same time, the less the two of you are with us the less chance there is of anything slipping out about our plans while she's present.'

Clarissa's suggestion seemed extremely sound as the less Oonas knew about our intentions the less opportunity she would have of proving dangerous to us if she did rat on me later. By the warmth of my thanks I tried to show Clarissa how very grateful I was to her and we strolled back to the hotel so that she could get on with her unpacking.

Oonas was in grand form over lunch. The Nile boat, on which we should have arrived, was due in that evening and she had arranged for her own car to be driven down from Cairo to meet her in Luxor. Her chauffeur had just reported to her and she said that now the car was here we could go on lots of expeditions in it.

After lunch I took the opportunity of introducing Oonas to the others and we all had coffee and liqueurs together in the lounge. The business went off better than I had expected.

Harry had no great brain but he was one of the most friendly people I have ever met and such a happy soul that it was second nature to him to be nice to everybody; without any deliberate effort he soon had Oonas talking and laughing. Clarissa backed him up with conscious skill and only Sylvia remained at first a little aloof; but directly she found that Oonas was interested in Egyptology she came out of her shell, and the five of us spent a very pleasant half-hour together.

Everything would have gone off quite splendidly if, just as we were breaking up, Sylvia had not said to me:

'If you're not doing anything this afternoon, Julian, I would very much like you to come for a walk round the town with me, because I want your advice on some things I have to see to.'

I guessed at once that she referred to the men Amin had got together for our expedition and she wanted me to vet. them before they were definitely engaged but, on the face of it, her invitation sounded as though she was just trying to carry me off for a quiet stroll.

As Oonas and I had not arranged to do anything and I knew that the sooner the job was done the better, I agreed at once; next moment I caught sight of Oonas' face and it was a positive revelation. She was staring at Sylvia as though she could cheerfully have killed her and, without another word, she picked up her bag and left us.

A rather awkward silence followed until Clarissa remarked that, having had to get up so early on the train, she was going to lie down; upon which Sylvia and I went off together.

To avoid any possibility of Oonas seeing what we were up to Sylvia had arranged that instead of the men parading on the steps of the hotel they should meet us down by the Nile boat landing-stage which was some little distance along the water-front. Amin was outside waiting for us and as we strolled along the Nile bank the two of them told me of the arrangements they had made.

The leading car was to take our guides and servants and the second, which would be driven in turns by Harry and myself, would also carry Sylvia, Clarissa and Amin. The other four vehicles were lorries containing our stores and water, each of which would need a driver and have a man on the box beside him to help with the general labour of digging the vehicles out of the sand when they got stuck, erecting tents, porterage and so on.

Amin produced a cook named Abdulla and two servants, Omar and Mussa; the last of whom could also act as chauffeur to the first car. We were to pick up our guides at the oasis of

Kharga but Amin had secured four reliable drivers for the lorries and four hefty-looking fellows to do the odd jobs.

Altogether we should number eighteen which was more than I really cared about but Amin said that as the lorry drivers could not be counted on to lift a hand outside looking after their vehicles it was essential to take at least three servants and the four labourers for general purposes. We had already worked out the amount of water we should require and two out of the four lorries were to be devoted entirely to it; that gave us an adequate supply for such a party but did not leave as large a margin against emergencies as I had hoped. The third lorry was to carry our petrol while the fourth would provide transport for our tents and stores.

I had not had much experience of engaging natives but I had a word with each of the men, impressing upon them the difficulties and dangers of the journey, and the replies of all of them were quite satisfactory. Sylvia, who really knew more about Gyppies than I did, agreed with me in this and I had enormous faith in Amin's judgment, so we duly signed them on for an exploration into the Libyan desert; the ostensible reason for which we gave as a geological survey of a portion of that vast, unknown region.

On the opposite side of the road from the landing-stage, right in the centre of Luxor's waterfront, rise the ruins of one of the finest temples in Egypt. It is not as big as the great temple of Amen-Ra at Karnak, although far larger than most Christian cathedrals, but having been built by Amenophis III, surnamed 'The Magnificent', in the 'great' period, its architecture is exceptionally fine; and, having done our business, Sylvia suggested that we should walk round it.

From the time of the fall of the Roman Empire, or in some cases earlier, right up to the middle of the last century all the temples of Egypt were left to fall into decay. The Coptic Christians, and later the Mohammedans, occupied miserable little corners of them for the worship of their less spectacular Gods and the rest of these vast, pillared halls were given over to the poorer towns-folk. Huts and lean-tos were built by the hundred in the courts and chambers, so that they became a rabbit-warren of slum dwellings and when these fell in others were erected on their debris.

By the 1850's, when the European archæologists first gained permission to excavate, the lower forty feet of the temples were entirely buried under a solid mass of refuse which had accumulated during some fifteen centuries. In addition, all and sundry were allowed to treat the temples as free stone-quarries and carry away any portion of them that they could manage to transport for their own purposes. When a law was at last passed to prevent this iniquity, one vandal had just made off with sufficient stone from a temple to build a sugar refinery; and it gives some idea of their immensity that in spite of these depredations which have gone on throughout the whole of the Christian era the greater part of most temples still remain to testify to the greatness of the people who built them.

The bulk of these ancient sanctuaries have now been cleared to their original ground level and as we wandered through the Luxor temple we saw, high up on one wall, the crude drawings with which the early Christians had defaced the beautiful Egyptian reliefs and, thirty feet above us in the corner of one courtyard, a mosque which is still used by an Arab congregation.

When the temple was cleared of refuse great efforts were made to obtain permission to demolish the mosque but the Egyptian Government would not grant it because a Mohammedan saint named Abu'l-Haggâg lies buried there; and Sylvia told me an interesting yarn about the excavator who had been foiled in his attempts to clear the whole temple.

The floor of the temple lies below the level of the Nile when the river is in flood and only about a hundred yards from it. Since the excavator could not induce the authorities to let him demolish this last incongruity which spoils the beauty of one of the courtyards, he planned so to arrange a new digging that there would be an 'accident' and when the Nile rose its waters would flood the whole temple, undermine the foundation of the mosque, now unprotected by refuse, and bring it crashing down. He completed his preparations and waited patiently for the Nile to rise but on the very night of the inundation, when he intended to remove the barriers so that the water would come rushing in, he died of a heart attack.

The Mohammedans, learning of his intentions afterwards, attributed his death to a miracle by their saint, Abu'l-Haggâg.

In any case, the mosque remains inviolate and still spoils the symmetry of the courtyard.

When I got back to the hotel I found Oonas sitting in my room staring out of the window. She had evidently been working herself up all the afternoon and, the instant I appeared, she treated me to a grand scene of jealous anger.

'How dare I', she demanded, 'leave her at the very first opportunity for that brazen, pasty-faced, yellow-haired Mademoiselle Shane?'

I assured her that I had not the least interest in Sylvia, or Sylvia in me, beyond perfectly normal friendship. But she raved on so that I could hardly get a word in edgeways, declaring that if I preferred that bloodless, flat-chested, gawky creature to herself, she was not prepared to submit to such an indignity; she would rather kill Sylvia and be killed herself than surrender me to her.

I pointed out that there was no question of her surrendering me to anybody but she became positively hysterical with jealous rage and accused me of having spent the afternoon in Sylvia's bedroom.

I took the only course possible with such a woman in such a state and lifting my hand I struck her with the flat of it sharply across the cheek.

For a moment her eyes goggled as though she was going to have a fit, then she burst into a violent storm of weeping; upon which I took her in my arms and kissed her.

It was a thoroughly unpleasant half-hour yet, owing to some strange twist of the female brain, the fact that I had administered the slap not only brought her to her senses but seemed to convince her that I really loved her, and by the time we parted to dress for dinner she was perfectly happy again.

In view of this jealous scene I thought it best that Oonas and Sylvia should not meet that evening so, after dinner, we just nodded to the others and went straight upstairs.

During the meal Oonas had suggested that next day we should make an expedition across the river; in consequence I ordered a picnic lunch to be packed for us and the following morning we set out together.

A motor-launch took us across the Nile and we were met on the other side by Oonas' chauffeur with her car which had been ferried across. It was a beautiful silver Rolls and it carried us in luxurious comfort through the fertile belt to the edge of the desert where many tombs and temples are situated beneath a long line of towering sandstone cliffs.

One of the most interesting spots is the beautiful temple of Deir el Ba'hari which is cut out of the living rock in three huge terraces. It was constructed by Egypt's greatest woman ruler, Hat-shept-sut, the Queen Elizabeth of Ancient Egypt. She lived in the time of the mighty XVIIIth Dynasty and married Thothmes II, who seems to have been such a weak ruler that, even as a young girl, she soon gathered all power into her hands. She later succeeded in deposing her weak consort and proclaimed herself the divinely-chosen heir of his dead father, Thothmes I; but her half-brother or possibly step-son—it is not quite clear which—was proclaimed Thothmes III by certain members of the powerful priesthood; upon which this determined lady married him too, in order to eliminate him as a rival.

Thothmes III, apparently, was a young man who did not like being dominated by his forceful and now middle-aged wife so he left her to combine with the exiled Thothmes II against her. She had some difficult years endeavouring to suppress the two of them but Thothmes II died and Thothmes III apparently decided that he had better give in to her, so he returned to Egypt and reigned with her as co-ruler although up to the age of 40 he remained entirely in the background and she ruled with absolute power for a period of untroubled years.

This was the more remarkable in that Thothmes III later proved to be the greatest monarch in all Egyptian history. When he was in his early forties Egypt's Syrian dominions revolted, so the Queen allowed him to go at the head of an army to suppress the rising. He was signally successful, and while he was away on this campaign she died. Released at last from the leading-strings of his elderly wife-stepmother-half-sister, he became the supreme ruler and reigned for another seventeen years, fighting fifteen campaigns and consolidating the Egyptian Empire from the Third Cataract of the Nile to the banks of the Euphrates.

The hatred which this great conqueror bore his consort, on account of the score of years during the prime of his manhood during which she had kept him idle and powerless, is recorded for ever by the vindictive manner in which, after her death, he defaced the monuments which she had erected.

Hat-shept-sut was a great builder and raised innumerable shrines to the gods where she was portrayed by carvings on the walls in the guise of a male Pharaoh divinely born, offering homage and incense to the local and national deities. With a fanatical thoroughness Thothmes III caused these images of her to be chipped out of the stone, together with her name which appeared in the Royal Cartouche beneath them. Throughout the length and breadth of Egypt he destroyed every memorial to her, with a single exception of one that is on a wall of the temple at Deir el Ba'hari; which he could not touch because the Queen is portrayed as a young girl being suckled by the cow-goddess Hathor and, since the two figures are linked together, he dared not deface that of the deity.

His efforts to erase the memory of the great queen from the annals of Egyptian history have proved quite unavailing, as the temples which she built are known and remain an abiding monument to the glory of her reign, while chief among them is this uniquely beautiful rock temple at Deir el Ba'hari.

It is here, along the inner side of one of the colonnades, that there is recorded the result of the first Egyptian expedition to the Land of Punt, as Abyssinia was called in those days. The Queen despatched five ships down the Red Sea and an exquisite series of carvings tells the story of the return of the expedition with ever sort of strange and valuable merchandise welcomed by a great multitude playing flutes and scattering flowers while there passes the procession of slaves and donkeys from the ships, laden down with gold, ebony, ivory, myrrh, living incense trees, baboons, apes, hounds and leopard skins.

Oonas and I spent the best part of the morning wandering round the temple and then retired to Cook's rest-house, which lies only about a quarter of a mile from it, to wash, eat our excellent picnic lunch and drink some of the best coffee procurable in Egypt.

We decided to spend the afternoon in the Valley of the Nobles which is in some ways more interesting than the Valley of the Kings as, although the tombs are much smaller, the paintings, instead of being confined to formal delineations of the Pharaohs and the Gods, are mainly scenes of family life as the Egyptians lived it and hoped it would be in the next world.

In many of them these paintings are of such an extraordinary freshness that although they were done over 3,000 years ago they have all the appearance of having been finished only yesterday. The scenes depicted, too, are so human that they bridge the great gulf of years and present the Egyptians as cultured, kindly people, very much like ourselves. The sort of episodes portrayed are: a nobleman fishing from a boat with his wife unpacking the picnic basket beside him while, as he leans over to spear a fish, his little daughter is throwing her arms round one of his legs for fear he might fall overboard; the overseer of a farm kneeling down to remove a thorn from a slave-girl's bare foot; a blind harper being fed after he has entertained a gentleman's family. In every tomb the husband and wife are pictured seated side by side on the far wall of the burial chamber with their arms twined affectionately round each other's waists.

One tomb appealed to us particularly; it was that of Sennufer, a prince of Thebes and superintendent of the Royal gardens. Unlike the others, the rock of its low roof had not been chiselled flat but left rugged; the whole ceiling had then been painted over with vine leaves and great bunches of purple grapes. Owing to the uneven surface it was extraordinarily effective and in the flickering light of the candles it really gave the temporary illusion that one was standing beneath a wide spread vinery where the grapes were just ripe for picking.

Climbing up and down the sides of the steep hills in which these tombs are situated, under the blazing sun, and scrambling down into their dark, narrow entrances was dusty and tiring work, so although our day was full of interest we were glad enough to re-cross the river about five o'clock and get back to the hotel for a badly-needed bath.

That evening, just as we were finishing dinner, Harry came over to ask if we would like to join up for coffee in the lounge afterwards and we naturally accepted. The usual nightly dance got going shortly afterwards and I danced with all three of the girls in turn. Sylvia was in excellent spirits although later it struck me that perhaps her gaiety was a little forced. While we were dancing together she chipped me a lot about my success with Oonas and, as I took it in good part, we were laughing most of the time that we glided round the room together.

It was that, I think, which upset Oonas again; added to the fact that she was an absolutely rotten dancer, heavy as lead and clumsy with it; whereas Sylvia, although much taller, was as light as a feather and danced divinely. She was obviously extremely fond of dancing, too, and as Harry was not particularly expert it was not surprising that a quarter of an hour later, when the band struck up an old favourite, she should suggest our dancing it together.

As I had only danced with Oonas once, this put the lid on it. She promptly stood up and declared sulkily that she was tired and going to bed. In common decency I could hardly say I was going with her and march off at the same moment so I wished her a polite good night and went on to the floor with Sylvia.

The incident served to change Sylvia's manner entirely. Instead of being amused she was annoyed and said at once:

'The stupid little fool! What does she think I want to do? Eat you? But I suppose she's so used to snatching other people's men that she thinks everyone is tarred with the same brush.'

'Now, now!' I laughed. 'Give her a chance. Although she's had a European education she's extraordinarily primitive in many of her idea and if you weren't so good-looking I don't suppose she would be so jealous.'

'Thanks for the compliment, but I'm no more attractive than three or four other girls you can see here if you look round the room. The thing is, if your little Gyppy friend considers herself fitted to mix with decent people she should learn our canons of behaviour. She ought to realise that girls like myself don't deliberately angle for young men who're obviously occupied elsewhere or want to rush off to bed with every man they meet.'

'She'll learn in time,' I shrugged. 'But I think what really got her was the fact that she's such a rotten dancer whereas you're quite obviously a star turn at the game.'

Sylvia thawed a little. 'I simply adore it and that's really what made me so angry. You dance awfully well yourself, Julian, and if this little minx hadn't come on the scene I should have had one of the best partners I've had for ages to dance with every evening. As it is, I suppose I've got to take a back seat, or else you'll have to pay for it by gruelling scenes of jealousy each night when you go along to that young woman's bedroom.'

'Why should you think I do that?' I asked.

'My dear, isn't that obvious? What possible attraction could she have for you otherwise? But don't think I blame you in the least. The tune they're playing at the moment is rather apt, isn't it, if you change the first word of its title? *She's Young and Healthy and You've Got Charm.*'

'You're young and healthy too.' I countered rather foolishly.

'Thanks. But I don't go in for that sort of thing. I'm not in the least prudish about other people's amusements, though. As a matter of fact, I think you're rather lucky to have Oonas fall for you because she looks as though she had been created for that sole purpose, and I wouldn't mind betting it's the breath of her life. The only thing that makes me so sick is her stupid and quite unwarrantable jealousy, because I do enjoy dancing with you quite frightfully much. Archie Lemming was pretty good but you're even better.'

'Lemming,' I repeated in surprise.

'Yes. As he was attached to father's outfit last winter we used to dance together practically every night except when we were up country on a "dig".'

It had not occurred to me till then that Sylvia and Lemming must know each other well and I asked if she had heard anything of him since his return to Egypt.

She shook her head. 'No. The poor boy must have gone crackers to get himself mixed up with O'Kieff, I think. Anyhow I was hoping you would take his place in giving me some dancing.'

'I'll do my very best,' I said, and although I really am terribly smitten with Oonas, I've no intention of letting her treat me like the proverbial slave. It won't do her any harm to learn that she can't have everything her own way.'

Afterwards I was rather sorry I had made that declaration as Sylvia took me at my word and, in the face of it, I could hardly make an excuse to get away and pacify Oonas; so I had to continue dancing, on and off, until the band stopped shortly after midnight.

Oonas was in a fine rage when I got upstairs and we had another blood-row on the question of Sylvia. The only way I could think of to quell the trouble this time was by refusing to discuss the situation or say one word until she had remained silent for a full five minutes and when she had come to the end of her abuse I sat there quietly smoking until the five minutes had ticked by. At the end of that time she was automatically reduced to a reasonable calm so I proceeded to give her a short but very forceful dissertation upon the difference between dancing and making love as understood in the Western world, together with an absolute assurance that I was not the least in love with Sylvia.

For the time being she accepted my assurance and became again the warm little cooing dove; but I felt that there was still 'Something rotten in the State of Denmark' since, after Oonas had left us that evening, the rest of us had agreed that we would eat our Christmas dinner in Luxor, and set out on our hunt for Cambyses' treasure on Boxing Day, which was in four days' time. What Oonas' reaction would be when she heard that I meant to leave her I simply dared not think.

19

The Tombs of the Kings

None of O'Kieff's or Zakri's people had shown up in Luxor so I was beginning to think that having failed to secure the lower half of the tablet they had decided to abandon the quest; more particularly, perhaps, because I had succeeded in dealing them some thoroughly nasty knocks, and knowing that I was now in touch with Essex Pasha they feared that there would be further trouble to come if they started anything else against us.

That did not really suit my book as my desire for full vengeance had by no means slackened. I wanted to carry the war into the enemy's camp but, for the time being, I could see no way of doing so. In the first place I had no fresh line to go upon except by making use of the information with which Oonas had supplied me; and that, for her sake, I could not do. Secondly I had involved myself in this treasure-hunt with Sylvia and the Belvilles. Earlier on it had seemed certain that O'Kieff and I would clash over that, which was just what I wanted, but now it appeared less likely I could hardly let the others down; and, I will confess, the whole problem of Cambyses' lost legions intrigued me immensely. By going off into the desert I might lose a few weeks but, as I had a whole life-time in which to track O'Kieff down, the loss seemed worth it.

Up to the moment it certainly looked as if we were to be allowed to get away from Luxor without further interference and I was quite definitely booked for the trip; but it was clear that I could not take Oonas with me, even if she were willing to submit to the hardships of the journey, which she would unquestionably loathe. Apart from the probable refusal of the others to have her along, anyhow, I did not need them to point out to me that in the event of our discovering the treasure we should be completely at her mercy if she chose to blackmail us afterwards by threatening to give away our activities to the

Egyptian Government; and, once her passion for me had died down, that was just the sort of thing she might attempt to do.

Although I knew that I ought to tell Oonas how things stood, I dared not risk an immediate blow-up with her in case she got active at once and threatened to disclose the secret purpose of our expedition right away. I had been dreading that she would make some reference to it but, apparently, she was so absorbed in our love-affair, her jealousy of Sylvia and the antiquities we were visiting that the reason for the Belvilles presence in Luxor had temporarily failed to trouble her mind. As far as I could see there was no alternative but to postpone the evil hour, conceal our preparations for departure from her and only tell her that the time had come to part just before we set off into the desert; meanwhile I endeavoured to shelve my uneasy forebodings as far as possible.

The following day Sylvia took the Belvilles to see the Valley of the Kings so we saw nothing of them; we got up late and spent a lazy day, contenting ourselves with a sail on the river in the afternoon. In the evening Oonas behaved rather well, I thought, because it would have been difficult to avoid the others, unless we had gone straight to bed, and she suggested off her own bat that we should return their gesture of the night before by asking them to join us after dinner.

The more I pushed Oonas round the dance floor, the more I appreciated the intervening dances which I had with Sylvia and Clarissa. I freely confess that I felt rather a cad about it and I did my level best not to show the way I felt; but it was quite understandable that the sight of Sylvia and myself moving like one to the rhythm of the jazz band must have galled Oonas terribly, after our own awkward attempts together, and to spare her as far as possible I broke the party up early on my own accord.

During the succeeding days I kept the two girls apart as far as possible by arranging expeditions so that they should not encounter each other, but having established the custom of our all spending the evening together it was virtually impossible to break it off without appearing flagrantly rude. Sylvia was unreasonable each time I tried to cut down my dances with her; and Oonas became sullen and openly spiteful on every occasion that I left the table for a few turns round the floor. Harry and

271

Clarissa did their best to smooth matters over and always by some tactful intervention succeeded in preventing an open and humiliating scene; but we were constantly on the edge of a flare-up. The two girls now did not even take the trouble to conceal their intense dislike for each other and I had more and more difficulty in persuading Oonas that Sylvia was absolutely nothing to me but a friend. My own position during these evenings was the unfortunate one so aptly recorded in Gay's lines from the Beggar's Opera:

> 'How happy could I be with either
> Were t'other dear charmer away.'

Sylvia and the Belvilles continued their preparations for our departure and although I was of little help to them I was kept informed of all that they were doing. By Christmas Eve everything was in readiness for our expedition down to the last detail but it was at the dance that night that the antagonism between the two girls boiled over. At about eleven-thirty I was pushing Oonas round the floor when she said that she was fed up with dancing and would like to go to bed so, although it was Christmas Eve, I made an excuse to break up the party.

It was then Sylvia who made trouble, I suppose because she was so passionately devoted to dancing and angry at having her evening's fun cut short; but with a lazy smile at me as we said good night, she murmured:

'Don't you think, Julian, it would be a good idea if you got the professional to give the Princess some dancing-lessons as a Christmas present? I'm sure she'd enjoy her evenings then ever so much more.'

It was a stupid, unkind thing to say and she flushed scarlet the moment she had said it. She apologised to me, too, most handsomely the next day and swore that the second the words were out she could have bitten off her tongue.

'Really! I don't think the Princess needs dancing-lessons,' I said quickly.

Oonas was almost white with rage but she controlled herself magnificently and had the best of the encounter since she looked Sylvia up and down calmly before she said:

'In my country women of position consider it beneath them

272

to dance for the purpose of alluring men. Only courtesans find it necessary to achieve Mademoiselle Shane's perfection in that respect.'

It was a nasty crack but Sylvia had asked for it and my sympathies were all with Oonas as I followed her from the room. True, when it actually came down to brass tacks, it was *she* who had flung herself at my head, but I'd done the running-up knowing perfectly well that she was a thorough bad hat. It takes two to make an *affaire* as well as two to make a quarrel and, having taken her on, she was my young woman as long as it lasted so I wasn't going to allow her to be slighted or made fun of.

Next morning Sylvia did the decent thing by sending her a large box of chocolates as a Christmas present and a note to say that when she had spoken of dancing-lessons she had momentarily forgotten that we were in Egypt. Oonas, not to be outdone, sent her back a diamond bracelet worth about £300, and when I protested that Sylvia would never accept it she showed me a note she was enclosing which read, 'Since we *are* in Egypt Mademoiselle Shane will, I trust, accept this trifle, as such offerings are not unusual between women in my country even if it is not the custom to make them in her own.' As Oonas was travelling with enough jewels to stock a shop it cost her nothing and gave her the last laugh as well as the satisfaction of remarking to me:

'Since the poor thing has nothing to wear except that rope of fake pearls, she will be as proud as a peacock of this when she can forget where it came from.'

Rather to my surprise Sylvia did acccept although afterwards I learned that she had put it aside to return later. Christmas Day passed without episode but its gaieties were marred for me by the knowledge that when night came I would have to break the news to Oonas that I was leaving her on the following day.

We had told the Manager of the Winter Palace that we were going up to the Oasis of Kharga, from which we intended to do a fortnight's camping in the desert and, instead of making a morning start, which would entail early rising for our final packing, we had arranged to set off in the late afternoon, covering the first stage of our journey in the cool of the evening.

273

By postponing the news of our departure until the following day I might have evaded the scene which I knew I was bound to have with Oonas. At worst I could have left her weeping on the terrace, but I felt that would have been a rotten thing to do and, quite apart from the fact that I had to get my packing done which she was sure to notice, I felt I owed it to her to let her blackguard me as much as she had a mind to in private.

When I broke it to her she at first appeared quite stunned and I had to repeat my words twice before she fully took them in; but once she really understood the situation her rage was unbelievable.

She had known quite well why the Belvilles and I had come to Luxor yet for some reason she had assumed that our preparations for the expedition would take ever so much longer and comforted herself with the thought that she would have ample opportunity to dissuade me from going on it before the time for my departure came. Now that she was faced with it without warning she was positively livid with me for not having told her of my plans earlier.

It was a frightful business trying to persuade her that I was just as distressed at our parting as she was and the greater part of my protestations were perfectly true. During the last ten days she had given me many wonderful moments which I felt I should never forget and I am quite sure that if it had not been for Sylvia's presence the whole of our time together would have been a blissfully happy one. I knew only too well that there were going to be many nights, not only out in the desert but in the months to come, when I should positively ache to feel her in my arms again. I had temporarily forgotten the evil side of her entirely and that only just over a week before she had plotted my murder; I could only feel now that I had treated her abominably and was behaving like the very worst sort of outsider in abandoning her like this.

In time her rage exhausted her and she was just a small, weeping bundle in my arms; sobbing as though her heart would break. It was nearly three o'clock in the morning before I could really make her understand that I was absolutely adamant in my determination to leave Luxor with the Belvilles and she began to show some signs of resignation.

We had been to the Valley of the Kings together two days

before but she suddenly reminded me that we had planned a second visit for the coming day and asked me, quite meekly, if I intended to rob her of that too.

Actually I had meant to cancel it, because there were so many odd jobs I had to see to before leaving Luxor; but, as things were, I simply had not the heart to tell her that the trip was off. I resigned myself to the prospect of scrambling through my packing early in the morning and determined to get back from the Valley as soon as I could in the afternoon.

It was a very subdued Oonas who met me in the lounge of the hotel some seven hours later at the time we had fixed for setting off on our expedition. On our previous trips we had never taken a guide because we knew most of the principal places of interest from having both stayed in Luxor, although at different times, during the previous winter. I was a little surprised, therefore, when we went out on to the terrace, to find a strange dragoman bowing before us and to learn that Oonas had engaged him for the trip.

'This is Sayed,' she said. 'The hall porter recommended him as I thought that today we might have a look at one or two of the less-well-known tombs which neither of us have seen yet.' I agreed at once and we went down to the launch which took us across the smoothly-flowing river.

We did the few miles across the fertile area in Oonas' car and, leaving Deir el Ba'hari on our left, entered a rift in the hills through which the track winds for a couple of miles to the famous Valley of the Tombs of the Kings. I had been through that barren, sun-scorched ravine quite a number of times before but I found it as overwhelmingly impressive as ever.

The rough road twists between great naked sandstone cliffs with precipitous sides and the innumerable huge boulders with which the bottom of the gully is strewn. It is indeed a Valley of the Dead since no living thing grows there and it is said that even snakes and vultures will not inhabit that wilderness of stone. Outwardly, perhaps, it differs little from many other valleys in the Libyan Hills yet it has an atmosphere all its own. Its utter desolation seems to cry aloud that it is the very end of the world and that beyond the shimmering heat-haze which rises from its rock-strewn vistas can lie only the gates of Hades. The very silence and mystery of the place make it incredibly awe-inspiring and, once in it, all sense of time is lost. The modern world seems a million miles away and at any moment one expects to come upon one of those great processions of white-robed, shaven-headed priests and brilliantly-clad captains which, long before the days of Rome or Athens or Carthage, passed that way with solemn chanting and regal pageantry to lay the Pharaohs of the Empire in their magnificent resting-places.

The Valley ends at last in a great pit surrounded on all sides. but for its narrow entrance, by glaring, reddish-yellow cliffs which are broken here and there by steep spurs running down into it; and it is under these that the Tombs of the Kings were cut out of the living rock.

There are about sixty tombs in all and very nearly all of them were robbed of their precious contents during the period of anarchy which succeeded the fall of the Egyptian Empire. Many of the empty tombs were already an attraction to tourists as far back as Graeco-Roman times but a great number of them were lost trace of by falls of rock covering their entrances during the centuries in which the Arab Dynasties made Egypt inaccessible to European travellers. In the middle of the last century only about twenty were known, but the archæological expeditions from European countries and the United States have since succeeded in opening up the rest with, it is believed, only two exceptions, which they have still failed to trace.

Of all the tombs so opened in modern times only two had escaped the tomb-robbers of the past and were found with the mummies and treasures in them just as they had been sealed by the priests after the burial.

That of Tut-ankh-amen, the discovery of which made archæological history, was one; and it escaped the depredations of the robbers only because it is an exceptionally small tomb and lies between two others in a place where there seems hardly room enough for a tomb at all. The great store of treasures found in this little tomb gives some idea of the immense riches which must have been looted from the others, many of which were at least twenty times its size. The other tomb which was found intact was that of Iuau and Thuau, the foreign parents-in-law of the 'Heretic Pharaoh'. This, too, was a comparatively small tomb but the riches in it form the second-finest collection of Egyptian antiquities in the world.

As even an energetic visitor can only manage three or four tombs in one morning, few people see more than eight during a fortnight's stay in Luxor since, apart from the Valley of the Kings, there are those of the Nobles and the Queens and half-a-score of the most important temples in Egypt for the enthusiast to cover there.

Only the half-dozen or so most important tombs have been made easily accessible to tourists by concrete steps, where they are necessary, hand-rails on the slopes and the installation of electricity. The others must be inspected by candle-light and one has to slither down in to them as best one can while holding aloft a guttering candle.

The period of a tomb can easily be guessed as they are of three quite different types. The Kings of the XVIIIth Dynasty, who were the earliest to be buried there, had constructed for them a series of deep pits sloping almost sheer down into the rock but joined by horizontal passages, the sarcophagus-chamber being right at the bottom and often several hundred feet below the surface of the earth. The XIXth Dynasty rulers modified the grade of the slopes so that one can walk down them without much difficulty, while those of the XXth Dynasty burrowed with only very slight slope almost direct into the sides of the hills.

Individually they vary in accordance with the length of the reign of the monarch for whom they were hewn. Directly a Pharaoh came to the throne he commenced work upon his last resting-place; a passage often as much as twelve feet square, was dug in to the cliff followed by a room of twenty feet or so wide. If the Pharaoh's reign was short, as in the case of Tut ankh-amen, this would be the sarcophagus-chamber. If the reign continued, side-chambers were often added and then another passage and another chamber further in the cliff face, which, in turn, became the sarcophagus-chamber if the reign was of medium length; but if the reign were a long one several passages and several chambers would be constructed so that the tunnel penetrated further and further into the rock as the years went by.

Not one of the tombs is finished; each ends in a jagged passage or a partly-hewn room. The moment the Pharaoh died work on his tomb was abandoned and one can still see the various stages of the walls where the work was left uncompleted. In turn there came the miners who hacked out a rough, rectangular passage, the masons who worked its surface to a polished smoothness, the priests who drew the sacred symbols quite roughly outlined in red paint, the artists who did a new and perfect outline over them in black, the sculptors who chiselled out the images and, lastly, the men who painted them in glowing colours.

The sculptures and wall-paintings are all of a religious nature, consisting of portions of the text and illustrations of the Book of the Litanies of Ra, the Book of the Gates, the Book of Him who is in Underworld, the Book of the Opening of the Mouth and the Book of the Dead, which together composed the sacred literature of the Egyptians. Their purpose was that when the dead King awoke from the sleep of death he should have before him in the hieroglyphics on the walls of his tomb, or those which embellished his huge granite coffin, all the magic texts and symbols which he would need to know in answering the many monsters who would bar his passage through the Valley of the Shādows before he could enter the Boat of Ra and sail to the Egyptian Paradise.

The earlier tombs, like that of Amenophis II of the XVIIIth Dynasty, are the more sombre and restful to the eye and the figures on their walls are not carved but only painted, although their artistry is very pure and beautiful. The XIXth Dynasty tombs show no falling off in the purity of their art and they have the added attraction that every figure and symbol in them was carved in relief before it was painted; their painting is also much more colourful. That of Seti I, who was the third king of the Dynasty, is perhaps the finest in the whole Valley. With the temple which he built to Osiris at Abydos it forms the highspot of all Egyptian art during the Empire period and can only be rivalled by the work of the artists of the Old Kingdom who wrought with such skill at Sakkara nearly two thousand years earlier. By the time of the coming of the XXth Dynasty a slight decadence had set in. The huge tombs of Rameses VI and Rameses IX, which are fine examples of the period, are even more colourful than those of the earlier Dynasties; but their vivid paintings make them a little crude and the draughtsmen of that era lacked something of the perfection of their pre-decessors.

Oonas and I had visited most of the important tombs before, either separately or together, but neither of us had seen that of Merenptah, which is very fine, so we went down into it and afterwards visited that of the general who usurped the throne on the death of Tut-ankh-amen, the Pharaoh Horemheb. Over an hour of our time had gone when we came up again into the sunshine out of the cool yet stuffy darkness. I did not think much of Sayed, the guide she had provided, but he seemed willing enough and quite a decent fellow.

'What would you like to tackle now?' I asked her. 'There are still any number of them we haven't seen although we've done the best ones.'

'How about Thothmes III?' she suggested.

The guide shook his head. 'I would not advise this one, my ladyship. There was a fall of rock in Thothmes III last year; so it is not very safe any more.'

'Is it shut now?' she asked.

'No, it not shut,' he replied slowly. 'But only the archæolo-gists make visit there. You no like—no interest.'

Thothmes III was the gentleman who, after remaining tied to Queen Hat-shept-sut's apron-strings for some thirty-odd years, had become the greatest conqueror in all the long history of his country. The idea of visiting the Egyptian Napoleon's grave had suddenly appealed to me, so I said:

'If the grave is officially open it must be safe and even if there isn't much to see I should like to visit it on account of the personality of the man who was buried there.'

Still, Sayed demurred. 'It is a long way from here, and one must go down ladders to get to it, my lord. It is much trouble-some to get. The tomb is down in a deep pit which we have to reach by climbing up into the hills.'

'I don't mind that, darling,' Oonas said, 'if you'd like to see it. I should, because his being such a great King makes it in one way really the most interesting tomb in the Valley.'

'Right ho! Let's go there, then,' I agreed.

Sayed shrugged his shoulders. 'If my lordship wishes I will

ask one of the guardians for the keys; but it is a long walk and he will tire my ladyship.'

The Arabs, generally speaking, are a lazy lot and I had a shrewd suspicion that Sayed was only raising objections because he was himself unwilling to undertake the exertion of getting there in the hot sunshine which was now grilling down upon us. In any case I knew that his talk of the place being dangerous must be sheer nonsense, otherwise the authorities would not have allowed the tomb to remain open to the public. Still grumbling and muttering he shambled off to see the tomb guardians about the keys.

A few minutes later he came back with one of them who proved equally averse to our making the visit. He said that there was no danger of the tomb itself caving in, as the fall of rock had been outside its entrance, but that .it meant a steep climb first and that in the descent to the entrance of the tomb afterwards one might have a nasty fall; only the professional archæologists ever bothered to go there and so far the tomb had not been opened even once this season.

The very fact that so few visitors to Egypt had ever been down into the tomb of the great conqueror made us all the keener and, as Oonas pointed out, if the way to it really proved too steep and dangerous we could always turn back; so the tomb guardian took one of the large keys off a big iron ring that he carried at his belt and handed it to Sayed.

Leaving the bottom of the Valley, where all the best-known tombs are situated, we followed Sayed slowly up a footpath that led along one of the spurs coming down from the ridge of hills. The way was very steep and ten minutes later we were a hundred feet above the valley bottom, moving in single file along a shaly track that ran parallel to the windings of a nearby precipice.

On our right, across the gulf, we could see another precipice and the two gradually closed in to form a narrow gully which ran deep into the heart of the mountain. It was the best part of half an hour before we reached its end and it was here, at the bottom of a perpendicular chimney, enclosed on three sides by sheer cliffs, that the entrance to the tomb lay. Evidently too, it could not be approached along the bottom of the gully as the only way down to it was by a succession of ladders tied to a rickety scaffolding precariously fixed in the cliff-face.

'Have you ever visited this tomb before?' I asked Sayed.

'Once, my lord,' he replied uneasily. 'I had to for the obtaining of my guide's certificate; but it is not a nice place and I had hoped never to have to go again.'

Here was the explanation of his reluctance to bring us there but I only laughed and promised him an extra good tip for the trouble to which we were putting him.

'How d'you feel about it now?' I enquired of Oonas. 'Is your head all right for heights? Or would you rather we chucked it up?'

She shook her head, smiled and she placed a small, soft hand in one of mine.

'It seems a pity not to go down now we are here after that tiring walk, and I shall not be frightened if you hold me firmly.'

'All right, then, I murmured, stepping on the ladder. 'I'll go first and if you'll come after me step by step my arms will be round you so that you can't possibly fall.'

It wasn't really such a difficult business and we reached the foot of the last ladder a little breathless but quite safely. Standing as we were now, at the bottom of the rock chimney, the entrance of the tomb still lay some twenty feet below us and the only way down to it was over a tumbled pile of jagged rocks.

'I will go first here,' said Sayed, 'and my ladyship can come after, putting a hand on my shoulder.'

We followed as he suggested and reached the iron doors built into the rock-face. He inserted the key in the lock which had evidently not been oiled since the previous winter, as he had some difficulty in turning it, but at last he got it open.

He then produced from his pocket some candles which we had used in the tomb of Horemheb and lighting three of them, gave us one apiece.

The tomb being of the XVIIIth Dynasty period was one of the very deep ones which go down almost perpendicularly into the earth and the first ramp was so steep that we could hardly keep upright as we shuffled forward, down into the pitchy, musty blackness. At its end we came to a flight of stairs, one side of which had fallen away into the depths of an unseen chasm below, so that in places only about nine inches' width of the stairway remained to tread upon. Negotiating this dangerous patch was a tricky and unpleasant business. We had to flatten ourselves against the wall and, as well as holding our candles, Sayed and I had more or less to support Oonas between us.

Her breath was coming quickly and I knew that she was scared but when I suggested that we had gone quite far enough and should turn back she would not hear of it and I admired her pluck tremendously.

We passed through a largish square chamber and then descended another steep ramp. At its bottom there was a short passage-way and I suddenly caught a hollow ring beneath Sayed's feet as he led us through it. Next moment he paused and lit a length of magnesium tape which gave a sudden, lurid flame. By its glare I saw that we had just reached a wooden bridge which spanned a wide chasm the full width of the passage. He motioned to us to peer down into the dark abyss and said:

'For the tomb robbers. The Pharaohs very clever. They make these pits in the middle of the tunnel and when the priests have buried the king they take away the bridge afterwards. The robbers come and they don't know that. They fall down in the dark and break their necks. When this tomb opened they find the skeletons of six men down there. Tomb robbers who have kill themselves or died of thirst because unable to get out.'

I had seen such pits before in other tombs and knew their purpose, and I was anxious that we should get off that narrow bridge so, with a quick word, I hurried him on.

He dropped the few remaining inches of the flaming tape into the great man-trap and, as it fluttered down into the unseen depths, we caught a glimpse of the shaft's sheer, perpendicular sides. On the far side of the bridge the passage took a sharp right-angle turn and, ten yards further on, turned again just before entering the sarcophagus-chamber.

Sayed lit another length of magnesium tape and on glancing round I saw at once that the tomb really was worth a visit for its own sake. More people would undoubtedly go there if it were not so difficult of access and the guides so reluctant to undertake the venture. It was decorated in much the same manner as the tomb of Amenophis II; painted texts and figures upon a dull ground; but in shape it was quite unlike the sarcophagus-chamber of any other tomb, as it formed a long oval similar to the cartouche in which the Pharaohs always enclosed the hieroglyphics representing their names.

'Burial place of King Thothmes the Third,' Sayed announced parrot fashion. 'Very great King. Make all neighbouring nations bow down to Egypt. Very long reign; fifty-four year. This one of the deepest tombs in whole valley. We are now three hundred feet below ground; over four hundred feet below cliff top. Tomb robbed and mummy removed long, long ago, but coffin still here.' With his hand he struck the sarcophagus a resounding blow which echoed hollowly round the chamber.

It was not a very big coffin compared with the hundred-ton affairs I had seen in some of the other tombs. On the floor near it I noticed a little heap of broken fragments from alabaster vases and carved faïsance figures which clearly showed that very few people ever visited the place, otherwise such interesting souvenirs would have long since been mopped up by the tourists.

Oonas remained standing in the entrance of the chamber as I moved forward with Sayed to examine the pile of pieces. Just as I was stooping over them she spoke.

'Well, now we're here, what do you think of it, Julian?'

'It's far more interesting than I expected,' I said. 'I'm awfully glad we came.'

'I wish we could see some more of the tombs together,' she said slowly.

'So do I,' I replied, 'but I'm afraid that's not possible as I have to get back directly after lunch.'

'You have quite made up your mind to go, then?'

'Yes; you know that. I can't let the others down.'

'Can't you possibly persuade them to let you take me with you?'

I straightened up and turned towards her. 'Now, please!' I said. 'Don't let's spoil our last few hours together by going into all that again. With the five of us, day after day, never out of each others' sight for weeks on end there would be the most frightful quarrels. You and Sylvia hate the sight . . .'

I got no further. By the light of the candle she was holding I saw Oonas' expression change with incredible swiftness from one of meekness to frenzied, diabolical rage.

'Sylvia!' she screamed. 'It is for her you are determined to leave me!' Next second she shrilled out a hysterical command in Arabic.

Before I could turn Sayed, who was standing just behind me, hit me a heavy blow on the back of the head with some sort of bludgeon he had been concealing in his robe.

I pitched forward on to the floor and for a moment I must have been knocked unconscious. A blinding pain seemed to split my head in two and when I could see again the sarcophagus-chamber was lit only by a faint glow barely outlining its entrance. Oonas and Sayed had disappeared and I could hear their footfalls as they hurried back along the corridor.

I tried to stagger up but fell again. With a supreme effort I forced myself to my knees, then to my feet, and lurched towards the fast-dimming square of the entrance. Filled with ungovernable horror at the thought that they meant to leave me there, I blundered out into the ante-chamber and across it. My feet seemed weighed down with lead and my head swayed limply from side to side on my shoulders. But the light was brighter here and somehow I managed to reach the middle of the passage where it was divided by the deep pit.

At its edge I fell again and a fresh access of terror shook me. I saw that Oonas and Sayed were standing on the far side of the gulf and had removed the plank bridge so that I could not cross it.

'Oonas!' I gasped. 'Oonas!' but a croaking whisper was all that I could manage.

She held her candle aloft so that I could see her face and the light glinted on her great, widely spaced blue eyes but they held no trace of mercy as she cried harshly:

'You thought you were going to have a fine time in the desert with that tow-headed stick of an English girl, didn't you? What a fool you must be to think that I would let you leave me for her. She loves you. I know that; but now she shall eat her heart out believing that you've thrown her over to remain with me.'

Before I could whisper a plea for mercy or attempt to reason with her, Oonas turned away. My strength was ebbing and the light from the candles faded as their echoing foot-falls receded in the distance. The pit now cut me off from them. Even if I had had the strength to rise again it would have been impossible for me to reach them before they locked the iron gates at the entrance of the tomb and passed out into the daylight hundreds of feet above my head.

My last thought, before I sank into black unconsciousness, was the appalling certainty that there was no hope of escape and that I must die there in the darkness.

20

Buried Alive

For the first few seconds after I came to I did not realise where I was or what had happened to me but, all too soon, full consciousness returned and my numbed brain recovered sufficiently to savour racing thoughts that made me shake with abject terror.

I was lying face-downwards where I had dropped in the passage-way with one arm dangling over the sharp edge of the shaft that had been cut nearly thirty-four centuries before to trap tomb-robbers. Withdrawing it hastily I scrambled up into a sitting position and shrank back against the wall. My head ached abominably from a dull pain which increased and diminished regularly with the rhythm of my pulsing blood. Very gingerly I felt the back of my head and the dampness my finger-tips encountered told me that it was bleeding; but my dark hair is thick and I thought it unlikely that my skull was cracked particularly as the blow had only knocked me out for a few seconds after it was first delivered.

An icy sweat had broken out on my forehead. As I brushed it away I knew that I must try to control my panic. Almost instinctively, with fumbling fingers, I searched for my cigarettes and lighter. As I lit one the flame threw weird shadows on the walls and, beside me to the right, I could see the black gulf of the pit.

For a moment I wondered whether I could get across in one desperate flying leap but almost as soon as I thought of it I knew that it was impossible. The part of the passage where I sat took a right-angled turn almost immediately on my left which meant that I could not get more than a two-yards' run and with a ghastly sinking of the heart I admitted to myself that I was trapped in the lower portion of the tomb. If I attempted to jump the pit I should only precipitate my end by falling short and crashing headlong upon its bottom.

The impossibility of getting across did not depress me quite so much when I'd had time to realise that had I been able to do so I should have been little better off. Even if I could have reached the iron gates of the tomb, situated as they were in the bottom of a gully a hundred feet below the track along the cliff which was their only approach, I might have shouted until my voice cracked but the chances were a thousand to one against anyone's hearing me unless they were actually descending the ladders to the tomb.

The chance that someone might pay the place a visit, and find me there before I died, seemed my only possible hope and I began to wonder how much likelihood there was of that. The tomb guardian had told us that the grave of Thothmes III had not been opened since the previous winter which showed clearly that visits to it were of very rare occurrence, while the bits of alabaster and pottery scattered about the sarcophagus-chamber substantiated the fact that it was almost unheard of for a casual traveller to come there.

Every Egyptologist worthy of the name would certainly inspect the tomb of such an important monarch at one time or another but having once viewed its unique oval burial-chamber there was nothing else to call for a second visit. Most of the members of the archæological missions then digging in the neighbourhood of Luxor were old hands and would have been down into my prison during their first seasons. It seemed that my hope of life hung upon the slender chance that some new-comer to one of the missions might decide on making the descent; or, perhaps, an Arab who had to do so once before he could qualify as a licensed guide. But unless one of them arrived in the next two days, which I reckoned was about the limit to which I could hold out without water, I felt that there was no chance of my ever seeing daylight again.

Curiously enough, by the time I had got that far in my speculations all panic had left me and for the time being, at least, I felt almost resigned to die. I have never been afraid of death; since it can only be one of two things; either a complete black-out into nothingness or a passing on, as all religions encourage us to hope, into some more pleasant state.

The black-out theory is argued very soundly by materialists but it has always seemed inconceivable to me that life should be quite meaningless and, if it is governed at all, the laws which govern it should be logical; in which case all effort towards mental growth automatically leads us somewhere and, as there is no adequate reward for striving visible in this present life, this postulates another where we shall reap what we have sown. Having once arrived at the conclusion that all the probabilities lie in favour of there being some form of life after death I had long since come to regard death as the beginning of the greatest adventure of all.

On the other hand, while I had no fear of death, I have always had a very great fear of dying. It is a regrettable fact that only a very small percentage of people are fortunate enough to die from old age, quietly in their sleep, or painlessly under an anaesthetic. The great majority are cut off before their time by some sort of violence which is almost inevitable painful or, perhaps worse, linger for weeks or months before they are finally carried off by some agonising disease.

Now that I began to think about dying as a personal matter which I should have to face within a time that could be more or less measured by hours, I shrank from the ordeal; particularly as it seemed that death from thirst must be my portion and by all accounts that is a very painful form of death indeed.

I wondered how I could circumvent it. If I had had my gun on me I could have blown my brains out, but I had left it in my room at the hotel. Whether I should have had the courage to put a pistol to my head and pull the trigger I do not know. Time is an illusion, as we see by our experience of everyday life, from the dreary dragging of school hours as opposed to the fleeting of lovers' moments; and I have often thought that although it may only be a fraction of a second in *our* time from the explosion of a suicide's pistol to the moment when he lies limp and dead, he may experience what seem to him hours of appalling torture as the bullet smashes in the bone formation of his skull and sears like a white-hot comet through the delicate membrane surrounding his palpitating brain.

I could always throw myself down the pit but it was far from certain that I should die instantly; I might quite well lie there broken, bleeding and in agony for hours before I actually expired.

Then I had an inspiration. I could open the veins in my arm with my penknife. In the dark I should not see the blood and as it drained away from me I should slip out of life by the easy road of gradual weakening till I fell into a state of unconsciousness. I recalled with some perturbation that a doctor had once told me the reason the Romans always lay in a hot bath when adopting this highly civilised form of suicide was because unless the body were kept at an even temperature during the draining of blood, which naturally lowered it, violent cramp was liable to set in. I had no hot bath in which to die gracefully like the immortal Petronius but I felt that the pains of cramp when I was just on the point of expiring could be borne with much more fortitude than countless hours of agonising thirst.

It cheered me a lot to think that opening my veins would always provide a way of escaping the worst horrors that beset me; but for the moment I was much too full of life to think of putting it into practice and with a sudden dread that later I might temporarily forget my bearings in the pitchy blackness and fall into the pit by mistake, I decided to make my way back to the sarcophagus-chamber. Taking out my lighter I snapped it open and by the aid of its tiny flame, which did no more than dispel the gloom for a few feet round me, I limped painfully down the passage into the big, oval vault.

As my hopelessly inadequate torch lit only a small section of the chamber I made a tour round it and found, as I already believed, that it was completely empty except for the stone coffin which had once contained the body of the Pharaoh, near its far end, and the broken bits of funeral offerings, the larger of which showed as faintly white patches upon the floor each time I lowered the lighter to see where I was stepping.

Only one thing came of my inspection, but that filled me with more elation than the finding of a casket of jewels would have done in the same circumstances. I came across the piece of candle which had fallen from my hand at the moment Sayed had knocked me out. It was a good five inches long and although I knew quite well that it brought me no nearer to any prospect of escape I regarded the finding of it almost as

Heaven's direct answer to a prayer. The petrol in my lighter was liable to run out at any moment; whereas the candle would at least ensure me several hours of blessed light.

Dusting a clear space on the floor I set it up carefully between two good-sized fragments of pottery, lit it and snapped my lighter shut; then I sat down beside it with my back against the big stone coffin and, as well as my aching head would permit, did my best to review the situation calmly.

My entombment by Oonas had clearly been a premeditated act. After she had exhausted herself in the violent scene to which she had treated me the night before she must have lain awake in bed beside me in the darkness plotting my death. She had left me about six o'clock in the morning and, instead of going to sleep for a couple of hours in her own bed, she must have dressed at once and gone out to find a man suited to her purpose. Perhaps Sayed had been her guide in Luxor the previous winter; in any case, she probably knew him already and that he was the sort of unscrupulous rogue who would be prepared to do exactly what she told him for a sufficient reward and the promise of her protection. She must have primed him beforehand to appear unwilling to take us down into the tomb of Thothmes III so as to avert any suspicion on my part that she was deliberately luring me there. Oonas was clever enough to know that just such reluctance by a guide to show something of special interest in order, apparently, to save himself a little trouble, was the one thing calculated to make me insist on seeing it.

I wondered how far, if at all, the tomb guardian who had given Sayed the key could be involved and decided that everything pointed to his being an innocent party. The tomb guardians all lived out here on the far side of the river from Luxor so Oonas could have had no opportunity to get at him early that morning and, as she had never left me from the time we entered the Valley, she had certainly had no chance to conduct such a delicate negotiation as bribing him to be a party to a murder while we were there. For a moment, that gave me renewed hope of rescue. Sayed would have to hand him back the key and if he noticed that whereas a man and woman had gone off to the tomb with Sayed only the woman had returned, he might make enquiries as to what had happened to the man;

and, if these did not prove satisfactory, perhaps come along later to verify them for himself.

A moment's thought dispelled that hope as I put myself in Oonas' shoes and considered what I should have done had I been in her place. Other than the gorge by which cars arrive at the great natural bowl in which the Tombs are situated, there is only one way out from it; this is by a steep track which leads up a spur into the mountains whereby, after three quarters of an hour's hard climb, one comes out upon a flat cliff-top five hundred feet above the rock hewn temple of Deir el Ba'hari. From this spot there is one of the most magnificent views obtainable in the whole of the Nile Valley.

Luxor can be clearly seen some five miles distant on the opposite bank; the river winds away for mile after mile on either hand and below, as though charted on a map, one can pick out the Colossi of Memnon, the Ramesseum, the ruins of all the temples of ancient Thebes. It is even possible to identify the lines of their outer courtyards and buildings which are no longer above the level of the sand, just as one can do from an aeroplane. From this cliff another steep track leads down to Cook's rest-house where most of the visitors to the west bank eat their lunch.

The beginning of this climb over the great cliff barrier coincides for its first half-mile with the track by which we had come up to Thothmes III's tomb. I knew that if I had been Oonas I should have sat down where the two tracks joined and told Sayed to leave me while he returned the key to the tomb guardian with the information that his 'lord and lady' were on their way over the cliff to lunch at Deir el Ba'hari. Sayed could then have seen our chauffeur, sent the car round to meet us, and returned to me; upon which we should have taken the track over the mountains leaving the tomb guardian to suppose that the third member of our party was still with us.

The chauffeur was Oonas' own man, so if anybody questioned him he would say exactly what she told him to; but what would she do when she arrived back at Luxor without me?

If she returned to the hotel alone the Belvilles would naturally want to know what had happened to me and she would have to put up a fairly water-tight yarn to allay their suspicions. She could, of course, say she had quarrelled with me, that I had gone off on my own and she had not the faintest idea where I had got to; that would give her time to get her things packed and clear out; but it could only be a very temporary expedient.

When I did not arrive back in time to leave Luxor with the expedition late in the afternoon my friends would naturally become anxious about me and delay their departure. If I failed to return that night they would promptly set enquiries on foot. The police would be called in, the tomb guardians questioned and a hue and cry raised after Oonas as the last person who had seen me alive. If that happened there seemed a fair prospect that the tomb guardian who had given Sayed the key would tell what he knew to the police as a result of which, within twenty-four hours, I would be found and Oonas would be charged with attempted murder.

On the other hand, would Oonas be fool enough to tell such a story? I did not think so. It was far more likely she would try to find some means of causing the Belvilles to set off that afternoon into the desert believing that I had let them down at the last minute.

It was hardly conceivable that they would swallow such a yarn unless she had some written message from me to show them in confirmation of it; and I did not think that she could have got one forged at such notice.

But was there any necessity for her to return to the hotel at all? She had her car and, directly she had crossed the river, she could drive north towards Assiut or south towards Aswan along the Nile bank. When she reached one of the towns on either route there was nothing to prevent her sending several telegrams; one to the Belvilles purporting to come from me, expressing my regret at having left them in the lurch and inferring that I had eloped with her; another to her maid, and two more signed with her name and mine to the manager of the hotel instructing him that her maid would pack our bags and bring them on.

That seemed much the soundest plan she could adopt and as far as I could see there were no snags to it. The Belvilles might be distressed about my ratting on them but they knew of her extraordinary attraction for me, so it would not surprise them overmuch to hear that I had abandoned them in order to remain with her; and if they were once convinced that I had elected to do so there was no reason why they should delay their departure. That I should be too ashamed of my weakness to face them and tell them the truth myself even added plausibility to the story; they would think I had just bolted and despatched a telegram from the first halt on my flight with Oonas.

Knowing we had shared a table in the restaurant and been constantly in each other's company the hotel management would also put two and two together on the receipt of the telegrams about our baggage. The maid would collect both our bills which Oonas would settle by cheque and the hotel people would have no more cause than the Belvilles to suspect that anything had gone wrong.

There was only one point that I did not quite see how Oonas was going to get over; and that was my body. It might be days, it might be weeks, it might be months before it was discovered; but sooner or later somebody was bound to come down into the tomb. The first thing they would find was that the plank bridge had been withdrawn to the outer side of the pit; the second, when they had replaced the bridge, would be my remains in the sarcophagus-chamber. The fact that the bridge had been removed would make it abundantly clear that I had not died through any accident or heart-attack when down there on my own, but had been deliberately trapped and left there to perish.

That would result in an immediate investigation; the tomb guardians would be questioned and the fact that I had gone down into the tomb with Sayed and Oonas established. Even if the man who kept the key had been bribed to keep his mouth shut in the meantime there could be no concealing the fact that I had left the Winter Palace with Oonas on the morning of my disappearance. A score of people, at least, had seen us either crossing the river together or in the valley of the Kings. Sayed and Oonas would be arrested and, as far as could see, they would find it a mighty difficult job to explain how it was that I had been left down there in the tomb with the bridge over the pit withdrawn so that I could not get across it, and found with dried blood all over the back of my skull!

Suddenly a ray of daylight pierced my abysmal gloom.

Oonas *dared* not leave my body in the tomb unless she wanted to face a charge of murder; she had *got* to come back and collect it.

The more I thought it over the more certain I became that that was what she meant to do. Perhaps she had taken an impression of the key of the tomb so that she could have another made and return with Sayed secretly at night; but, in any case, sooner or later they would come back, replace the bridge over the pit, carry my body out to hide it in some cleft in the hills and cover it with rocks so that there would be little chance of its being discovered for years, or perhaps generations.

If they *were* coming back, when would they do so? That was the question which now agitated my feverish mind. The longer they left my body in the tomb the greater the risk of its being discovered; once that happened they would have to face a charge of murder. It seemed to me that they would not dare to delay the removal of my body for more than a few days, at most. The time of their return would have to be judged by them very carefully; they must leave me there long enough to ensure my death but not a moment longer.

Yet would they wait even so long when every hour meant a lengthening of the shadow of the gallows which was reaching out towards them? Perhaps they would only wait just long enough for hunger and thirst to sap my strength until I was reduced to such a state that I was incapable of resistance; then return to drag me out and finish me off outside in one of the little-frequented gullies.

As I thought of that my pulses quickened. If I were right there was still a chance that I might live until they returned and then escape from them. But how could I possibly conserve my strength sufficiently to put up a fight when they came to get me?

I could hardly hope they would leave me there for less than a couple of days and, by that time, if I were not a raving lunatic from thirst I would certainly be so weak that I could barely crawl and coherent thinking would be an impossibility; therefore my sole chance of getting away alive lay in my concocting some plan to outwit them while my brain was still keen and active.

Gone were all thoughts of meeting death half-way by open-ing a vein in my arm. I was determined now to see the matter through whatever agony it might cost me. In my mind I turned over a dozen plans until I hit upon one which I thought might give me the chance I needed.

It was quite warm in the tomb and whether the rocks three hundred feet above were red hot with the blistering heat of an Egyptian summer or swept by the cold night winds of winter the vault was so deep down in the heart of the mountain that its temperature remained unchanging through the centuries. Knowing that, I began to undress right away in order to put my idea into operation.

When I had finished my preparations against the return of Sayed and Oonas I looked at my wrist-watch, which by great good fortune was one with a luminous dial that I had bought in Cairo specially for the expedition, and I saw that it was a quarter-past two. It seemed that I had already been entombed for so many dreary hours that immediately assumed it to be a quarter-past two in the morning, but suddenly my eye fell on the candle. It had been over five inches long when I found it and about three inches were remaining. We had made our descent into the tomb at a little after twelve so by my reckon-ing I had been there some fourteen hours; yet the fact the candle was still burning showed that to be quite impossible. If it were really the middle of the night the whole five inches would long since have been consumed; so it must be a quarter-past two in the afternoon. Incredible as it seemed, I had been down there only just over two hours.

If my plan of escape were to have any chance of success I should need the candle later on; I quickly blew it out and was instantly wrapped round again with the Stygian darkness.

Sitting down in the dust of ages that softened the hardness of the rock floor, I began to wonder how best I could possibly support the forty-eight hours or more of torture that lay be-fore me. The place was silent with that deathly stillness which can almost be felt. So far that had not troubled me because when I first came round my head had been too painful for me to think of much else; when the pain had eased a little my brain had been fully occupied with the horror of my situa-tion, and later, for the last hour at least, I had been moving about so that the sounds I myself made had reverberated round the oval tomb-chamber; but now I knew this eerie, unbroken quiet was going to play the very devil with my nerves.

Somehow I had to defeat it and there were only two ways in which to do so. I must either sleep or occupy my brain with something else. Manual labour would have kept my mind busy but there was none that I could do, and even if there had been I knew that I should have been unwise to do it; exertion of any kind would tend to exhaust me quicker; worse, it would create thirst—the thing that was my most deadly enemy. I remembered newspaper accounts of men in exhibitions who for the stunt purposes had gone without food for upwards of forty days, and that although the pangs of hunger were said to be severe during the first sixty hours or so, they then faded away leaving the faster in a weakened but untroubled condition. Thirst, however, was a very different matter and, as far as my memory served me, no man could hope to survive more than three or four days without some form of liquid.

Just as I had reached this point in my deliberations I let out a scream of such terror that the whole vault seemed to quiver round me. I leapt to my feet and stood shaking there while the perspiration broke out on my forehead and the hair seemed to rise on the back of my scalp.

I had not imagined it, I was quite certain. Something had come up out of the impenetrable darkness and brushed softly against my lips as I was sitting there.

With shaking fingers I fumbled for my lighter and relit the candle. The sarcophagus-chamber was as empty as before. I picked the candle up, tiptoed all round the vault and even out into the passage-way as far as the pit. But there was nothing there and as I listened the dread stillness of the grave remained unbroken.

Returning fearfully to the burial chamber I went over to the big stone coffin, the edge of which was nearly as high as my shoulder, and peered down into it. The bath-shaped piece of granite was quite empty except for a triangular piece of its broken lid. With considerable labour I had managed to carry a larger portion of the lid out into the corridor some time before as part of my plan against Oonas and Sayed; and with even greater exertion, had slightly shifted another great lump that was resting on one end of it so that it only just balanced and would fall on the floor if I gave it a quick tilt. The pieces were just as I had left them and there was nothing lurking under the shadowed sides of the coffin which could account for the horror I had experienced.

For a few awful moments, while I mopped the dampness from my brow, I was terrified by the thought that some horrible, supernatural thing must be an inhabitant of my prison. If ever there were a place suited for a ghost to haunt, surely the desecrated tomb of a Pharaoh was one. I recalled the stories of archæologists who had been overtaken by a sinister fate which the superstitious ascribed to the revenge of the dead spirits whose graves had been tampered with.

Having dabbled a little with the occult in my Oxford days I knew enough of it to be convinced that although many of the people posing as mediums are nothing but charlatans others possess powers which are quite inexplicable and that spontaneous supernatural manifestations do occur. Yet somehow I had the feeling that there was nothing of that kind about this place. Its deadly stillness was a natural thing; it had no suggestion of that sinister chill that nearly always accompanies any evil thing which has broken through the thin veil protecting us from the unseen earth-plane. In some curious way the mild warmth of the vault gave it an almost friendly atmosphere; or perhaps it would be better to describe it as impersonal. It was just an empty room with attractive decorations on its walls—no more, no less; and it gave one the impression that it was simply a shell from which any personality or spirit that might once have inhabited it had long since departed. In spite of my terror I had a deep-seated conviction that no hostile, psychic force lingered in it.

Yet to be on the safe side, I did a thing which may sound stupid as I write it but which was done with all earnestness at that time. I set the candle on the floor and standing with my arms outstretched before me so that my hands were above the level of my head, which was the attitude adopted by the Ancients when they prayed, I addressed myself to Thothmes III; telling him quite seriously, as though I were addressing a person, that I had only visited his grave in reverence and that being confined there against my own will I begged his forbearance for my intrusion and his protection during my hours of trial.

Another quarter of-an-inch of my candle had burnt away by this time and although I hated to do so, it was so precious to me that I positively forced myself to put it out.

I knew pretty well what was in my pockets so I had not bothered to run through them before, but now I thought the time had come to make a full mental list of all the things I had upon me. The feel of them was quite enough to tell me what they were and so, sitting down again, I ran through them in the darkness.

There were my keys, some Egyptian coins, mainly silver, a pocket-knife and my lighter in my trousers pockets. In my coat I had half-a-bottle of fruit-drops that I had bought from the chemist in Luxor and these I counted my greatest treasure as I knew that by sucking one every few hours I should be able to relieve the dryness of my mouth when thirst set in. There were also some old hotel bills, a pencil, a few pounds in Egyptian bank-notes, my cheque-book and my cigarette-case which contained nine cigarettes; while round my waist I had my money-belt which still contained a good sum in English tenners. It was not until I felt in the ticket-pocket of my coat that I discovered something I had completely forgotten and for which I was boundlessly grateful. It was a small, flat bottle of aspirin tablets, about two-thirds full; these, I realised with immense joy, would ensure me a sound sleep and the longer I could sleep the longer I could conserve my energy. It seemed almost as though the spirit of Thothmes III had interceded with the Great Ones for me and they had sent an answer to my prayer.

For a little I thought with regret of my hip-flask which I nearly always carried when I went on an expedition but by chance had neglected to bring that morning; yet on consideration I felt that perhaps it was for the best that I had not got it with me as I was extremely doubtful of the effects of neat brandy in quenching a fiery thirst. I was rather inclined to suppose that it would have done more harm than good; and if I started to suffer from thirst really badly it might have proved a greater temptation than I could resist.

I looked at my watch again hoping that it might be time for me to get a sleep but to my amazement and distress it was barely three o'clock. I nearly broke down and wept as I thought of the almost inconceivable way in which time crawled in my dark and silent tomb. Yet time could mean nothing to me for the next two days at least. Dawn and dusk ceased to operate beyond the iron gates of the tomb nearly a quarter of a mile above the place where I was sitting; there was no reason whatever why I should wait until nightfall before I attempted to exclude my fears and miseries by the blessed expedient of sleep.

It was then that the Thing came at me again; it was light as a feather-duster, but as surely as though it had been a ton of bricks I knew that something had brushed over my hair. I did not scream this time but started violently back, knocking my still aching head on the stone coffin against which I was leaning. The pain, which had died down a little although it had been present the whole time as a monotonous nag in the background of my thoughts, now started up again with renewed vigour and for a little it racked me so that I was too miserable to be quite so much afraid; yet my terror of that unseen Thing which had come at me twice out of the darkness was still so great that I quickly lit the candle once again.

Picking it up I made a further search; determined this time to run the horror to earth unless it was indeed some supernatural manifestation: I made the round of the chamber again and quartered it, holding the candle high, but I found nothing and was about to give up when a faint squeak caught my ear. Looking up at the low ceiling I saw the solution of my mystery —a little brown bat was clinging there.

If I had not been so overwrought I should probably have thought of bats before. How they exist without water in these great underground caverns is more that I can explain but perhaps they feed upon some tiny insects which are almost invisible to the human eye, as one certainly never see flies, spiders or any other creatures of that kind in the tombs. On numerous occasions before I had seen small bats, apparently asleep, on the roofs of the passages and chambers in other tombs that I had visited.

Bats are unpleasant creatures but only because they carry vermin and I was so relieved to know that my funk had had a natural cause that I found myself laughing a little inanely. These little brown creatures are an entirely different species from the blood-sucking vampire variety so I had no cause to fear that they might attack me while I slept.

Dowsing my candle again I made myself as comfortable as I could on the ground and took out my little bottle of aspirin. There were fourteen tablets in it and I decided that while eight would not be sufficient to harm me they would ensure a real long sleep. One by one I swallowed them. The bat touched my face twice again, but I brushed it off and after what seemed an hour, but was actually probably less than a quarter of that time. I feel into a dreamless slumber.

When I woke I found from my watch that it was a quarter-past six and I wondered if I had slept three hours or fifteen. In view of the quantity of aspirin I had taken I felt pretty confident it was the longer period, particularly as ever since my arrival in Egypt I had hardly had a full night's undisturbed rest, and the number of turns it took to rewind my watch confirmed my impression.

My head had stopped aching and, all things considered, I felt extremely well. Although I had not eaten for getting on for twenty-four hours I did not feel particularly hungry, just that I would have welcomed a good, hearty breakfast but no more. On the other hand I badly needed a drink. But I put the thought firmly from me, knowing that I should only need it worse if I began to visualise large cups of tea; and I started to employ myself in thinking how I could best occupy my mind during the day.

If only I had had some light there were a dozen ways in which I might have kept my mind off my anxieties and appet-ites. Two or three hours at least could have been spent in exam-ining the wall-paintings of the large, oval chamber in detail and trying to puzzle out the meaning of the many symbolic pictures portraying the Pharaoh's journey through the under-world and his trial before the gods. Then, even at the cost of defacing some of them, I could have drawn things myself, or worked out complicated sums, or scribbled lines of verse, just as prisoners have done on the walls of their cells from time immemorial; yet all such activities were barred to me because I dared not burn more of my treasured candle-stump except for special purposes.

One thing I was determined on and that was to write an

account, on the backs of the bills I had in my pocket, of how Oonas and Sayed had left me there to die; so that if I were dead by the time they returned there would be some chance of their being brought to justice even if my body were only discovered in a cleft of the hills years later. But I decided to reserve that until the afternoon.

I took out a cigarette and lit it. The sight of its glowing end, like a firefly in that impenetrable darkness, cheered me a little but I got no joy at all out of the tobacco; it did not seem to taste of anything and the smoke from it was invisible. In the belief that tobacco is a form of nourishment I smoked it to the very end by the old expedient of sticking its butt on a pin which I found in my lapel.

The silence began to get on my nerves again so I started to hold a sing-song with myself and if anybody had entered the tomb early that morning they would have been extremely surprised to hear the strains of 'Flat-Foot Floogy' or 'Mademoiselle from Armentières' echoing up from the sometime resting-place of the Napoleon of Egypt. I can't remember how many songs I sang before my voice got tired but it must have been several dozens and I occupied some hours that way as my watch showed it to be ten o'clock by the time I got so husky that I had to chuck it up.

The unbroken quiet settled down round me once again and never have I known such utter stillness. It was eternal night with not even the tiny noises of small, scurrying animals or the drip of water on a rock which one would have heard in the most desolate country above ground.

By midday thirst was beginning to worry me so I sucked one of my fruit-drops, turning it round and round into every corner of my mouth. That relieved me for the time being so, while the going was good, I decided to try to get another sleep, on the theory that he who sleeps, dines.

The hard ground on which I had to lie, eased only a little by its coating of sand and dust, was no aid to slumber but I pillowed my head on my arm and after what seemed an interminable time of twisting and turning, drifted off.

I don't know what time I woke again as I made up my mind that I would remain there dozing as long as I possibly could; but eventually my increasing thirst got the better of me and I felt that I could no longer resist allaying it a little with another fruit-drop. Actually I had done better than I thought as I had managed to hang out until nearly five o'clock.

I was hungry now and try as I would I could not stop myself from thinking, with an appalling longing, of a good square meal including all my favourite dishes. I smoked again and sucked another couple of sweets.

Somehow I managed to get through the next two hours and at seven, with almost ritual solemnity, I lit the candle for the purpose of writing my denunciation of Oonas on the back of the bills.

That filled in only a bare half-hour as, although I would have liked to cover every inch of paper with minute writing, I could not possibly afford the light for more than a meagre outline of my story.

Although I knew it was too soon to do so, I tried to sleep again; but sleep simply would not come and it occurred to me that a little mild exercise might keep me employed for a bit, so I started to walk up and down. It was a queer sensation as at first I was constantly afraid of banging into something in the darkness; and walked only a few cautious steps each way with my head held back and my hands thrust out instinctively before me. But after a time I got used to it and started a steady, senty-go, fifteen paces forward and fifteen paces back, striding out with gradually-increasing confidence as I learned better how to turn exactly in the dark without losing my sense of direction and cannoning into the sarcophagus or the wall. Once I got into the rhythm of the thing I started to count, making up my mind to do five thousand paces, which I estimated would be about three miles. The rhythmic movement did me good and I could have gone on much longer if I had not thought it essential to conserve my strength.

It was half-past nine when I sat down again, had another cigarette and followed it with two more fruit-drops. To my annoyance I did not feel the least bit sleepy and the exercise had had the regrettable effect of increasing my hunger; so I tightened the strap at the back of my trousers while I endeavoured to put away from me the vision of hen lobsters, roast duck, asparagus and bubble-and-squeak.

As those visions of luscious dishes simply would not leave

me I hit on the idea of making them serve me to while away a little time, and in my mind I planned a series of magnificent banquets, selecting for each course its appropriate wine. This led me to making up after-dinner speeches for various occasions, and among them the most amusing were proposing the health of a rival politician in whose cup one would have liked to put poison, and the welcome extended by King Bongo-Bongo to the Lord Mayor of Dunderhead preparatory to eating his own guest.

Only those who have tried sitting for even a short time in a completely darkened room can appreciate how swiftly thoughts come and go, so that in the space of a few minutes one can visualise a dozen scenes; and all too soon the brain gets tired of creating imaginary situations. Between half-past nine and eleven I must have followed out literally hundreds of such episodes in my mind and found that it was beginning to lose its power of concentration; yet I knew that if I were to stand any chance of securing another long sleep I must not settle down too early, so I hit on the idea of turning somersaults in the dark. Unfortunately it wasn't a very good one as I very soon grew dizzy and had to give it up.

I fished out another cigarette but just as I was about to light it the thought struck me that it might help to sustain me better if I chewed the tobacco instead. I had never chewed tobacco before and I did not like the sharp, bitter flavour at all. After I had masticated the first mouthful for some moments it dawned on me that I would have to spit it out, which would mean a considerable loss of saliva, and saliva was more precious to me than gold or rubies. That thought put the lid on chewing any more tobacco and to get rid of the unpleasant flavour I sucked another sweet.

My next idea was to try to count as far as possible all the people I had ever met, ticking them off on my fingers; but when I reached seventy I got hopelessly confused and could not remember if I had already put in certain people who kept on recurring to me; so I started off on a new game, which was to select belated Christmas presents, regardless of cost, for all the people that I could think of.

That set me wondering if I should live to see in the New Year; reckoning the odds up anew they seemed very long indeed. It was, after all, only a theory of my own that Oonas and Sayed would return to collect my body before it was likely to be discovered by anyone else. Even if that were their programme, seeing that the tomb was so rarely visited, they might well consider it perfectly safe to leave me there for a week; while, if my best hopes were realised and they got the jitters to the extent of returning for me while I was still alive, my chances of outwitting them still remained pretty slender. I tried to force myself to think that they would be certain to come, and come soon, but it was a horribly difficult business.

I glanced at my watch again, dreading to see how slowly the minutes had crawled by, but to my joy it was after midnight so I felt that I might now reasonably hope to get a sleep. For ages, as it seemed to me, I debated with myself whether I should take the last six aspirins in one go or reserve some of them for the following night, but I had a grim foreboding that by that time I should be in such a ghastly state that two or three aspirin would be much too mild a dose to bring me any appreciable relief; so I swallowed the lot and settled myself as comfortably as I could.

Blessed sleep came quickly and owing, perhaps, to my now weakened state and empty tummy, the aspirin had a more than usually strong effect. I slept right though the night until half-past eight.

Waking to a new day in the eternal night of that silent grave was one of the most terrible things I have ever experienced. With utter despair I thought of the endless hours of torture that lay before me and I am not ashamed to say that so overwhelming was my distress that I broke down and wept. Yet, even as I did so, I greedily licked in the salt tears that ran down my face for my mouth was now dry, furry and horribly parched. Cursing myself for a spineless fool I managed to pull myself together again and tried to breakfast off a cigarette; but the invisible smoke now burnt my lips and tongue and, as I inhaled, I choked which sent me into a violent fit of coughing; so I had to stub out the cigarette before it was one-third consumed.

Three fruit-drops bettered my condition for a little and I sought to plan my day. An hour's exercise first, then a bit of a sing-song if I could manage it, after that a recital of all the poetry I could remember, a little mental arithmetic involving such problems as I could conjure up in my head. That might bring me to midday if I were lucky, but even as I named the hour to myself I knew that such a programme would barely carry me to ten o'clock. I groaned with self-pity and was near giving way to tears again.

To get away from my thoughts I began to pace rapidly up and down the chamber, but after a couple of dozen turns I had to give up. Hunger had got me now and a beastly pain stabbed in my stomach each time I moved. I drew in the tab at the back of my trousers to its fullest extent but that didn't seem to ease things very much so I lay down and, undoing my clothes, began to massage my stomach. On and on I went, rhythmically smoothing it up and down until my wrists ached so much that I simply had to stop; but the pain was better and I was able to do two thousand paces which killed a fraction of my day.

The sing-song did not prove at all successful as my throat was now so dry and parched that it was a strain to get out every note, and my efforts were pathetic compared with those of the day before. Eventually I stopped trying and just repeated the words over to myself while humming the refrains in my brain. When I could not think of any more choruses that I knew I tried mathematics, but the only problem I could think of was: 'if a herring and a half cost three-halfpence . . . ?' the answer to which I already knew.

As I sat there with my back against the Pharaoh's bath-shaped coffin I realised that my tongue was constantly licking over my dry lips just as one sees a snake flicker its forked tongue while it considers some object which may prove a suitable prey. By eleven o'clock I was muttering to myself half-crazily but soon after, quite unaccountably, I fell asleep.

It was half-past three when I woke again. I had been entombed for over two days or, to be more exact, some fifty-one-and-a-half hours. I sucked at my mouth spasmodically and, when I popped a fruit-drop into it, only a conscious effort enabled me to move it round my tongue.

The afternoon seemed never-ending. I did my best to prevent myself from looking at my watch too frequently but in spite of all my efforts I never managed a longer interval than eight minutes between half-past three and six o'clock. Sometimes I

walked up and down, sometimes I endeavoured to sleep, sometimes I just sat there staring wide-eyed into the surrounding
blackness, swallowing and swallowing and swallowing my ever-
decreasing saliva and striving to ease the tension of my
gradually-closing throat. For much of the time I must have
been light-headed through the pains that constantly stabbed
at my belly and my never-ceasing craving for some form of
drink.

It was some time early in the evening when I forced myself
to take stock of the situation and the result was only an appalling fit of despair. I was convinced now that Oonas would never
come back. There were a score of other schemes which she
might have adopted. Her subtle brain was quite equal to devising any number of explanations as to how my body came to be
in the tomb when it was discovered there weeks later. It was
quite a possibility that they had not locked the entrance-gates
on going out and would say that I had gone back to get something which I had dropped, sending them on over the river
when I had made my farewells, as it had been arranged that I
should set off into the desert that afternoon. In any case the
expedition would have to cross the Nile before it started and
I might quite well have planned to have my things packed for
me and join it only when it reached the western bank.

Such theories did not account for the withdrawal of the
bridge over the pit, but by then my brain was too bemused
for me to think clearly. I remember scrambling to my feet and
staggering up and down in a semi-hysterical state, cursing
Oonas long and bitterly in hoarse, gasping whispers for this
thing she had done to me.

During my hysterics I had lucid intervals but while they
lasted the pain in my stomach prevented my thinking clearly.
It seemed to gnaw at my very vitals so that at times I rolled in
agony upon the floor; my attempts to stop it by further massage now proved futile and I lay there semi-conscious for hour
after hour moaning and muttering to myself through my
cracked and swollen lips.

How the time passed I do not know but I came to my senses
soon after ten o'clock and I did my very best to get a hold on
myself because I knew that if I failed I should certainly go mad.
I thought again of taking out my penknife and slashing the

veins in my wrist to let the blood flow so that I might sink away into a final unconsciousness, which would have been an overwhelming relief. But it was night again and, if they came at all, I felt convinced that it was by night they would come. With a gargantuan effort I forced the temptation away from me and resolved to support another ten hours in the tomb if I possibly could.

My mind weakened again and became a prey to strange fancies. I had O'Kieff pinioned under me and was battering-in his head; time had gone backwards and Oonas as Cleopatra occupied the throne of Egypt, while I was Caesar, the lover of her youth; I was back in England and a few years had dropped away so that I was throwing a party once more at the Quaglino's to a few of those many friends I had had before I became an outcast; I was in the Diplomatic Service again, rising by extraordinary feats of skill to the post of British Ambassador in Berlin and, by a brilliant *coup*, preventing the outbreak of another world-war while still under forty.

The visions faded and I slept. I was awoken by a piercing scream.

21

Escape

Apart from my periods of sleep I had been clinging to my sanity for over sixty seemingly endless hours by the single thread of hope that I might hear that cry at last.

Now that it had come it cut across my stupor like a clarion call rousing me to instant and automatic action. In one movement I was on my feet, thrusting blindly at the great slab of granite, shoulder-high beside me, which formed part of the coffin-lid; it tilted and went over, crashing to the floor with a thud that seemed to shake the vault. The echoes reverberated round the oval room shattering the momentary stillness which had succeeded that harsh cry of fear.

Next second there was another scream from the corridor but unlike the first, which had been deep and guttural, this was high and shrill. It was followed by further cries of terror and the noise of stampeding feet as those who had come to get me fled in utter panic.

My head was light and buzzing while my tongue, now thick and swollen, clung to the roof of my dry mouth. For an instant I lost my sense of direction and, missing the candle stump in the darkness, fumbled wildly for it; yet I knew I must force myself to act calmly. Life and death alternated on the balance. Only by keeping my head and drawing unsparingly on any reserve of strength that I might have left could I hope to reap any advantage from this one chance of escape that had been given me.

I found the candle, lit it and went out into the passage. Propped up against the wall there I saw the thing that I had made over two days before when I still had my full wits and strength about me. Seen in the dim light cast by a candle I did not wonder that the sight of it had filled Sayed and Oonas with stark terror. By balancing the smaller fragments of the great coffin-lid one upon another against the wall, I had managed to construct a rough pillar of broken stone. On this I had draped my white shirt and drawers, crowning the pile with my panama stuck up on end so that on its crown, with spittle and dust, I had been able to draw the bold outlines of a face.

Coming upon it suddenly round the corner from the pit-shaft and finding it barring their path only six feet distant in the uncertain light, first Sayed and then Oonas had, as I intended, taken the effigy for my ghost. The loud thump of the coffin-lid which I had engineered immediately afterwards must have completed the impression that my angry spirit was active there and about to exact vengeance on my murderers.

Such an experience might well have shattered the nerves of two tough European criminals and, knowing the superstition-ridden mentality of all Egyptians, I could well imagine the devastating effect it had on Oonas and her thug. I could still hear their flying footsteps in the distance as small portions of rock and rubble clattered down the steep slopes above.

Although I knew that in their panic they would never have paused to withdraw the bridge over the pit again, I was un-utterably relieved to find it in place, and I hurried across it.

Everything depended now on whether they would have recovered themselves sufficiently, by the time they had reached the entrance of the tomb, to lock the iron gates behind them. In an attempt to spur them on through an access of fresh terror so that they would not pause to do so, I tried to shout; but only a husky whisper would come from between my cracked lips, and every time I took a breath a frightful pain seared like a hot iron down my burning throat.

Whether they heard me coming after them or not I do not know but since I could not use my voice I made all the noise I could by stamping my way along the corridors and banging at the walls with my free hand. Even if I had been capable of running I should not have dared to do so as my candle would have gone out, and it would have been almost impossible to negotiate the half-fallen stairway without it. Swaying from side to side, groaning and gasping, I staggered up the steep ramps and broken stairs with all the speed I could muster.

At last a faint lightening of the darkness ahead told me that I was nearing the entrance of the tomb, and almost before I knew it I was there. The gate was open and I was through it, staring up from the bottom of the twenty-foot hole where the entrance lay, past the dark cliffs on either side, to the blessed stars above.

I would have given the world to have sunk down there on the jagged rocks and just sucked in the fresh night air which was so gloriously refreshing after the close stuffiness of the tomb; but I was not yet out of danger. If they returned to find me lying in the tomb entrance they would slit my throat, as in my hopelessly weakened condition I could not possibly put up a fight against them.

I listened intently for any sounds which might indicate that they were still about but once out of the tomb they must have fled up the ladders as though all the devils in hell were after them. Somehow, I had to mount those ladders myself as they were the only way out from the deep rock gully in which I stood; and if I could not secure water the chances were that I should be mad or dead before morning.

How I accomplished it I shall never know. I must have been within an ace of falling and breaking my neck a score of times, but somehow I managed to drag myself out of the deep hole, scale the ladders and reach the cliff-top. The friendly starlight showed me the rough track round the tongue of the gully and across its further precipice. Aching in every limb, my eyes protruding from their sockets, I stumbled along, falling at times and crawling on my hands and knees until, by a new effort which every time seemed the very last, I succeeded in dragging myself to my feet again.

I slid and tumbled the last two hundred yards down into the valley bottom; another hundred yards and I had crossed it. The last effort, which all but finished me, was a fifty-foot climb up a steep slope to the little building above Tut-ankhamen's tomb where the guardians of the valley have their quarters. Most of them sleep in the village several miles away but a few are always left on night-duty; and, unable to cry out, kneeling there in the dark utterly exhausted, I hammered with my fists upon the wooden door until I roused them.

It was fortunate that they were Arabs. Europeans might have given me the great draught of water for which I was so desperately craving, and that would have killed me. Instead, knowing the proper treatment for a man found in the desert dying of thirst, they only bathed my face and lips. One of them put some fresh dates in a cup with a little water and pounded them up into a soggy mass, after which he forced small portions of it into my burning mouth.

It was not until, with the most frightful agony, I had swallowed a good part of this moistened mixture that they allowed me to drink a few drops of water from a bottle of Evian taken from the excavators' stores; and then, my pain having eased a little, I fell asleep.

When I woke it was full day. I was naked and lying on a low bed wrapped in blankets. I vaguely remembered, as in some hideous dream, the tomb guardians stripping my pain-racked body the night before in order to sponge it all over with cool water; and the clothes in which I had escaped from the tomb were folded in a neat pile beside me.

As I stirred, an Arab who had been sitting cross legged on the floor at the foot of the bed rose and gave me a drink; then he left me to return a few minutes later with an elderly Englishman.

My visitor asked me how I had come to be in such a state but it was all I could do to croak out my name; and in any case I wanted a little time to think out what sort of statement I should make.

'All right, old chap,' he said kindly. 'Don't bother to talk just yet.' And taking a bowl of stuff like junket from the Arab who had just come back into the room, he began to feed me with it.

'When you've had some of this you'll feel better,' he went on. 'It's *leban zebadi,* the curdled milk of the female *gamoose*. It's light as a feather on the tummy but crammed full of every sort of vitamin; the more sensible Arabs have it for their evening meal during the month of Ramadan, when they have to fast from dawn to sunset each day, instead of gorging themselves half the night as the stupid peasants do.'

He gave me another drink of water, then left me to sleep, and I did not wake again until late in the afternoon. The Arab was no longer there so I had a chance to concoct an account of myself which would prove adequate for the enquiries which it was certain I should have to face. If I told the truth, it meant charging Oonas with attempted murder and, in spite of the way

311

in which I had suffered at her hands, that I was not prepared to do.

I had no reason to believe that she would ever have attempted to injure a hair of my head if I had stuck to her and, even after her passion for me had died down, the chances were it would have remained a pleasant memory, so that I should have at least retained her goodwill if I had dealt fairly with her. She *might* have ratted on me and sold us out to Zakri, but I had no proof of that and felt it was only just to give her the benefit of the doubt. As things were, it was *I* who had ratted on *her* by telling her of my intention to leave her at only a few hours' notice. It was not unnatural that a girl of her violent temperament should have been quite convinced that Sylvia was the reason for my doing so.

If Oonas had had more time she might still have plotted my death rather than give me up to another woman, but it would probably have been a quick ending by poison or the knife in the good old Eastern tradition. The torture she had inflicted on me during those incredibly dreadful hours in the tomb was not through any deliberate desire to cause me a slow and painful death, but had occurred because at such short notice she could think of no other way in which to stop my going on the expedition without laying herself open to a charge of murder.

In consequence, when the English excavator visted me again, about five o'clock, I told him that I had made a visit to the Valley with Oonas three days earlier during which I had decided at the last minute not to go with some other friends on an expedition into the desert which was due to set off later in the day. Not wishing to tell them myself of my decision to back out, I had left her to inform them of it and, after visiting the Valley, we had parted on the track which led over the hills to Deir el Ba'hari; our arrangement being that she would return to Luxor at once while I was to wait there until my friends had departed. During the afternoon I had got bored with sitting up there on the cliff-top so I had gone off to explore a ravine some few miles distant. Night had overtaken me before I could get back to the Deir el Ba'hari track and in trying to find it I had got lost and had wandered about without food or water for over sixty hours until, on the third night, when I was virtually at the end of my tether I had once more stumbled on the Valley of the Kings.

This story seemed to fulfil most of the possible contingencies and the excavator, whose name I learned was Mason, swallowed it readily enough. He then asked me if I felt up to making the journey back to Luxor that evening and when I said I did, he went off to make arrangements.

As I pulled on my things I wondered if he had noticed that, except for my vest, I lacked underclothes but he appeared not to have spotted my strange shortage of garments, and it was a fairly safe bet that it would not have meant very much to the Arabs who had undressed me. Later, of course, the shirt, pants and hat with which I had decked out the effigy of my ghost were certain to be discovered and would doubtless raise some interesting speculations in the minds of the people responsible for looking after the tombs. By that time I hoped to be out of Luxor and on my way to join the Belvilles, if not already with them hundreds of miles out in the desert. If the worst came to the worst and they were found immediately, I could always put up a yarn that I had a vague recollection of having found the tomb open during my delirious wanderings and had taken refuge there from the scorching midday sun, not realising how near I was to the Valley of the Kings; but that my undressing there and rigging up a guy with part of my clothing must have been owing to some mad freak of my thirst-crazed brain of which I had no remembrance.

I was still so weak from my ordeal that the journey back to Luxor proved a trying one although the kind Mr. Mason did everything he could to make it as easy for me as possible.

The hall porter at the Winter Palace looked almost comically shocked and upset when I arrived back there at half-past seven, and he certainly had good reason to be so in view of the state I was in. The Arabs had dusted down my clothes as well as they could but they were incredibly dirty and torn in half-a dozen places from my attempts at turning somersaults in my prison and the many falls I had sustained after my escape. As I saw, too, when I had a chance to look into a mirror a little later, my experience seemed to have aged me by ten years; there were great, dark hollows under my eyes while my cheeks and temples had fallen in and the whole of my scalp was ingrained with dirt. I looked a positive caricature of my former self and I was not at all surprised at his amazement.

On my asking about my room he said at once that they were under the impression that I had given it up four nights before, and my theory as to Oonas' tactics proved correct. The management had received a telegram purporting to come from me instructing them to have my baggage packed and handed over to Oonas' maid who would take it on with her mistress' things to Cairo. I neither confirmed nor denied having sent the telegram but asked to be accommodated as soon as possible; and seeing the state I was in the *chef de bureau* wasted no time but had me taken along to a room where I ordered a light dinner and went straight to bed.

Next morning I had a visit from the manager and set his mind at rest by telling him not to worry about my baggage as the Princess had only carried out my instructions while I, unfortunately, had upset all our arrangements by getting myself lost in the Libyan hills.

I was afraid that I might also receive a visit from the police, whose curiosity might have been more difficult to satisfy, but they did not appear and, after all, there is nothing criminal about getting oneself lost; so apparently Mr. Mason, the excavator, had not considered it his duty to report my misadventure.

Owing to Oonas' maid having made off with my baggage I hadn't a rag to my back except the ruined suit I had arrived in, and that afternoon I got the hall porter to send out to the local shops for a few of my most urgent requirements. Having slept the best part of the day I was much stronger by the evening so I had a really good meal sent along to my room and put in another night's sound sleep.

By the following morning it was getting on for sixty hours since I had escaped from the tomb, which was nearly as long as the time I had been confined in it, and as I had spent the best part of the period since my return to the upper world in life-giving sleep I was now feeling much more my own man again. The hollow under my eyes had disappeared and having shaved off my five-days' beard I found that my face was nearly restored to normal. My one remaining suit had been mended by the local tailor and cleaned and pressed. It presented a rather woebegone appearance, but it was good enough to go out in; and my shopping list of the previous day had included a shirt, collar, tie and underclothes, so I dressed myself and left the hotel for the purposes of purchasing a completely new kit.

My first visit was to an Arab tailor and I chose some of his less alarming cloth with which to have some suits made as, unlike European tailors, Arabs will work all night and run up two or three suits in twenty-four hours if it is for a customer who is prepared to pay them well. Unfortunately they have no idea of cut at all but if one can provide them with any sort of garment as a pattern, they will copy it with a faithfulness which would not disgrace Savile Row, and the additional blessing that no time has to be expended on fittings.

I changed into a ready-made suit there and then leaving my own as a pattern for the tailor, and spent the next two hours in making a great variety of other purchases. Owing to the limitations imposed by the small number of shops in Luxor and the lack of variety in their stock, my new kit was almost entirely composed of makeshifts, and as ready-made suitcases were quite unprocurable I had to buy hand-woven native baskets to pack it in; but when it was all assembled in my room at the hotel I felt that it would serve me well enough for the trip into the desert.

The next problem which face me was how to catch up the Belvilles. They had left five nights before, as arranged, evidently after having been informed by Oonas by telegram or some other means that I did not intend to make the trip. There was only one way to do it. I must charter an aeroplane and trust to luck that I should overtake them before they had penetrated very far into the desert. Fortunately I still had plenty of bank-notes stuffed into my money belt and in the afternoon the hall porter sent one of his underlings with me to the Luxor Air Port where I succeeded in chartering a 'plane for the following morning.

The loss of my kit was extremely trying but one thing at least had been salved from it—this journal which I had written up at odd moments. Not wishing Oonas to see it, as she might well have done owing to her frequent presence in my room, I had handed it to the manager of the hotel for safe keeping. Having received no instructions about it, he had not

sent it on with the rest of my luggage and it was still in his safe.
I wrote it up to date, resealed the package and returned it to
him with instructions that if I did not either claim it or write
to him within two months he was to destroy the second portion,
which I had just written, but forward the first part to Essex
Pasha.

It was New Year's Eve but, apart from the gala dinner, I did
not participate in any of the festivities. A couple had turned up
whom I used to know well in the old days and I did not want to
come face-to-face with them as they would certainly have
recognised me now that I no longer had my protective beard. I
finished my packing, got a good night's rest and was in the air
before nine o'clock next morning.

The 'plane which I had succeeded in hiring was a small four-
seater of a type which has now been superseded on the Egyptian air-lines run by the Miza Company, but my pilot was a
young Gyppy who seemed to know his job. From Luxor we
headed south by west following the course of the river, which
bends sharply there, for about twenty miles; then leaving it to
fly due west over the Libyan Hills until nothing but sandy
wastes stretched below us. By 'plane the journey to the Great
Oasis is not a long one and in just under an hour we picked up
the misty green streak, running north and south in the yellow
sands as far as we could see, which is the outer edge of the
fertile region of Kharga.

Many people have the idea that an oasis is no more than a
group of a few dozen palm trees with a mud-hole in their
centre, but while this is so in many instances, the Great Oasis
runs for nearly two hundred miles from north to south and in
one place it is over forty miles wide; so its belt of verdure
stretches as far as from London to Ilfracombe or Liverpool to
Norwich. There are many villages in it and two fair-sized
towns, Beris in its centre and El Kharga near its northern extremity. The latter is even connected with the Nile Valley by a
light railway, for the transport of the date crop which is the
principal means of livelihood of the Oasis dwellers.

We came down outside the town of El Kharga although I
had little hope that I should find the Belvilles there. Travel is
very slow in the Sahara and such business as securing guides is
subject to every sort of irritating delay, but even so I did not

think it could have taken six days for my friends to get their papers vetted by the local officials and to complete their other arrangements before proceeding further into the interior.

Enquiries elicited the information that the party had left El Kharga three mornings before and had taken the caravan-route for the Oasis of Dakhla.

An hour later we were in the air again and passing over another dreary stretch of sand, but by midday we had reached the outskirts of the Dakhla Oasis which, although smaller than the Great Oasis, is still nearly as large as the county of Dorset.

Coming down at the town of Mut, near its centre, we made fresh enquiries and learnt that the Belvilles had left there the previous morning. We then flew on a further twenty miles to the little town of Qasr Dakhla which is on the northern edge of the Oasis only to find that they had moved on from there at dawn.

Caravan-routes leave Qasr for the north going to the Great Oasis of Farafra, or north-east to the Nile; but to its south, west and north-west there lies absolutely nothing but the *Grande Mer de Sable*, or Sea of Sand, which stretches in those directions unbroken by any habitable land or even occasional water-holes for over four hundred miles. For travellers advancing from the east, therefore, Dakhla is to all intents and purposes the end of the world.

Far away to the north-west across the sand sea there lies the Oasis of Siwa which in the old days was known as that of Jupiter Amon and was the rich goal of Cambyses' legions; but through the centuries the rare expeditions which have reached it have always done so *via* a chain of oases far to the north or by coming down from the Mediterranean coast. The direct route, which necessitates a journey longer than that from London to Edinburgh through a completely trackless and waterless desert, has never been attempted since Cambyses' day.

Knowing that the Belvilles could not now be far ahead of me I persuaded the Egyptian pilot to fly me out in search of them; and we set off again, now penetrating the fringe of the great no-man's-land of Africa. I had hoped that it would be quite an easy matter to pick them up from the air until I realised that they would be certain to halt during the midday heat and that it is very difficult indeed to identify any object which is not moving in the sort of broken ground that lay below us.

For over an hour we circled back and forth, flying low over each long, waterless *wadi* as we came to it in the hope of spotting their camp. At last we located it in a narrow defile where the rocks on one side gave a little shade from the burning sun.

My pilot landed me on a flat stretch of sand about two miles away and helped me unload my baggage. Some of Harry's people had seen the 'plane land and I saw through my binoculars that he and Amin were coming out to investigate. As the pilot was anxious to get away I said good-bye to him, watched him take off and then set out to meet my friends. As soon as the distance had decreased sufficiently for them to recognise me in my strange clothes they both began to wave and shout excitedly; and their surprise at my having suddenly dropped on them out of the blue can be imagined.

Reserving my full story for a more appropriate time, I just said that I had been unavoidably detained, and Amin went back to get porters to fetch my baggage. I then told Harry that Oonas had set a pretty little trap for me out of which I had only just managed to wriggle and that I would give him all the details later.

Clarissa was unfeignedly glad to see me when we reached the camp, but Sylvia commented sarcastically upon my washed-out appearance and said I looked as though I had been having a few nights out with a vampire.

I didn't disillusion her for the moment but inquired how things were going with the expedition. One of the porters had chucked his hand in at Kharga having, apparently, only started out from Luxor with the idea of getting a free trip to the Oasis because he wished to visit his family who lived there; and another, having inadvertently trodden on a cobra, had departed from this vale of tears in a distinctly unpleasant manner; but Sylvia had succeeded in getting two good men to replace them and two guides for whom the local Sheik had vouched.

The four lorries and two cars, all of which had enormous balloon tyres, these now having been found more satisfactory for desert travel than caterpillar tractors, had put up a good performance although they were pretty heavily laden. Their loads, however, would automatically decrease as we advanced.

The worst trouble my friends had met with, apart from the grim business of endeavouring to soothe the last moments of the poor fellow who had died from snake-bite, was having been badly bitten themselves by insects. The oases swarm with mosquitoes and, although the nets keep most of these at bay during the night, the sandflies which are almost as great a pest so infinitesimal that they will penetrate even the finest netting. Harry had been singled out for particularly viru-lent attacks, probably on account of the rich alcoholic content of his bloodstream, and he declared he had not had a single hour's sleep since he left Luxor owing to the infuriating dron-ing of the little devils; but now that we were entering the sterile desert it was to be hoped that we should get free of them. I was given a belated lunch and at about four o'clock the cara-van set off again.

Progress was slow as there was no question of our going straight ahead on a compass course; every mile covered meant a scouting expedition either on foot or in one of the cars to survey the lie of the land ahead and decide which way to bring up the convoy. Sometimes long détours had to be made to avoid the low ranges of hills, and at others one of the vehicles would get stuck in a patch of soft, treacherous sand. When that happened we had to unroll forty-foot strips of canvas into which wooden battens were sewn, in front of the two fore-wheels of the vehicle to give them something to grip on, and hitch it on to one of the others with a tow-rope to give it a start; in the worst cases, when a lorry was badly stuck, we had to get our shovels and dig it out.

There is a special technique for driving through desert country and our drivers had been picked for their previous experience so they did not get stuck very often. The idea is to follow the course of each *wadi*, zigzagging from one to another, roughly in the direction in which you wish to go; but in the *wadi* bottoms lie lovely, smooth stretches of yellow sand which are highly deceptive; these must be avoided like the plague so one has to drive along their edges where the hard ground slopes up to the ridge on one of the *wadi's* sides. This means that the car is nearly always running along at an angle of about forty-five degrees and one is in constant fear that it may turn over. Added to this, there being not the slightest suggestion

319

of a track, one bumps and jolts violently the whole time one is moving; so it is difficult to imagine a more thoroughly uncomfortable and exhausting mode of travel.

We pitched camp at sundown. The others had already experienced several days' desert journeying in their trip from Luxor to Kharga and Kharga to Dakhla; but even this single afternoon's run was enough to show me that the expedition in which I had involved myself was very far from being a picnic.

By a rough reckoning we were satisfied that although the actual mileage of the convoy was much greater, it had accomplished about thirty miles along its compass course northwestward since the morning. We could have got considerably further if we had been using camels, as the caravan could then have followed an almost direct route up hill and down dale; but, on the other hand, we should have required a great number of animals to carry all our stores, which would have meant more men, and both camels and men would have required more water; which, in turn, would have meant yet more camels and yet more men; and that, of course, is the reason why the Arabs have never attempted to cross the *Grande Mer de Sable*.

Our cars and lorries were considerably slower but they afforded the only possible means of making a prolonged desert journey in which fresh supplies of water could not be obtained. Actually we were not displeased with the thirty-mile stage we had accomplished, since, if we could keep up that average, we reckoned that we ought to be able to reach our destination in about ten days.

We were now in hostile, or at least lawless, territory as bands of Bedouin, who are fanatical Christian-haters and responsible to no man, roam the fringe of the desert. We posted sentries to keep a look-out for such unwelcome visitors and the rest of the men settled down to their meal of dry bread and dates washed down by great quantities of incredibly strong black tea; while our cook, Abdulla, prepared us a simple but good evening meal.

After it was over I told my friends how extraordinarily lucky I was to be with them, and the full story of the grim happenings which had prevented my setting out with the expedition from Luxor as I had originally intended. Just as I had guessed, Oonas had sent a telegram signed with my name, saying I had changed my mind at the last minute and decided to return to Cairo with her. She had even had the forethought to include a line in it saying it was my wish that Amin should accompany the Belvilles, to make quite certain of getting him out of the way as well.

Sylvia was considerably chastened when she had heard the true reason why I was looking so washed-out and ill; and she said that it would give her considerable pleasure to convert Oonas into a brazen image by sticking into her 3,600 drawing-pins, being roughly one per minute for the time I had spent imprisoned in the tomb.

It had been grilling hot when I had joined the party that afternoon, and all through our trek most of us had been perspiring as we stumbled up the low hills to seek a way for the convoy, or bumped and bumped, and bumped on the seats of the cars; but with the coming of night the temperature had fallen with extraordinary rapidity. In that barren waste there was no wood to make a camp-fire; our cooking was done on crude-oil stoves and these had to be put out immediately it was finished in order to economise fuel; so, although we all had heavy coats to wear in the evenings, we shivered where we sat on the floor of the bell-tent we were using as a mess-house. It was the cold that broke the party up, soon after I had finished recounting my adventures, as we were all longing to crawl into our warm flea-bags.

In the great stillness which enwrapped us I felt very far away from the turmoil of the modern world. O'Kieff and his minions seemed infinitely far removed from this blessed peace of the barren lands which have remained unaltered by man since time began. As we had foiled him in his attempt to secure the lower half of the tablet we had no cause to fear his sending out a rival expedition and, as I had kept a most careful watch from the 'plane earlier in the day, I was quite certain that he was not sitting on our tail, expecting us to guide him to the treasure, as I had thought he might. I thought a little about the treasure and our chances of finding it, which I felt were small; a little about Sylvia, and a lot about Oonas; then I fell asleep.

22

The Great Sea of Sand

Amin woke us at five next morning. The two servants, Omar and Mussa, brought us tea and fruit, after which I gave the order to strike camp. That fell within my province owing to an arrangement which we had made when I had joined the party the day before.

There were no passengers in our convoy and Harry, Clarissa, Sylvia, Amin and myself had more or less agreed upon the duties we would each undertake when we had first discussed the expedition in Cairo. My failure to set out with them had upset things rather so Amin had had to take on most of the jobs that should have been mine between Luxor and Dakhla but now we were able to readjust matters.

Before he had married, Harry had been a motor-salesman and although he had not proved by any means a spectacular success at selling cars, there was very little that he didn't know about their insides; so he was transport chief and had the drivers immediately under him.

Clarissa was in charge of our stores. She issued the rations at each halt, gave Abdulla and the other servants their orders, looked after our feeding arrangements and provided us with such minor comforts as were possible.

Sylvia's province was that of navigation officer; she took the altitude of the sun each day at midday with her sextant, worked out our position from her books of logarithms and gave us our compass course for our next trek forward. She spoke Arabic much better than I did and the guides came under her, advising on which course the convoy should advance as it moved from one grim, sun-scorched valley to another.

I was camp-master, a job that Amin had been doing before my arrival and in which he still assisted me to some extent although he now had time to help with other work as well. It

was my job to select the places where we should halt during
the midday rest and for the night, superintend the loading and
unloading of the baggage and, while we were on the march, to
supervise the porter's operations whenever any of the vehicles
got stuck.

All five of us naturally helped each other out whenever possible and, as neither Clarissa nor Harry could speak any
Arabic, Amin spent a good part of his time with one or other
of them making known their wishes to the drivers or servants
when the Arabs' small stock of English proved insufficient.

By six o'clock we had resumed our journey and it was about
half-past eight when two men on camels appeared over a rise
ahead of us. Halting their beasts on its crest they remained
there waiting for us to draw nearer. Presently they were joined
by a dozen others all of whom also brought their long-legged
beasts to a halt and sat perched upon them staring at us but
making no sign of greeting, friendly or otherwise.

Our guides, who had gone on a little way ahead, came running back to us with excited cries and Amin translated their
Arabic, which was partly dialect that I could not follow. The
camelmen who had appeared so silently and with such startling
suddenness out of a blank horizon were Toureg. I had noticed
they were all veiled and swathed in blue *burnouses* and I remembered then that such a costume was always worn by this
scattered tribe of fanatical nomads who roam from oasis to
oasis throughout the whole of the North African hinterland
attacking ill-armed caravans and murdering peaceful traders.

There is no law in the desert except that of strength. We
knew before we started that we could expect no quarter if we
had to fight some such band of cut-throats, and the little group
on the hill-top about six hundred yards away was strangely
menacing from its very stillness.

We were well supplied with arms and ammunition. Every
one of our fourteen men had a modern rifle as also had Harry
and myself; besides which we two and the girls were all equipped with automatics. The Toureg were reported to be wonderful marksmen and they carried long, old-fashioned pieces slung
over their shoulders, so that the barrels in some cases projected as much as a foot above their heads; but if it came to

a showdown I did not think we should have much difficulty in driving them off with our modern magazine-rifles.

I halted the convoy, formed it into a rough circle and, using it as a screen, we took up our position behind it with our rifles at the ready; but we had no need to use them. Seeing that we were prepared to put up a fight, the tallest Toureg kicked his beast into motion and turned it back down the far slope, upon which the whole band disappeared as silently and mysteriously as it had come.

We continued our march rather warily and put out sentries when we halted for the midday rest about three hours later. Our camp had only just been formed when one of our sentries gave a warning cry and we saw that another party of camel-men had appeared on the horizon. They were more numerous than the first and on studying them through our field-glasses we could see that many of their camels were laden with great bales of stuff and that most of the riders wore the white *burnous*; so it appeared to be an inoffensive trading caravan.

Half-an-hour later a fine old man, who was its leader, rode up to us crying, *'Aselamu! Alaikum!'* in friendly greeting, and we duly replied, *'Marhaba, marhaba!'* in welcome. He introduced himself to us as the Sheik Abu Hafiz of the Oasis of Farafra, and ordered his people to pitch their camp near our own.

Between peaceful travellers desert custom entails boundless hospitality and whenever two caravans meet they must always offer each other a full share of all food and drink they may be carrying. We immediately placed our supplies at the old gentleman's disposal and he promptly returned the compliment; but on its becoming clear that neither caravan was in want, the ceremony boiled down to an exchange of presents. We sent the Sheik a handsome gift of tea and sugar, sugar being particularly highly prized in the desert and regarded almost as a form of money; while he sent over to us a branch bearing about twenty hands of bananas and a package of sherbet which we found most refreshing.

We settled down to our respective midday meals some little distance apart but during them we again exchanged courtesies by sending him some of our tinned Irish stew in return for a big dish of *fatha* which is an Arab concoction of carrots, bread and eggs. Knowing the fierce religious fanaticism of all desert-travellers, Sylvia had withdrawn on the approach of the caravan, taking Clarissa with her, and when the two girls appeared for the meal they were both wrapped in the long cotton *barracans* worn by native women, and veiled. Sylvia had brought these garments in her kit against just such an encounter and, I learnt later, they had used them to avoid causing offence during most of the time they were travelling from Luxor through the two Oases.

Seeing that the faces of our women were respectably hidden, the Sheik asked us to join him for tea after we had finished eating, so we walked the fifty yards which separated the two parties and sat down in the soft sand beside him and his two sons.

Tea-drinking among the Bedouin Arabs takes the place of the cinema, the race-course, the dance-hall and practically every other form of entertainment. It is a solemn ritual and is begun by the servants filling a large teapot half-full with sugar; another quarter of it is filled with the tealeaves and the remaining space filled with water. They then boil the mixture, pour it into another pot, reboil it, add more water, pour it back again and so on, tasting it frequently until the strong, sweet brew is to their liking. It is then drunk out of small glasses with much gusto and noisy sucking of lips to show appreciation.

While the tea-drinking is going on, host and guest discuss every subject under the sun in a pleasurable and leisurely manner until, when the giver of the party feels that the time has come to make a move, he adds some mint to the teapot and the guests take this as a sign that they should say 'Farewell' after having consumed a last, mint-scented ration of the potent brew.

The Sheik told us that he was going south to the small Oasis of Ballas, a little over a hundred miles from his home territory, and that for quickness' sake caravans such as his own skirted the edges of the great Sand Sea with some frequency although they never attempted to cross it.

He was a splendid-looking old pirate with a fine, white beard, a hooked nose and up-turned moustaches. At his belt he carried an old-fashioned revolver with one of the longest barrels I have ever seen on such a weapon, and a dagger in a richly-chased sheath the point of which turned up like the tail of a capital J. His two sons were also armed and I noticed that a number of his men had long, old-fashioned rifles, but I thought it as well to tell him of the band of Toureg we had seen that morning.

Gravely inclining his head, he expressed his gratitude for the warning but said he was not the least perturbed as he had half-a-dozen Sudanese soldiers in his retinue. These coal-black Sudanese are mercenaries hired out by the great lords of the desert to such caravan-owners as will pay for them. They are lazy, greedy, vicious brutes and will not do a single hand's turn on a journey, but they are indomitably brave and will fight to the death if a caravan to which they have been attached is attacked. In consequence the Toureg, knowing this, will nearly always refrain from molesting a caravan that has a Sudanese bodyguard and it has become a custom for nearly all caravans of any size to take a few of these vicious but redoubtable black warriors with them as a sort of insurance.

We spent the best part of two hours at this ceremonial tea-drinking and after many cordial good wishes on both sides for a safe and successful journey, our two caravans packed up and parted. Half-an-hour later the Sheik's long string of laden camels disappeared over a low range of sandy hills and his people proved to be the last humans outside our own company that we were to see for many days.

That night we camped in a valley bottom on the edge of a long stretch of smooth rock which the wind had blown free of sand. After dinner we got out our portable radio and having listened to the news, tuned into a London dance-band; upon which Sylvia suggested dancing. It was rather heavy going on the hard rock but it served to keep us warmer than we had been the night before and between pauses for cigarettes we kept it up for the best part of an hour.

Since the previous night, when I had told the tale of Oonas' abominable treachery, Sylvia had thawed out quite a lot; she no longer aired the sarcastic witticisms to which her dislike of Oonas had driven her when we were in Luxor, and I found her easier to get on with than at any time since I had met her. She was not a particularly brainy girl except in her one particular subject of Egyptology and I rather suspected that her keenness about that was only the outcome of her long association with her father and his work; but she could be very amusing when she chose to exert herself and since she was very strong and healthy the desert life seemed to suit her and bring out all her best qualities.

On our third day out from Dakhla we entered the real Sea of Sand. Before then there had been plenty of sandy stretches but these were always broken here and there by rocky outcrops or higher land formations which could be definitely identified; whereas now we had begun to penetrate a region which had the additional desolation of lacking even the smallest landmark. It consisted of just line after line of sand-dunes about half-a-mile apart and with sandy valleys in between. On an occasional higher crest we were able to see several miles before us and the ridges of dunes stretched away interminably towards the horizon without any break or variation whatsoever; but most of the time we could see no further than the next ridge as we traversed each shallow valley.

It was no longer possible to follow a zigzag course from one valley to another as the lines of hills stretched for mile after mile in an unbroken series of billows at a diagonal angle across our path. In one way the going was better because it was not so bumpy and, since there was no alternative, we kept a straight course according to our compass; but this necessitated our mounting each fresh ridge which lay before us and going right over it.

As the ridges averaged some five hundred feet in height above the valley bottoms, this meant that, through constantly going up and down, our mileage was actually about half as much again as it would have been on a flat surface; so we did not gain very much by no longer having to make any détours. Moreover, some of the slopes were very steep ones and now and then one or other of the lorries failed to make them, which necessitated our unloading a lot of the gear from another lorry and using it to give the one that had stuck a tow over the crest; after which there was the tiresome business of reloading.

Although our water-supply was ample and we did not suffer from thirst we saw the usual mirages which desert travellers report, with some frequency. Usually they took the form of a large placid lake lying in the centre of a valley bottom we had just sighted, and this is easily enough explained from the shimmering of the hot air on the burning sands. Often they had a greenish tinge round their edge which suggested grassy slopes and sometimes palms, mud-walled villages or even distant cities with white-domed mosques and minarets. There is a theory that these illusions are due to refraction in the extraordinarily clear atmosphere which reflects actual places situated at a great distance; but I am more inclined to think that such mirages are only a trick of the human imagination which, aided by the shimmering heat waves, conjures up the sort of landscape it is craving so desperately to see as a relief to the interminable monotony of changeless sandy vistas.

Our long treks were exhausting work when carried on day after day without intermission and all of us had to go about in sunglasses or our eyes would soon have suffered from the constant glare, but the life was a healthy one as the waterless wastes which have been baked for centuries are entirely free of every sort of germ; the air is clean and exhilarating and we all felt well and cheerful. Very soon the sun had coloured us up to a pleasant brown, although in poor Harry's case it proved too much for his fair skin and on our fourth night out he became badly blistered, which necessitated Clarissa's ministrations and a considerable inroad into our supply of witch hazel.

It was on the fifth day that we came upon the first traces of Cambyses' lost regions. About ten o'clock in the morning one of our guides pointed out a great patch in one of the sand dunes that varied in colour from the rest. It was the only break in the monotony of the yellow ocean which we had seen for over two days so we went out of our way to inspect it.

To our considerable excitement it proved to be the remains of one of the huge dumps of water-jars that Cambyses had had planted out in the desert in advance of his army. Few of the jars were still unbroken and the great patch, which stretched for a mile or more, consisted almost entirely of thousands upon thousands of largish pottery fragments half-burried in the sand.

We spent over an hour there, turning them over and pulling out only partially damaged specimens in the vague hope that we might come upon something else; but evidently the army had only halted there for the night and then passed on, as we could not find a single thing other than these countless pot-sherds which were all of the same colour and material. Yet it was a thrilling thing to find this absolutely definite confirmation of Herodotus' report and to realise that the last human beings, and perhaps the only human beings, who had ever stood upon that spot until our coming were those Persian soldiers who had camped there so many hundred years ago.

Apart from the sticking of our vehicles in soft patches of sand or on the slopes of hillsides the principal inconvenience we suffered was the intense cold of the nights and periodical sandstorms which blew up from the south. The *gibli*, as the sand-laden south wind of the Libyan Desert is called, struck us four or five times after we had entered the *Grande Mer de Sable*; on each occasion it was necessary to halt the caravan and close the windows of the cars but, even so, the sand penetrated everywhere and a fine golden-red dust made us cough and choke while a thin layer of it coated us and all our belongings, causing us acute discomfort. These storms never lasted long and were not serious except for one which was heralded by the approach of half-a-dozen dust-devils, great columns of sand caught up in the swirling wind which carries them, like moving towers, at a terrific pace over the hills and valleys.

Directly we saw them we hurriedly made our preparations to meet the storm, closing up the cars and wrapping veils round our faces, but we were held up for over an hour during which we could not see any further than one can in a pea-soup London fog; and the storm was of such severity that the driven sand had the effect of emery-paper. When we were at last able to leave the cars again we saw that it had taken every scrap of paint off the windward side of them.

Appearances did not bother us but we were greatly pertur-bed about our engines as if these had become choked we should have had considerable difficulty in getting them going again; but we had taken the precaution of having the engines enclosed in special sand-protectors before leaving Luxor and, much to our relief, we found that these had functioned satis-factorily.

Experience soon taught us that Clarissa was not a very efficient quartermaster as far as keeping a check on our stores was concerned, so we placed Amin in charge of that very important department. She was, however, an admirable caterer when it came to devising our menus and, owing to he ingenuity and the trouble she took in explaining dishes to Abdulla, we fed much better than might have been expected seeing that nearly all our food came out of tins.

It was just as well for us that Clarissa was such an enthusiast about food since Sylvia would have proved quite hopeless. Soon after we had entered the Sea of Sand she told me one day when we were walking on ahead of the convoy together, that she simply loathed anything to do with cooking and had never been able to raise the least enthusiasm for household management. On my remarking that her dislike of such things would prove a handicap if she ever thought of getting married, she replied:

'That's just the trouble. I should never be any good as a poor man's wife and yet I do want tremendously to marry and settle down. I'm sick to death of the wretched existence I've been leading for the last few years—never enough money, always having to scrape and save; trying to keep up appearances because of Father's position by living in expensive hotels, yet having to beg managers for special terms and suffer the constant humiliation of under-tipping servants because one hasn't enough to do the job properly. We've never had a proper home since Mother died and I'd give my eyes to have one of my own instead of making a parade that I can't afford out here in the winter, and pigging it in some rotten little boarding-house at home each summer.'

I was a little surprised at this outburst as it showed me a completely different side of Sylvia and an aspect of her life that I had not suspected although I knew that her father had been far from rich.

I nodded sympathetically. 'That sort of existence must be pretty wearing; but surely if you'd wanted to marry you must have had lots of chances? Even if you'd been hard up yourself, you've been moving in moneyed circles out here and I should have thought that in the last few winters you would have come across quite a lot of likely lads.'

'I can understand your thinking so,' she agreed. 'But somehow it doesn't pan out that way. You see, most of each season

I've been stuck away up country with Father in some dirty little "dig" and the only men one meets in such places are the young excavators, who're full of enthusiasm for their job but haven't got much money. Then, as far as Cairo or Luxor is concerned, only rich people can afford to come so far afield as Egypt for a holiday and the great majority of visitors are middle-aged or old.'

'But hang it all,' I protested, 'You're terribly good-looking Sylvia. You know that as well as I do; and you *must* have had some chaps fall for you.'

'Oh yes; but the ones with money have been twice my age or married already and the only man I really cared about hadn't got a bob. He was an excavator and even his expenses out here were paid by one of the University Archæological societies, although he was one of the most brilliant young men Father ever had on his staff. I had a darned good mind to burn my boats and marry him; but Father said he'd sack him if I did, and I just couldn't face starting married life practically on the dole.'

'I think you were right about that,' I told her. 'Love in a cottage can't be much fun after the first few weeks, and there's always the possibility of children turning up to make things more difficult than ever.'

She turned a glowing face to me. 'Oh, but I adore children. And that's one of the reasons I'm so terribly keen to marry. I'm determined to have at least four and I wouldn't mind working my fingers to the bone in the nursery. I'm sure I'd make a good wife, too, because I am the faithful kind and I've learnt to be economical. It's only this wretched business of thinking up meals and cooking which I hate so much; and if I couldn't afford to have servants to do it for me I should be driven stark, staring mad after the first few months.'

'Couldn't you get some sort of job yourself which would help pay for a couple of servants?' I suggested.

'I thought of that ages ago but there are so few jobs I'm fitted for which would bring in decent money. My only special subject is Egyptology and there are plenty of young men from the Universities or the wives and daughters of archæologists who're able and willing to do that sort of clerical work for nothing. I'm no good at modern languages and I've never learnt shorthand so I couldn't get a post as secretary. I could serve in a shop or become a mannequin, I suppose, but the pay wouldn't amount to much and if I were out at work all day, who would look after the children? No, Julian; my one real hope is this expedition. If it's successful I'll have enough to live decently and marry anyone I choose. If it's not, this will be my last season in Egypt and I'll have to drop out of things to become a daily-breader at about two pounds a week living in some London suburb.'

'What happened to your chap?' I asked.

'I don't know,' she said bitterly. 'He quarrelled with Father, mainly about me; and he went home to try out some scheme by which he hoped to raise the wind; but he's not very practical, poor darling, and from the last I heard of him I'm afraid he's made a mess of things. It's not easy to get rich quick on an academic education and I've pretty well given up hoping that he'll ever come back into my life at all.'

After this chat Sylvia and I seemed to slip quite easily into a much greater degree of intimacy and she told me a lot about the wretched shifts to which they had been put in order to maintain her father's position in the eyes of the outer world, while looking twice at every penny expended on food and clothes.

One is always inclined to regard a very pretty girl as an exceptionally fortunate person because one assumes automatically that her good looks more or less place the world at her feet, and that she can get anything in reason that she sets her heart upon; but I saw now that it didn't necessarily work out like that. In spite of her natural attractions Sylvia seemed to have had a rotten deal and my sympathy for her drew us together during the many hours we spent in each other's company.

In the minor crises, which are natural to such expeditions, she never lost her head; and I admired tremendously the calm way in which she brought order out of chaos among the jabbering, excited Arabs. I felt she was right, too, when she had said that she was the faithful kind and would make a good wife. I wondered what the chap was like whom she had fallen for and decided that, in any case, if she fell for someone else, he would be a darned lucky fellow; providing he had just sufficient income to provide her with servants for her kitchen which, after all, wasn't a very unreasonable thing for a girl to ask when brought up as she had been.

She seemed impervious to sunstroke and while we sweated under our solar topees she went about bare-headed most of the time, her pale gold hair gradually bleaching to an even lighter *blonde cendrée* in the strong rays of the sun. I had thought her attractive from the beginning and the sight of her tall, slim figure clad in riding-breeches, top-boots and an open shirt, which was never long out of my range of vision, consoled me more and more as the days went on for the lack of variety in the landscape.

Day after day we trekked over the endless sand, mounting crest after crest to see wave after wave of others, undulating before us. Sometimes we managed only a little over twenty miles in a day and at others nearly forty, according to the amount of time we had to devote to getting the cars and lorries out of soft patches where they had stuck.

It was on our eleventh day out from Dakhla that we arrived at our destination. Somehow I had vaguely expected that there would be something to indicate it, just as a child thinks that the North Pole must really have an ice-coated flag-staff set up to show the Arctic explorer that he has really reached his goal. I don't know what I expected, a bit of ruin or a small oasis, perhaps: but I was quite disappointed when, an hour and a half after we had set out from our midday rest on the eleventh day, Sylvia called a halt and said: 'Here we are!'

The column drew up on a ridge and in every direction as far as the eye could see, the landscape was the same incredibly monotonous waste that we now seemed to have been trekking through for half a life-time—just endless waves of hump-backed, yellow dunes.

I moved the convoy down into the next valley in order that our camp should be sheltered from the wind as much as possible and, when I had started the porters setting up our tents, I trudged back up the hill. Sylvia had taken her usual observation of the sun at midday but she was now taking another as a final check on our position, which she worked out by the same process, having allowed for the difference of time registered on our chronometers.

'We're not far out,' she said when she had done. 'The actual point is about three-quarters of a mile further south along the ridge here, as near as I can make it.'

With Harry and Clarissa we walked along to the place she had pointed out and began to look about us; hoping that even a casual survey might enable us to find a solitary spearhead or some other indication of the thousands of men who had perished there. But the sands were as smooth and unbroken as those of the innumerable dunes we had traversed in the preceding days.

Although I had not said so, as I did not wish unduly to depress the others, I had never felt particularly optimistic about the success of the expedition after Sylvia had told me in Cairo something of the natural laws which govern the sands of the Libyan Desert. Apparently, although the countless waves of dunes appear quite stationary, they are actually in slow but constant movement. This is caused by the prevailing wind which gradually shifts the sand from the windward sides of the dunes, over their tops to their leeward sides, which has the effect that, in the course of time, the whole of each dune turns right over, gradually moving forward as it does so. As every ridge does the same the whole sandy ocean slowly advances in one direction. During a period of centuries the dune upon which we were standing might gradually have rolled to its present site from a spot many miles further north-west of us. In consequence, the bottoms of the valleys also change their position so that one section of low ground is un-covered at one time and another a few years later, which results in any particular point being alternately an exposed valley bottom or buried five hundred feet deep below the crest of a dune which consists of millions of tons of sand.

The last camps of the lost legions would obviously have been in the valley bottoms of their time so that the legionaries might get as much shelter from the bitter night winds as possible. Within a few months, or at least years, of their foundering, all traces of their camps would have been obliterated by the moving forward of the nearest dunes. Year after year the sand above their remains would have got deeper and deeper, until they lay buried hundreds of feet below its crest. Then, after a further period of years, the sand that buried them would gradually have moved on until they were fully exposed in a new valley bottom once more.

How often they became exposed was difficult to calculate and perhaps if one had flown in an aeroplane over the spot upon which we were standing in the year of Queen Victoria's jubilee one might have seen mile upon mile of metal debris stretching along the valley bottoms for anyone to pick up who came along. On the other hand, in that particular year all traces of the lost legions' passing might have been at their maximum depth below the sand; or again only buried some ten feet deep, in which case they would be comparatively easy to get at.

I had no doubt whatever that the stuff was there but it seemed to me that the whole success or failure of our expedition hung upon the blind chance as to how deep it was buried during the particular year in which we had arrived on the scene. The only thing really in our favour was that an army of 50,000 men would have occupied a very considerable area, more particularly as they must have scattered at the last in their desperate endeavours to find a way back out of the trap into which they had fallen; so, although many of their remains might be buried beyond all hope of recovery others might possibly be found in these or neighbouring valleys.

We spent a couple of hours prospecting the valley in which we had set up our camp but none of us could find anything at all and, as Sylvia pointed out, even a small miscalculation on the part of the Egyptian astronomer on whose bearings we were relying to find the spot where the treasure had been abandoned, might have thrown us out by several miles. Taking the site of our camp as the centre of operations, therefore, our next job was to go out in the cars during the succeeding days and survey the whole territory within as big a radius as we could, section by section.

The following day we set about it, taking the south-eastern sector over which we had advanced as the most likely; for this would be the direction in which the army would have retreated. Harry suggested halving our labours by letting the two cars take different directions but I would not agree to that as I thought it was much too dangerous. Even on picnic expeditions from the Nile Valley the Egyptian Government have made it a law that not less than two cars may proceed into the desert, since if one breaks down its occupants may lose themselves in trying to get back, and formerly the government was put to much expense in having to send out aeroplanes to locate stranded parties. We had no aeroplane to search for one of the cars if anything went wrong with it or even if it got stuck in a bad patch of sand, and if the second car failed to find it that might cost the occupants of the stranded car their lives. In consequence, I had my way and it was agreed that both cars should set out together.

As time was an important factor, now that we had arrived in the area where we believed the treasure to be, we decided to take our lunch with us each day and carry on through the rigours of the blazing noontides, in order to cover as great amount of ground as possible. Without the lorries we were able to go much faster, covering up to seventy miles a day, but although we scoured the surrounding valleys, literally from dawn to dusk for the next five gruelling days, we did not find a single thing; and at the end of that time we were beginning to fear the expedition would prove a failure.

Each of our two water-supply lorries was equipped to carry 300 gallons and they had been filled to capacity with filtered water before the expedition had left the last wells in the Oasis of Dakhla. Their horsepower was capable of transporting a much greater weight of water over roads but we had deliberately, and wisely, cut their loads down to the maximum we thought they could carry through trackless country. On a basis of a gallon per head per day for all purposes the 600 gallons were calculated to last the eighteen of us just over 33 days. When we had first settled upon the quantity we should take we had hoped that our caravan would be slightly fewer in numbers, and that, reckoning ten days for the journey from Dakhla to the site of the treasure and ten days for the return journey, we should have well over a fortnight in which to prospect the territory in which the army had foundered and put in the necessary digging to collect as much of the treasure as we could carry, if we could find it.

Unfortunately the water-ration of the additional men whom Amin had considered necessary reduced our time limit on the spot by a day or two and, as we had taken eleven days to get there, I felt that we ought to allow ourselves at least twelve to get back, in case of accidents. That cut our stay on the spot down to ten days; five of them had already gone without result and only five were now left us if we adhered to our original arrangements.

A gallon a day per head for all purposes was a fairly liberal allowance seeing that the natives did not wash; but they used considerable quantities in their cooking and as, apart from the two guides they were not desert-bred men, they were apt to be careless and wasteful of water in spite of the strict supervision exercised wherever possible by Amin and myself. Even so, we should have been well in hand if the radiators of the motors, which were constantly boiling over in the steep climbs up the sand-dunes, had not consumed much more than I had reckoned upon. That about evened things out so on this, our sixteenth night out from Dakhla, we had just a decent margin over half our original water-supply remaining.

Petrol did not worry for, in addition to a whole lorry devoted to it, each vehicle had set out with a full tank and an additional reserve lashed to its carrier. In our journey we had not consumed anywhere near half our supply and for the last five days the four lorries had been idle, so we had more than sufficient to continue our exploration in the cars and get the whole convoy back.

Water was the difficulty. If we did not strike lucky in the next few days we should have no time left in which to dig, unless we increased the length of our stay on the spot and I knew that there would be overwhelming temptation to do so should we come across any indications of the lost army. To remain there longer, once we were due to set out on our return journey, meant one of two things; either cutting down our daily ration of water, which could be done but might prove a very dangerous proceeding if some unforeseen occurrence held us up on our return journey; or heading north by west for the Oasis of Siwa instead of south-east to Dakhla.

Siwa lay only about eighty miles distant and was by far the nearest inhabited territory in any direction; we could reach it in three days at the most instead of the eleven days we should need to get back to Dakhla. This possible alternative would give us another clear week at any 'dig' on which we might be working; but, as against that, Siwa is the capital of the fanatical Senussi who fought against the British and played such havoc with our columns during the Great War.

A state of peace now exists between the Senussi and the Egyptian Government but Siwa is still a forbidden city to Europeans. The Sheik who rules this powerful people and is, at the same time, the head of the strictest of all Mohammedan sects, will not endanger the morals of his nation by allowing the infiltration of Whites who carry the forbidden alcohol and the taint of commercial slavery to native races wherever they penetrate.

It has been only with the very greatest difficulty that a few European explorers have managed to secure permits to visit Siwa, even in recent years, and to do so without the signed warrant which shows one to be under the direct protection of the Lord of the Oasis would be to court death in the outlying villages, since Christians are still regarded as the living images of the Devil by its fanatical inhabitants.

It seemed to me, therefore, that whatever happened, we must turn back in another five days, or six at the very outside, although I knew how bitterly Sylvia would feel about having to do so. The failure of the expedition meant so much more to her than to the Belvilles or myself as, after Clarissa's capital outlay had been repaid from any treasure that we might find, she had expressed her willingness that Sylvia should have the lion's share of the spoils.

When I thought of the dreary existence she had led through lack of money and the fact that somewhere within a few miles of us there must lie literally millions of pounds' worth of antiquities, gold and jewels, I could well understand how she must be feeling. Even a tiny fraction of such a vast treasure would be sufficient to pay the costs of the expedition and set her up with a pleasant income of her own for life. Sir Walter had had practically nothing to leave her and now that he was dead she would have little further chance of even meeting likely young men with a certain amount of money. After this last flutter in Egypt she would have to go home and eke out a microscopic income by buckling down to any sort of job she could get. Therefore to her our success or failure meant either a new lease of life with the realisation of some, at least, if not all of her dreams; or the grim outlook of a search for work at some unskilled job which would leave her little leisure and barely keep her when she got it.

It was this knowledge and my absolute insistence that we *must* turn back after six more days which led me, very much against my better judgment, to give way to Sylvia and the others when they pressed that, nearly half our time already having gone, we should, in future, divide our forces and let the two cars take different routes each day so that we could prospect double the amount of ground.

The cars having been specially equipped for such work were as fool-proof as possible and Harry always ran over their engines personally each morning before they went out, so there was really very little danger of a breakdown. The principal risk was getting in a soft patch of sand but the huge balloon tyres with which the cars were fitted considerably lessened the chance of this misfortune, and having had over a fortnight's experience of desert driving we were now able to judge with considerable accuracy the good sand from the bad by the slight variation in its colour. In the last event, if we did get stuck, we felt that although it might necessitate a long and tiring walk, we should not be in any really serious danger because we could always follow the tracks of the car back to our camp.

Unfortunately, however, it proved that there were one or two eventualities of which we had not thought.

23

Lost and Found

Next morning I set off with Clarissa in one car and Harry with Sylvia in the other. We had already surveyed all the valleys for some fifteen miles round our camp so for the first part of our journey we kept together. When we reached fresh territory we planted a pole with a *burnous* tied to its top on the crest of a ridge to mark the place as a rendezvous, and parted, having agreed to meet there again at four o'clock in the afternoon so as to return to camp in company.

Clarissa was a cheery companion and no misfortune overtook us but our day's prospecting proved as profitless as the ones that had gone before, and when we met Harry and Sylvia at the rendezvous shortly after four o'clock we learnt that they too had drawn blank.

The following day we set out again, this time changing partners so that Sylvia came with me, and we took a more southerly direction after parting from the others than we had the day before. Yet not a trace of the lost army met our ever-searching eyes as we drove slowly from hill to valley and valley to hill over the never-changing sand.

It was just after lunch that misfortune overtook us. We were skidding half-sideways down a not particularly steep hillside; there was nothing at all unusual about that as this wretched desert driving consisted almost entirely of brief, straight rushes and short, sideways slides; but without warning one of the tyres on the side of the car which was further down the slope seemed to hit something. There was a terrific bump; the car overturned, somersaulted twice and came to rest upside-down in the soft sand of the valley bottom.

The steel roof of the car prevented our being pinned underneath it but we were badly flung about. I got a nasty crack on the head that made me see stars for a moment and when I pulled Sylvia out we found that she had twisted her ankle.

As soon as I had a chance to take stock of the situation I didn't like the look of things at all. The car was reposing where it had come to rest, roof-downwards and wheels in the air, and I knew at the first glance that on our own we certainly had not the strength to turn it right way up again. We were almost at the limit of our day's prospecting and had been talking only a few minutes before of turning back; so we were the best part of thirty miles from our camp, and some twelve from the rendezvous where we had stuck up our flag-pole again and arranged to meet Harry and Clarissa at four o'clock. The twelve miles' tramp back along our track across the sand-dunes would have been an exhausting undertaking but we should have been able to accomplish it before sundown if it hadn't been for Sylvia's sprained ankle; that was the real trouble and I knew from the pain it caused her even to hobble that we were stuck.

However, I was not unduly worried as, when we failed to arrive at the rendezvous I knew that Harry and Clarissa would come out to find us; a matter which presented little difficulty as all they had to do was to drive along the tyremarks our car had made. I thought Harry would be able to cover the distance in about three hours, so even if he waited until half-past four before setting out, he ought to reach us sometime about sundown. The journey back would have to be made in darkness so it would be slow going as we should be sunk if we once lost our track and the head-lights would have to be kept constantly on it. That meant it would be early morning before we got back to camp. But apart from missing our dinner and sleep it didn't look as though we had much to worry about.

Sylvia very gamely insisted that she could walk and although I tried at first to dissuade her I eventually agreed to let her see what she could do as the nearer we could get to the rendezvous the quicker Harry would find us once he set out.

She put up a very good show to start with as she hobbled along with her arm round my shoulders but after a time we had to stop for her to rest with ever increasing frequency. I tried carrying her for a spell but those elegant limbs of hers weighed ever so much more than I had bargained for and wading through soft sand with nine stone of tall young woman hanging round my neck proved no joke. One way and another we covered about a couple of miles and despite my pleadings and her obvious pain she would go on to the very last lap; so I wasn't at all surprised when she burst into tears on my shoulder and begged me to forgive her because she could not manage another step.

It was already two o'clock and I endeavoured to cheer her up by saying that Harry and Clarissa would be along in a few hours' time but secretly I wished that she hadn't been so insistent on making the effort as, had we remained near the car I could have made her much more comfortable with some of the things in it whereas, having abandoned it, we could only sit on the barren sands without even the ease that its shelter would have given us from the sun.

An hour drifted by and then I noticed Sylvia sniffing apprehensively. I knew at once what was causing her to do that as it struck me at the same moment. The air was hotter than it had been although quite a strong wind had suddenly started to get up. The dreaded *gibli* was coming, and within another couple of moments it was upon us.

Covering our faces with our clothes we lay down huddled together while the sky to southward grew as black as though night were approaching and eddies of sand began to swish into the air all about us.

It was not, thank God, a bad sandstorm as such storms·go although we suffered horrible discomfort for the next half-hour; but when it had passed and we were able to see the surrounding country again, all traces of our life-line had been obliterated. The tracks of our car, which Harry must follow if he were to find us, had been completely wiped out.

If the storm had caught him too, as it almost certainly must have done, he might be hours getting back to our rendezvous instead of reaching there at four o'clock, and if he then set out to find us it would be like looking for a needle in a haystack to search for two human beings, not knowing the direction they had taken, among those countless waves of sand all looking so similar that they might have been turned out from one machine.

I looked at Sylvia and Sylvia looked at me. We said nothing for the moment, but each of us knew that only a miracle could save us from dying there just as Cambyses' legions had perished twenty-four hundred years before.

It suddenly struck me with grim, ironic humour that the Fates had decreed for me a death by thirst; it seemed a particularly raw deal, though, that having suffered all the agonies of approaching death that way only a fortnight before in Thothmes III's tomb, I should be called upon to go through the same ordeal again. As I thought of it I made up my mind that this time I would cheat the Fates, as far as the last hours of torture went, anyway. We would hang on as long as we had a drop of water in the hope that the slender chances of the Belvilles finding us before we died were realised; but, when our water gave out, I would shoot first Sylvia and then myself.

I instinctively put my hand to my belt to feel for my gun and it was only then that I remembered I had given up carrying it a few days before because there did not seem the most remote likelihood of an occasion arising where I might need it, and it was an additional weight which added slightly but persistently to the toil of ploughing about in the sands under the hot sun. Sylvia saw my movement and interpreted it correctly.

'You left it in the mess-tent,' she said. 'I saw it there before we started; but even if you had it I wouldn't let you shoot me. I'm not going out that way.'

'I hope we're not going out any way,' I replied with more conviction than I was feeling. 'We've got our water-bottles and there's a reserve supply in the car so we ought to be able to hang out all right until the others find us.'

She nodded. 'I hope you're right, although I know you don't believe that. Now our car tracks have been wiped out there's not the least indication as to where we've got to and these wretched dunes are as like each other as the rows of pins in a paper packet. They limit the range of vision, too, so much. You know yourself that you can rarely see more than the half-mile from one crest to another. There's about as much hope of their locating us as there would be of a trawler picking up a rowing-boat in the English Channel with a high sea running.'

'Don't let's take too gloomy a view,' I pleaded. 'And if the worst does come to the worst there's an easier way out than letting thirst or a bullet finish us. I had plenty of time to think of it when I was cooped up in that filthy tomb.'

'Perhaps, but I've told you already that I'm not having any. While there's life in us there's always hope; and I've got my own reasons for preferring even the most painful death to suicide.'

'What are they?' I asked curiously.

'I don't believe that any of us are ever called on to suffer more than we can bear,' she said slowly. 'And although we should avoid suffering by any normal means we can, we've got to take it when it's thrust upon us, because it's a kind of test of our spiritual strength; and if we can succeed in passing it we get good marks for it later on.'

'You mean, in some future life?'

'Yes. Anybody who's had to study ancient religions as much as I have must realise that the ancients held much more logical beliefs about the hereafter than those usually accepted in the modern world. It would be so frightfully unfair to judge everybody on just one microscopic span of about sixty-odd years and then award them either a harp and crown or eternal damnation for the countless millions of years which go to make up eternity.'

'You believe that we have many lives, then?'

'Yes. Here or elsewhere.'

I knew a little about the purer Buddhism myself and our conversation about the possibilities of what might happen after death became so intriguing that for the next few hours we almost forgot the desperate situation we were in.

Gradually the sun sank down like a fiery ball to the western horizon, the magnificent colourings which we had seen night after night during our journey through the desert again filled the sky. Slowly the afterglow faded and we were wrapped in darkness.

Both of us had water-bottles with us and I had a packet of chocolate in my pocket so we took a modest drink and shared the chocolate between us for our evening meal.

There is a strange fascination in sleeping out in the desert; the utter stillness brings a feeling of complete peace and in the crystal-clear air the myriads of stars twinkle in the heavenly canopy with a brightness hardly believable to those who have only viewed them from the streets of cities.

Our long talk about the possibility of lives to come had fortified us both to a most astonishing degree. There was nothing that we could do to save ourselves and for the time being we had accepted the fact quite calmly that it lay on the knees of the gods whether we were rescued or must die there.

Our only discomfort at the moment was the chill that had crept into the air after sundown and the knowledge that it would increase to a bitter cold before morning. With a view to protecting us from it as much as possible I scooped out a shallow trench with my hands about six feet long, eighteen inches wide and a foot deep.

'There you are,' I said to Sylvia when I had done, 'Lie down in that and cover the lower part of your body with the sand. It ought to protect you from the cold a bit, and I'll dig another for myself near by.'

'We should be much warmer together,' she remarked quietly.

I knew she was quite right although I hadn't liked to suggest it, so I broadened the trench and we lay down in it side by side; then I put my arm round her neck so that she could rest her head on my chest and be more comfortable.

We lay there in silence for a bit and the warmth we gave each other with the sand over our legs was just sufficient to dispel the cold we had been feeling. I was not the least sleepy and lay there on my back studying the patterns of the constellations; but I thought that Sylvia had dropped off, when she moved her head a little and spoke.

'You know, Julian, when we met that first night out by the Pyramids I thought we were going to have a love-affair.'

'So did I,' I agreed. 'But you had a quaint idea of showing it in the way you treated me when we got back to the Semiramis.'

She laughed softly. 'Well, you must confess that little trip through the cotton fields was enough to fray any girl's temper; and of course you couldn't know then that you had ruined one of my few presentable dresses and that I was much too hard-up to buy another.'

'You poor dear. That was pretty hard. If only I'd known I would have bought you a dozen.'

'How lucky you are to have lots of money, Julian.'

'Surely you don't need telling that money doesn't necessarily bring happiness.'

'It can carry one the devil of a long way towards it.'

'I suppose that's true; but no amount of money could ever set *me* on my feet again, unfortunately.'

'You *are* a mystery-man, aren't you?'

'Are you tired?' I asked.

'Not a little bit. It's only about half-past eight and I shan't sleep for hours yet.'

'Then if it would amuse you I'll tell you now about my murky past.'

'I wish you would.' She wriggled herself down more comfortably beside me. 'I've got all the average female's allowance of curiosity and you've no idea how many hours I've spent wondering what the mystery is that you've kept hidden so carefully from us all.'

I told her then about my brief career in the Diplomatic Service and its tragic termination. She seemed to think that I was making mountains out of molehills and behaving like an idiot to hide myself under an assumed name. As she said, the whole thing had been appallingly bad luck and nobody could possibly blame me if they knew the full story.

I pointed out that the tragedy of it was, that I couldn't possibly tell *everybody* the full story; I could let my personal friends know the truth and any fresh friends that I made but that wouldn't stop other people who didn't know the facts believing me to be the worst sort of traitor who had sold his country's secrets.

'Just think for a moment,' I said. 'How would you like to be the wife of a man who was constantly being cut by all sorts of people and have to face a never-ending situation in which, as soon as you started to make new friends, they heard some beastly rumour about your husband and dropped you like a hot brick?'

'I shouldn't mind,' she said firmly, 'If I loved him. Two people who really love each other don't need anybody else, and the few real friends one had would know the truth and continue as friends just the same.'

'You would make a grand wife, Sylvia,' I said suddenly.
'Is that a proposal?' she laughed.

'No, my dear. I'm afraid it's not. In spite of all you say I'm
not quite such a blackguard as to contemplate asking any
decent girl to share the furtive sort of existence that has been
thrust upon me. And anyway, you don't love me.'

'How do *you* know?'

'Because you told me yourself only a few days ago that you
were still bats about that young excavator you had such a
hectic affair with.'

'That's quite true. I'd marry him tomorrow if I were safely
out of this and we had just enough cash to start a little home
together with a reasonable prospect of not having to starve.
But there are different sorts of love, aren't there?'

'Of course,' I said slowly.

'I loved him in every way; mentally and physically. We
lived together for nearly three months but I knew with an
absolute conviction that when our passion had worn off we
should still be immensely happy together. That's real love
and if only we had had the money to get married I should
have been absolutely faithful to him. There is the other kind,
though; just physical attraction. One knows quite well that it's
not going to last but it can play the very devil with one's
imagination while it does.'

'You needn't tell me.' I smiled. 'I've only just got over the
attack I had with Oonas.'

'You wouldn't have married her, then, if you hadn't got
your unfortunate past, and she had been just the same but
free of her appalling criminal instincts?'

'Good lord, no! She was a simply marvellous mistress but
her crookedness apart, we should have tired of each other
in a couple of months at most.'

'Yes, I know just what you mean. At times like that one's
hardly responsible for one's actions.'

'You seem to have been bitten by the same bug yourself
sometime or other,' I remarked.

'Well, I'm twenty-six, you know, and although I don't
think you could really call me a bad lot, I had rather a rotten
break when I was eighteen. I knew next to nothing and the chap
was rather a swine. Having once taken the downward path

there were two occasions later on when, having really fallen pretty hard, I went off the deep end again of my own free will. It wasn't real love in either case although, of course, I persuaded myself that it was at the time. I admired them both tremendously too, and I had rather the same sort of feeling for them as I had for you when you pulled me out of that hellish place down at Ismailia.'

It was, I suppose, our acceptance of the virtual certainty that we were going to die out there in the desert that made us talk with such absolute freedom. There seemed no point whatever in observing any sort of conventionality or hiding anything from each other any more. Neither of us was in love with the other in the real sense but we had been strongly attracted from the beginning, and I said thoughtfully:

'I'm not going to tell you that I regret the Oonas episode because I don't; but I do feel that both of us have missed something through her coming on the scene. We *did* make a good start along the old, old road, that night out at Mena and by the time I had got you out of the House of the Angels I had as good as fallen for you. Even if I could have, I'm not saying that it would ever have got to the point where I should have asked you to marry me, because I honestly don't think we've got enough in common to hitch up for life together; but I am quite sure that I shouldn't have been able to resist making love to you if I hadn't left Cairo in such a hurry to contact Oonas on the Nile boat.'

Sylvia moved her head slightly and turned her face up to mine. Her eyes were shining in the starlight as she said:

'I wouldn't marry you, Julian, even if we were out of this and you asked me. There's only one man in the world whom I would marry. But I don't see any reason why you shouldn't kiss me good night.'

One kiss begets another and although the Angel of Death was hovering over us we defied him because youth and life were still pulsing in our veins. It was late when we finally dropped asleep like tired children after play.

In the morning we were woken by dawn flaming in the eastern sky; no sound disturbed the stillness and no hoped-for figures broke the utter desolation of the sand-dunes. We took a swig of water apiece from our flasks but had nothing left to eat and I knew that we must now attempt to get back to the car if we could find it.

During the previous afternoon and evening we had shifted our position a little from time to time on the top of the ridge so we should not even have known which way to set out if it had not been for the sun which gave us our direction roughly. Sylvia's foot was stiff and ached a little but was no longer acutely painful and now that we were no longer trying to beat the coming of sunset, as we had been when we started out on the previous afternoon, we were able to take our time. Leaning on me she managed a slow limp quite easily and I made her sit down and rest for a few moments every quarter of a mile.

Fortunately I remembered that in our effort to get back as far as possible along our own track to the rendezvous we had crossed four ridges, so when we made our way slowly down the far slope of the fourth I knew that it was the valley in which misfortune had overtaken us; but the car was not in sight.

Both of us felt we had gone a little too far to the right so we turned left and walked along the valley bottom. After covering about two hundred yards Sylvia noticed a dark object sticking up in the sand some little way ahead of us and as we came nearer I thought it was a small brown rock. Even the sight of such an ordinary object quite excited us when our eyes had looked upon nothing but sand for so many dreary days and we experienced something of what Robinson Crusoe must have felt on coming upon Man Friday's footprint. On stooping down to examine it we saw that it was not a rock at all, and when I went to pick it up it fell to pieces in my fingers.

Closer examination showed that it had once been a thick. bowl-shaped piece of leather but the passing of endless years had blackened it and made it so brittle that it fell into dust as we handled the broken pieces. All that remained worth looking at was an iron rim and a round, iron stud which had been in its centre. We knew then the strange trick that Fate had played us. Cut off from our base, hopelessly lost in the Sea of Sand. almost resigned to the prospect of the death that was stealing relentlessly upon us, we had at last found our first real trace of the lost legions of Cambyses. The thing which had fallen to pieces at our touch had once been the crude leather helmet of a Persian infantryman.

'Isn't it amazing that the leather should have lasted all this time,' Sylvia said. 'But probably it's lain undisturbed for centuries until yesterday's sandstorm uncovered it. Let's look about and see if we can find anything else.'

'No, you mustn't waste your strength,' I demurred. 'Our first job is to find the car again. Then if the others do find us after all we can always come back here.'

But as we walked on down the valley we found quite a number of other remains scattered in our path. They were mostly broken pieces of the same brittle leather from helmets, belts and shields; or pieces of crude iron, being the studs from these and the heads or grips of spears. But we found one javelin and a rather nice belt-buckle of chased brass.

It was about half an hour after our first discovery that to my great relief we sighted the car, and another twenty minutes' slow walking brought us to it. The first thing we did was to take stock of its contents. There were two quart bottles of Evian in it, as a reserve without which the cars never left our camp, and one bottle of Perjac orangeade left over from the previous day's picnic lunch. We also had our reserve supply of food which consisted of iron-rations enough to last us for two days. In addition there were our coats which would help to keep us warm at night and various other oddments which might come in handy for rendering our situation a little less disagreeable. As Sylvia pointed out, too, when we had exhausted our supply of bottled water we could always drink that which was in the radiator of the car. It would mean smashing a hole in it to get the water out as the car was upside down, but we had the tools with which I could manage that; and, allowing for evaporation, it would give us at least another half gallon, so it looked as if we should be able to hang out for four or five days. That seemed to give us a slightly better chance than we had reckoned on as Harry would be searching for us from dawn to dusk each day.

Yet I was very far from optimistic. Taking the camp as the centre of a circle, since we were 30 miles from it, the circumference of that circle upon which we stood must measure 180 miles. Harry knew that we had gone roughly south-west so he would concentrate his search on that quarter of the circle, but, even so, he had a front to cover of 45 miles in extent. In each journey he could only see approximately half-a-mile to either side of his route and we were so far out that he could not make more than one journey each day. With five days to go the odds were exactly nine-to-one *against* his finding us.

As we had so far eaten nothing we made a modest breakfast off some of our tinned supplies and when we had done I decided to have a look at the thing which had caused the car to turn over. I now had a pretty shrewd idea as to what it might be, and leaving Sylvia sitting in the shadow of the car I went off up the slope to see if I were right.

I was. There was a biggish black object protruding from the sand which I had noticed the day before, and as I had suspected this was more of the Persian loot we had been after.

Before the car crashed it the thing had been a large, iron-bound leather chest. The top had been dashed to fragments by the wheel of the car but inside it I saw the stuff that had given it sufficient solidity to turn us over. It was full to the brim with a dinner-service of ancient plate.

I picked one of the pieces up and looked at it, coming quickly to the conclusion that it had little value except that which it might fetch in the sale-room as an antique. It was certainly not gold or silver but some dullish metal not unlike pewter with a faintly reddish tinge.

Gathering up a pile of this first real treasure-trove I hurried with it back to Sylvia; both of us would have been extraordinarily thrilled by such a find only twenty-four hours before, but even if the edge were taken off our excitement by the small likelihood of our ever being able to make use of our find, we still got quite a kick out of it.

We always carried a couple of spades in each of the cars so that we could start to dig at once if we found anything on any of our prospecting trips, and I thought that in any case a little digging would serve to keep our minds off the anxiety which always lay like the pain of a nagging tooth at the back of them: so I assisted Sylvia up the slope, settled her comfortably and began to dig.

There was quite a lot of stuff round about the neighbourhood of the chest and within a few inches of the surface of the ground. Most of it was practically unidentifiable, having rotted to bits with the shifting of the sand; but I unearthed a small armoury of spearheads, javelins and swords; and by digging round it for the best part of two hours, a queer contraption that looked something like the remains of a sedan-chair.

Sylvia suggested that it probably *was* a carrying chair for some high officer who had been wounded or was too gouty to mount his horse; so we knocked off the top of it and started to clear the interior by baling the sand out with our cupped hands.

So far I had not come across a single bone or anything that might be taken for a portion of mummified human body. In the immense length of time that had elapsed since the army had perished, the bodies would have rotted and even the bones would have calcined during the periods when they had lain exposed in the valley bottoms to the burning sun and the constant friction of wind-driven sand; but before we had got very far down in the sedan-chair we came upon an extraordinarily gruesome spectacle; the remains of the dead man were still in it.

Evidently he had died there, either because he was too weak to get out or had decided at the last to meet death philosophically and at least sheltered from the blazing sun by the roof of his carrying-chair. Unlike the bodies of his servants and companions which had been exposed to the ever-shifting grit, his had been protected by the framework of the chair in which he was sitting until it had gradually silted up and his body had become mummified in the warm, dry, stationary sand.

As soon as we got to the level of his shoulders the old boy's head fell off and as I lifted it out it weighed almost as light as a feather. We dug down further hoping that he might have had things of value on his person and our patience was rewarded. When we got to his chest we found a beautiful ornament of uncut rubies set in gold. Still lower, we unearthed his scimitar which was a lovely thing with semi-precious stones which we could not identify in its hilt. Lower still, down at his feet, where we imagined it had dropped from his hands as he died, we came upon a statuette of Osiris. It was of pure gold, about ten inches high, and had tiny sapphires inlaid for its eyes. Evidently it was part of the loot which the Persians had taken with them from Ancient Thebes, and Sylvia declared that such a piece would fetch infinitely more than its gold content; two, or perhaps three thousand pounds, she thought.

Besides these three really valuable finds we came upon his belt-buckle, a number of silver and gold buttons from his tunic and some strips of paper-thin gold which Sylvia said were used as money. Evidently he had been someone of importance and the dinner-service which had overturned the car must have been part of his baggage, so we had great hopes of being able to locate the rest.

By this time the sun was high in the heavens; almost overhead. We knew that it was about midday and our work had given us a decidedly worrying thirst so we decided to knock off for the time being. Taking our principal treasures with us we went back to the car and made a light meal, after which we decided that we would sleep during the worst of the heat and set to work again later in the afternoon.

As the car was upside-down I arranged its cushions and our coats to form a couch on the inside of its roof. When I had done we crawled into it through one of the windows and lay down together. Few ways of spending the afternoon could have been more pleasant if only we could have been a bit more hopeful about our prospects of being rescued, but with thoughts of the previous night in mind we turned instinctively towards each other and forgot our anxieties for a time in very sweet and gentle love-making which yet had an eerie quality of romantic unreality as if we were actors rehearsing a part. After which we cuddled up together and drifted off to sleep.

We both woke at the same instant with the roar of an engine in our ears. For a second I thought that it must be Harry in the car dashing over the nearest sand-dune and coming straight at us; but almost instantly I realised that the noise came from overhead and that its note was the steady hum of an aeroplane engine.

Scrambling out of the car I looked up into the sky and there she was circling right over us. Sylvia crawled out beside me and we both waved frantically while shouting with all the strength of our lungs.

Almost at once out hearts leapt in exultation. The people in the 'plane had seen us and it was coming down. It slowly circled into the wind and, dropping gently, bumped along the valley bottom coming to rest within a hundred yards of where we stood.

In her excitement Sylvia forgot the pain in her ankle and grabbed me by the hand as we both ran forward to it. The 'plane was quite a small one and looked like a four-seater but it meant precious life to us.

When we were within twenty yards of it the door of the 'plane swung open and an Egyptian in European dress jumped out. He carried a rifle and with quick movement brought it up to his shoulder. I had barely time to let out a gasp of amazement when I recognised a second figure who had followed the first. It was Sean O'Kieff.

24

At Grips

A third figure stepped from the 'plane; Zakri Bey, plump, oily, smiling. The strong-arm man had us covered with his rifle; evidently they had come down believing us to be armed and had made up their minds not to take any chances of our shooting at them first.

Sylvia and I halted in our tracks some fifteen paces from them. Our excited hails had died upon our lips; the almost crazy joy that had seized us at the sight of the landing 'plane had been snuffed out like the flame of a candle in that one devastating second when we had recognised its occupants. As though blasted by lightning and struck dumb, we stood there stupidly, our mouths agape, staring at O'Kieff.

Although the sands were sizzling hot in the glare of the afternoon sun he was not clad for a visit to the desert. A Trilby hat concealed his grey hair and a single-breasted grey tweed overcoat, more suitable for London wear, hung loose on his tall, raw-boned figure. I remembered as I noticed his get-up that in the old days he was always complaining of the cold.

A little smile flickered across his thin-lipped mouth as he addressed Sylvia:

'Good afternoon, Miss Shane. You may remember that we met in Ismailia a few weeks ago, when I had the privilege of entertaining you for a short time. Unfortunately I had to leave in rather a hurry, so I had no opportunity to wish you good-bye.'

Sylvia stared at him hard-eyed but made no reply; while Zakri, his plump face wreathed in smiles, tittered in a horrid, false way, unlike a man but on a note approaching that of a eunuch or a schoolboy.

'And here is Mr. Julian Day,' O'Kieff went on, transferring his glance to me, 'who took such an interest in my doings when we were passengers in the "Hampshire". I see now that we also met for a few moments in the House of the Angels, although I did not realise at the time that it was you with whom I was exchanging shots—owing to the removal of your beard. I only had a feeling that your face was vaguely familiar.'

He paused a moment, then suddenly stepped forward. 'Good God! I know you now. You're Du Crow Fernhurst!'

I nodded. 'That's right; and I've never had any desire to conceal the fact from *you*. Day is only the name I took to make life bearable among decent people after I was slung out of the Diplomatic Service through your filthy scheming.'

He resumed his normal calm. 'That explains a lot. I felt sure you were not tied up with the police or any of the Intelligence Services; and it's puzzled me a great deal as to why a young man named Julian Day should concern himself with my affairs and pursue me with such bitter but quite inexplicable hostility.'

'Yes,' I agreed. 'You've got me to thank for the closing down of Gamal's dope-joint in Cairo and the smashing-up of the House of the Angels; from both of which feats I derive enormous pleasure.'

He smiled again. 'My dear boy, *you* should know better than to imagine that such pin-pricks could seriously inconvenience *me*. Gamal deserved all he got for his stupidity in allowing a stranger like yourself to collect dope from him; and the loss of eight young women with the house at Ismailia is a matter of very minor importance. As an old friend of yours I'm really rather distressed to think that circumstances may prevent you from getting any more fun out of your purity-campaign. By it you have succeeded in bringing to my notice one or two weak links in my organisation. This is a valuable service and I am not ungrateful; as I propose to prove to you. What sort of success have you had in your search for Cambyses' treasure?'

It was impossible to try to conceal our 'dig' so I shrugged and glanced back towards the exposed sedan-chair and chest of plate sixty yards away up the slope.

'You can see for yourself. We've found a few things but nothing of much value.'

'I also see that you have had an accident.' He pointed towards the overturned car. 'And unless I'm much mistaken you're marooned out here.'

For a second I hesitated, wondering if we had better tell him the truth and throw ourselves on his mercy, but I knew him to be merciless. His talk of 'gratitude' was pure sarcasm and I did not believe there was one chance in a million that he would give us a lift back to civilisation in his 'plane. It would be better to pretend, for the time being at least, that although we were unarmed our friends would appear on the scene at any moment.

'Oh no, we're not marooned,' I laughed as lightly as I could. 'The Belvilles and the rest are digging some other stuff up in a near-by valley. We had a spill on our way out this morning, but as we didn't get back after lunch they will be coming along any time now to find us.'

'How nice that would be for you if it were true. But you seem to have forgotten that I arrived here in a 'plane. If your friends had been anywhere in the neighbourhood we couldn't have failed to see them. What's more, you haven't shaved today, my young friend; and Miss Shane hardly presents her usual impeccable appearance. That car was overturned yesterday and you spent the night out in the desert. You're lost and you would have died of thirst here if I hadn't happened to find you.'

'Then you'll take us back?' said Sylvia suddenly.

He shrugged his bony shoulders. 'I'm afraid that may be a little difficult. As you have perhaps noticed we only have a four-seater 'plane and with our pilot all four seats are already occupied.'

I felt certain that the brute was only playing with her but I didn't dare to say anything just in case there was a chance that he might take her with them; although I was dead certain that he would never lift a finger to save me.

'But a four-seater 'plane can easily take six in an emergency,' Sylvia protested quickly. 'You can't leave us here to die.'

'I could,' he said quietly. 'But I don't propose to do so. Now, I think, we will inspect the treasure. But first I would like to make quite certain that you are not carrying any arms.'

He signed to the man with the rifle. 'Just run over them, Daoud. I've a feeling that neither of them really likes me and we don't want any accidents.'

Daoud leant his rifle against the plane and, drawing an

automatic, came round behind us; after patting us over he nodded to O'Kieff and we all moved off in the direction of the place where I had been digging.

O'Kieff was keenly interested in antiques and had some very beautiful old pieces in his house in Brussels. He began to examine our finds with quiet enthusiasm and there were so many facets to his strange personality that within a few moments he seemed to be a different man entirely. Exerting that erudite charm which had deceived so many people, he soon had Sylvia talking so freely on Egyptology and similar topics that it was quite clear she had forgotten for the moment that he was responsible for her father's death and her own abduction, and not just a very nice, well-educated, middle-aged gentleman.

After a little he turned to me, his grey eyes twinkling behind his pince-nez.

'And now, perhaps, you would care to show me the rings and other trinkets which must have been on this poor fellow's mummy when you unearthed it?'

We had the valuable items down by the car and I knew that it was no use arguing. Unfortunately they were all together in one heap so we could not show him one thing and conceal the others while he would never have believed me if I had told him that the man in the sedan-chair had not had a single thing of value on him.

At the car O'Kieff examined the jewels and the golden Osiris we had found, with the greatest interest. He then handed them all to Daoud with the remark:

'I think we had better put these in our 'plane for safe keeping.'

Sylvia's sextant had been lying near the jewels and Zakri had picked it up.

'We shall need this to register the exact latitude of this place before we leave,' he lisped passing it to Daoud. 'I think you had better take it to the 'plane as well.'

As the gunman moved off carrying the spoils and Sylvia's sextant, I said hoarsely:

'That's all right by me, if you're taking Miss Shane with you.'

O'Kieff shook his head. 'I'm afraid that wasn't quite my idea. You see, you two young people have been very foolish.

If you had let well alone after I had secured the first half of the tablet and given me time to get the second half in some unobtrusive manner, I should have formed my own expedition and you would not find yourselves in your present awkward situation.

'As it was, you forced my hand by taking Essex Pasha into your confidence so I had to act quickly and send Miss Shane on that little trip to Ismailia. Essex Pasha prevented my getting the second half of the tablet from the bank on the letter that Miss Shane so kindly wrote for me; but, even so, given another day or two and a few, perhaps rather unpleasant experiences at the hands of my Arabs, Miss Shane would probably have told us all we wanted to know herself; or if she could not have remembered the details of the tablet sufficiently well, we might have held her to ransom against it.

'You elected to interfere again which placed the second half of the tablet once more out of my reach. There was only one thing that I could do—let you set off on the expedition yourselves since you were so determined to do so. Given a week or so out here, I thought it was probable you would even save me considerable trouble by locating the treasure and digging some of it up for me. All I had to do then was to come out here in an aeroplane and collect it.

'I had a little more difficulty in finding you than I expected and this is our third day's flying, but now the whole affair has resolve itself most satisfactorily. You have led me to the spot where Cambyses' army foundered and provided me with a few interesting souvenirs to take back with me. I can now return at my leisure and dig over the whole of the valley for the great fortune which must lie in it. You will agree, I think, that your present position is entirely due to your own pigheadedness in having persistently thwarted me from the beginning. The only thing which remains to be done at the moment is to show you my gratitude for your various activities in saving you both from the peculiarly horrible death brought about through excessive thirst, by er—shooting you.'

'Damn you!' I roared, trembling with fury. 'You can keep your gratitude *and* your bullets. We're stuck here and we'll be dead inside a week but we'd rather stick it out and you can save your fireworks.'

Zakri chuckled, and piped up in his thin falsetto, 'Your friends must be somewhere. Surely you don't think we would risk their finding you still alive here? Oh no, no! You know too much to live. You know many things that the Princess Oonas told you. She has informed us of that.'

O'Kieff nodded. 'I see you've quite recovered from your experience in the tomb where she trapped you. When she told us about it I guessed the trick you had played on her and went down there afterwards to have a look at the figure you made to represent your ghost. That was a most ingenious idea and it gave me great amusement. The poor Princess and her man were scared out of their wits; and it may interest you to hear that in the belief that you were a Catholic she is now spending a considerable amount of money in having Masses said for the repose of your soul. Still, as it turns out, she had only been anticipating your demise by a little under three weeks, and the Masses may serve to save you a few thousand years in Purgatory.'

'As I'm not a Catholic she's wasting her money,' I said grimly. 'Why didn't you tell her I'd escaped?'

His wintry smile again flickered over his thin lips. 'You seem to have forgotten that I have some reputation as a necromancer. I allowed her to suppose that I had temporarily laid your ghost and had removed your body from the tomb. You see, the Princess Oonas is in a position to be very useful to us but she is regrettably unreliable; witness the manner in which she endangered our plans owing to her sudden passion for yourself. Knowing my occult powers she will in future prove more amenable to discipline because she believes your spirit to be under my control and that I can raise it when I wish to terrify her into insanity.'

'You ingenious swine!' I muttered. 'But let's get back to the present. I haven't used anything that Oonas gave me against you.'

'You might if you ever had the opportunity and, frankly you bore me. I no longer find that attraction in you which you possessed as a young diplomat.'

My hands clenched and unclenched spasmodically. I itched to fling myself at the sneering brute's throat but I knew that the others would riddle me with bullets before I could kill him with my bare hands; and restraining myself I said thickly:

'All right. Have it your own way about me, then. But you've got nothing against Miss Shane. For God's sake do one decent act in your life and take her out of this with you.'

'And give her the chance later on to make a statement to the police that she was an eye-witness to our shooting you out here in the desert? No, thank you, my young friend. Both of you have reached the end of your tethers. Daoud! Get on with it. Shoot the woman first.'

With a quiet smile Zakri intervened. 'You can settle him, Daoud. I'll attend to her.'

Anyone could guess that Zakri was pathologically abnormal and Oonas had told me that, in addition, he was an inveterate woman-hater. The note of sadistic joy in the little swine's voice conveyed the horrible, perverted pleasure he expected to derive from the murder of a clean, good-looking girl like Sylvia.

I had been within a fraction of hurling myself upon O'Kieff since, if they were going to shoot us anyhow, there was no point in standing there waiting to be butchered like sheep; but the oily little Egyptian's revolting murder-lust filled me with such loathing that at the last second I changed my mind and, swerving, went for him.

As his hand went to his pistol I shouted:

'Run, Sylvia!' and leapt at him across the few intervening yards of sand.

My own last-moment change of plan saved me from Daoud's bullet but nearly brought about my death from another quarter. At the second I sprang a solitary rifle cracked somewhere nearby and the bullet from it tore through my jacket, while I was in mid-air, landing up with a smack in the over-turned car.

Zakri had drawn his gun but the report on the rifle upset his aim and he fired over my shoulder. With sudden, unholy glee I saw the stark fear in his black eyes just a second before my fist crashed into his face, pulping his nose and sending him flying backwards.

Anticipating a bullet in the back from Daoud or O'Kieff, the instant I regained my balance I swung about, but O'Kieff was no longer there. Razor-sharp wits must have saved his life on many a previous occasion and on the instant the rifle cracked he must have realised that it would be death for him to linger in that exposed position, an easy mark for an unseen enemy. He was already racing across the sand towards the 'plane with the tails of his grey overcoat flapping out behind him.

Daoud could have killed me; he had the chance and as I swung about his pistol was actually pointed at me; but he was no longer looking in my direction. Having caught sight of O'Kieff's swift movement in his rear he had turned to look after him, and was hesitating whether he should stay to settle me or make a swift get-away too.

His hesitation was his undoing. Two, three, four rifles cracked. With a sharp cry Daoud spun about, lifted his arms and fell, the red blood gushing from his mouth on to the sand.

Half-a-score of rifles were in action now but I could not wait to see if O'Kieff was hit. Zakri was on his feet again, half-blinded by tears and with blood streaming from his broken nose, but he still held his pistol.

Before he had time to raise it I charged him again. Catching his slender wrist I twisted it with such violence that he screamed with pain; I felt the bones snap and the pistol dropped from his nerveless fingers. With my free hand I jabbed him violently under the heart and next moment we fell together.

The thought of mercy did not enter my head; he would have killed me without compunction that night I had slept with Ooonas in the marquee at Tel-el-Amarna; he would have killed Sylvia a bare fifteen seconds before if those blessed riflemen had not intervened. He was as evil as something that had escaped alive out of hell and he was one of the Seven who had caused Carruthers' suicide.

I got my thumbs into his little fat neck just below his double-chin and I rammed them home with all the strength of my muscular hands: I took no pleasure in the deed and I averted my face as his eyes started right out of their sockets; but I killed him just as I would have killed a venomous snake that had attacked me. Two minutes later one out of my seven enemies lay a huddled heap, dead at my feet upon the ground.

Our rescuers were still firing but as I looked towards the 'plane I saw that O'Kieff had reached it and his pilot had the engine running. A bullet thudded into its tail just as it ran forward but a moment later it was in the air.

With shouts and cries the Arabs from our convoy now appeared in a straggling line on the top of the ridge of sanddunes. They were blazing away at the 'plane as it rose. but they must have been a pretty poor lot of marksmen to have let O'Kieff escape them when they had him as a clear target over a straight, hundred-yard run; and if any of them succeeded in hitting the 'plane the bullets did no serious damage as it was soon high in the sky and, wheeling westward, passed out of range.

Sylvia had had the good sense to fling herself flat when the firing started but when she saw her rescuers she had jumped to her feet and rushed in a limping run up the slope to meet Harry the moment he appeared over the crest.

My meeting with him was almost like that of Wellington and Blücher after Waterloo as, without a shade of self-consciousness we wrung each other's hands; except that we were breathless and laughing from our exertions and excitement. Clarissa came running down towards us a moment afterwards waving her pistol in such a dangerous fashion that it went off as she flung her arms round my neck; but apart from half-shattering my ear-drums, it fortunately did no damage, the bullet ploughing up the sand a dozen yards away. Meanwhile, Sylvia was kissing Harry as though he were her long-lost sweetheart.

When our excitement had eased a bit we learnt that it was really O'Kieff who had unwittingly been the means of saving us. Upon our failing to arrive at the rendezvous on the previous afternoon, Harry and Clarissa had come out to try to find us, got lost themselves on being overtaken by darkness and only succeeded in finding the camp again by a miracle of luck at one o'clock in the morning. Nevertheless, long before dawn Harry had mobilised all five remaining vehicles in the convoy, unloaded their stores so that they could travel lighter, and set off the second there was enough light to see by, taking the centre of a line himself and placing two lorries on each of his wings at half-mile intervals so that by advancing in the same direction simultaneously the five vehicles could sweep a belt of territory about three miles wide.

His right wing had missed us by a couple of miles half an hour before O'Kieff's arrival and, as he said, there was such a huge area to cover that it was most unlikely he would have come anything like so near us again in the succeeding days; but they had seen O'Kieff's 'plane and had watched it circle round and come down a couple of miles behind them and some way to their right. Knowing there was absolutely nothing in the desert to come down for, Harry had assumed that the people in the 'plane must have spotted us, so he had immediately turned his line of vehicles round and hurried back towards the place where the 'plane had disappeared behind the dunes.

If O'Kieff had not been so interested in the Persian remains, we should have been dead before Harry had reached us; as it was, when his own car had topped the dunes a little in advance of the others and unobserved by us, he had recognised Zakri and, realising our danger, backed twenty yards down the ridge, halted the rest in the valley and hurriedly ordered the men to come up on foot with their rifles. It had been his shot which had nearly hit me but had saved us by routing O'Kieff's party almost at the last moment.

Unfortunately O'Kieff had made off with all our most valuable finds but Harry, Clarissa and our grinning Arabs were tremendously elated on discovering that in spite of our nearly fatal misadventure, we had at least discovered some of the Persian treasure. All our baggage was still dumped in our original camp and it was now too late in the day to go back and fetch it, but each vehicle carried its supply of emergency rations so we decided to remain where we were and sleep out under the stars that night.

As there were still a couple of hours of daylight to go after we had brought the vehicles over into the valley where Sylvia and I had crashed, and the men had righted our overturned car, and buried Zakri and Daoud, we started to dig again at once.

Many hands make light work is a true old saying and even the lorry-drivers, who ordinarily would not do a thing outside their job, were so excited by our discovery that they willingly lent us their assistance. By sundown we had tuned up over thirty ancient weapons, three of which were fine specimens, and quite a pile of other junk; but we found nothing more of value that evening.

After a picnic meal we held a council. It was now the evening of the eighth day since we had started our hunt for the treasure, so if we adhered to our previous programme. we had now only two days left in which to dig before we must turn back. That was little enough when one considered that although we might turn up plenty of old iron and rotten leather, the ordinary Persian soldiers would have had little of value on them. We must find the remains of more people like the officer in the sedan-chair if we were to secure anything of real worth; and it might take many hours of digging before we came across another haul like our first.

If we left after our tenth day was up we should be allowing twelve days for our return journey whereas it had only taken us ten-and-a-bit on the way out; so we had a little margin there in addition to which we were just a bit in hand on our water-supply, so if we increased our two days' digging for the actual treasure, now we had found it, to four we still ought to be all right; but as a precaution against accidents we decided that we could cut down our water-ration by a third which would not cause us serious inconvenience and would leave us an emergency supply in hand for the journey back.

Next morning Harry set off with the lorries to collect our stores from the old camp, leaving Sylvia, Clarissa, Amin and myself with six of the men to dig. I went up the valley to prospect other likely spots and marked down five of them, while Sylvia directed the digging on our original site. When I got back within sight the girls hailed me with cries of joy, having just made a splendid find.

After clearing out the whole of the sedan-chair and removing the remains of the mummy, Sylvia had found an inlaid ivory casket of Egyptian workmanship, with several other objects, in a sort of cupboard under the chair's seat. As she had lifted the casket from its resting place one side of it had fallen out and a whole stream of bracelets, rings, necklaces and other ornaments had gushed from it on to the sand at her feet.

Over our picnic lunch we endeavoured to assess their value Some of them contained uncut precious stones of considerable size; in others the stones were of little actual worth but the ornaments themselves would fetch high prices on account of their antiquity and the great beauty of their workmanship. Altogether there were fifty-six items and we reckoned that, by and large, they could not possibly be worth less than £25,000.

Among the other things under the seat of the Sedan-chair we found a considerable quantity of the paper-thin gold strips used for money, two fine drinking-cups of solid gold and an enormous quantity of coloured beads which originally had probably been sewn on to some sort of stuff to form a highly-decorated garment.

As far as we knew our natives were reasonably trustworthy but it would have been foolish to have tempted them by leaving the jewels about; so on Harry's return with our equipment, Sylvia, Clarissa, he and I divided them up between us and at my suggestion the girls set to work sewing our respective shares into the linings of some of our garments.

While the girls were busy and a new camp was being formed I took Harry aside to tell him a thing that had been worrying me the whole day; O'Kieff's statement to me that he had deliberately let us set off to find the site of the treasure with the intention of coming out to get it himself later on. When he did return it was clear that he would bring a considerable number of his henchmen with him, and he had spoken of digging over the whole valley, although to do that, the question of water-supply would make it necessary for him to come out to the place a number of times over a period of several weeks.

'I don't think we need worry,' Harry shrugged optimistically. 'We can't remain here for more than another three days now, ourselves. Today's only January the 19th so it's still quite early in the digging season and he's got to get his outfit together. It's hardly likely he'll come back again before we've gone.'

'I agree about that,' I said. 'But I think we ought to take precautions.'

'What sort of precautions *can* we take?' he asked.

'For one thing, we can have a man posted up on the ridge all the time we're digging to keep a look-out for his 'plane; and for another, we can dig a deep trench so as to be able to take cover in it if we're attacked.'

Accordingly it was decided that we should make the trench

on the following morning and in doing so we killed two birds with one stone. As a lot of sand had already been turned up from the spot a little way up the slope where we had unearthed the sedan-chair, we made this the centre of our trench and dug a big ditch, clearing the ground to either side of it.

It wasn't an easy business as the sand filtered back in a most infuriating manner, nullifying our work as soon as we got a little way down; but we managed to make quite a good job of it in the end by riveting the sides of our ditch with some of the packing-cases which held our stores and the water-containers which we had already emptied.

As we got further away from the sedan-chair even the objects of minor interest we were turning up became less frequent, so in the afternoon we tackled two of the other sites that I had marked down. One of them produced a fine suit of armour and a handsome metal helmet which must have made a gallant figure of some officer who had lived and loved and fought in the dim long ago. But although we worked like heavers for many hours on the two sites we did not succeed in finding anything that really counted.

Having now only two days to go we made a very early start the following morning and attacked the other three sites I had selected just as dawn was breaking. Two of them proved unfruitful except for spearheads and javelins which we now had by the score; but in the third we found the remains of a chariot, three more helmets, two bronze shields, several small idols, a ring, a heavy bracelet set with semi-precious stones and four small bars of gold that weighed about ten ounces each.

Rather reluctantly we knocked off for lunch and were hurrying through our meal in order to get back to this promising dig as soon as possible, when our watchman up on the ridge let out a shout and, jumping up, pointed to the sky towards the west.

From our camp in the bottom of the valley we could see nothing, but in that great desolation inhabited neither by man nor beast nor bird, we knew that the alarm could only mean one thing. O'Kieff was descending on us and, next moment, we saw his plane.

25

Death in the Sands

The men were having their meal on the far side of our camp
and were a good three hundred yards further from the trench
than we were. I shouted to them to get their rifles and we began
to run.

The 'plane was a much bigger machine than the one in which
O'Kieff had arrived three days before; a great twin-engined
monster capable of carrying twenty people. It was flying at
only about two thousand feet. As we dashed up the slope it
dived and came straight down at us.

Harry and I had grabbed up our rifles but the men were still
getting theirs from the lorries when a sharp *rat-tat-tat-tat-tat*
rang out through the valley. The great 'plane was armed with
machine-guns. That was worse than anything I had bargained
for and, sick with apprehension, I pulled Sylvia away from a
line of little puffs where the bullets were spraying up the sand
within ten feet of us.

We four reached the trench in safety and jumped down into
it at the same moment as our sentry, a porter named Kait who
had come charging down the hill; but the rest of the men were
a long way behind. The 'plane zoomed right down over our
heads, blacking out the bright sunlight on the sand around
us for a second with its huge shadow. Its arc of fire had passed a
little to the left of our entrenchment but it impinged direct on
the camp a hundred yards away. How many machine guns
were in operation I could not tell but we heard the bullets
smack like a storm of huge hailstones into the tents and lorries.
I saw two of our men fall hit and one of them began to scream
as he writhed in torture on the ground.

The first attack was over before we had got our breath.
Harry and I barely had time to send a shot apiece from our
rifles winging after the plane as it flashed over the opposite

ridge and was momentarily lost to sight. A second later we saw it again climbing steeply.

The men had taken refuge under the lorries but I knew that our only hope of defeating the enemy was by concentrated fire which might bring the plane down when next it flew low overhead. I yelled at the top of my voice for them to leave their temporary shelter and hurry to us while the coast was clear. To my horror that order proved our undoing.

It was not altogether my fault, as if they had come at once they could have covered the open ground in safety; as it was they were naturally scared half out of their wits and Harry and I had to shout ourselves hoarse for the best part of two minutes before we could get them to make a move. Only Amin and Mussa, the more intelligent of our two servants, started towards us without delay and the two of them reached the trench breathless but safe. The other nine who remained unwounded hesitated and then began to run up the slope in a ragged bunch.

The 'plane had made a wide half-circle, veering off towards the south, but with quick dismay I saw that instead of completing the circle and coming at us from over the hill again, it had descended into our valley and was heading straight for the camp, flying very low. It had entered the valley about two miles away and came streaking up with its machine-guns blazing. Our wretched men were caught half way between the camp and us. In the next ten seconds there was the most appalling massacre. Shrieking, cursing, stumbling, they were mown down by that devastating fire.

We were too horrified even to shoot at the 'plane ourselves as it flashed past us. Where there had been a group of running natives only a moment before, there was now a writhing heap of twisted, moaning bodies. Out of the whole nine only one of them a driver named Hamid, remained unhit and he had dropped his rifle. His eyes were staring out of his black face with terror as he cast himself headlong down into the trench among us.

Some of the men who had been mown down were only wounded and I knew that we must get them in if possible. Harry, having the same thought, had begun to climb out of the trench but I pulled him back again.

'One of us must stay with the girls,' I said. 'I'll go out and do what I can.'

With flying feet I dashed down the slope but when I reached the group of dead and dying I hardly knew which to aid first. Two of them were already dead, three others were clearly past help; the rest had leg wounds and I grabbed the nearest by the arm to pull him up and help him up the slope. His ankle was shattered and he fell again. At that moment there came a cry of warning from Sylvia. Repeating its previous tactics the 'plane had circled and was rushing up the valley once more.

I flung myself flat beside the wounded man as the machine-guns opened. On my other side was Abdulla, our cook, stone-dead from a bullet through his heart. With lightning speed I grabbed his body to me and rolled over with it so that it was between me and the approaching 'plane. The bullets hummed, whined and spattered to right and left of me; the cries of the natives who were still living rose in a crescendo of fear and pain.

When I dared crawl out from underneath Abdulla's body I found that three more of the men were now dead including the poor fellow whom I had tried to help. One, mad with fear, was staggering back to the camp dragging a wounded foot that left a trail of blood in the sand; and the other two were rolling about clutching their stomachs with wounds that I knew were fatal.

My own escape was miraculous, even with Abdulla's body on top of me which had saved me from two bullets in the groin as I saw by his freshly-shattered head and shoulder. There was nothing more that I could do there.

The fourth attack came only a moment after I had regained the trench and, having massacred the natives who were in the open, O'Kieff now made the trench his objective.

'Heads down!' Harry yelled as the first bullets sent the sand spurting up a few feet in front of us, and we crouched there in the bottom of our ditch while the shots clanged and thudded into the water-containers and packing cases which formed our parapet.

It was appallingly hot, which I put down to our exertions, and it was only later, while we were crouching there as the 'plane circled to come at us again and again, that I noticed how stifling the air was and that the day had turned exceptionally sultry.

Time after time the guns in the great 'plane raked the trench, and each time it swooped at us we were unable to retaliate until it had passed since had we exposed ourselves to do so we should have been shot to pieces. All we could do was to blaze off a few rounds apiece in the frightfully short interval between it passing over our heads and flashing out of sight across the ridge behind us. The porter, Kait, was killed by a bullet through the top of the skull at the seventh attack and at the ninth Harry was hit in the left shoulder. As he could no longer use his rifle he started potting at the 'plane with his automatic, although it must have been out of range most of the time he was firing at it.

We had made the girls lie dead flat in the bottom of the trench although they both kicked about it, but it kept them out of danger; the rest of us put up a desperate but ineffective defence with an increasing sense of hopelessness. According to our own account given out in Luxor, Kharga and Dakhla, we had merely gone into the desert to survey a portion of it, so no one knew where we were; and if we failed to return people would only assume that we had got lost and died of thirst just as had happened to many other exploring parties before us. O'Kieff could murder us all without the slightest fear that it would ever be brought home to him. We could hope for no help in that great desolation so many hundreds of miles from any human being and there was not even any likelihood of our remains being discovered for centuries.

It could only be a question of time before O'Kieff wore us down and out ammunition became exhausted; nightfall might have saved us temporarily but the 'plane had appeared shortly before one o'clock and so there were yet many hours to go before sundown. Grimy, sweating, panting for air in the awful heat, and spattered with the blood of our casualties, all we could do was to stick there while we were picked off one by one.

At the twelfth attack Amin was wounded in the neck and in spite of all we could do he lost blood so quickly that we knew the wound was mortal. He died in my arms five minutes later. Although I have said very little of Amin, his death shook me most terribly. He was such a splendid fellow, quiet, good-humoured, brave and kindly. During the many weeks we had spent together I had come to regard him as a true friend, and it was I who had drawn him into this wretched adventure.

I suppose I should have felt sorry, too, about all the other poor fellows who had been killed that afternoon on our account; and I was, in a general sense, both distressed and horrified at the fate which had overtaken them solely because we had hired them for our expedition; but there was nothing personal about that sorrow. Amin's death was somehow different and it touched me to the very roots of my being.

We were now reduced to two rifles, my own and Mussa's, as Hamid, the driver who was with us through being the one man to escape the first massacre, simply crouched in the bottom of the trench gibbering with fear and was too frightened to expose his head for a moment even when the 'plane had passed over.

It swooped twice again after Amin died and then it roared away and suddenly its engines were cut off. For a second I hoped that one of our bullets had hit it in a vital spot but the engines came on again and we could hear them humming although we could no longer see the machine as it was now behind us over the crest of the slope we occupied.

The engines were cut out again and I knew that the 'plane must be landing in the next valley. Evidently, now our fire was reduced to two rifles, O'Kieff had decided that the time had come for a closer form of attack in order to finish us off more quickly. For an hour or more the insistent drone of the 'plane's engines had either sounded from the distance or increased to a great roar each time it sailed low overhead, so the renewal of silence seemed quite unnatural. It was desperately hot and we all took a swig of water to quench our thirst while we waited for O'Kieff's next move.

It came within ten minutes of the 'plane's landing. Each previous attack had been delivered from our front as we stood facing down into the valley; now it came from the higher ground behind our backs. O'Kieff's gunmen had occupied the ridge and they began to pour a steady stream of bullets into the trench from above.

It was no longer possible to stand upright, even for a

moment, and we had to remain on our knees to avoid the shots that peppered the cans and cases which had previously formed the front breastwork of the trench. All we could do was to save ourselves for a last, desperate stand when they found that they could not kill us that way and left their cover to take the trench by storm.

The attack did not develop as I had expected and the firing from the ridge was not very fierce. It was maintained quite regularly but consisted only of single bullets at short intervals and a burst of machine-gun fire about every couple of minutes. We had been crouching under it for over a quarter of an hour, fighting for breath in the stifling heat when Clarissa said that she could smell smoke. Harry agreed with her and I could smell it myself after sniffing the air a little. Very cautiously I raised my head a few inches and popped up for one swift glance over the paapet down into the valley. I understood then why O'Kieff had been content for the time being to let his men only force us to keep our heads down by a steady fire instead of driving them on to finish us. He was busy looting our camp and destroying it.

As we had all our most valuable finds upon us I knew that he would not get much from the camp except the two gold cups and a fine collection of old weapons; but, with what seemed to me senseless fury, he and half a dozen of his thugs had poured our remaining petrol over our lorries, tents, and stores which were now going up in one huge bonfire.

The second I popped my head above the edge of the trench a blast of hot air struck it, which I took to be the intense heat radiating in all directions from the flaming camp, and as I ducked down again Sylvia exclaimed, 'Just look at the sky!'

I saw then that the sky had taken on a strange, reddish tinge and that, too, I put down to the raging furnace just below us as a steady wind was now blowing the smoke and sparks in our direction.

'It's our camp,' I said. 'O'Kieff's soused everything with petrol and the whole outfit is going up like tinder.'

'So that's his game,' muttered Harry.

'It seems a pretty pointless one,' I replied. 'He'll have to form a camp here himself if he's going to dig the valley over, and the sensible thing would have been to keep our stuff for his own use. Destroying everything like this is just stupid vandalism.'

Harry shook his head. 'Not a bit of it, old man. They haven't hit one of us since they've been firing from the ridge. O'Kieff knows now that he can't get us that way as long as we stay here and any attempt to finish us off means a hand-to-hand scrap in which some of the devils are sure to get killed. He doesn't mean to risk the skins of his people.'

'I get you,' I nodded. 'He's thought of a way to do us in without losing a single man. Having destroyed the whole of our supplies he'll fly off again and come back in a few days' time knowing that by then we shall all be dead from lack of water.'

Clarissa groaned. 'We're scuppered, then. There isn't a hope in hell of our being picked up here or being able to reach an oasis, is there?'

'Siwa is the nearest,' Sylvia sighed. 'But that's the best part of a hundred miles and it might as well be a thousand for all the chance we've got of reaching it on foot and with no drink except what we've got in our water-bottles. Just look at that sky.'

Great clouds of smoke had been drifting over for the last couple of minutes but now the wind had dropped entirely and the smoke hung above us in a thick pall which had a livid red background. With the dropping of the wind the stillness seemed almost uncanny. We could still hear the crackle of the flames down in the valley but some other noise was missing. It dawned on us then that the almost regular crack of the rifles on the crest above us and the thudding of the bullets into the breastworks of the trench only a foot above our heads, had ceased.

Suddenly the wind came again, a steady, searing blast increasing in velocity until it was tearing at us, even where we crouched below the level of the ground, and whipping up the sand all round the trench like sheets of fly spray.

'The *Gibli!* The *Gibli!*' gasped Sylvia, and even as she spoke her voice was almost drowned in the hideous moaning of the wind rushing down the valley. The moan increased to a high, screaming note and next second the full violence of the desert hurricane was upon us.

I knew then why the firing had ceased so abruptly; the men on the ridge had seen the approach of the dreaded sandstorm when it was still a few miles distant, whereas we had been caught by it without even a moment's warning. We were enveloped now in dense clouds of sand which made it impossible to see more than a few feet in any direction and were safe from the enemy's bullets but threatened with suffocation unless we could secure some sort of cover.

Instinctively we all started to climb out of the trench. Our sun helmets had been whipped from our heads in the first fierce blast and now the scorching fingers of the red-hot wind tore at our clothes as though it would strip them from us. For a second we staggered about uncertainly, covering our faces with our hands in a desperate endeavour to keep the sand out of our eyes. Sylvia bumped into me and I grabbed her arm, yelling at the top of my voice:

'Over the ridge! Over the ridge to their 'plane!'

Harry, Clarissa, Mussa and Hamid were near enough to hear my shout, even in the screaming of the storm, and the six of us, who were all that now survived of our party, began to blunder up the sand-dune; clutching at each other as we went for support against the frightful buffeting of the sand-laden gale which threatened every moment to overthrow us.

At last we reached the crest and began to slither down the other side. I had no idea where the 'plane was and through the fog of sand it was quite impossible to discern even the outline of the valley bottom; yet the storm had come up so suddenly that I believed O'Kieff and most of his men had been caught by it while still burning our camp, and so were even further from the 'plane than we were. If we could reach it before they did, the odds against us might not be quite so hopeless.

But could we reach it? Blinded as we were, we could only stagger forward down the slope praying that we might bump into it. We reached the valley bottom, as we knew by the fact that the ground beneath our feet had started to slope up again, and we halted there in desperation not knowing if we should turn to right or left. The decision was made for us. Another figure came rushing past us in the darkness and mistaking us for some of O'Kieff's people, called in a panic-stricken voice:

'This way, you fools! this way!'

In a second we were blundering after him and almost at once the bulk of the great 'plane loomed up in the reddish murk ahead. The man who was leading us cannoned into another who stood, holding a tommy-gun, by a short ladder that led up to the door in the 'plane's side.

Letting go of Sylvia's arm I drew my pistol and rushed towards them. The one with the tommy-gun had his left hand over his eyes to protect them from the sand. In the fiendish wailing of the storm he neither saw nor heard me coming. With my left hand I grabbed his gun and jerked it from him; my right, which held my own pistol, smashed into his face. The other man was equally unprepared and Mussa clubbed him with his rifle.

The door of the 'plane was vaguely discernible above, and from behind its glass panel a third man must have been keeping a look-out. Seeing the two men below him attacked, he threw the door wide and opened fire with his automatic. Hamid lurched against me shot through the head and slipped to the ground without even a moan. Clarissa screamed and fell, hit in the thigh; but Sylvia, who was just behind me, had raised her pistol and fired at the same moment. The man above clutched at his tummy, doubled up and crashed forward on us, knocking Harry over.

Mussa was the first up the ladder and I tumbled into the 'plane right on his heels.

'The pilot!' I gasped. 'For Gods' sake don't shoot him!'

'Right, boss!' he panted and with his rifle at the ready he charged forward between the two rows of seats in the saloon of the 'plane to the door which gave on to its cockpit. I thought the saloon was empty and was just about to follow when a small figure swathed in dark veils sprang up from one of the low, armchair seats. The second she had ripped away the veil which hid her face I saw that it was Oonas.

For an instant she stood there staring at me in the dim, uncertain light; her great, widely spaced blue eyes were starting from their sockets. Suddenly she screamed and cowered from me in abject terror. There can be no doubt that she believed it was my ghost she saw and that I had come back to earth to claim her. In a second her face had changed from its serene loveliness, as I had first glimpsed it when she had pulled away

the veil, to the contorted features of a mad-woman. Again and
again she screamed upon a high, piercing note until I thought
her shrieks would shatter my ear-drums.

I took a step forward and stretched out a hand to reassure
her with my touch that I was real, but she sprang aside as
though my hand was the head of a striking cobra. Next instant,
before I had a chance to stop her, she had leapt through the
open doorway of the 'plane.

As I reached it I only caught a fleeting glimpse of her
through the blinding sand. She had picked herself up and was
dashing away into the reddish darkness as though the Fiend
himself were at her heels.

'Quick, Julian!' Sylvia was calling just below me and I saw
that she was endeavouring to carry Clarissa up the ladder.
Harry was behind them but he could give little help because
of his wounded shoulder. In a moment I had the two girls in
the 'plane and Harry slumped in after them, dragging the door
shut with his good hand.

Brushing the dust from my red and aching eyes I stared out
through the window at the place where Oonas had been
swallowed up in the black night that was now all about us. I
had no scruples about O'Kieff or his hirelings but I could not
leave her to choke to death out there in the whirling sand.
Whatever her faults and crimes, which God knows were many,
there was no doubt that she had loved me for a brief season.
The others were safe now, and it was up to me to go out and
get her.

As I gripped the handle to open the door again, Sylvia
guessed my intention and flung herself upon me.

'No Julian! No!' she shouted. 'It's absolute madness! You'll
never find her and it would only be chucking your own life
away.'

I had not noticed Mussa come back into the saloon to see
that we were all safe on board; but the 'plane was now vibrat-
ing and I could hear the roar of its engines.

'Let me pass!' I yelled, but as I thrust Sylvia aside the 'plane
began to move.

It bumped twice on the valley bottom, then lurched sicken-
ingly so that those of us who were standing were thrown off
our feet. With incredible swiftness the 'plane flashed out of

the sandstorm into the clear, bright sunshine, but for the next few minutes it behaved like a crazy thing, and we were flung from side to side as it switchbacked and floundered through the airpockets caused by the violent disturbance below.

When at last the bumping eased a little and we managed to sort ourselves out I knew with bitter certainty that as we could not see the contours of the ground it was quite impossible to land again until the storm was over.

The floor of the 'plane was three inches deep in sand and everything in it was covered with a thick coating of golden-yellow dust. We could hardly see from end to end of the inside of the saloon and all of us were coughing from the frightful irritation in our throats and lungs, but the air began to clear when the 'plane had been in motion for about five minutes.

Clarissa was stretched out at full length on the floor. Harry and Sylvia knelt at either side of her endeavouring to ascertain the extent of the wound in her thigh. She was in considerable pain and on cutting away her clothes we found that the bullet had torn her outer leg-muscle badly, but fortunately it had not touched the bone. On discovering that she was in no immediate danger I left the others to staunch the blood and bind up her wound while I hurried forward to the cockpit.

Mussa, who had served us so splendidly, was squatting there on his haunches with his rifle at the ready just behind the pilot; whom I found to be a white man although his tanned face showed that he had been living out of Europe for some time. He was quite a young fellow with rather a devil-may-care expression about him, but he eyed me with considerable uneasiness as I said:

'How are you off for petrol?'

'I've enough for another five hours' flying,' he replied gruffly. 'We fuelled to capacity before we started.'

'What'll she do?'

'Cruising speed's 160. We came from Dakhla and I could get her back there in about a couple of hours.'

'How about Luxor?'

'That's roughly 500, say three hours and a quarter. Let's hop to it, shall we? I know a young woman in Luxor.'

His flippancy was doubtless partially due to nervous apprehension as to what was likely to happen to him when we landed. I ignored it and asked, 'Who does this 'plane belong to?'

'That swine O'Kieff,' he muttered.

'Are you in his regular employ?'

'No. His own man went sick on him and I was offered a thousand pounds to take this job on with the proviso that if I didn't keep my mouth shut afterwards I'd get a knife in my back.'

'You knew what they meant to do out here?'

He shrugged. 'One doesn't get a thousand pounds for a few hours' flying and I needed the money. But of course I shall deny that if you mean to charge me. You can't force me to take you back, if I decide not to.'

'Can't I? That's all you know.' I tapped the pistol at my belt. 'I assume you'd rather fly us where you're told than have a bullet in your head?'

'I'd risk that and break all your necks rather than go like a lamb to the slaughter.'

'I don't think you'd be quite such a fool as to crash the 'plane if it came to a show-down,' I said quietly. 'But we've got two wounded people in our party and I want to get them in as quickly as I can. As you didn't participate in the actual shooting I'll make a bargain with you. If you'll fly us back without any argument I won't hand you over to the police for complicity in this ghastly business?'

'That's decent of you,' he grinned. 'Where d'you want to go, Luxor or Dakhla?'

'Neither for the moment. I want you to cruise round until this storm dies down because there's just the chance that some —some of our wounded may have survived and if so we must pick them up.'

I left him with Mussa still on guard and rejoined the others. Clarissa was easier now and they had her settled in one of the long, low, comfortable chairs. All of us were suffering from the most appalling thirst and Sylvia was busy bandaging Harry's shoulder, so I went through to the rear compartment of the 'plane hoping I should find some sort of pantry and a stock of drinks there.

It proved to be a small kitchenette and an open cupboard showed a rack with a good array of bottles but as I stepped through the door I almost fell across the body of a man. There. trussed up on the floor, lay Lemming.

'Hello!' I exclaimed. 'What on earth are you doing here?'

'Good God!' he gasped. 'That shooting! It was you capturing the 'plane. Is Miss Shane with you, and the others? Did you all get away all right?'

'The four of us made it and one of our Arabs but your friends succeeded in murdering thirteen poor wretches,' I told him grimly.

'But I tried to stop them,' he moaned. 'I tried to stop them when they opened fire. They were too many for me. They tied me up and threw me in here.'

'I see. You got an attack of conscience at the last minute,' I said sarcastically. 'Somehow when we met before I didn't think you would make a very full-blooded sort of crook. '

'I'm not a crook!' he declared angrily. 'I went in with O'Kieff's bunch to try to find out what they were up to and then land them.'

If any story could have appealed to me that one should have. It was the very thing I had tried to do myself a couple of years before; but for the moment I didn't believe him, although I remarked, a trifle more amiably:

'You don't seem to have done very well at it.'

He sighed and wriggled into a sitting position. 'The swine was a damned sight too clever for me. I only learnt by chance that he was coming out to Egypt on some business connected with Sir Walter so I offered my services to him as an Egyptologist, and he took me on. When I heard about Sir Walter's murder I got the wind up, but I thought I'd better stay in with O'Kieff to see if I couldn't land him with the murder. I meant to take that bit of tablet to the police but you put the lid on that by preventing my getting hold of it. Then I tried to get away with one of the photographs, but they found me out and locked me up in a house in Cairo. I've been cooped up in a filthy cellar there till two days ago when O'Kieff turned up with some stuff you'd found out here, to get my opinion on it. Then he offered me the choice of being strangled by one of his thugs or coming out here to advise him on his digging. Naturally I wanted to save my neck, so I accepted.'

His story now seemed to have a ring of truth about it. Get-

ting out my knife I knelt down and cut the cords that bound
him, as he went on:

'I wasn't certain if your party was still out here or not so
I didn't know if we should run up against you; but I was
simply praying for a chance to help you out of it if we did.
Are—are—are—all of you really all right?'

'Both the Belvilles are wounded, but Miss Shane and one
of our servants and myself got through untouched.'

'Thank God for that,' he murmured.

'There's one thing, though,' I went on, 'that doesn't quite fit
in with this yarn of yours. How about the three thousand
pounds you blackmailed out of the Belvilles before they left
England?'

'Oh, that!' He stumbled to his feet and began to shake the
thick coating of dust from his clothes. 'Yes, I plead guilty there.
But Sir Walter was an old screw and although he was entitled
to it as the head of last year's expedition, it was I who found
the tablet. We quarrelled but I didn't see why I should lose
my share of the loot on that account. As a matter of fact,
though, I didn't think there was any real chance there would
be any. That's why I cashed in by the only way I could think
of while the going was good.'

'Right ho,' I said. 'You had better come and tell the Belvilles
that yourself, and help me carry along some of these drinks.'

He fished a tray out of the cupboard and set some glasses
on it while I collected a good assortment of bottles, then I led
the way back into the saloon. As we appeared Sylvia looked
up from tying a sling she had made for Harry's arm.

'Darling!' she exclaimed. 'How wonderful!'

I thought she was referring to me and the drinks so I grinned amiably, but Lemming pushed past me and, setting the
tray he carried down in Harry's lap, seized Sylvia in his arms.

'Where *have* you sprung from?' she babbled on. 'They told
me you were in Alex. But what are you doing here?' Her voice
quavered off in uncertainty and distress as it struck her that
Lemming must have been on the 'plane the whole time and
was one of O'Kieff's associates.

In a wild spate of words, as he kissed her again and again,
he was explaining how he had been eating his heart out with
worry for her during the last month while O'Kieff had kept

him in a cellar, and telling her how he had been overpowered when he tried to prevent O'Kieff attacking us from the 'plane.

Within a few moments everything was straightened out between them with the exception that no mention had been made of Clarissa's £3,000; but recalling all Sylvia had told me of her young archæologist, the truth about that was as clear as daylight. The Belvilles had not been friends of Lemming's and as far as he was concerned were only the capitalists who were financing Sir Walter's expedition. Since the old man had refused to let Sylvia marry him he had recklessly resorted to blackmail in order to provide his Sylvia with a cook and enough cash to enable them to get married.

Doubtless he still had the money safe in his bank at home, but in any case we had got away with about twenty-five thousand pounds' worth of treasure which would be ample to reimburse Clarissa and provide Sylvia with a nice little private income which was all she needed to realise her dreams of marriage and children.

There was one moment just after we had passed round the drinks when she threw me a sudden anxious glance; but I knew that our few hours together had only been a sort of very delightful desert madness. As I was sitting behind Lemming I put two fingers to my lips and smiled at her; which little gesture she could interpret both as a good luck salutation and an indication that I was not the sort of chap who would ever kiss and tell.

I took some drinks through to Mussa and the pilot who asked me how long I meant him to go on circling round and round above the place from which we had risen. Looking down I saw that 4,000 feet below us the storm was still raging. None of the ridges of the dunes were perceptible and as far as the eye could see we appeared to be sailing over a vast stretch of pinkish-yellow cloud which was in constant, violent motion.

'Leave a good margin of petrol to get us back,' I said. 'But I would like to fly out the storm over this spot if it's at all possible.'

I felt there was little likelihood now that Oonas or any of our wounded me could still be alive down there but I was determined not to leave the place, unless we absolutely had to, without making quite certain. With a heavy heart I rejoined the others in the cabin.

We managed to wash some of the worst of the dirt off ourselves and an hour sped by while Lemming gave us a more detailed account of his unfortunate adventures. Having played a lone hand against O'Kieff myself I could sympathise with him now, and on closer acquaintance I found him to be a very decent fellow.

Sylvia was half-way through an account of our excitements, for his benefit, when Mussa came along to the cockpit to say that the pilot wanted to see me.

I went forward at once and he pointed downwards. While we had been talking the air below had suddenly cleared and the great storm of sand was whirling away to the northward like a huge bank of dense, yellow fog. The longer ripples of dunes which from our altitude looked little larger than the ridges upon a tide-washed beach were now visible again in the clear air below us.

It was impossible to tell from that height in which valley our camp had lain but the pilot assured me that we could not be far from it and should pick it up when we got lower. We descended to 1000 feet and continued to circle over valley after valley but every one of them was exactly similar, without break or marking to distinguish it from its neighbours.

We flew still lower and in half an hour prospected a dozen or more valleys, one of which must certainly have been that from which we had ascended, but the storm had been of such severity that it must have lifted millions of tons of loose sand, burying all trace of our diggings, our burnt-out camp and the dead who lay there.

I knew than that the dunes had moved again, rolling over a little in their slow but relentless march under the pressure of the winds. It was, after all, sheer luck that Sylvia and I had tumbled on a portion of Cambyses' treasure. As Zakri had stolen Sylvia's sextant we had been unable to work out our exact position during the time we were working on the 'dig', and the Egyptian astrologer's figures only gave us the site of our old camp some thirty miles to the north-east. A dozen more expeditions might be fitted out and search those endless vales of sand for months before actually locating the place where our camp had been or coming upon any other booty.

We had recovered only a tiny portion of the immense wealth looted out of Egypt; the remainder lies buried there still with the lost legions of Cambyses for those to recover who have the patience and the bravery to go out and search for it.

'It'll be Dakhla or nothing soon! I've only got about three-and-a-half hours' petrol left,' said the pilot. 'And I know a young woman in Luxor.'

I too, had once known a young woman in Luxor and the thought of her beauty and her laughter thrilled me still, although she was as far removed from me now as if she had been buried two thousand years ago in the Valley of the Queens. My voice was shaking and my attempted lightness a hollow sham as I said:

'All right, then. "Home, James, and don't spare the horses."'